Dear Readers,

Many years ago, when I was a kid, my father said to me, "Bill, it doesn't really matter what you do in life. What's important is to be the *best* William Johnstone you can be."

I've never forgotten those words. And now, many years and almost 200 books later, I like to think that I am still trying to be the best William Johnstone I can be. Whether it's Ben Raines in the Ashes series, or Frank Morgan, the last gunfighter, or Smoke Jensen, our intrepid mountain man, or John Barrone and his hard-working crew keeping America safe from terrorist lowlifes in the Code Name series, I want to make each new book better than the last and deliver powerful storytelling.

Equally important, I try to create the kinds of believable characters that we can all identify with, real people who face tough challenges. When one of my creations blasts an enemy into the middle of next week, you can be damn sure he had a good reason.

As a storyteller, my job is to entertain you, my readers, and to make sure that you get plenty of enjoyment from my books for your hard-earned money. This is not a job I take lightly. And I greatly appreciate your feedback—you are my gold, and your opinions *do* count. So please keep the letters and e-mails coming.

Respectfully yours,

William W. Johnstone

WILLIAM W. JOHNSTONE

SPIRIT OF THE MOUNTAIN MAN

ORDEAL OF THE MOUNTAIN MAN

PINNACLE BOOKS
Kensington Publishing Corp.
http://www.kensingtonbooks.com

PINNACLE BOOKS are published by

Kensington Publishing Corp.
850 Third Avenue
New York, NY 10022

This novel is a work of fiction. Names, characters, places, and
incidents are either the product of the author's imagination or
are used fictitiously. Any resemblance to actual persons,
living or dead, or events is entirely coincidental.

All Kensington Titles, Imprints, and Distributed Lines are available at special quantity discounts for bulk purchases for sales
promotions, premiums, fund-raising, and educational or insti-
tutional use. Special book excerpts or customized printings can
also be created to fit specific needs. For details, write or phone
the office of the Kensington special sales manager: Kensington
Publishing Corp., 850 Third Avenue, New York, NY 10022,
attn: Special Sales Department, Phone: 1-800-221-2647.

Pinnacle and the P logo Reg. U.S. Pat. & TM Off.

First Pinnacle Books Printing: March 2006

10 9 8 7 6 5 4 3 2 1

Printed in the United States of America

SPIRIT OF THE MOUNTAIN MAN
7

ORDEAL OF THE MOUNTAIN MAN
285

SPIRIT OF THE
MOUNTAIN MAN

1

Sliding languidly, in big, oily swirls, over a few submerged sandbars, the red-brown surface of the Colorado River glided past the low, native stone buildings on the isolated knoll. The complex rested well above the sandy, ochre flood plain, beyond the maximum high water mark. According to the Army engineers who designed the structure, it made the ideal location for a prison.

For that was the purpose of this high-walled, forbidding construction. Yuma Territorial Prison; it housed the hardest of hard cases, the most unrepentant road agents, bank robbers, and highwaymen, the wife and baby killers who had escaped from other institutions to kill again and never show a flicker of remorse. At the quarry, guards' shrill whistles announced the noon hour and the men working on the rock pile lowered their hammers and drills. They shambled wearily through the shimmering mid-day desert heat to find what solace they could in the shadows of an overhanging wall of the strip quarry. Among them, three men stood out from the rest.

Victor Spectre could never be mistaken for a drifter or a highwayman. A graduate of Yale, he had the look about him of a businessman, albeit one who kept himself in excellent condition. Trim, with hard muscles, in his mid-forties, he had only the beginnings of a pot belly. The latter had developed quite a lot during his seven years in various prisons. He used to be the brains behind, and leader of, a large outlaw gang that operated in Missouri, Kansas, and Colorado.

He had lived the good life, in luxurious splendor, in a fancy St. Louis hotel, and directed the actions of his vast gang from there. That is, until his greed and the viciousness of his underlings attracted the wrong sort of attention. That's when he met up with *trouble*. And it was spelled *Smoke Jensen*. They had a series of violent encounters.

Since that time, Spectre's thick shock of black hair had a white streak to the left of his part, caused by a bullet fired by Smoke Jensen. The slug had knocked him unconscious and saved his life. His eighteen-year-old son, Trenton, had not fared so well. Originally sentenced to hang, Victor Spectre's money and influence got his death warrant commuted to life in prison. With icy green eyes and thick, bristly brows which met in the middle of his forehead when angered, he quickly became the head cock on the yard at any institution in which he had been incarcerated. It also earned him frequent transfers when enemies and rivals among the prison population turned up mysteriously dead. No different from previous occasions, Victor Spectre had assumed leadership over his two companions.

Ralph Tinsdale was a contemporary of Victor Spectre. He had a thick build, going somewhat to pot with advancing years and a starchy prison diet. He used to be a big land speculator, who obtained prime ranches and city properties by the simple expedient of having the owners killed and dealing with the widows. He had been in the process of acquiring from a silver-haired dowager a choice square block in the heart of the business district of Denver when he discovered that the late Harrison Tate had been a close personal friend of one Smoke Jensen.

Quite quickly, Smoke Jensen wrote *finis* to the evil machinations of Ralph Tinsdale. In their final confrontation,

Smoke had left Tinsdale for dead, at the bottom of a deep ravine, with two bullet holes in the belly. Tinsdale had survived with large scars and a permanent limp. Smoke found that out when called to testify at the trial. When the guilty verdict came in and the judge sentenced him to life in prison, Tinsdale cursed Smoke hotly in language unbecoming the stylish clothing the swindler wore. His time in prison had failed to mellow him. Tinsdale had grown slack behind bars, so that his once lustrous hair had turned a mousy brown, poorly cared for, and his once natty pencil-line mustache had been replaced by a scraggly wisp of its former self. Only his hatred of Smoke Jensen gave him a semblance of youthful vigor. Enough, though, that he was accepted as second in command of the unholy trio.

Olin Buckner had nearly ten years on his associates. His auburn hair, which had faded to mostly gray, was worn slicked back tightly on a long skull. He had a porcine appearance, enhanced by a jowly face, with a pug nose and small, deep-set black eyes. An over-large mouth and big ears added to the illusion. He had already developed a middle-aged spread. Once, though, he had been trim and almost compulsively active. He had owned an entire town in south-central Montana. Most of it he had acquired by unlawful means, and he ruled with an iron fist—until he tried to drive out the daughter of a mysteriously and recently deceased friend of Smoke Jensen.

Smoke went after Buckner with a particular vengeance. Olin Buckner replied by hiring an army of gunfighters, putting a bounty on the head of Smoke Jensen, and sitting back to enjoy the results. Buckner might have been a fine, skillful fisherman, but he had never hooked a shark before. When Smoke Jensen got through with him, he had lain in a hospital bed for five months before he could stand upright, and another three before he could be brought to trial. Like the others, his residual wealth and influence bought him a commutation of sentence. The hangman was cheated and Buckner went to the worst prisons in the west.

He ended up in Yuma and soon found a common bond between himself and the other two.

Now, this trio of the lowest form of human debris stood quietly in line to take a bowl and tin cup in turn, and shuffle past the trustees who dispensed the mid-day meal. Each inmate received a large dipper of a thin soup, purported to be chicken, but lacking even the sight of a speck of meat, and half a round loaf of sourdough bread. Then they retreated to the blessing of shade. As always, the topic of conversation among Spectre, Tinsdale, and Buckner centered on Smoke Jensen.

"I hate that bastard," Olin Buckner spat. "I've not been able to enjoy a day or night without pain since Jensen shot me. I want him dead—no, crippled and suffering would be better."

"You both know I have ample cause to despise Smoke Jensen," Ralph Tinsdale spoke in precise tones, as his stomach cramped and growled in protest to the food. "I was a man of consequence and ample means before Jensen thrust himself into my affairs. Since then, I have not been able to eat a meal without terrible agony. And prison has further destroyed me."

Victor Spectre gave a snort of amusement through his nose. "And you have destroyed a few of them, from what I hear."

Tinsdale sniffed disdainfully. "I was not afforded the respect I deserved."

"Well, whatever," Spectre muffled through a mouthful of bread. "I have no reason to love Smoke Jensen, as you well know. He maimed me and murdered my son, took everything from me. The only thing is—"

"Quiet down there," a guard snarled. "No talkin' among the prisoners. You three know the rules."

After the guard turned away, Victor Spectre repeated himself. "The only thing is, there is not a thing we can do about it from inside here. Smoke Jensen is free as a bird to go and do anything he wants, with no harm to him."

"I'd give a hell of a lot to see it otherwise," Buckner growled. He spooned the thin soup into his mouth.

Ralph Tinsdale studied Victor Spectre while he munched on the chewy sourdough bread. "Are you proposing we find a way to get out of here?"

"I think that would go a long way toward accomplishing our mutual goal, to bring an end to the career and life of Smoke Jensen."

"It won't be easy," Tinsdale offered.

"No," Victor Spectre agreed. "And, as I said, we can't do it from here. We will have to find a way to escape."

Suddenly the guard rounded on them, his Winchester no longer on his shoulder, but held competently at high-port in a menacing manner. *"No talking among prisoners!* I warned you three jailhouse lawyers once. This is the second time. There won't be a third. You'll be taken direct to the Sun Box."

Silenced by that most effective threat, the three master criminals froze in silence. They knew all too much about the ingenious variation on solitary confinement employed at Yuma Territorial Prison. Four coffin-like boxes of sheet iron and rock had been constructed in the center of the Yard. They were so small a man could not lie down, could not even sit properly with the door closed and locked. The only openings were tiny, barred holes in the upper part of each door. Each of the recent arrivals at the institution had heard the screams, wails, and blubbering of men driven mad in the heat of a Sun Box. Finally, the warden turned away to snarl at other offending prisoners.

Buckner, by far the most devious of the trio, leaned forward and whispered, "Find some way this afternoon to be sent to the infirmary. We can talk freely there."

Spring had awakened new buds on the aspen trees of the High Lonesome, which had unfolded into tender, pale green leaves. The meadows and pastures of the Sugarloaf had turned emerald. Warm, soft breezes called longingly to those with sufficiently sensitive natures. One of those was a tall, broad-shouldered man with faint streaks of gray in his hair. He breathed deeply and savored the winey fragrance of renewed life. Then he set his coffee cup on the plank flooring of the porch and came to his feet.

"I think it's time to go fishing," he told the lovely woman beside him. "I'll take Bobby along and get in three or four days on Silver Creek, and over Honey Spring way."

His wife looked up with a frown of protest on her forehead. "That boy has yet to finish his studies, Smoke."

Smoke Jensen smiled a wide, white smile in a sun-mahoganied face. "Sally, there's a universe of learning out there in this magical country. He can learn biology, botany, even weather studies."

Sally Jensen broke her stern visage with a giggle. "Also a lot about rainbow and brown trout, I'll wager."

Smoke took her outstretched hands and raised her from the wooden rocking chair. He remained amazed that she had never lost her youthful figure. The years and five children should have done some damage, yet he could detect none at all. "And right you would be, my dear. The last day we'll catch a mess and bring them home to you. Have some fresh biscuits waitin'. And a pie. We have to have a nice pie."

"I've a Mason jar of cherries left, and a couple of blackberries. Which would you prefer?" Sally asked sweetly.

Smoke patted her on one shoulder. "Whatever you pick will be all right with me. Now, I'll go get Bobby and we'll round up our gear."

Bobby Harris had been living with the Jensens since he became an orphan at the age of ten. His stepfather had been beating the boy's pony and Bobby had been tearfully pleading with the drunken brute when Smoke rode up to the small homestead outside of Thatcher, Colorado. Smoke Jensen could not abide any man who would harm an animal and watched in growing anger. When the abused critter stumbled to its knees, the lad became hysterical. Smoke stepped in when the stepfather decided to turn the length of lumber on Bobby.

After a thorough beating, administered by the hard fists of Smoke Jensen, the drunken sot had gone for Smoke with a pitchfork. Bobby's shouted warning saved Smoke's life and cost that of the stepfather. Smoke was on the way to give assistance to old and true friends in Mexico at the time and at last decided on sending Bobby and his pony north to the Sugarloaf. A year later they made it official by adopting the orphaned boy. He was bright and energetic, although at times a bit forgetful of the limitations of a small boy. He was doing such now, risking any future progeny on the saddle of an unbroken mustang, when Smoke came upon him at the big corral.

Sugarloaf riders had located the wild horses a month earlier, still snowbound in a box canyon. They patiently constructed a barricade across the mouth of the chasm and waited. When the snow melted and the animals calmed somewhat, flankers along the herd's edges brought them in to provide a new bloodline to the prize horses raised by Smoke and Sally on the Sugarloaf.

Grunting and squalling, the wild bang-tail crow hopped and sunfished under the small, tightly gripping legs of Bobby Harris. Smoke rode in close and held his peace, gloved hands folded on the saddlehorn of his big 'Palouse stallion, Thunder. Two more jumps and a tornado spin later, Bobby tasted corral bottom. The spunky lad came to his boots after only a lung-jarring grunt, dusted off his jeans and chaps, and spat grit from his mouth. "Damn," he followed it with. Then he saw Smoke Jensen. "Oh, sorry Smoke. I—ah—" He grinned sheepishly.

"What's a damn or two between two friendly men?" Smoke asked lightly. Bobby literally glowed. He wore his hero worship of Smoke Jensen for everyone to see. "I thought you might be in a mood for something a little less strenuous."

"Like what?" Bobby limped to the fence and squirmed through the two lower poles.

Smoke teased him shamelessly. "My nose and my mountain man instincts tell me it's time to go hog out a few rainbows. Think you'd like that?"

Bobby dusted his hands together, then adjusted the angle of his pint-sized Montana peak Stetson. "Would I? You bet, I would. Where would we go? How long?"

Smoke raised his chin and spoke as though just thinking of it. "I thought we'd angle up Silver Spring a ways, then head over toward Honey Spring. Be gone three, four days."

Bobby's eyes went wide. "That's stupendous, Smoke, I'll git ready right away."

"Stupendous?" Where the hell do they get these words? Smoke wondered silently.

Grinning from ear to ear, Bobby Harris turned in the saddle. "This is really great, Smoke." He breathed deeply, filling young lungs. "It smells so good up here. I can tell pine an' blue spruce, grass a-growin' like crazy. There's water up ahead, I can smell it, too. We never had nothin' to smell around Thatcher, excect dust."

"Whoa! Get a rein on that enthusiasm. And remember the grammar Sally has been drilling into your head."

Bobby made a face. "Along with Miss Grimes at Punkin' Head School," he lamented. "Study, study, study. That's all we do."

Smoke pulled a wry expression. "Then how'd you manage to come home with that big bag of marbles at snow closin' last winter?"

Eyes fixed on the skirt of Thunder's saddle, Bobby slid out his lower lip in a pout and dug at his pug nose with a knuckle. "We only got to play during our nooning, Smoke, honest."

"Then you must be the best marble player in all of Big Rock."

"I'm . . . good, right enough. Sammy an' me played some when I boarded at his folks' house."

Here, in a land of big and early snows, school was held on a reversed schedule, from the fifteenth of April until the fifteenth of October. Tutoring made up for the other three months of class work. Sally Jensen, who had taught school at one time, held group lessons for Bobby, the children of ranch hands, and neighboring youngsters. It vexed her students mightily, Smoke knew, yet they showed up and behaved extraordinarily well. A broken leg had prevented Bobby from starting in Big Rock this April and, now out of his cast, cabin fever had set in.

What else would account for the boy undertaking the hazards of breaking mustangs? Smoke asked himself. Well, in a week, two at most, he would be headed for Big Rock and the little red schoolhouse at the end of Main Street. It had been arranged for him to live with his best friend, Sammy, and the Weisers expected him no later than that. For all Bobby's protestations, Smoke noted, he and Sammy had managed to get enough time away from the classroom the last summer to acquire a decent browning of their hides. A faint yellow-brown tinge of high altitude tan still colored Bobby's cheeks and forearms. Given this summer, he would be free forever of the unhealthy pallor which had accompanied the boy to the Sugarloaf. The high altitude sun soon cured normal skin like leather, with about the same color.

"We gonna build a lean-to or sleep out under the stars?" Bobby asked.

Smoke smiled back. "We can do whatever you want."

An animated face answered Smoke. "Then can you tell me some stories about you and Preacher? About back when you were my age?"

Smoke leaned over and lightly tapped Bobby on one shoulder point. "I didn't know Preacher when I was your age. I was fourteen, I think, when I wound up lost out here and on my own."

"So? Go on."

"Tonight, over fish and biscuits."

"That's a promise, Smoke?"

"Promise."

Toward mid-afternoon, Smoke Jensen called a halt to their journey. A small stand of silver-barked aspen beckoned. On his own land, Smoke could be certain of being safe, yet training and experience compelled him to pass up that inviting shelter. Instead, he used a short-handled axe to cut down a dozen forearm-thick saplings, bundled them and tied them off behind the packhorse. They traveled on to a moderate clearing, with plenty of grass for the horses, and shaded by a big old blue spruce.

It towered a good sixty feet into the air, and had, for at least 250 years, miraculously escaped the attention of the fierce lightning that crashed through these mountains and valleys each summer. With Bobby's help, he quickly constructed a roomy lean-to and covered the long, slant back and square sides with overlapped layers of pine bough. They stood back, hands on hips, and admired their handiwork.

"Not bad for a couple of amateurs, eh?" Smoke opined teasingly.

Bobby made a face that indicated he knew his leg was being pulled. "Aw, Smoke, you must have made hundreds of these before."

"Thousands, more like," Smoke agreed. "Now, it's your job to fetch firewood, while I bring stones from the creek for the fire ring."

Bobby cocked an eyebrow. "Who says we're gonna catch anything?"

"We have to cook *something*, don't we?"

"Yep. But who says I've got to get the firewood?"

"*I says.* Is that good enough for you?"

Bobby gave a fake gulp. "Yes, sir, yes it is."

He scampered off to do as bidden. Smoke turned toward the creek, located a suitable distance from their camp to muffle its noisy gurgling. As he neared the bank he heard lazy splashes from the sparkling water of Silver Creek. The rainbow trout would be thick enough to almost walk on, and hungry after the long winter.

An hour before sundown everything had been laid out in readiness. Outfitted with a Mason jar of live dragonflies and some of the newfangled artificial dry flies hooked into their shirt collars, man and boy set off to the east bank of Silver Creek.

At first sight, Bobby almost forgot himself and cried out in excitement. The water swarmed with mossy green backs. Hundreds of finny creatures filled the stream. Their deep color faded along their sides to the dividing line of rainbow colors. Beyond that their white, speckled bellies flashed brightly when one or another would roll gracefully after surfacing to snap up a winged insect. Bobby's eyes danced.

"Let's get to work," Smoke suggested.

Within half an hour they had a dozen pan-sized trout. The larger ones they had unhooked and thrown back. Those they caught tomorrow would be filleted and smoked. This intimate time together would teach Bobby many mountain man tricks. Smoke got the fire going while Bobby cleaned the fish. Smoke made biscuits and put the pot of beans he had put to soaking over the fire on a trestle arm. Bobby looked on and asked endless questions about camp cooking, while he peeled onions brought from the root cellar at the Sugarloaf headquarters, washed and sliced potatoes, and put a large skillet of them on to fry. At last, when the coals undulated with just the right red-orange glow, he put the fish on to fry.

They ate it all, wiped the skillets with biscuit halves, belched and patted full bellies. Then Smoke leaned back and lighted a thin, hard, dry cigar. Bobby returned to his first interest.

"Tell me about you an' Preacher."

"Oh, my, where to begin? I had to be about fourteen when Preacher hooked up with me and Pa in Kansas. Now, mind, we did not hit it off at the first. Preacher was old. Nearly as old as God, the way I saw it. He was crotchety, set in his ways, and about as foul-mouthed as any ten men could get. He could fill the air with blue smoke when he took to cussin'." Smoke paused to consider. Yep, Preacher had been all of that, and much, much more, too. "He was the best friend anyone could have, man or boy.

"Preacher was also kind, loyal, astonishingly intelligent, and absolutely convinced that life, as he lived it in the High Lonesome, was the best sort of life anyone could ever have. He took me in after Pa died."

"Tell me about one of you and Preacher's famous gunfights, Smoke?" Bobby interrupted.

Smoke sighed. "All right. Just this once. I recall the time when Preacher and I had to fight off eleven tough outlaws, the last of a gang that had been preying on immigrant trains along the North Platte. It was in the 'Sixties then, and the Army had mostly gone back east to fight for the Union. So, boarder riff raff grew bolder and bolder. This particular bunch had holed up in one of the trading posts they had also victimized. Preacher an' me had to go in after them. . . ."

Preacher eased his head up over the fallen log and peered closely at the tumble-down shack that housed the eleven vicious highwaymen. This weren't no dance for a seventeen-year-old tadpole to join into, he reckoned. But Smoke was here and rarin' for a fight, so what could he do? He cut his eyes to where Smoke Jensen crouched between some fat granite boulders, some twenty yards away.

Good boy, Preacher thought approvingly. He'd learned the lad about not bunchin' up right early in their time together. "The main idea is to give whoever is shootin' at ya more air than meat for targets," the mountain man had explained to a wide-eyed boy of almost fifteen. "Fact is, they's always more air than meat, as you'll find out when you are on the give side of that equation."

That had been near four years ago. Now all the lessons on surviving in the Big Empty were about to be put to the test. Preacher fervently wished that Charlie Three-Toes and some of those other never-quitters among the trapping fraternity had come along for this showdown. Best to have all sides of a building covered. Whatever, there was nothin' for it now. Preacher slid the barrel of his .56 Hawken over the fallen tree and took aim on a square of thinly scraped hide that served as a window pane. Behind it, kerosene lamps and flickering candles projected the head and shoulders of a human figure. Preacher eared back the hammer of the Hawken.

Sure, he could have hollered out for these scoundrels to surrender, to come out with their hands up, but he reckoned that such a move would only bring him and his young companion to more grief. So he fined his sight picture and squeezed the trigger. The Hawken made a sharp, clean report and shoved into Preacher's shoulder. The conical bullet went straight and true.

From his vantage point, Smoke Jensen saw a small black dot appear in the skin window and a moment later the human figure popped out of sight as though pulled by a rope. As instructed, he fired at the doorway when the flimsy pine board panel flew open. An unseen man screamed and then Preacher bellowed at the top of his lungs.

"That's two down! You men in there best come out and surrender. We've got you surrounded."

Well, at least on two sides, Preacher eased his conscience over straying from the whole truth.

"Like hell we will," came a belligerent reply. "We been watchin'. There's more of us than you."

By then Preacher had his Hawken reloaded. "Not for long," he bantered back as he again took aim on the window.

A crash and tinkle, and one clear, bell-like note followed

his shot. To Preacher's right, Smoke put a round through the open doorway. His reward came in hurried orders.

"Drag Rafe back out of there, we've gotta close that door."

Weak, though clearly audible to Smoke Jensen, Rafe spoke from the floor of the shack. "I'm gut-shot, Doolie. I ain't gonna make it."

Anger, colored by fear, filled the reply. "Then crawl outten that door so's we can close it."

"It hurts too much, Doolie."

The crack of a pistol shot answered him, then Doolie's growl. "Now, drag that body outten the way an' let's get to business."

Preacher had trained him well. Smoke was ready for that. He winged another man who bent over the dead Rafe. The hard case made a yelp and a startled frog-leap obliquely to the doorway. "Oh, dang, they got me in the cheek, Doolie."

"Can't be much, you can talk all right," the outlaw leader muttered.

"It's the other cheek, Doolie. Oh, damn, it hurts."

"Stop yer belly-achin'. We got to get 'em. By my count, they's only two. I say we rush them."

Doolie and his henchmen did not get the chance. Preacher's next blind shot through the opaque window shattered a kerosene lamp and the whole shelter went up in flames. Clothes afire, two men ran from the doorway, their weapons forgotten. Preacher dropped first one, then another with a pistol ball from his Model '60 Colt. Smoke fired at a third who went to one knee, shot through the side. Smoke's rifle sights still had him shooting low. Doolie and a couple more stubbornly insisted on fighting it out from inside.

When it was all over, only five of the eleven remained alive, all wounded. The shack burned to the ground with Doolie in it. And that's how Preacher handled that. . . .

Smoke Jensen looked down at Bobby Harris to find the boy with his head on one crooked arm, eyes closed, breathing deeply in a sound sleep. Smoke chuckled, then asked himself aloud, "Was I that boring?"

The boy did have a long, hard day of it, he reasoned. Tomorrow there would be more adventures. Smoke settled in his soogans and closed his eyes under the starry sky.

2

Darkness lay in a heavy blanket over the Yuma Territorial Prison compound. Droopy-eyed guards stood watch in the eight turretlike towers atop the walls at each corner and in the middle of each span. The two on the river side would be their targets, it had been decided. When he judged that alertness had sufficiently drained from the sentries, Victor Spectre forced a spate of coughing that would signal the other two to put their plan into operation.

Spectre's plan was simplicity in its most distilled form. They would incapacitate the turnkey, get out of the cell block, knock out the guards and pitch them over the side, then follow them on ropes made of torn blankets. To that end, when the cough ended, Buckner began to bang the bars of the cell he shared with Tinsdale with a tin cup. When he received no response, he called out.

"Hey! Hey, turnkey. There's a man sick in here."

No answer. Not even a light at the end of the corridor outside the open-fronted cells. Buckner, the most guileful, drew breath and yelled again. "Damnit, I mean it. He's powerful sick."

At last a light came, weakly from a hooded kerosene lantern. "Stow that racket."

"My cell-mate is powerful sick," Buckner wheedled. "It's

that rotten pork we had at supper. He's about to die on me."

"Have him report to the infirmary in the morning."

"He is not going to *last* until morning, Boss. Please, come take a look for yourself. He's all gray and green, eyes are rolled up. Hurry!"

Grumbling, the turnkey complied. He had a rolling gait, a leftover from his years before the mast on a clipper ship. When he had left the clipper ship service, he swore he never again wanted to see a body of water he could not hurl a rock across from bank to bank. He wound up here, at the top of the Rio Colorado delta, where the river ran a mile wide. He muttered to himself about the whims and petty annoyances of his charges as he approached the cell. He looked inside and saw a man who could indeed be on the edge of death.

Unadvisedly, he unlocked the cell and stepped inside. To his credit, he locked it behind him before he crossed to the bunk. He had no way of knowing that the pale, gray-green face had been achieved by mixing whitewash powder with scrapings from an ancient copper deposit in the quarry. When he bent to get a closer look, Olin Buckner snaked an arm around his neck and began to squeeze.

In less than two minutes Buckner had quite thoroughly throttled the prison guard. Ralph Tinsdale took the man's keys and helped to lift him onto the bunk in his own place. They gathered their makeshift ropes and slung the coils over both shoulders. Then Tinsdale unlocked the door and stepped out under the overhang of the second tier catwalk. Buckner followed and they locked the cell behind them.

They went directly to the cell that held Victor Spectre. Spectre waited for them at the bars. His cell-mate had awakened and suddenly realized what was at hand. "Take me along," he pleaded. "Hell, man, I'm doin' life like the rest of you. You gotta take me."

"We do not have to take you anywhere," Spectre told him coldly.

A crafty light glimmered in close-set eyes. "You don't take me, I'll make a fuss, get you caught. It's a floggin' an' another five years for attempted escape. Best be takin' me."

Resignation blossomed on the face of Victor Spectre. He nodded curtly, and gestured toward the cell door. "You win. To prove there's no hard feelings, you can go out first."

A lust for freedom glowed in pale blue eyes. "Now, that's mighty white of you."

When he stepped forward to stand at the door, Victor Spectre slid a hand-fashioned stone shank out of the sleeve of his shirt, gripped the cloth-wrapped hilt, and drove the needle point deep into the right kidney of the other prisoner. Swiftly he slashed from side to side, withdrew it, and destroyed the second vital organ. The man would bleed to death internally in less than four minutes, Spectre knew.

"Let's get going," he commanded as he eased the wounded man onto a bunk.

Once outside, the trio headed for the barred stairway at the opposite end of the corridor from where the turnkey had appeared. They moved on tiptoes to reduce any chance of discovery. Fortunately for them, the prison authorities insisted that all metal objects be well tended and frequently oiled, to ensure swift entry into the yard or cell blocks in the event of trouble. The key turned noiselessly and the bolt slid back.

Stealthily, the three escapees traversed the stairs and came upon the first guard in his corner tower. His chin rested on his chest and soft, wet snores rumbled up from his throat. Buckner bashed him in the side of the head to ensure he would not awaken for a while, then hoisted the slumped body and dumped him over the side. The other pair crawled along the parapet to the middle watch post. They found this guard staring out toward the river, contrary to his standing orders to look inward at the prison.

On a signal from Spectre, they swarmed over him and knocked him out without raising any alarm from the other watchers. In a second, he joined his fellow guard at the foot of the wall. Spectre motioned Buckner forward and began to fasten one end of his rope to a roof support of the mid-wall tower. Tinsdale did the same as did Buckner when he reached them. They slid down the rampart with surprising ease, only to find their ropes some fifteen feet short. The barrier had been footed in bedrock and the yard was that much higher than the ground outside.

Not liking it, though liking the alternatives even less, Victor Spectre let go and dropped to the rocky ground below. Good fortune went with him. He did not twist an ankle on any loose stones. Tinsdale came next and hit on his rump with a solid whump. Lastly, Buckner let go and plummeted to earth. Sharp pain shot through his left ankle.

He had severely sprained it. "What do we do now?" he bleated.

"Go on as planned. Ralph and I will find a boat, bring it here, and pick you up."

Twenty minutes later, the blunt prow of a river punt came into view through the limited starlight. Biting back shafts of pain, Buckner hobbled to the gunwale and his companions hauled him aboard. Cloth-padded oarlocks moved with a soft rumble and thump as they pushed out into the stream, leaving the guards behind, one with a broken neck. They headed northeastward, although Mexico lay a scant few miles the other direction. It had been Tinsdale's contribution that they would stand a better chance by going the long way, which would be least expected, rather than south into sure capture by the Rurales in Mexico. All in all, it proved a clever twist in their plan.

On this third day of their fishing trip, Smoke Jensen sat on a large, water-smoothed, flat rock and watched Bobby cast his line in lazy serpentines across the surface of Honey Spring. Smoke leaned on one elbow, took a puff on a cigar, and reflected on their time alone together as the gray white streamers drifted upward from his mouth. He felt he had made some progress with the boy.

Bobby had opened up to him, more so than any time in the past. For the first time the boy had released the pent-up sorrow and horror over his mother's death and freely grieved for her. She had not abandoned her son, as Bobby fantasized, rather she had been taken away by Rupe Connors. Rupe had been a brute and a sadist and had turned out to be a coward. He had abused the woman and the boy and in the end he had killed her with his fists and boots. And, for his cowardliness, as much as his savagery, Smoke Jensen had killed Rupe. Bobby understood those things more clearly now. Sally had been right, as usual, in saying that Bobby had transferred his large store of unexpressed love and hero worship to Smoke. The last mountain man only hoped that he had enough years left to see Bobby grow into a man. A sudden movement on the water brought Smoke abruptly upright.

A big old brown broke the surface and went for the man-made dry fly at the end of Bobby's line. The boy was a natural fisherman, more so than Smoke. He knew instinctively just when to set the hook, how hard to yank and how long to play the catch before landing it. He was in the process once again of doing so when his bare foot slipped on a mossy rock and with a shout, Bobby fell into the water.

"Ow! Ouch, my ankle," Bobby cried immediately. Then, "Get him, Smoke. Hurry or he'll get away."

Trout, line, and pole had started away from the shore of the pond. Smoke bounded into the water and snagged the cane rod by the butt, yanked and retrieved enough to fight the fish. Over one shoulder he called to Bobby, "Get out of the water. Now. You'll catch your death."

"'Kay, Smoke, if you say so. Oh! Ouch. That really hurts."

"Don't be a baby," Smoke teased.

Bobby glared at him. "I ain't a baby. But I'm cold, an' my foot really hurts."

Dripping, Bobby climbed from Honey Spring pond and

stood on shore, which prompted Smoke to be bossy again. "Get out of those clothes and wrap up in a blanket. I'll build a fire after I catch your blasted fish."

Twenty minutes later found them drying off beside a hat-sized fire. Bobby's teeth still chattered and he had a blue ring around his lips. Water dripped from his longish blond hair and the sharp points of his shoulder blades could be seen through the blanket that covered him. All of that did not keep him from a fit of giggles when Smoke described what he had been forced to do in order to land the brown trout. The titters dried up and Bobby looked seriously at Smoke.

"It's sure too bad that these mountain waters aren't like those around Model and Timpas. I mightily long to go for a swim."

Smoke sighed. "That's something you'll have to live without in this part of Colorado."

"Aw, darn." Then the boy brightened. "Don't you think, maybe by July, the water'll be warm enough? It is in Big Rock."

Shaking his head, Smoke patted Bobby on one shoulder. "It might be for you, but to me it's too dang cold. Now, get to work at warming up."

When the shivers ceased, Smoke examined Bobby's ankle. What he saw troubled him. "I don't think it's broken, but that ankle is swollen too much to get it back in your boot. Get dressed while I think on what to do next."

"Yes, sir."

When Bobby had restored himself in his clothing, he turned an anxious face to Smoke. Smoke Jensen rubbed his jaw with long, thick fingers. "You're not going to be able to keep on out here. Thing to do is turn back to the Sugarloaf."

Bobby frowned. "What about the fish you were going to smoke?"

"I figure they'll get smoked like we intended."

"How?"

Smoke smiled and explained. "I figure since you know

where the house is from here, and you're big enough anyway, you can ride on in by yourself."

"Really?" Bobby squeaked. "You mean it?"

"Yep. That's the long and the short of it. I'll help you load up and see you on your way, then come back and pull out a nice mess and get to it. Tell Sally I'll ride in late the day after tomorrow, right before supper."

Bobby all but jumped with excitement. "I really get to ride in by myself? It's—it's . . . stupendous!"

Fifteen minutes later saw the injured boy on his way. Bobby had a .38 Colt Lightning tucked in his waistband and his Stetson sat at a jaunty angle on his straw-colored hair. He waved confidently to Smoke, who chuckled and waggled his hat in the air. Smoke wanted very much to give the lad confidence in his ability to care for himself. After all, he was thirteen now. *"He'll do fine,"* Smoke said gruffly to himself. "Just fine."

Early morning revealed that not only humans had responded to the siren call of early spring. While Smoke fished the shore of Honey Spring for big browns, a shaggy, ill-tempered grizzly awakened from his hibernation. Belly rumbles prompted him to crawl out of his cave and go in search of something to eat. Instinct aimed him toward Honey Spring.

Alone now, and content with it, Smoke continued to fish into mid-morning. When he made a dozen casts and failed to get a single rise, let alone a strike, he decided to quit until evening feeding time. He had already smoked two dozen and would set his morning's catch to a smudgy aspen and hickory fire right after his noon meal. With what he could catch this afternoon, he would have a fair supply to take home the next day. With his mind made up, he began to roll the line onto his pole. With his gear packed up, he turned to head for his camp.

Right then, a very hungry bear, fresh out of hibernation, ambled down to the water for something to eat. Its small, myopic eyes did not at first take in the figure of a lone human. The grizzly snuffed the wind, grunted and tossed its head in bad humor. That sure put Smoke in a dilemma. A fishing pole was no defense whatever, and a handgun—even a hefty .45 Colt—would hardly be enough to take on a bear. A moment later, the bruin discovered Smoke.

In its ill-tempered mood, the grizzly saw the man as a threat to its territory. With a thunderous roar the animal charged.

Far from being a starry-eyed animal lover, Smoke Jensen had never seen any purpose in the wanton killing of animals. So, he took flight, his creel and pole left behind. It soon turned into a close race, with the speedy grizzly closing ground with each bound of its oddly articulated hind legs. Smoke won, though only by a hair.

He scaled the first twelve feet of the slender pine without even a grunt of effort. Once beyond the reach of the bear, he dug in his heels and shinnied up five more feet, grabbed the lowest branch, and pulled himself higher. With a powerful swing of his strong body, Smoke swung himself up to where he could straddle the branch. Now the sweat broke out. Smoke found himself panting for air. Below him the grizzly roared and assaulted the tree.

It made a good five feet, then began to slide back from sheer weight. Snuffling and tossing his head, the bear began to circle the pine. Above him, Smoke hung on and tried to think of something good happening.

After a third pass around the trunk, the bruin followed his nose to the wicker creel of trout and ripped it open. Voraciously it consumed every one, then went to the shore of the pond and waded out a ways. Competently, its long, sharp claws began to flash under the surface and come back out with a fat trout that flew sparkling through the air to land on the grassy bank. A disgruntled Smoke Jensen sat where he was and watched the bear work for an hour.

When it had its fill, perhaps it would amble away, Smoke reasoned. That would give him time to get down, get Thunder, and get the hell out of there.

Nightfall found the grizzly still there. He growled, yawned, grunted in frustration, stomped the ground, and made frequent trips from tree to pond and pond to tree. Smoke hung on and sweated. He removed his belt and fastened it around the trunk and retreaded the buckle. At least he would not fall asleep and become bruin breakfast. The ursine grumbling went on until a thin sliver of moon appeared to float majestically through the plethora of stars in an inky sky. At last, he fell asleep. So did Smoke. His last thought echoed in his head. *Maybe tomorrow will be a better day.*

A squat, bow-legged man, with grizzled, thinning hair, looked up from his kitchen table at the sound of a hollow thump that came from the small dock he had constructed out into the Colorado River. Visitors. And wouldn't you know it, right at breakfast time. Hiram Wells cut his eyes to the cloth-draped larder. He knew by heart what was within it.

Plenty of slab bacon. Only two eggs. Chickens had been acting offish lately. Flour for biscuits. Cornmeal, too. It would serve, and he could come out of it with a few cents in hard money. That would come in handy. Hiram pushed back his chair and came to his feet as he heard boots thud on the planks of his dock. He reached the door in time to count three men approaching at a stiff gait. One of them, he noted, limped. Too long in a boat, Hiram judged.

Yeah, but from where? And all night? The questions plagued him while the strangers approached. They came straight on, not even a howdy. The one in the lead nodded pleasantly.

"Mornin'. We'd be happy to pay if you could fix us something for breakfast."

Hiram pondered a moment. They stood and carried themselves like men of quality. Businessmen or the like. Yet they wore the thread-bare pull-over shirts and butternut linsey-woolsey trousers, with the broad black stripes that marked them as escaped convicts from the prison down-river at Yuma. A sudden chill struck him. Had he let them get too close already? Hiram decided to hedge.

"I'm a tad light on supplies, gentlemen. But I reckon I can whip up some bacon and some scrambled eggs. Biscuits or cornbread. I've some honey."

"Fine, fine," the apparent leader said rapidly. "Anything will do. We're rather hungry."

He had that cultured way of speaking, Hiram noted. Could be he was mistaken about the clothes. They might be some back-Easty fashionable hunting togs. "Come on in, then," he invited.

Hiram went to the stove and turned his back to them. That way he failed to note the quick exchange between the trio. His cartridge belt and six-gun hung on a peg in the wall. Above it hung a shotgun and a use-shiny Winchester. Hiram heard a soft footfall and then the strident click of sear notches as a hammer ratcheted back.

Hiram did not hear the bark of his Model '60 Remington conversion revolver. The bullet beat the sound to his head by a split second. Hiram Wells slammed sideways into the wall and fell dead to the floor. Quickly, Ralph Tinsdale undertook the duties of the cook. He provided a warm meal in minimal time. Victor Spectre had to cut Olin Buckner out of his boot, then all three sat down to consume the food hurriedly. They included that which the late Hiram had prepared for himself.

With their bellies full, they took the flour, cornmeal, sugar and salt, a tub of lard, and the remaining portion of the bacon slab. Done up in a flour sack, the provender accompanied them as they went to the small barn in search of horses. An hour after sinking their escape boat, Victor Spectre and his partners rode off without a trace.

* * *

Morning found Smoke Jensen still literally up a tree. He awakened to loud growling—from the bear and from his stomach. He had not eaten since the previous noon. Smoke opened gummy eyes and rubbed them, then looked down to find the grizzly reared back on his haunches, staring up. He had a hungry expression. A night in a tree without even a blanket had induced a lot of stiffness. Smoke hoped that it would not make him a quick snack for the bear. Abruptly, the bruin came to all fours and resumed his circular post around the pine tree.

With each pace on the left side, the grizzly emitted fearsome growls. Each with the right, disturbing rumbles. Smoke looked on and considered his chances of killing the creature with six loads. At least he might incapacitate the animal and not have to track it down later. He had about resigned himself to having to shoot the creature when it stopped pacing abruptly and reared on its massive hind legs.

Its small, pig-eyes stared myopically while it turned its head from side to side, as it listened to slight sounds as yet unheard by Smoke. Gradually, Smoke made out faint hoofbeats and snatches of conversation. The bear's ears twitched, the black muzzle pointed in the direction of the sound. Dropping to all fours, the animal bolted for hiding in a lumbering gait as two riders cantered into view. Within three minutes, Smoke recognized them, grateful for the help, yet wishful that it had been anyone else but these two.

A laughing Monte Carson reined in under the tree. His face wreathed in mirth, Hank Evans sat beside him. "Hoo-haw! Look what we have here!" Monte chortled. Mid-morning sunlight winked off his sheriff's badge.

"What do you suppose got him up there?" Hank asked through a titter of laughter.

"Couldn't be that bear, could it?" Monte queried rhetorically. "That big ol' grizzly bear?" He held his sides and howled with merriment.

"You mean that little-bitty fur ball that got scared off by our horses?" Hank kept up the badinage.

"That's it. That's the one," Monte guffawed.

"This is it!" Smoke corrected, while he brandished a big, knobby fist. "This is the one that will smack you right between the runnin' lights when I get down out of this damned tree."

"Oh, why, come right ahead," Monte taunted.

Smoke glowered at them. "Do you think you two could stop cacklin' like a barnyard full of hens long enough to give me a hand getting down?"

Hank snaked a rope up to Smoke, who draped it over the limb. Then the last mountain man released himself from his emergency sling, restrung his belt and swung one leg over the branch. Balanced sideways, he inserted a boot toe in the loop of the lariat and turned around to hang from his hands.

"Lower away," he gave the sign.

In less than a minute, Smoke had returned to solid ground. His mood had not improved the least while Monte Carson and Hank Evans plied him with questions about how he had been caught off guard by the grizzly. Hank laid a fire and filled a coffeepot with fresh water. He set that to boil and broke out Smoke's skillet.

"I'll bet you're hungry, right?" he asked Smoke dryly.

"Don't even mention it."

"Bacon, eggs, an' fried tatters?" Hank prompted.

"A pound of bacon, a dozen eggs, and two pounds of potatoes with onions, if you please," Smoke answered calmly. "And that's just for starters." Then his temper caught him out again. *"And I don't like bein' done for!"*

His voice echoed across the water in the silence that followed. As though on a signal all three men broke up in side-splitting laughter. Finally, Smoke choked out a sensible reply. "I'll tell you about it after the first cup of coffee."

Monte stepped forward, extending a silver flask in one hand. "I've got a little rye to spike it with."

"Good," Smoke grumped. "Damn good. Then you'll hear it all."

3

After Smoke had recounted his incident with the bear, with frequent interruptions of sniggers and out-and-out hee-haw braying laughter, he got around to asking Monte what had brought the lawman out from Big Rock. Monte took a pull on his coffee, rubbed his chin in a contemplative manner, and turned his sky-blue eyes on Smoke.

"Well, it might not mean anything at all. It's something I picked up from the telegraph. Only, the names were familiar, and I did want an excuse to sample some of Sally's great pie, so I rode out to tell you about it."

"Well, then, stop chasin' around Murphy's barn and do it," Smoke responded in mock irritation.

"All right, I will. Three men have escaped from Yuma Prison."

It left Smoke unimpressed and unconcerned. "There's more than that has gotten out of there."

Monte ignored Smoke's teasing interruption. "These three went together. Beings as how you put all of them behind bars, I got to thinkin' that maybe you should know."

"Who are they?'

Monte named them. Smoke listened and shook his head. "I remember those three right well. I had no idea they had gotten together in prison. How'd a thing like that happen?"

Right at home with this sort of situation, Monte called off the list. "Attempted escape can get a man transferred. So can a killing inside prison that a certain convict cannot be proven to have done. Or just being a constant pain in the ass. There's plenty of causes. And, considering the Territorial Prison at Yuma is the hellhole of the entire system, no doubt the worst all wind up there eventually."

Smoke nodded affirmatively. "You've described Buckner, Spectre, and Tinsdale perfectly, Monte. They are all killers, they would no doubt contrive to escape, and beyond any doubt, they are all huge pains in the ass."

"There's more. They badly injured one guard, and killed another and a turnkey on the way out."

"Yep. I had no idea they'd been put together, like I said, but with these killings, it makes it clear that they're up to no good. Now, let's put out this fire and go look at a piece of that pie."

After the noon-hour rush, business had slackened off at the Grand Canyon Saloon, in the Arizona town of the same name. Five cronies sat around a green baise-topped table playing a desultory game of poker. The hands took forever to be played and the largest bet was half a dollar. At another table, one sequestered in a shadow-darkened corner, Spectre, Tinsdale, and Buckner sat conducting business. They had been in the settlement on the rim of the Grand Canyon for less than a day. They had as yet to pay any notice to the spectacular view. Bored with the lack of activity, Buckner nodded toward the card players.

"Last of the big-time spenders."

Victor Spectre studied him over the rim of a whiskey glass. "I'd not sneer, were I you. Up until we killed that old man on the Colorado, the most you've had in your pocket for the last fifteen years is lint, Olin. You would have sold your soul for fifty cents cash money."

Buckner flushed deep red. That had hit too close to home.

He had sold his soul, or at least it seemed like that, when he was younger and his need for tobacco had become overwhelming. He had stolen it. The first theft of his life. He lost his chance to make a testy reply when a tall, lean, hard-looking man approached their table. The stranger appeared to be in his mid-twenties, and did not remove his hat or act in the least servile, Olin Buckner noted. At a distance of three feet, the man stopped and cleared his throat.

"I hear you're lookin' to hire some men."

"We are. Are you, by chance, interested?" Victor Spectre responded.

A fleeting, icy smile spread full lips. "Not by chance, by lack of other employment. What is it you are hiring for?"

"We need men good with their guns. And I like to know the name of any man I'm talking business with."

"My name's Jaeger. Gus Jaeger. M'given name is Augustus, but it's a lot to work your tongue around, so I shortened it. And who might you be?"

"I am Victor Spectre, these gentlemen are my partners in this little endeavor. Ralph Tinsdale and Olin Buckner. Now, Mr. Jaeger, take a seat and we can discuss this a little further."

When Jaeger took one of the straight-back chairs, reversed it and seated himself, Spectre signaled the bartender for a round. When that had been duly delivered and the apron absented himself, Spectre steepled his fingers on the green table and spoke in a low voice.

"It did not take much initiative or effort for us to do a little research. I suppose your current unemployment has something to do with the three years you spent in prison for stagecoach robbery, Mr. Jaeger. The others in the gang got considerably more time, am I correct?"

Gus Jaeger went white from anger and clenched a fist before answering. His cold, hazel eyes burned under black brows. "You're right about that. The reason is I hadn't pulled as many jobs with the boys as they got caught for. What business is it of yours to go snoopin' into a man's past?"

"Oh, we did not do anything so shady, believe me. We

simply went through some of the sheriff's old wanted posters and reviewed past issues of the newspapers. Your name came up, along with some others. We left invitations in their postal boxes, like the one you received. So far, you are the first to respond."

Jaeger's full, fleshy lips pulled wide in a rueful grin. He removed his Montana Peak Stetson, revealing thick black hair, and sailed it toward a row of hooks on the near wall. It caught and held. By then he had recovered himself enough to speak calmly.

"I'm surprised there has not been more interest. What exactly do you have in mind?"

"There is this man. He needs doing away with," Spectre evaded.

Jaeger looked them over with a puzzled frown. "You want to hire a killing? There's three of you. Why don't you simply find him and do it yourselves?"

"It's—well, it is not quite that easy." Spectre still tried to avoid naming the target.

"Why not? Is he a gunfighter?"

"Yes, Mr. Jaeger, he is."

Smiling, Jaeger knocked back his whiskey and tilted his chair away from the table. "Well, then, you needn't worry about any other applicants. There's not anyone around that's better than me in a one-on-one shoot-out. I could even handle two to one, if necessary. If you gentlemen are satisfied, you've got yourself all the gunhand you'll need. By the way, who is this gunfighter?"

"It's—ah—Smoke Jensen," Spectre regretfully gusted out.

Jaeger's chair legs banged noisily back onto the floor and his jaw sagged. Belatedly, he closed his mouth and swallowed hard. "If I weren't so hard up for work, I'd tell you just how crazy you are and high-tail it out of here."

Tinsdale responded dryly. "You've heard of him, I gather?"

"*Heard* of him? I grew up readin' penny dreadfuls about

Smoke Jensen. If only a quarter of it was true, he's pure hell on wheels. Not anyone I'd want to go up against alone. Hell, I'd be afraid to even try to back-shoot him."

"It is wise to have a healthy respect for an adversary," Spectre stated flatly. "Though hardly good to fear someone you are engaged to dispose of. Are you sure you can conquer your awe of Jensen long enough to make an end of him?"

After a long moment of careful thought, Jaeger made reply. "Of course I can. Especial, I've got me three or four good boys to back me up."

Victor Spectre responded almost primly. "We were thinking of more like twenty. Very well, Mr. Jaeger, consider yourself hired. We will, naturally, pay for your hotel accommodations and meals, with a two dollar a day stipend until we are ready to move on."

"Is Smoke Jensen here, in Arizona?"

"Not that we know of. We assume we will need to do something to flush him out of his high valley ranch in the Colorado Rockies. Until we are in a position to do that, we must build up a sizable gang to make things happen as we want them to. Now, you can do us a first service. Spread the word to those of like inclination. Tell them we are prepared to be most generous." He paused a moment and pinned Jaeger with his cold eyes. "Only don't tell them who they'll be facing."

After Gus Jaeger departed Olin Buckner spoke what was on all their minds. "A good thing that old man was a miser, or we'd not be able to be so generous."

"Yes, quite," Spectre answered. "We will have to act quickly to replenish our purse after our recruiting is ended here, Olin."

"What did you have in mind, Victor?" Tinsdale asked.

"We have engaged the services of an expert highwayman. I think we should find out all we can about the stage lines coming into here and what they carry."

Buckner brightened. "Yes. And there are banks along the way, too. By the way, where are we going?"

Spectre spoke in a tone that suggested he had been thinking on the subject for a long while. "North. Perhaps as far as into Wyoming. There's a place there guaranteed to make Smoke Jensen come to us."

"Where's that?" Tinsdale demanded.

"Later. You will all know when the time is right."

Over the next three days, they learned all that could be expected about the stage lines. Spectre and his partners also interviewed close to twenty-five men. Among them certified hard cases, murderers, and a number of outlaw wanna-bes. They rejected all but two of the latter, and one of the killers, who had an odd cast in his eye that made him appear to be studying them for the best method of making their deaths long and excruciating. That left the trio of vengeance-hungry felons a total of seventeen gunhands.

"We'll get more along the way," Spectre advised them philosophically.

"Why do we need more?"

Spectre smiled patronizingly. "Simple, Olin. We have to have a veritable army to take over an entire town."

Eyebrows climbed Buckner's forehead. "What town?"

"In due time, Olin. At the right moment, everyone will know. Please, do not bring up the subject again. Uh—Mr. Jaeger, notify the others that we will be leaving early tomorrow morning."

"Right away, Boss. And—ah—call me Gus, everyone does. And I can call you . . . ?"

"*Mister* Spectre," Victor interrupted.

An hour after first light, the eighteen hard cases rode out of Grand Canyon with the partners. They left by twos and threes in order not to attract unwanted attention. Twenty miles out of town, where the trail disappeared around the curved base of a large hill, Victor Spectre called a halt.

"Men, Gus here has considerable experience at holding up stagecoaches. Miller and Brock, as I understand, have some acquaintance with the technique also."

An erstwhile thug named Huntoon screwed up his face and, in an Appalachian accent, asked a baby-faced gunfighter named Carpenter next to him, "What's that feller say?"

Carpenter cut his pale ice-blue eyes to Huntoon. "He says Jaeger, Miller, an' Brock have robbed themselves a few stages."

Brow furrowed, Huntoon considered this. "That a fact?"

Spectre ignored the aside and went on. "In a short while, a stage, heavily laden with the payroll for the Valle del Cobre mine, will be coming around that curve. We are going to rob it. In order to do this, you will follow the orders of Mr. Jaeger. Misters Miller and Brock will direct the two phases of the operation. Obey them as you would myself and we shall all enjoy the spoils."

"We gonna split it up share for share?" Huntoon raised his voice to inquire.

"No. My partners and I shall use the proceeds to pay you your new wage of ten dollars a day."

An excited murmur ran through the outlaws and thugs. The only objection came from Huntoon. "Now that's mighty generous, Mr. Spectre, but we'd prefer equal shares."

Victor Spectre's face flushed dark red. Fury burned in his green eyes, and sparks crackled in his voice. "And would you also prefer to be left stone dead beside the trail?"

"Uh—no, sir. Not at all, nosir."

"Then leave the financial affairs of this jolly band to your betters, Mr Huntoon."

Huntoon's mouth almost got him dead after all. "What d'y'all mean my betters?' Y'all may talk lak a dandy but you ain't nothin' more than another jailbird on the run. I done seed the flyer in the post office."

Thunder rumbled and lightning flashed in Spectre's

harsh rejoinder. *"We are your betters,* you hillbilly trash, for the simple reason that we can read and write and we do not dally with our cousins and sisters."

Had it been any other man, or had he not seen Carpenter, a feller he thought of as a friend, put his hand on the butt of his Colt, Huntoon would have dragged iron. Instead he lowered his eyes and spoke softly as he would to his father. "Yes, Boss. You're right, Boss." It didn't keep him from brooding on the idea of a future feud.

Victor Spectre did not even attempt to hide the smirk on his lips. "Very well. Gus, divide the men according to your needs and get them in position. We haven't much time."

Twenty minutes later the keener ears among the gang picked up the faint jingle and slap of chain and tack over the rumble of hooves and crunch of iron-shod tires. Before long the creaking of the coach could be heard. It surprised Victor to see the nervousness of so many among his band of desperados. He trusted that they would perform better than it looked like they could.

The flying manes and outstretched necks of the coach horses came into view around the curve. At once, men rode out of the brush and trees to either side of the trail and fired at the men on the driver's bench. Others blocked the roadway and two of them reached for the lead horses. A shotgun boomed and one of the outlaws screamed horribly. More gunshots crackled from the robbers and the guard slumped dead.

A moment later, the driver dropped the reins and threw up his hands. He pitched forward over the dashboard and fell to the tongue. The horses came to a calamitous halt, the hind four ramming forward into the rumps of those ahead. Swaying wildly, the coach juddered to a halt. From inside, a lone passenger fired a futile, unwise shot. Three rounds answered him.

Silence followed. Then, the unseen passenger groaned

as the masked men walked their mounts to the coach. Fin Brock dismounted and opened the door. The wounded passenger leaned outward and two highwaymen helped him from the stage. They sat him against a boulder and ignored him thereafter. It took little time to discover the three large strongboxes filled with gold and silver coin.

Men cheered at the sight. At the direction of Gus Jaeger, the stage horses were unhitched and their harness altered to serve as pack bearing tack. One iron-banded crate went on each of three, alone with some of the load from the gang's pack animals. With loads lightened, the hard-faced men removed their bandana masks and rode off without any thought for the wounded passenger.

4

Spectre, Tinsdale, and Buckner remained very much on the mind of Smoke Jensen as he rode into Big Rock to telegraph the prison for more details. An emergency breeched foal and other ranch minutiae had prevented him from returning to town with Monte Carson. Now, a week later, he dwelled on the circumstances of the men whose criminal careers he had interrupted. There wasn't a one of them who did not get what he deserved.

With such dark broodings filling his head, Smoke ambled spotted-rump Thunder onto the northern end of Central Street, the main drag of Big Rock. The recent craze for naming every street in the small community amused Smoke. He considered it *pretentious,* one of the fancy words Sally had taught him. He did not think what he discovered halfway down the first block of the business district to be pretentious, nor did it amuse him.

A burly man, a stranger to these parts, stood between the driver's seat and dashboard of a heavy wagon. Muscles rippled in his thick shoulders as he plied a whip to lash the daylights out of a pair of scrawny, sway-backed mules, trapped in the harness of the overloaded rig they pulled.

"I'll learn ya, gawdamnit, you stubborn, stupid critters. When I say haul, you by damnit haul. Now git to movin'."

Smoke Jensen just naturally bristled at this unnecessary cruelty. He eased his 'Palouse stallion closer and tipped the brim of his hat back on his head. For all his sudden anger at this abuse, he kept his voice polite.

"Excuse me." The huge teamster ignored Smoke. "I said, excuse me. I don't think you will achieve the results you expect by beating these starved, worn-out animals any longer."

The burly driver turned to face Smoke. "Mind yer own gawdamned business. These lazy bastids, all they do is eat and sleep and crap. Hell, they even sleep standin' up. Now, git on outta here and leave me to what I have to do."

When the teamster turned away and applied his whip again, Smoke edged Thunder closer to the wagon. He reached out with one big hand and lifted the man off his feet. With a touch of his heels, Smoke backed Thunder clear of the buckboard and released his grip on the astonished wagoneer. Then Smoke calmly dismounted while the astonished lout dropped to his boots in the dusty street.

Blinded by rage, the foolish man went at Smoke with the whip. In one swift move, Smoke deflected the lash with his left forearm, grabbed the braided leather scourge and yanked it from the man's grasp. Smoke's right hand got right busy snapping short jabs to the thick lips of the dolt. Rocked back on his heels, the errant teamster belatedly brought up his arms in an effort to end the punishment. Smoke Jensen merely changed targets.

Hard knuckles dug into the puss gut of the abusive dullard. Coughing out air, the man did manage to land one blow that stung Smoke's left cheekbone. Smoke responded with a looping left that opened a cut on his opponent's right brow. A red curtain lowered over the teamster's right eye. He uttered a bull-roar of outrage and tried to grab Smoke in a bear hug.

Smoke danced back from it, and popped his target on one fat jowl. He felt teeth give beneath the layer of fat. Then the stranger tried a kick to Smoke's groin. Smoke side-stepped it and grabbed the offending leg. He gave it a quick yank upward.

"Phaw!" the teamster bellowed when his rump contacted the hard-packed street.

Smoke closed with him and battered his head seriously. Groggy, the owner of the mules tried to stand. Smoke knocked him flat on his back with a left to the jaw. Satisfied that he had taken all of the fight out of the man, Smoke turned his back and strode toward Thunder. He barely heard the scrabble of boot soles on the pebble-strewn street as the battered man came at Smoke with a knife.

Bert Fowler had never been given such a humiliation in his entire life. Always big for his age, he had bullied and brow-beaten even children older than himself. As he grew, he had filled out, both in muscle and in flab. Bert loved to eat. Six eggs, two pork chops, a couple of slabs of cornmeal mush, and a half dozen biscuits he considered a light breakfast. He routinely ate a whole chicken when he sat down to be serious about it. That came with the better part of a serving bowl of mashed potatoes, a quart of gravy, and more biscuits to mop up the run-over. Bert liked his run-overs.

By the time he was a man full-grown, he stood an inch over six feet and weighed 257 pounds. When Smoke Jensen lifted him off his wagon, he had increased that to an even 300. Now, bruised, cut, and bleeding, his ribs and gut aching pools of fire, Bert got set on revenge. From his boot top he retrieved a long, thin-bladed dagger and pushed himself upright. Wiping blood out of his right eye, he went directly for the back of the man who had assaulted him so viciously.

Smoke heard the rush of boot soles at the last moment. He jumped to one side and slapped instinctively at the hand that held the knife. Bert Fowler staggered a bit off course, but whirled in time to confront his enemy. Smoke

Jensen saw no reason to kill this lout. Even though faced with the danger of a knife, he eschewed the use of his trusty .45 Colt Peacemaker. In the fleeting instant when both men stood in locked study of one another, he decided to give the errant teamster a taste of his own medicine.

Cat-quick, Smoke bent at the knees and recovered the handle of Fowler's whip. He came up with the lash seething through the air in a backward motion beside his ear. He sensed when it reached its maximum extension and brought his arm forward. Fowler screamed when the nasty little lead tip he had affixed to his bullwhip bit into the flesh of his right shoulder.

He retained his grasp on the knife regardless, and lunged forward with the tip extended toward the heart of Smoke Jensen. Smoke cracked the whip again. This time he cut through the front of Fowler's shirt and left a long, red welt on pallid flesh. Fowler howled with pain. He took two more staggering steps toward his hated opponent.

Smoke met him with another rapid, three cut criss-cross that opened the entire front of his assailant's shirt. Blood ran from the rent flesh. Fowler reversed the knife and made to throw it. Smoke Jensen sliced the dagger from his hand. Relentlessly the flogging went on.

Smoke moved from side to side, the strap cut into the bulging shoulders of Bert Fowler, tore away the remains of his shirt and began to checker his back. He bent double, intent now on merely protecting his face. Smoke had no intention of marking him there, and laid on the flail with unemotional exactness. The trousers came next.

Long gaps in the trouser legs showed equally white human legs beneath, albeit stout as beer kegs. They did not remain so for long. By the time Smoke Jensen had cut the cloth away at mid-thigh, in the manner sometimes worn by small boys, those legs had become rivers of blood. This would be one beating Smoke determined the man would never forget. Fowler went to his knees, howled pitifully, then finally cringed into a whimpering mass of cut and bleeding flesh. Smoke Jensen relented.

Stalking over to the badly mauled teamster, Smoke tossed the bloody whip into the wagon box and stared down at the product of his efforts. "Tell me," he asked politely, "did you enjoy feeling like your mules must have?" Then he turned away, remounted Thunder and rode off down the street.

Smoke Jensen tied off Thunder outside the telegraph office at the railroad depot in Big Rock. His boots rang on the thick two by six planks of the platform as he crossed to the door. Inside, the telegrapher sat in his bay window that overlooked the tracks. Coatless, he had sleeve garters to hold up the long sleeves of his light blue shirt with the white vertical pinstripes. Three cigars protruded from the upper pocket of his vest. A green eyeshade obscured his face. He looked up as Smoke approached the counter.

"Afternoon, Mr. Jensen. What can I do for you?"

"I'd like to send a telegraph message."

Rising from his chair, the telegrapher came to the counter. "Do you have it written out?"

"No. I'll do that now."

An octagonal-faced Regulator clock ticked out the seconds while Smoke wrote his query on the yellow form. It was clear, concise, and direct. He hoped the answer would be the same, and come quickly. When he finished, he handed the missive over to the telegraph operator, who glanced at it and raised an eyebrow.

"You—ah—expecting company, Mr. Jensen?"

He remembered when the famous Smoke Jensen and Monte Carson had stood back to back and battled a nest of outlaws in the streets of Big Rock. They had cut them down mercilessly and driven the remainder out of town. The village had been right tame since then.

"I don't think so. And, I'm going to do my best to see nothing unusual happens."

Relief flooded the face of the railroad employee. He counted the number of words. "That'll be two and a quarter. I'll get this out right away. If a reply comes in soon, where can I reach you?"

"I'll be over at Monte's office." Smoke paid him and left.

Back astride Thunder, Smoke ambled along the main street to the low, stone building next to the town hall. He looped the reins over the tie-rail and gained the stoop. Inside the stout, thick door, Monte Carson sat at his desk, a report form from the night man in one hand, a steaming cup of coffee in the other. He glanced up as Smoke entered.

"Didn't take you long to decide to look into that a little more, did it?"

"No, Monte. It just sat in my head and gnawed until I had to find out all I could."

"Pour yerself some java. Herkimer just got in some fresh beans over at the Mercantile." Then he noticed the disarray of Smoke's shirt. "What did you get into?"

Smoke snorted and tugged at his shirttail. While he poured, he told Monte about the stranger and his mules. Monte listened, nodded at the proper spots, and then rendered his judgment. "It's a wonder the feller didn't get himself a sudden case of the deads."

"If he had pulled a gun, instead of that knife, he would have."

"That's cold, Smoke, downright cold," Monte said with a twinkle in his eyes.

They drank coffee and talked about the latest goings on in Big Rock for a quarter past an hour. Monte was in mid-sentence, telling Smoke about how Bluenosed Bertha, one of the bar girls at the Follies Saloon, had gotten her finger caught in a mousetrap, when the door swung outward.

"What's this?" the lawman demanded.

In the opening stood a boy of about eleven or twelve. Barefoot, he had a thick thatch of carroty hair above a balloon face of rusty-orange freckles. His unfastened trouser legs ended at mid-calf, which gave him the look of an urchin. "For Mr. Jensen, Sheriff. We got an answer back from the folks out in Arizona Territory."

Smoke took the folded, yellow form and handed the boy a dime. The lad's eyes went wide. "Oh, boy! A whole dime. Thank you, Mr Jensen."

He scampered off down Central Street, no doubt to the general mercantile and those inviting glass jars of horehound drops and rock candy. Smoke opened the message and read from it. His eyebrows rose and he whistled softly at the conclusion. He gestured toward Monte Carson with the sheet of paper.

"They've learned a bit more since that first telegram. The warden verified that they killed two guards and seriously injured another in their escape. The search has been fruitless in Mexico. But a hermit, by the name of Hiram Wells, who lived up-river from the prison was found murdered and his horses missing."

"That fits with what the warden says a trustee told him. Which is that the three of them formed an alliance to get revenge on some unnamed man responsible for them all being in prison. A man who lives somewhere up in the mountain country."

Monte Carson looked hard at Smoke Jensen. "He didn't have a name, huh?"

"That's what it says. Although it doesn't take a whiz at arithmetic to add up one and one and get two."

Brow furrowed now in concentration, Monte reached a conclusion. "I think you an' me, an' a couple of good deputies had ought to ride up to the Sugarloaf and fort up. That's what I think."

Smoke shook his head. "No offense, Monte, but I don't think that's such a hot idea. No sense in bringing the fight home with us. In fact, the farther I can keep Spectre, Tinsdale, and Buckner from the Sugarloaf, the happier I will be."

Genuine concern for his long-time friend colored Monte's words. "What do you have in mind?"

"I reckon to head into some friendly territory up Wyoming way. Say, maybe Jackson's Hole. I can settle in, make my presence known, and let the word get out. Then let them come."

"Think they'll do it on their own?"

"No, Monte, they'll bring along help. Spectre used to run a large band of outlaws, numbered around forty. He's known along the Owl Hoot Trail. If he feels the need, he can get all the men he needs."

"Why do you single him out as the leader of all this, Smoke?"

"Because I came close to blowing out his brains in the showdown we had. And I killed his only son. But look at it this way. When they come for me, and they will, I'll have these would-be avengers on ground I am well familiar with and they know little about. That'll go a long way toward evening the odds."

Monte could not let it go. "I hope you're right. I sure's hell do."

Hanksville, in Utah, hovered on the edge of Ute country. As yet, the native dwellers of the sparse ground had not been corralled and driven onto a small, unpromising reservation in the southern corner of Colorado. They roamed free. It was doubtful that more than a handful of politicians in Washington knew that they existed. Not until the arid land they occupied offered something of value would they come under the scrutiny of the Bureau of Indian Affairs. Hanksville had a white population of fifty-seven and a scattering of Mexican and halfbreed residents. It also served as a transient haven for men on the run.

Victor Spectre came there to recruit more guns for his

gang. He had little difficulty in achieving that. Eleven hard cases signed on. Men with shifty eyes and a day or more growth of beard, they found the pay acceptable and the promise of a bonus for killing just a single man satisfying. There were no saloons in Hanksville, so the outlaws drank in their rooms and Victor ordered a quick departure when he had all of the reinforcements he could expect to obtain. So far their travels had paralleled the Colorado River. Here they would make a change.

Five miles outside of town to the east, he halted the growing band and gathered them around. "We're heading north from here."

"How far north?" one fellow with an over-fondness for the desert asked with a gimlet eye.

"Quite a ways."

"Thought you said this feller we're to kill lives in Colorado?"

"He does, but we're not going there."

Upon hearing that, Fin Brock looked hard at Spectre, doubt clear in his narrow face. "Then how are we gonna get him?"

Spectre's answer was simple enough for anyone. "We make him come to us."

Farlee Huntoon got in his nickel's worth. "Easier said than done, I reckon. 'Specially if he finds out how many of us there is."

Others agreed. Huntoon pushed his luck. "One man alone, he don't have to come up again' us, lessen he chooses to."

Victor Spectre's voice crackled in reply. "There are ways, Mr. Huntoon, to make a man do anything you want him to. If you weren't such a dolt, you'd know that."

"Say what? Was you tryin' to insult me, Mr. Spectre?"

Victor spoke lightly, his face unreadable and his tone dry. "No, Mr. Huntoon. I was praising the remarkable lack of genius engendered in the terminally inbred."

"Well—ah—okay, I reckon that's no insult then. Ain't often I get praised."

"No, I expect not." Spectre turned away.

One of the new men, Judson Reese, better spoken and dressed than the average, touched his hat brim in a sort of salute. "If we cannot have the exact location, can you at least give us a general idea of our destination?"

Spectre beamed at him. "I admire a well-spoken man. Yes, I'll answer that, since you've put it so nicely. In the short term, I feel you men need some recreation. Especially after being in that straight-laced place. We shall pay a visit to the Utes. I hear there is a prosperous trading post not far north of here. Then we will be going on to Wyoming, perhaps even Montana. But, rest assured, wherever we go, Smoke Jensen will come to us."

Back on the Sugarloaf, Sally Jensen knew something had gone terribly wrong for her husband the moment he rode up the lane to the main house. His usually high, smooth brow wore lines of furrows. He kissed her somewhat absently, then hugged her tightly to his chest as though it would be the last time.

"What is it, Smoke?"

Neither he nor Monte Carson had mentioned the real cause of Monte's visit to the ranch a week earlier. Now Smoke found himself at a loss as to how to explain. So, he used the time-honored tactic of husbands everywhere. He evaded.

"It's nothing important. I'll tell you over supper. And—ah—ask Bobby to take supper with us, too, please."

That worried Sally even more. Good wife that she was, though, she remained quiet about it. She fixed them a choice rib roast from a steer recently slaughtered out of the small herd kept for that purpose—Smoke would like that—and mounds of mashed potatoes—Bobby would like that—with pan gravy, turnips, and a half gallon, blue Mason jar of wilted lettuce put up last summer. She had already baked a pie.

They ate and Smoke related only the gossip he had picked up in Big Rock that he knew would interest Sally. Then, over a second piece of pie and a cup of coffee, Smoke grudgingly drug out the topic he least wanted to discuss.

"Sally, do you remember when Monte rode out here a while ago?"

"How could I not? It was only last week."

"What you are not aware of is why he came." And he went on to give her a highly edited version of the escape and the backgrounds of the men involved. When he had finished, Sally sat with her hands in her lap and stared at the checked tablecloth. At last, she raised her head and spoke somewhat shakily.

"What is it you are going to do?"

Smoke frowned. Now came the hard part. "I am going to be gone for a while. It's me they want, not you, or the hands, or even Bobby. Odds are they are unaware he exists. I'll put some distance between us and then let it be known where I am. The word will get to them. They'll come. And then I will take care of them the way I should have the first time around."

Sally said it plainly enough that its tone of resignation nearly broke Smoke's heart. "You'll kill them."

"If that's what it takes." He broke his hazel gaze from her steady, demanding eyes. "We can hope it ends otherwise."

Bobby suddenly charged into the conversation. "I want to go with you, Smoke."

"No. That's out of the question. I have to do this alone and not endanger anyone else. Monte even offered me deputies and his own help to defend the Sugarloaf. I told him no. My way is the best."

"I'm big enough," Bobby protested. "You've gotta let me come. I can shoot and I've been practicin' with rifle and six-gun. Ike says I'm a far above average shot, even from horseback. And you taught me how to live in the mountains."

Smoke needed little effort to sound stern. "Not another word, young man."

Sally got right to the most painful item. "When?"

"I'll leave first thing tomorrow morning."

Tears swam in Sally's eyes as she cleared the table, and she brushed them away angrily. He was her man and he would do what he thought best. Though if he would listen to anyone, it was she. Sally tried to use that power sparingly. His feelings hurt, Bobby excused himself early to go to the bunkhouse.

That night, laying in bed, Smoke reached out and tenderly took Sally in his arms. She came eagerly and they had a long, tender, passionate parting. The one in the morning would be a facade, a formality for the hands who would witness it.

Pale gray hovered over the eastern ridge as Smoke Jensen came from the kitchen door and took up the reins to his pack horse and Thunder and turned back to the open doorway. Sally hesitated only a second, then lifted her skirt and apron and ran to his embrace. He held her tightly and she did a remarkable job of holding back the tears.

Stuff and nonsense, she thought angrily as she felt the burning behind closed lids. She had seen her man off to danger a hundred times before and not acted so childishly. She pulled back and they kissed hungrily.

"You take care of yourself, Smoke Jensen."

"Yes, ma'am, I'll be sure to do that," Smoke said with wry humor.

They kissed again and Smoke swung into the saddle. He looked around, wondering why Bobby had not come out to see him off. With a light-hearted wave he parted from his wife and set out down the lane to the main gate of the

Sugarloaf. As he neared it, he saw a forlorn figure waiting for him there.

Bobby did not argue or even plead. His looks said it all. His throat worked to fight back the lump, his big, blue eyes pooled with tears. He worked lids rapidly to fight them back, determined not to shed them in a shameful display. After all, if he was going to prove he was big enough to go with Smoke, he had to be too old to cry like a baby. Hope died hard in the breast of a thirteen-year-old. It crashed suddenly and swiftly for Bobby when he heard Smoke's soft, sincere words.

"No, Bobby, you still can't go. I'll see you when this is over."

Bobby had to force the words past the thickness in his throat. The effort caused his hat to fall from his head and hang by its string. "Wh-When will that be, Smoke?"

"Only the Almighty knows that, son."

"Then don't go, Smoke. Please don't go."

Smoke Jensen shook his head at the intensity of the boy's concern. "I have to, Bobby, there is really no other choice. Some day, something will happen in your life and you'll know for yourself. Now, goodbye."

Fear clutched Bobby's heart. "No. Don't say that. Just say so long."

Smoke reached out and ruffled Bobby's snowy hair. "All right. So long, pardner."

Then he turned Thunder's head and rode off to the north.

5

Smoke Jensen no sooner got out of the basin that sheltered the Sugarloaf than he discovered that the word had gotten out on the owl hoot telegraph. It came at him in the form of two proddy young gunhands who trotted along the trail toward him. They reined in and touched fingertips to hat brims by way of greeting. Then, the one on the right who had carroty hair and buckteeth below pale green eyes the color of arctic ice, spoke with the over-confident sneer of youth.

"You familiar with these parts, old-timer?"

Old-timer? Although there was a touch of gray in his hair, Smoke hardly thought of himself as an old-timer. It brought forth a testy response from him.

"I might be, depends on who's askin', sonny-boy."

Chill eyes flashing, the punk leaned toward Smoke in a threatening manner. "I'm askin', old man, and you'd best be answerin', hear?"

There was that word again. Damn! "What is it you'd like to know?"

"We were wonderin' if you might know where we can find a man we're lookin' for."

Smoke shoved back the brim of his Stetson with his left hand, Thunder's reins held slackly in the fingers. His right hand rested lightly on his thigh. "It would help if I had a name. There's not many folks this far from town."

"Yeah. We done asked at Sulpher Springs. A gent in the saloon said the man we want lived down this way. His name is Smoke Jensen."

Smoke tensed, but didn't let it show. "Might I ask what you want with Smoke Jensen?"

. That bought him a surly answer. "That's none of yer business, you old fart."

That did it! Smoke dropped all pretense at civility. "Well, I just happen to think it is my business, being that I am Smoke Jensen."

The lout beside the orange-haired one cut his eyes to his partner. "Gol-dang, Lance, what do we do now?"

"Go for it, Lonnie!"

That had to rank as the stupidest mistake Lance had ever made. He had barely closed his fingers around the butt-grip of his Smith .44 American when he looked down the muzzle of the .45 Colt Peacemaker in the hand of Smoke Jensen. His eyes went wide and his mouth formed an "O," though he yanked iron anyway.

Smoke shot him before the cylinder of the tilt-top revolver cleared leather. The bullet punched through Lance's belly and burst out his right side. Reflex fired the Smith and the would-be gunfighter shot himself in the leg. Smoke swung the barrel of his Colt to cover Lonnie. The kid had his Merwin and Hulbert .44 clear of leather, but not aimed. Smoke's second round ripped through the youth's liver and angled upward to shatter a portion of rib before exiting from his back. Desperation fought long enough for him to trigger a round.

At such close range it was nearly impossible to miss a man-sized target, but Lonnie did. Hot lead cracked past the right side of Smoke's chest and splattered on a granite boulder behind him. Smoke fired again and pin-wheeled Lonnie in the breastbone. Shards of bone slashed the young lout's aorta on the way through to break a vertebra between his shoulder blades. He was dead before he hit the ground.

Bleeding profusely from stomach and thigh, Lance forced himself to draw his left hand gun for another try. Smoke reached out and batted the weapon from the wounded thug's hand.

"Give it up, Lance," he told the adolescent. "You're dying as it is."

Lance's defiance came through gritted teeth. "Go to hell, Smoke Jensen."

Smoke ignored it. "Out of curiosity, why did you draw on me?"

Lance swung his good left leg over the saddle, put both hands on the horn, and slid off his mount, his face white with agony. His right leg gave and he slumped to the ground. The horse jittered and danced a few steps away. Through the entire brief and bloody action, the only movement Thunder had made was to twitch ears at each gunshot. Smoke dismounted and ground-reined the 'Palouse stallion, then knelt beside the dying saddle trash.

"You might as well tell me and go off to the Almighty with a clear conscience."

"You taken to preachin' sermons lately?"

"No, but the man who raised me was called Preacher. He taught me to shoot, too."

"Did a—a damn fine job of it."

"Save your breath to answer me. Why did you pull iron on me?"

Lance turned those icy green eyes on Smoke. "The word is out that a whole lot of money will be paid for your head."

Smoke had a fair idea he knew who had made the offer, though he had to ask. "Who's supposed to pay?"

"A man named Vic . . . tor . . . Spectre," Lance choked out before he died.

* * *

High up along the Colorado River, in the corner of Utah, the gang led by Victor Spectre and his partners found the Ute Indians. Their number had grown to twenty-eight. They hungered for whiskey and women in this strict Mormon land. From a distance they eyed the low, brush lodges of the Utes and the square outline of a trading post. The trader would be the Indian agent, Spectre had told them.

"I suggest that three or four of us ride up there first. We can size up the place and distract the agent. The rest of you be ready to come on full tilt when I give the signal," Spectre told them.

Gus Jaeger and several others nodded sagely. Gus prompted, "Do you want me to come along?"

Victor Spectre cut his eyes to the lean outlaw. "No. You stay here, lead the men."

"Good enough."

Spectre picked two of the gang, then he and Tinsdale rode off toward the distant building. The remainder of the gang waited behind a low ground swell.

When they reached the front of the building, which faced east, they saw two burros tied off out at the hitch-rail. The four outlaws dismounted and entered, to find only three white men occupying the trading post. Two of them had the look of prospectors, the third wore a white shirt, with sleeve garters, dark trousers and a string tie. The agent/trader, Spectre judged. Three Indian women stood at a dry goods counter, haggling with the proprietor over a bolt of cloth. No problem there, the gang boss thought. Spectre stepped up to address the Indian agent.

"I say, sir, might you have some whiskey we could purchase?"

"Nope. Ain't allowed where there's Injuns."

Spectre cocked his head and gave the fellow a "man of the world" look. "Oh, come now. My companions and I are fairly parched after being a week in Utah. Surely you must have a little—ah—private stock set aside?" A hand in one pocket, he let the jingle of gold coins sound clearly.

Avarice glowed in the gray eyes of the trader. "I might be able to find something. It'll have to be after I get rid of these wimmin. Can't have them knowin' there's liquor around. They're Utes and their bucks would burn this place down for a swallow apiece."

"Very well, then." Spectre crossed to the door and stepped outside. From a vest pocket, he took a highly polished gold watch and lined the open face cover up with the sun. The flash could be seen clearly by the waiting outlaws.

They came down on the trading post like the Tartar warriors of Gengis Khan. By then, Victor Spectre had reentered the trading post. He crossed to the agent/trader and grabbed him by the front of his shirt.

He put his face close to that of the suddenly frightened man and growled at him. "Your strongbox. Where is it?"

Consternation registered a moment before anger washed it away. "You are going to rob me? You'll not get much, and you'll not get away with it. Harvey, Lem," he called to the sourdoughs at the small bar across the room.

Harvey and Lem could do little to help him. They faced into the drawn six-guns of Ralph Tinsdale, Nate Miller, and Judson Reese. Squawking like pudgy hens, the Ute women made for the door. Victor Spectre dragged the spluttering trader across the room and rammed him against a wall.

"Tell me now and I might let you live."

Raising a trembling hand, the meek Indian agent pointed to the bar. "There, under the counter. It just has a key lock."

"Where's the key?"

"In it, during business hours. It's where I keep my whiskey."

Spectre motioned to Reese and Miller. "Clean it out."

That's when shouts of alarm in the Ute language came

from outside. The outlaws swarmed around the agency trading post and began to shoot down the helpless Ute men, who were armed with only lances, bows, and arrows. Women screamed and the children ran in panic.

Laughing, Farlee Huntoon took aim on a boy of about nine and shot him between the shoulder blades. He eared back the hammer to pot the child's little brother, then yelped in pain as an arrow creased the upper side of his left shoulder.

"Owie! That damn buck done drew blood," he bellowed as he turned to one side and fired into the face of the Ute who had shot the arrow. "Owie," he repeated for emphasis.

Those among the Ute men who had not already been killed or seriously wounded began to flee. They dragged along what women and children they could. The gang spread out and methodically began to exterminate the remaining males. The old women they let go. The young ones they corralled in the Council lodge, a large brush shelter. Back inside the trading post, Victor Spectre examined the booty.

"You were correct about one thing. There isn't a lot of gold here," he said to the proprietor. "Too bad. Had there been money enough, I might have been persuaded not to do this," he added casually as he lifted his revolver.

"No! Oh, please, no!" the Indian agent pleaded. "There's—there's more whiskey. In the root cellar," he bargained with his life.

"We'll find it," Spectre assured him, then shot the man dead.

By the time the two prospectors had been killed and stripped of their small pouches of placer gold, the last of the Ute men had run off with the women and children they had rescued. Gus Jaeger gathered the gunhawks and tolled them off by twos to make their pick of the young Ute women and girls. The female population of the Ute village began to shriek and wail the moment the first pair were dragged from the Council lodge.

* * *

Sally Jensen sat in the old wooden rocking chair on the front porch at the Sugarloaf. The rocker played a game of tag with the tail of a plump, orange-and-white tabby that lay at her side. So far the cat was winning, the wooden bow had not yet made contact as the tail whipped in and out beneath it. She glanced up at the angle of the sun. The hands would be in for supper before long.

She looked across the open yard to where the ranch cook bent over his pots of spicy beef stew, thick gumbo, and New Orleans-style rice and beans. A Cajun who had drifted north and west of his native bayous, he had proven to be a natural with the hearty fare of the High Lonesome country. Though where he obtained the okra she would never know. The summers were too short and mild to grow it here. He looked up and saw the expression she did not know she wore. A wide smile flashed in the swarthy Acadian face and he spoke with words he hoped sounded reassuring.

"Won't no harm come to Mr. Smoke, Miss Sally. I gar-ron-tee it."

How did he know I was worried about Smoke? Sally gave a little shiver and looked expectantly toward the direction from which the hands would ride up on the headquarters as she answered him.

"I know that, Jules. I was . . . only thinking."

"He be one brave mon, Miss Sally. Smart, too. He not be steppin' in front of some *sacre bleu* outlaw bullet." Jules Thibedeux nodded his head in confidence and understanding and went back to his cooking.

Sally heard hoofbeats then. She came to her boots and marched to the head of the steps. She paused on the second one, her face lighted by the gold-orange of a lowering sun. Riding beside Ike Mitchell she recognized the slender figure of Bobby Harris.

Bobby had taken to sleeping in his old room in the main house in the five nights since Smoke's departure. His attitude bothered her. He had not as yet returned to school in Big Rock, and although content to teach him at home, she worried about his adjustment to children his age.

Impatient with herself, she banished the thought and put a smile on her face. Bobby would be moody enough. He saw her worried about Smoke also. She ran fingers through her dark hair and tossed the curls to give them springiness. Then she stamped her foot in vexation when a tiny voice in her head asked her where Smoke was right then.

Smoke Jensen drifted into Wyoming that day at midmorning, near the small town of Baggs. He had been slowed because of a pulled tendon on his packhorse. The normally sure-footed animal had stepped into a prairie dog hole and badly strained its canon tendon. It limped and fought the lead. He would have to rent another one or trade off at the livery in Baggs.

With that decided for him, he stopped thinking about it. The skyline of Baggs seemed to grow out of the tall, waving prairie grass. He saw the tall spire of a grain silo rearing on the horizon, then the slender one of a church. The town had grown since he had last passed through. Then the blocky shapes of the business district crept above the rim of the world. At a half mile distance, Smoke heard the barking dogs. Shrill cries of children came next. A cow mooed in a backyard. A wagon, badly in need of axle grease, shrieked its way along the main street. Smoke counted half a dozen new houses.

Smoke felt his initial tension sloughing off. Too early, he realized as he swung off of the trail onto a maintained roadway. Two local farmers, their wagons stopped opposite one another to swap tall tales, looked hard at him with open suspicion. Beyond them, at the first house on the edge of town, three children, barefoot, shirtless boys, stared solemnly. The youngest popped a thumb into his mouth as

Smoke rode by. A buxom woman rushed from the side door to scoop them up and hurry them inside. Something, or someone, bad had been here recently, Smoke reasoned. He guided Thunder to the livery first.

He found it where it had been before. The same bent, stooped old man came forward to take the reins of Thunder when Smoke dismounted. The sturdy, buckskin-clad gunfighter nodded toward his packhorse.

"I've got a horse with a strained tendon. I'd like to trade him or rent another if I have to."

"You got his papers?"

"Sure do. He's prime stock. Raised him myself."

"Say, you've been here before, ain'tcha?"

"That's right. Last time about two years ago."

Thumb and forefinger massaged his whiskered chin. "As I rec'llect yer name's Johnson, Jennings, something like that?"

"Jensen. I breed horses down in Colorado."

A light gleamed in aged eyes. "Yeah. Do a fair bit of gun-fighting, too, as I recall."

"Huh! Let's keep that between the two of us, all right?"

Thin lips spread to reveal toothless gums and the old man cackled. "I ain't got any problem with that. M'lips are sealed." He went to the roan gelding and ran an experienced hand down the forelegs. He lifted a thick lip and studied the teeth. His keen eyes noted that even with the heavy pack load, the back remained straight and firm.

"If he comes from your stock, you've got a deal, Mister—ah—Smith." He pointed to the corral beside the livery barn. "I got me a fine little mare out there. I'll let her go for the swap and thirty dollars. She's a Morgan an' been broke to a packsaddle."

Smoke gave him a genuine smile. "I've been wanting some Morgan blood in my remount herd. I'll sign the papers over and we can seal it with a drink on me."

"Fine as frog hair by me. My name is Issac Rucker. Put it on the transfer an' I'll get you Debbie's papers." He winked.

"I could feel it weren't broke. I had me a sharper dope a horse with a broken leg with laudanum and try to pass it off as only a strain."

Their transaction completed, Smoke and Issac walked toward the saloon at the corner of Spencer and Lode Streets. The Bucket of Blood looked exactly as it did when Smoke last paid it a visit. Green and white bunting decorated the balcony railing. Cut out letters of green blotting paper spelled out *Erin Go Bragh!* above the center of the back bar. The piano tinkled mournfully, playing *The Minstrel Lad.* It had been *Danny Boy* when Smoke had been here last. A huge, portly, handlebar-mustached man stood behind the mahogany, a spotted white apron folded double and tied around his ample middle. He saw Smoke and recognized him immediately.

"Ah, faith an' it's Kirby me lad. C'mon me boyo, cozy up an' take a wee dram. Jensen may not be a name from the auld sod, but yer an honorary Irishman whenever you are in me darlin' place."

Smoke winced. If he had any hope of going unrecognized, Sean Doolin's big mouth had ruined all that. If anyone in here connected the name Kirby Jensen with Smoke Jensen, the word would be all over the town in five minutes. He and Issac Rucker crossed to the bar. Doolin slapped down two large, fish-eye shot glasses and poured them with pale amber Irish whiskey and added a tot to his own. He set the bottle aside and raised his glass in a toast. Smoke and Issac joined him.

"Up the Irish!"

A surly punk halfway down the bar raised his head and glowered at them. "Up their backsides, I say."

Smoke turned to stare at him. He saw a long-haired, trashy piece of barely human refuse, of about twenty-two years, whose lank, greasy hair showed no familiarity with brush or comb. He had a snotty sneer smeared on his thin-lipped face and a two-day stubble of pale, yellow beard. He wore a six-gun slung low on his right thigh, secured by a rawhide thong. The holster, an old, worn military one, had its cover flap cut away to give quick access to the butt of the .44 Colt Frontier it held. Probably considered himself a gunfighter, Smoke appraised.

The sad thing was that he would most likely die without ever knowing how wrong he was. Smoke looked again at the hateful expression, tiny, mean eyes, and unshaved jowls, then decided he might as well try to enlighten the lout.

"Who or what are you?"

Smoke's words hung in the air a long moment before the punk worked his mouth and deliberately spat tobacco juice at Smoke's boots. "If you don't know, you've got a treat comin.' I'm Tyrone Sayers. Folks here-about generally tremble when they learn that."

Smoke slid into his black, leather gloves as he forced his voice into a high, squeaky register. "Oh, I am trembling. Don't you see? As far as I can tell, your name is spelled S-H-I-T."

"Back me, Norvie!" Tyrone Sayers erupted in instant violence. His hand dropped to the butt of his revolver and began to yank it free, while Sean Doolin grabbed up a bung starter and started for Sayer's companion. "Take it outside, boyos," he commanded.

Sayers ignored him. He had not cleared the back-plate of leather when Smoke went into action. Instead of drawing, he rapidly stepped forward and slammed a hard right fist into the punk's mouth. Sayers flew backward and the small of his back smashed into the top rail of the bar. His gun-arm continued moving and he freed the long-barreled Colt. That's when Smoke hit him again. The revolver thudded on the sawdust-covered floor. His friend went for his gun then.

A loud *thop!* sounded as Sean brained Norvie with his wooden mallet. He went rubber legged and slumped to the floor, his head resting on a spittoon, while birdies sang in his head. Smoke did not even hesitate during this one-sided exchange.

He waded in on Sayers. His elbows churned back and forth as he worked on the exposed gut of the stupid lout. Sayers wheezed and gasped and tried to escape along the bar. He stumbled over his fallen comrade and had to duck fast to escape a sledgehammer blow to his head. Lightning fast, Smoke recovered and smashed a vulnerable nose.

Blood flowed in twin rivers from Tyrone's mangled beak. His eyes watered and he pawed at them to clear his vision. Smoke went back to Tyrone's middle again. Tyrone decided he had had enough of that. From a soft pouch holster at the small of his back he drew a stubby .38 caliber Herington and Richards and whipped it toward Smoke Jensen.

Chin down to protect himself from any retaliation by Sayers, Smoke did not see the little gun coming until it lined up with the middle of his belly. "Smoke, look out!" Issac Rucker shouted.

Smoke reacted instantly. With his left he batted the small revolver out of line with his body. It discharged through empty air in the same moment that Smoke Jensen drew his .45 Colt and jammed the muzzle into one ruined nostril on the face of Tyrone Sayers.

He didn't have to say it, the tiny .38 was on the way to the floor already, but he did anyway. "Drop it."

Through his pain-dulled mind, Tyrone Sayers finally made the connection between names. "Jesus Christ! Smoke Jensen!"

"Nope. It's just Ike Rucker . . . and Smoke Jensen," the liveryman said through a chuckle.

All of the strength went out of the legs of Tyrone and he sagged to the floor. He barely caught himself on the edge of the bar. "I didn't know. For the love of God, *I didn't know!* Please, Mr. Jensen, don't kill me."

Smoke eased off a little. "I think you've learned some manners. Get a hand on your partner there and clear the hell out of here."

Tyrone Sayers could not take his eyes off the six-gun

burrowed into his nose. "Yes, sir, anything you say. Yes, sir, right away."

With a grunt he came to his boots, grabbed the unconscious lout beside him by the shirt collar and dragged him to the bat wings. When they disappeared through the batwings, Sean Doolin slapped a big palm on the bar.

"By all the saints, that was a sight to behold. Another round on me."

By the time Smoke Jensen had consumed a substantial meal to rid his head of the buzz brought on by the Irish whiskey and ridden out of Baggs, Tyrone Sayers had cleaned up and his friend had regained consciousness. Tyrone was full of plans, which he quickly shared with Norvil Yates.

"Norvie, dough dit Billy Beterson nund br'ng hip here." Tyrone talked funny because he had twin fat lips, and two rolls of cotton batting stuffed in his nose with a heavy layer of tape to hold them in place.

"What do you want Peterson for?"

Tyrone explained in his mushy voice. "There's a bounty out on Jensen. Big money, we're gonna collect it."

Right then, it seemed to Norvil Yates that his friend would not fare well in the prophet business.

6

Back at the Sugarloaf, a worried Monte Carson dropped in on Sally Jensen. He stood on the porch, hat in hand, and related what he had learned the previous day in Big Rock. His expression revealed the level of his discomfort.

"I have some more news about those escaped convicts."

Sally nodded. "Not good from the looks of you."

Monte tugged at one side of his walrus mustache. "That's a fact. They have cut a bloody path across Arizona, following the Colorado River. It is suspected that they are in Utah now."

Sally had seen outlaws come and go, had faced terrible odds herself. For some reason she could not bring herself to be overly concerned about these men. "Just how much havoc can three men create, Monte?"

"It's not three anymore, Sally. They have a regular gang. There's more than twenty of them. And it appears they are heading northeast. Could be to here. I'd feel better if you came into town, where I could keep an eye on you."

"Honestly, Monte, I don't think that's necessary."

"Smoke would never forgive me if something happened to you."

Sally forced a light laugh she did not quite feel. "And I

would never live it down if I picked now to turn delicate and vaporish."

Caught on the horns of the proverbial dilemma, Monte fingered his hat nervously and brought up a lame excuse. "Well, if you hear from Smoke, pass along what I told you." He took his leave and cantered off down the lane.

After Monte had ridden out of sight, Sally remained standing on the porch, looking after him. She ran over in her mind what he had said and his offer to provide protection. Then she looked through the curtained window into the living room. A golden oak shelf clock ticked steadily, its brass pendulum hypnotic in the stillness. The hands would be in soon, she mused. She would take Bobby aside and tell him to be cautious. She might even tell him why, Sally decided.

Twenty minutes later a loud clatter arose in the barnyard. Hungry hands tied off their mounts to a corral rail and made for the row of washbasins along one side of the bunkhouse. Sally made herself keep her peace until all had eaten and some sat back with quirleys sending ribbons of blue-white tobacco smoke into the noon sky. Then she went out and gathered in Bobby Harris.

They walked a distance from the hands before Sally spoke what was on her mind. "Something has come up that makes me feel I should caution you to be very careful when you are away from here. In fact, I think I will rescind my rule about wearing a gun. Take your Colt Lightning when you go out this afternoon."

"Why? What's happened?" the boy asked eagerly. "It's Smoke, isn't it?"

"No," she hastened to assure him, then read the disbelief in his clear, youthful face. "Well, yes, somewhat." She had allowed herself to be mousetrapped and it angered her. Reluctantly she related all that Monte Carson had told her. Fire blazed in Bobby's eyes when she finished.

"I should have gone with him," Bobby said stubbornly.

"No, Bobby. Smoke is not hurt. We don't even know if he

is in danger." Unwilling to hurt the boy, she unwittingly did just that. "Believe me, there's nothing you could do to help him more than staying here, being armed and keeping a sharp eye."

Bobby's face turned red. *"Yes, there is!"* He turned away from her and started for the house. "I'm takin' my stuff back to the bunkhouse."

Suddenly apprehensive, Sally called after him in a rush. "You don't understand, Bobby. I'm asking you to keep a watch out for me as well as yourself."

Bobby turned his head to throw back a hot retort. "I can do that well enough from across the ways. Right now, the hands are better company than you are."

Gus Jaeger crawled back down the slope of the ridge to where the gang waited. The long, thin wisp of hairs that descended from his lower lip moved in agitation when he spoke. "There can't be more than three families living there. They've got 'em a palisade around the houses and barns. Brats runnin' around in the yard. Didn't see sign of but two grown men."

Victor Spectre showed his appreciation of such skill with a big smile. "You did a good job. How far are we from the Great Salt Lake?"

"It's about fifty miles north and a bit west," Gus answered.

Spectre nodded. "This must be one of those outposts— what do the Mormons call them? Desseret Towers?—that are strung across Utah. That means they will have quite a lot of valuables. No handy bank to go to after closing shop for the day. Get the men ready, Augustus, we'll take them, like we did those Utes."

Twenty minutes later the outlaw band stormed down on the Mormon encampment. Too late, they discovered the place to be a regular fort. Their rude awakening came in the form of a screeching in the air, followed by an explosion some thirty yards in front of the lead element of the gang. The heavy roar of an artillery piece followed.

"B'God, they've got a six pounder in there." Gus Jaeger accurately named the weapon.

Spectre reined in when the outlaw foreman did. He frowned, perplexed. "Does that mean trouble?"

"If they have any grapeshot or canister, it sure as hell does," Gus opined.

So far the residents of the small community had not bothered to close the gate in the stockade that surrounded their dwellings. Another shell burst close by and the cannon roared again. A staggered line of smoke clouds rippled along the parapet and rifle balls cracked through the air around the hard cases. Some looked around nervously.

In their trade of banditry, they were not accustomed to organized resistance. These Mormons had quickly proven that they were nothing to be trifled with. Victor Spectre studied the next volley of fire from the wall.

"How many grown men did you say?" he asked Jaeger.

"Two's all I saw. There could have been more inside buildings."

"Looks to me like everyone over the age of ten has a rifle and knows how to use it. We had best come up with something better than a frontal assault."

Gus Jaeger considered that a moment. "They can only point that cannon one direction at a time. And if they're puttin' all their guns on the side opposite us, it could be we should ride around the place like Injuns and look for a weak spot."

"Good thinking," Spectre approved. "See to it. I'll take five of the best sharpshooters and keep them busy over here."

Jaeger liked that. "Now you're talkin', Mr. Spectre."

He had it set up in two minutes. While Spectre and his two partners and the marksmen provided covering fire, Gus started off with the remaining twenty-three gunmen.

Again the cannon opened up. This time, tiny plumes of dust spurted upward from the hard ground in the midst of the riders who fired at the walls as they angled across the defended portion of the wall. Grapeshot.

Three horses went down shrieking, their riders and two other men wounded by the one inch balls. One of the outlaws sat slumped in his saddle and tried to put his mangled intestines back inside his body while he groaned horribly. While the attackers recovered from this new turn of events, the gate swung closed. Shouts came from inside and the crack of a whip. Slowly the black muzzle of the cannon appeared as it rolled up an incline and leveled on a rammed earth platform, the barrel protruding over the spiked tops of the barricade.

In frustration, two of the sharpshooters fired on it. Their bullets rang on the cast barrel and flattened, to moan off harmlessly skyward. With only poor targets to choose from, the snipers had little effect. Victor Spectre watched the gang disappear out of sight around a corner of the stockade.

At once a fusillade erupted as more rifles joined the defense. "Who are they?" Spectre asked rhetorically.

Again the cannon spoke. The grapeshot crashed into the earth less than ten yards from where they had positioned themselves. It made Spectre's skin crawl. He made a quick, disappointing estimate of their chances. He rose in his stirrups and called to the marksmen.

"This will never do. We're too far outnumbered. Ride clear of that place and then join the others. We're breaking this off." The cannon barked again to give his words emphasis.

When the withdrawal began, the gate opened and armed, mounted men swarmed out. Considering himself fortunate to have escaped with such light casualties, Victor Spectre increased the gait to a gallop and streamed after his gang. The Mormons obliged him by doing the same.

It became a horse race, rather than an assault. One that

they barely managed to win. Victor Spectre was pleased to discover that Gus Jaeger had correctly anticipated him and led the gang away to the north. He and his partners streamed along in their wake. The crack shots along with them turned to fire at the angry Mormons.

Gradually the distance closed between the leaders and the outlaws. When Spectre got within hailing distance, he shouted gustily, "Keep going. Take that notch ahead. I don't think they will follow us beyond that point."

"You had better be right," Gus Jaeger said through gritted teeth, softly enough not to be heard.

A vast sea of tall, lush grass extended to the north, east, and west for as far as the eye could see from the last ridge that overlooked the Great Divide Basin. Smoke Jensen made camp in a small clearing in the midst of a large stand of lodgepole pine. To his northwest lay the small town of Wamsutter, Wyoming Territory. After hobbling Thunder and Debbie, he set about gathering windfall for a cook fire.

Rabbits bounded away at his footsteps and a quail called his mate. A rookery of crows turned a gnarled old oak black with their bodies and the air blue with their grating complaints. The air smelled sweet and clean. To his satisfaction, Smoke did not detect a hint of wood smoke. No one else shared this empty place with him. He could do with it that way for quite a while.

Smoke Jensen had always been a loner. At fourteen or so, Smoke Jensen had, in mountain man parlance, been to the mountain and seen the elephant.

His early life had been hard. A hardscrabble farm that grew more rocks than crops, always being hungry, and never enough clothing to keep warm in winter had been his lot. But then, everyone else had lived the same during the Civil War, especially in Missouri. Young Kirby had never eaten a juicy steak or a grapefruit. Didn't even know what the latter was until years later when he had seen one in the breakfast room of a fancy San Francisco hotel.

No, his past life had not prepared him for elegance. It did teach him to survive. So he took up a notch in his belt and began to trudge along the trail with Preacher . . .

That had been a day to remember. When Kirby first saw Preacher, the man looked to him like one of the horrors out of a story by the Brothers Grimm. Preacher hadn't shaved in several days and a thick, dark stubble covered his cheeks and chin. He was dressed all in skins, with Indian beadwork on the shirt, which he wore loose, outside his trousers, kept in place by a wide, thick leather belt. From that latter hung a tomahawk, the biggest knife the boy had ever seen, and a brace of revolvers in soft pouch holsters. A possibles bag hung over one shoulder by a rawhide strap, and a bullet mold dangled below that.

There was a brass compass tied to it by a thong, and a powder horn. Preacher wore buckskin leggings over trousers of the same material, with high-top, lace moccasins. The uppers of those had been done in ornate quill and bead work.

Preacher wore his hair long, and lockets of other human hair had been braided into the fringe of his shirt. A skunk-skin cap covered the crown of his head. His mustache was months overdue for a visit with a pair of scissors, and covered his mouth in a shaggy droop. Had young Kirby Jensen been four or five years younger, such an apparition would have made him pee his pants. Then he saw the twinkle in those flinty eyes and the mouth opened in a white smile.

Preacher took him under his wing and saw to his upbringing, and his education. Before a year had passed, Kirby had read from Shakespeare and from the *Canterbury Tales* of Chaucer. He had improved his ciphering to the point he could deal with fractions in his head. He also learned to trap beaver, mink, otter, and raccoons. He proved to have a natural eye and became an expert marksman within two years. He could ride a horse nearly as well as a Cheyenne boy born to it. All in all, he concluded as he arranged tinder and kindling in a ring of rocks, he had a well-rounded education. . . .

For which he would be eternally grateful, he vowed as he lighted the fire with a lucifer. When the twigs blazed merrily, he fed thicker chunks of wood until he had enough, then left the small fire to find himself some fresh meat for his supper. It didn't take long. In a land rich in animal life, Smoke soon found a covey of plump quail.

With a cunning learned from Preacher, he called them in close enough to swiftly grab up three and wring their necks. He took them back to camp, plucked them, gutted the carcasses and threaded them on a green sapling to roast over the coals. Then he made biscuits. He had some dry hominy, which he had put to soaking when he first reached his chosen site. All that he wanted for was some gravy. To achieve that, he put the tiny giblets of the birds to boil with some wild onions and some crumbled sage leaves. Coffee came next.

Smoke's stomach began to growl as he smelled the savory odor that rose when the sparse fat on the birds began to drip into the orange glow beneath them. He poured coffee the minute it had boiled enough. Sighing, he sat back against his saddle and sipped with lowered eyelids.

Tyrone Sayers peered through a thick screen of gorse and blackberry brambles at the man who lay in the clearing in such confident repose, his saddle for a pillow. Tyrone knew they would find him. A wide smile spread on his face, which made him wince as the cuts in his mangled lips split open again. *You're gonna git yers, Smoke Jensen,* he thought in triumph as he slid back to where the others waited.

Despite the distance and the obvious fact that their target was catching a quick nap, Tyrone mush-mouthed his announcement in a whisper. "Fellers, we've found us Smoke Jensen."

Billy Peterson's brow furrowed. "Yeah? Where?"

Billy's patch was shy a few punkins, Tyrone reflected, but he did what he was told and didn't give any back-talk. That moderated the erstwhile leader's outlook toward the awkward lout.

"Jist beyond that little ridge, Billy. He's camped in this little clearing in a stand of pine. Right now, he's takin' a snooze. So, what we're gonna do is split up, take our time at it, an' work our way through those pine trees until we're right on top of him. Then we're gonna make ourselves rich men."

Billy could not suppress a giggle. "You sure talk funny, Tyrone."

"Go suck an egg, you little shit!" Tyrone fought to gain control over his mangled mouth and succeeded in part. "Listen to me. We got a chance at this."

Not understanding, Billy continued to press for details. "How we gonna capture him? I hear he's mighty fast and a whole lot mean."

Tyrone looked at the younger boy with disgust. "We ain't gonna capture him, dummy. When we git in place, we open up and fill him full of holes."

Wonder filled Billy's eyes. "We gonna call him out?"

"No, peabrain. We git him while he lays there."

"Tyrone, that ain't right," Billy protested.

Anger succeeded where willpower had failed before and Tyrone spoke almost clearly. "Look at me. He did that to me. Do you think I'm gonna let him get away with it?" Then he quickly outlined where he wanted them to take up position. Then he concluded, "I'm gonna kill Smoke Jensen if it's the last thing I do."

Pleasant smells from the cooking quail gave Smoke Jensen another stomach rumble that pierced his light sleep. He came to his boots and carried the soaking hominy off a ways to drain it. Then he set about finishing his meal.

Lard from a paper tube melted in a cast iron skillet. It would serve to make the biscuits and fry the hominy. It would provide for gravy, also. Smoke worked with an economy of effort and movement that marked his mountain man upbringing. He soon had dough mixed and the hominy sizzling in the pan. He put the biscuits in a Dutch oven, popped on the lid, and hung it low over the coals on a trestle arm. Then he poured more coffee. For a short while, he forgot about what had brought him so far from home. Everything seemed to have been put here just for his enjoyment.

To the west. a flood of gold had spread from north to south, and extended up to the bloated red ball of the sun. Birds called in the distance. His horses grazed on the thick, green shoots and made low, whuffling sounds. A doe and fawn stepped timidly from the tree line and the female turned large, black eyes on the man by the fire. Smoke watched them till they moved out of sight, then ladled up his meal and began to chew in a mood of contentment. The peacefulness lasted through the meal.

When the last dark, tender flesh of the final quail disappeared down his gullet, Smoke bent to mop up the last of the gravy with a biscuit half when a bullet cracked out of nowhere, slammed into the bottom of the skillet, and ripped it out of his hand. Pain shot up to his shoulder. The sharp report of a rifle quickly followed, accompanied by the detonation of at least two other weapons.

Another bullet barely missed Smoke's head and threw a shower of sparks from the fire. A third slug moaned off the rounded surface of a boulder beyond the fire pit. Hand stinging from the impact of the first round, Smoke propelled himself backward and landed on his shoulders. He had his Colt free and it bucked and roared in the direction from which the first shot had come. The hot lead smacked solidly into a tree. A flicker of movement put his second round right on target. A scream answered him.

Then, "Oh God, Tyrone, he got Billy! Billy's bleedin' like a stuck hog!"

"Shut up, ya idiot! He can find ya from your voice." Smoke's next round clipped a small branch from an aspen right over the head of Sayers, who yelped in alarm. "See what I mean?"

Smoke came to his boots and ran after the second shot, as had his would-be assassins. He dived behind a large boulder and picked his next target from the blunder through the brush. His .45 Peacemaker spat flame. The first, high, hysterical voice shrieked again. "Yiieeee! He got me now."

"Shut up, Norvie!"

Smoke's keen hearing let him refine his sight picture a little. Norvie Yates did not leave this world with a bang, but rather with a whimper. Shot through the throat at the tender age of eighteen, his last intelligible words were a gurgle of self-pity. "Mommy, help me, Mommy."

Tyrone Sayers, would-be gunfighter, emptied the cylinder of his six-gun in panic. He hit exactly nothing.

"Goddamn you, Smoke Jensen!" he ranted, mush-mouthed. "Goddamn you to hell."

"Give it up, punk. It's not worth dying for," Smoke advised him coldly.

"You're the one who's gonna die. You're gonna make me a rich man."

Smoke did not reply. Silence, he knew, had its own strong medicine. Instead he moved again, to come to ground at the base of a large pine. The magic of his sealed lips began to do its work.

"Answer me, goddamn you. I'm gonna collect the bounty on your head."

By then, Tyrone Sayers had reloaded and came out of the brush in a bound that landed him beside the fire. He slip-thumbed four rounds from his Smith American before he discovered he had ventilated an empty bedroll. He slowly turned on one heel, his face a mask of confusion.

"Come out. Show yourself like a man. Face me, you bastard," Tyron wailed through puffy lips.

Smoke Jensen stepped out into the clearing behind Tyrone Sayers. "Surprise."

Sayers spun and brought up his .44 Smith. Smoke had emptied his right-hand .45, which he wore low on his leg, and now drew his second revolver from the holster slanted across his left hip at belt level, butt forward. Before Tyrone Sayers could trigger his .44, Smoke completed hauling his iron. He lined it up, squeezed the trigger, and blasted a pinwheel hole through the heart of Tyrone Sayers.

Sayers rocked back on his heels. His eyes began to glaze. He squinted as his life swiftly ebbed away, and tried to focus on his target. His arm would not raise. Then his knees gave way. He sank down hard on the ground and teetered for a long second. Then with a faint gasp, he rocked backward and fell, to land on his head.

Ever cautious, Smoke Jensen made a careful check to determine that only the three had come after him. Then he reholstered his Peacemaker and addressed his remarks to the corpses.

"Only damn thing is, now I have to gather up the bodies, lift them by myself and strap them on a horse." They would serve as an excellent message to anyone who might follow.

A rabbit munching its way through the clearing awakened Smoke Jensen in the still, gray light of pre-dawn. The bunny froze when Smoke rolled onto his back, threw off covers, and sat upright. He yawned and stretched, then drew on boots. The furry critter missed becoming breakfast by its second instinctive alternative. It decided to flee.

Smoke stood up, stretched again and headed for the kindling to build a fire. While the coffee built, he considered what to do. He would take the other horses and all of the weapons and ammunition. His pack horse could easily carry the load. It might be better not to travel the main roads. If word of Spectre's price on his head had traveled this far, the less he saw of anyone, or they of him, the better. The sooner he got to Jackson's Hole, the quicker his trail would grow cold. Smoke fried bacon and mopped up the grease with leftover biscuits. He drank three cups of coffee, used the dregs to drown his fire, then buried what was left. He broke camp twenty minutes later and rode out.

At mid-morning, Smoke noticed a thin white column rising beyond the near ridge. He crested the rise and looked down on a tidy little cabin, located on the shore of a small lake, formed by Lost Creek. A low barn and corral had been built against the shelter of a round-topped knoll. Smoke rode in cautiously and stopped fifty yards from the buildings when a stoop-shouldered oldtimer stepped out on the narrow porch.

"Hello, the cabin," Smoke called out in a friendly tone.

"Hello, yerself," came the reply. "Be you alone?"

"That I am."

"If yer friendly, ride on up. I've coffee on the stove an' I'm cookin' up some eats for noon. Yer welcome to partake."

"Obliged." Smoke rode in and introduced himself simply. "My name's Jensen."

"Morgan Crosby. It's nice to see a friendly face. Don't get many folk out this way often. There's water at the barn. Tie up yer critters there and come on in."

They sat at a linoleum-covered table and Crosby told of moving to this part of Wyoming after the War. His slight Southern accent put a capital on the word. "Yep. I rode with ol' John Mosbey and the boys," he remarked on his service for the Confederacy. Crosby gave Smoke a cold eye. "I suppose you was with the Union bluebellies?"

"No. I didn't take sides in the war. I've lived in the High Lonesome since I was a boy. I never developed feelings for one side or the other," Smoke informed him.

"Well, now, that sounds mighty fine. You headed anywhere in particular?"

Smoke considered it only a moment before answering. "North. Up around the Yellowstone River."

Crosby poured them more coffee. "I never lost anything in that country, so I've no reason to want to go there."

"It's beautiful. Quiet and peaceful, and what people do go through there are, for the most part, friendly."

A light twinkled in the eyes of Crosby. "Then there's a few others that ain't?"

"Like everywhere," Smoke agreed.

Morgan Crosby roused himself from the chair. "All I've got's some fatback an' beans, creamed onions an' taters." An elfin twinkle came to his eyes. "But I had me some dried apples I put to soak early this mornin'. Made me a pie."

"Sounds good," Smoke encouraged him.

After they had eaten, with both men working on a

second piece of dried apple pie, Smoke Jensen stiffened with the fork halfway to his mouth. A split second later, Morgan Crosby did the same.

"Seems this is the day for visitors," the old-timer muttered.

"I make it to be four or five of them," Smoke advised.

"Yer hearin's keener than mine," Crosby admitted. "I wonder what's on their minds."

A moment later, they found out. "You in the cabin, come out with your hands up."

Smoke moved to a window with fluid speed. He peered around the corner of a scraped hide pane. "Is it the law?" Crosby asked.

Unlimbering his .45 Colt, Smoke shook his head. "Not unless the law around here looks like grave diggers. There's five of the scruffiest saddle trash out there that I've seen in a long time."

"Not friends of mine, then." Then Crosby added, "You seem to attract the most unpleasant sort of company."

Ruefully, Smoke had to agree.

"We'll give you two minutes, then we fill the walls with holes," came the warning from outside.

She had looked everywhere. Early that morning, Ike Mitchell, the foreman, had come to the house to tell Sally Jensen that Bobby Harris had not slept in the bunkhouse the previous night, nor had he shown up for his work assignment. Immediately she checked upstairs. His bed had not been slept in either. She expanded her search to the area around the ranch headquarters.

That had been an hour ago and still no sign of Bobby. Sally went to the corral and slipped a hackamore bridle on her sturdy mare, Blue Bonnet. She led the animal out and fetched a saddle.

"Blue, girl," she told the horse, while she saddled it, "we've got some searching to do." She retrieved the reins and swung astride.

Sally rode in widening spirals out from the Sugarloaf headquarters. Noon beckoned from close by and still no sign of the boy. Sally began to wonder if he had taken it into his head to go after Smoke.

"Surely he wouldn't," she told herself aloud for more assurance.

Her survey took her in the general direction of a low knoll with an ancient, huge, blue-green Douglas fir atop it. How the inviting target had escaped a lightning strike for the more than hundred years it had grown, neither she nor Smoke could guess. While she approached it, with Blue Bonnet bucking in protest to such prolonged activity after two days of idleness in the corral, Sally began to make out the shape of a figure at the base of the tree. At first it appeared to be a jackrabbit hunkered down in the low grass.

After a while, Sally could tell that more was attached to the earlike shape than a mere rabbit body. At fifty yards, she could see the profile of a human face. Closer still, she recognized Bobby's pug nose and slight frame. His horse grazed peacefully down the reverse slope and his bedroll lay rumpled at his side. Relief swallowed anger but, even so, she spoke harshly when she rode up and he did not even acknowledge her presence. In fact, he deliberately turned away to gaze off toward the 14,000-foot peak that towered to the west.

"Young man, what possible right do you think you have to put us to all the effort to find you?"

"I was right here," Bobby told her through his pout, tears formed in his big, blue eyes.

"That's not even a reason." Sally dismounted and walked to his side. "You have your duties with the hands. Also, you are entirely too old for this sort of behavior."

Bobby turned to look at her then. It was immediately obvious to Sally that he was about to lose his battle with his tears. "And I'm old enough to have gone with Smoke, too," he stubbornly maintained.

"*No, you're not!*" Sally snapped back, small fists on her

hips. The split skirt of her riding habit swirled violently as she resisted the urge to stomp a foot. "This fantasy of yours has gone on long enough. I'm sorry, Bobby, but you are going to have to look at this realistically." She softened her tone, surprised at how harsh it had grown. "If you intend to remain on the Sugarloaf, as our adopted son, or even as merely a ranch hand, then you have to learn to face facts.

"You must take responsibility for your acts." She paused, sighing. Was he absorbing any of this? "And most of all, to obey orders given to you. Smoke and I both love you, and we don't want to see any harm come to you."

"Then maybe I won't stay," he answered coldly, then stomped away to his horse.

Smoke Jensen and Mogan Crosby found themselves under siege as rifle slugs cracked through the thin hide windows of the cabin. Smoke strode to the door, yanked it open, and made a quick response. A yelp of pain answered him. Then four slugs slammed into the thick log walls. Horse hooves clopped in the barnyard.

Smoke moved also. At one window, he lifted a corner for a quick look. He caught two of the hard cases in the act of entering the barn. That left three more. One no doubt wounded. They would be taking up positions also. He cut his eyes to Morgan.

"I got me a good shotgun an' a bag of buckshot," the old man suggested.

"We're in for a siege. I'm more worried about water and food."

Crosby chuckled, a sort of squeaky *he-he-he* sound, and pointed to a squarish wooden structure on one end of the sink counter. "I dug me my well first, then built the cabin around it. 'Tweren't nothin' but Injuns out here then. I spent me many days and nights forted up in here. I've got a tunnel to my root cellar, too. And another to the barn."

Smoke raised an eyebrow at that. "That's one you might live to regret."

"Oh, you mean them fellers out there? Won't be any problem. The door is built into the bottom of a grain bin an' locked from this side. I keep just enough grain in there to hide it."

Smoke scratched his head in wonder. "Where did you come up with all these ideas?"

"I went to Europe when I was young. Saw what they did in all those castles. Some of them, those with wells, were never taken by siege."

"I am impressed. Now, our only real problem is if they send the wounded man for reinforcements. It would be nice to know where they came from."

"Yep. I allow to as how it would, though the Basin has been crawlin' with proddy fellers for the last four, maybe five days. Dependin' on whether they're locals or not, could be we're in for a rough time of it."

Ace Delevan had been a liar and thief all of his life. He became a killer at the tender age of twelve. Since then he had killed thirty men and maimed twice that number. He figured that made him an ideal choice as the one who would get Smoke Jensen. Though a vicious thug, none would say Ace Delevan was stupid. That's why he brought along four of his cronies. Now Hank had a nasty bullet scrape on his upper left thigh and sat in a stall of the barn whining like a baby.

Maybe it hadn't been a good idea to come on like lawmen? They had heard in Baggs that Jensen had passed through. And that three local punks had gone after him— and hadn't returned. Delevan and his friends rode on until they came upon a horse overburdened by three corpses. They backtracked the animal and picked up the trail of a man who had to be Smoke Jensen.

Although Smoke Jensen was reputed to have been on

both sides of the law at one time or another, Ace Delevan
knew that he most often sided with the law. Which gave him
his big idea. If Jensen thought them to be lawmen, his respect for the breed would get him out in the open so they
could blow him to doll rags. Ace accepted that one or two
of his partners would buy a bullet. But he knew himself to
be fast and accurate. At least as much so as anyone he knew.
He would still be the one to collect that reward on Jensen's
head. A silhouette moved across one of the vellum windows
and he fired in reaction.

A hole popped in the scraped animal skin. No response
from a wounded man. One thing bothered Ace. He had
no idea how many men were in there. Jensen for sure, he
had gotten a glimpse of a broad-shouldered, ash-blond
man in the doorway. A man so quick and steady he put a
slug along the side of Hank Graves's thigh. A groan came
from the wounded man as Ducky Yoder finished bandaging the limb.

"How's he doin', Ducky?"

"I'm doin' miserable, Ace," Hank answered for
himself.

"He can ride, if that's what you want to know," a surly
Ducky Yoder growled.

Ace Delevan slitted his eyes. "Who said we were gonna
ride anywhere? Smoke Jensen is in there an' we're gonna
git him."

Ducky cut his eyes to the open barn doors and the cabin
beyond it. "Who says that's Jensen in there?" He meant,
"besides you."

Ace chewed on the drooping left end of his mustache. "I
say it's him. For that matter then, you tell me what man
could fling open that door, jump into the openin', bust off
a cap, an' pop back outta sight without even gettin' a shot
at him if it ain't Jensen."

That silenced Ducky for the moment. Ace eased through
the shadowy interior of the barn to where he could see
through a crack. Burl Winfree and Pauli Hansel had taken

up good positions that covered the front door. They had the back covered. A clapboard add-on had been tacked to the rear, to allow for a kitchen and wash house. The door to that hung open a slight bit. Ace sighted in.

A billow of gunsmoke obscured his results for a while. When he could see clearly, he found only a neat little hole. He fired again. Something made of glass broke inside. There followed a shout of anger, then a cloud of wood splinters that cut at his face. The boom of the shotgun got drowned in his curses.

Ace plucked a splinter from his cheek as he turned to the other ruffians. "There's at least two of them in there."

"Then we'd better think up some way of getting them out or us in," Ducky Yoder suggested.

Ace shook his head. "We ain't gonna do that, just the five of us. Hank, can you ride well enough to go round up the Joiner brothers an' Wally Eckert?"

Hank winced. "I reckon. Iffin I can reach my horse."

"Might oughtta find Jake Brock an' Jose Suarez, too."

Ducky Yoder put in his two cents worth. "Jeez, that's scraping the bottom of the barrel, isn't it?"

Ace blinked. "Ya mean Jose?"

"Naw. I mean Jake. He's a hopeless drunk."

The trio laughed. Ducky helped Hank to his feet. "Go out the side door an' cut through the corral. Your mount is at the water trough," he told Hank.

"We'll lay down cover fire," Ace offered.

Hank hobbled away at the best speed possible under the circumstances. When he reached the double door to the corral, he swung it wide, ducked as low as the pain in his leg would allow, and made straight for the far side. Ace and his companions opened fire. Hank made it to the rump of his horse when Smoke Jensen drew a fine bead and let go with a round from his Winchester.

Hank's head exploded in a shower of blood, bone, and brain tissue. He went rubber-legged and fell in a pile of smoking horse manure. From beside him at the back door,

Morgan Crosby let go with first one barrel, then the other. Double aught buckshot slashed the plank wall of the barn.

"You bastard," Ace shrieked. "You put two pellets in my left arm."

In answer, he got three fast rounds from a Winchester. This was going to be one long afternoon, Ace thought bitterly.

Smoke Jensen shoved cartridges through the loading gate of his Winchester. He had seen movement in the corral and tracked the wounded thug to his horse. He had managed to finish him and get back to the semi-detached kitchen in time to give the others a nasty surprise when one of them shouted at Morgan Crosby. Now if that saddle trash out there would only do something else stupid, Smoke considered.

He weighed the safety of their position and made a suggestion in the form of a question. "Morgan, don't you think we're a little exposed out here? Those clapboard walls are nowhere near as thick as those of the cabin."

Crosby pondered on it a while. "Yep. I suppose yer right. But we've still got us at least two in the barn. Which reminds me, if it's only two, where's the other pair?"

Smoke had already gone into motion. "Out front, no doubt."

He reached the front room of the log structure moments later. Right in time, Smoke discovered, to watch the man Ace had called Pauli Hansel get brave.

When no return fire had come from this side of the cabin, Pauli correctly deduced that no one was guarding it. A recent immigrant from Germany, a former Bramen dock waif turned killer, he had fled from the German police. It had been natural enough for him to throw in with the criminal element in New York. Ace Delevan had proven a good leader, and when things got too hot, Pauli had agreed to move west with the gang leader. So far it had been easy.

There were fewer stores to rob, but the banks bulged with gold. And people out here were all so trusting. Pauli compared it to stealing from children. Only this time they had come up against someone a whole lot tougher than most residents of the frontier, and a whole lot meaner. From his vantage point, Pauli had seen what happened to Hank Graves. When the firing increased from the back of the building, it convinced Pauli that he could close in on the defenders from their blind side and finish it once and for all.

He had not counted Smoke Jensen into his equation. Pauli Hansel had taken three long strides toward the building when he saw a slight flicker of movement at one window. He swung his rifle to his left shoulder as a tongue of flame licked outward in his direction. Something hit him hard in the chest, with enough force to drive him to his knees. Pauli tried to contain the fiery ache long enough to sight in. He had the target lined up, palms sweaty, breath in short, agonizing gasps, when another hammer blow smashed into the butt-stock of his Marlin .38-40. The slug rammed through and blew away the lower portion of his jaw. A cascade of lights went off in Pauli's head and his shot went wild, a good five feet above the roof-tree of the cabin. An instant later, he fell dead in a welter of his own blood.

"Hey, Ace," Burl Winfree shouted. "They done got Pauli."

Nothing for it but to rush the cabin, Ace thought. He relayed his plan to Ducky Yoder. Then yelled to Burl Winfree.

"Burl, listen to me. We're gonna have to take this place damn fast. When you hear us open up, blast the front of that place and take the door. You got that?"

"You gone crazy, Ace?" Burl protested.

"No, I ain't. But at this rate, they're gonna git us one by one. Jist do it, y'hear?" This had indeed turned out to be a terrible afternoon.

8

This was more like it in Smoke Jensen's book. When the volume of fire increased, he made ready. Braced at the edge of the window, protected by two-foot-thick logs, Smoke shoved the muzzle of his rifle out the edge of the sash. He had not located the remaining hard case, only had a general idea from the sound of the voice. Smoke expected the man to charge for the front door when those in the barn opened up. That Burl Winfree did not choose to follow his orders to the letter nearly cost Smoke his life.

When the thugs in the barn began to blast furiously at the rear of the house, Smoke Jensen stepped away from the protection of the thick wall and tore apart a square of the window covering. At the same moment, a bullet snapped past his right ear. It took Smoke a fleeting second to locate the shooter. When he did, the Winchester tracked onto the target and bucked in Smoke's hands. It had been a hasty shot, one Smoke did not expect to be fatal. The hot lead did tear through the shoulder of the charging hard case. He bit off a groan and kept coming.

Burl had emptied his rifle magazine and shifted the Marlin to his left hand. The Colt in his right bucked and roared as he advanced, somewhat falteringly as blood soaked the back of his shirt. Smoke Jensen crouched below the window, waiting. Boot soles thudded on the small stoop porch and the weight of a body crashed against the door.

It shook and rattled in its frame, but the latch held for the moment. Increased effort cracked the slide bar and it began to splinter on the third powerful kick. Smoke exchanged his rifle for a .45 Colt and waited. The door, which ordinarily opened outward, vibrated violently and cracked apart at the middle, between two upright planks. Another kick and a muffled cry of pain followed and the divided halves flew inward.

At once, a man followed. Smoke raised his six-gun and fired. "Good," he told his target. "But not good enough."

Burl Winfree slammed back against the doorjamb, an astonished expression on his suddenly pale, grayish face. Slowly he slid down the side post to a sitting position. He left a glistening red trail behind. With effort he worked his mouth and breathy, gurgles came from deep in his chest.

"Are . . . you . . . Jensen?" he asked with his last gasp.

"Yep. One and the same."

Smoke Jensen watched the man until he died, then hurried to the aid of Morgan Crosby. The old man did not seem in much need. He had the remaining pair pinned down. One lay sprawled behind a feed bunker, badly wounded in the left shoulder by a load of buckshot. He kept up a steady fire, though, that crashed through the kitchen and smacked the cabin wall. The other man was not in Smoke's line of sight.

Then a rifle cracked in the hay mow and Smoke found his target. Two fast rounds from the Colt drove Ace Delevan away from his vantage point. He went down the ladder hand-over-hand and zigzagged his way to the big, open doors. Morgan Crosby fired at him as he cut away at a sharp oblique angle. The shot column hissed past inches from his chest.

Smoke Jensen fired at the movement also, with greater effect. His bullet took Ace low in the gut. Ace doubled over in blinding pain and stumbled into a pile of burlap sacks.

Those gave him a softer landing than he expected. Biting on his lower lip, Ace rolled over and swung his six-gun toward the threat from the cabin. He was seriously hit, though not as badly as he could have been. He waved feebly to Ducky Yoder, stretched out in the yard.

"Ducky, cover me."

"Sure enough, Ace."

Ducky opened fire, blazing away where no one waited anymore. Ace forced himself upright and began a shambling run toward the cabin. When he passed by Yoder's position, the last of his men came to his boots and followed. Both wounded, their chances for success lay somewhere between slim and none. Yet, they came on.

Three pellets of 00 buckshot, from a load fired by Morgan Crosby, tore into Ducky's left hip. Pain, suddenly numbed by icy shock, made him veer off course. Canted to one side to ease the hot agony in his abused flesh, Ducky angled toward the south corner of the house. Seeing that, Ace had a sudden change of heart. He reversed his course and ran back inside the barn. He returned with two horses.

"Quick, mount up. We've gotta get out of here," he yelled at a dazed Ducky Yoder.

"Go . . . on. I ain't . . . gonna last . . . no how," Ducky declared.

Ace used the mounts to cover himself as he ran up between their scourge and themselves. He jammed the reins on one bang-tail into the hand of Ducky Yoder and used that big ham fist to literally toss his last companion into the saddle.

"Keep low," Ace declared as he swung atop his horse. Following his own advice, Ace spurred his mount to a fair to middling run and they raced away from danger.

After five minutes, Smoke Jensen and Morgan Crosby came out into the yard. The old man went from one dead piece of trash to another. At last he shook his head, massaged his chin with one gnarled hand and looked Smoke hard in the eye.

"B'gosh, we done did it. Run them right off. By the bye, they ain't local."

"I've handled more," Smoke confided without bravado. "And alone for that matter."

Crosby knew he had to ask. "Humph! I figgered that. You know, the name Jensen is a right common one, sure enough. But this little fight's put me to wonderin'. Mighten you be *the* Jensen? Smoke Jensen?"

Laughing, Smoke nodded in the affirmative. "None other. And I'll say it was a pleasure to fight alongside someone who can handle a shotgun in so masterful a manner."

"Careful. Talk like that'll git me a big head," Crosby grumbled good-naturedly. "Well, seein's as how you are Smoke Jensen, I'm obliged to let you know that there is something in the wind that don't blow good where you're concerned. It'd be best if you watched your back-trail real close. An' to check every curve before you round it."

"I appreciate that, Morgan. I've heard something to that effect before."

Crosby spat a long, brown stream of tobacco juice. "This ain't in the past. I'm talkin' about the here and now. I reckon these proddy little pissants were lookin' to collect on that money's been put on yer head."

"No doubt. Some others tried just yesterday," Smoke informed Morgan. "And I do know who's put up the bounty."

Morgan Crosby cackled and slapped a thigh. "I figgered you did. A feller in your position don't live as long as you have, lest he's mighty smart. Now, you take care, Smoke Jensen. I'll deal with these bodies."

"You could use a hand digging holes," Smoke offered.

"I ain't that old that I need help. Besides, who said I was gonna bury them? We've got plenty hungry coyotes and buzzards around these parts. All I have to do is drag the bodies away from here."

Smoke took his leave. "Thank you for the good meal and for lending a hand with this trash."

"It's me who's thankin' you," Crosby came back. "I

haven't had me that much excitement in a long time. Makes me feel twenty years younger."

With an exchange of friendly waves, Smoke Jensen turned Thunder down the lane and rode off northward from the cabin. Morgan Crosby bent to fix a rope around the crossed ankles of the late Hank Graves to make ready to drag the corpse out of sight and smell of the cabin. He'd harness up old Rose. She was steadiest for chores like that. It had indeed been a good day, he thought with a crooked smile on his lips.

"So this is Dutch John," Ralph Tinsdale declared as the outlaw gang rode into the outskirts of a small town nestled in the Uinta Mountains, located in the northeast corner of Utah. "What are we stopping here for?"

Victor Spectre told him at once. "When I was last here, they had recently opened a nice little bank. I figure by now it should be rather prosperous. What some of you are going to do is make a withdrawal."

Tinsdale's eyes scanned the streets. Every man in sight wore a six-gun or had a rifle or shotgun close at hand. Even the purses of some of the women bulged in a suggestive manner. More Mormons, he reckoned, still shaken by the ferocity of the fight they had been forced to run from. From what he saw here, these people seemed equally competent. He made his unease known to Spectre.

"Are we all going to be in on it? These people can handle themselves. We could be caught in these streets, trapped here while they cut us down to the last man."

Victor Spectre gave him an encouraging smile. "Nothing to be alarmed about. We'll designate six to ten men to rob the bank, while the rest of us avoid the business district and ride out of town a ways. There we will prepare a greeting for any posse that might follow." He reined in and turned to the other side.

"Gus, pick nine good men and split off from the rest.

You'll enter the main part of town up ahead in twos and threes. Do nothing to attract attention. At precisely eleven fifty-nine, you will enter the bank with five men. Close and lock the doors, draw the blinds and then take everything."

"How come we gotta do it right then?" Farlee Huntoon blurted out.

If looks had the capacity for murder, the thunderous expression Victor Spectre turned on Farlee Huntoon would have had him dead and buried, six feet deep, and a headstone erected. "For one thing, Mr. Huntoon, you will not be going along. However, I'll answer your question for the benefit of any others who might be unaware. In these small communities, every business, with the exception of eating establishments and saloons, closes down over the noon hour. The bank will be no exception. That should give you the better part of an hour to thoroughly loot the place."

Fin Brock and Judson Reese rubbed their hands together in anticipation. Grinning, Reese spoke for them both. "I like that. Just take our time and git it all, eh?"

"Precisely, Mr. Reese," Victor told him. "The five who remain outside will provide a delaying action once the robbery has been discovered. Those carrying the money will ride by the most direct route to the northern edge of town and take the high road in the direction we have been following. You will know when you have caught up with us."

Brock sniggered. "We'll know it even more when any posse catches up."

Spectre suppressed a smile. "That we will. Now, Gus, pick the men you want and we will start off. Those participating in the ambush will take varying routes out of this residential area, with none, I repeat, none entering downtown. Good luck."

"And good fortune," Olin Buckner added with a jaunty salute.

* * *

Walter Higgins looked up from his large, roll-top desk as two men entered the double front doors of the Merchant's Bank of Dutch John. Through the open doorway of his private office he could see the large hand on the clock click over to 11:59. With perfect timing, the chief clerk intercepted the rough-edged customers.

"I'm sorry, gentlemen. We are about to close for the dinner hour. Can you possibly come back at one this afternoon?"

The better dressed of the pair spoke in well-rounded tones. "We won't be long. I promise you that."

It was then that Walter Higgins noticed three more men crowd in behind. They had the disreputable appearance of saddle trash. *Oh, God,* the banker thought, *we are going to be robbed.* Sure enough, the last one in turned around, shot the bolt, and drew the blinds. Higgins sent an unwilling hand to the drawer that contained his revolver.

That was when weapons appeared in the hands of the desperados. The softly spoken one put steel in his voice this time. "I wouldn't finish that reach, Mr. Banker."

For some unaccountable reason, Walter answered through trembling lips. "Higgins. My name is Higgins."

"Now, that's quite all right, Mr. Higgins. You see, we've come to make a major withdrawal." Gus Jaeger gestured with the muzzle of his Colt to the teller cages. "Get to it, boys."

To add insult to injury, the outlaws stuffed all the cash and coin into canvas bank bags and secured the leather tops to buckles by their straps. Although he had never had his bank robbed before, Walter Higgins felt certain that he was behaving in the proper manner. If only he could keep his mouth shut.

"You'll not get away with this. The Mormon Militia has an outpost not far from town. They'll hunt you down, you know."

Two of the lowlifes sniggered. "Watch us tremble, *Mister* Higgins," Jaeger sneered.

This could not be happening. The tall, thin one who had been speaking pushed through the rail that divided the working part of the bank from its lobby and went directly to the vault. Walter Higgins half-rose from his chair.

"There's nothing in there," he blurted in a chill of anxiety.

"Let's let me find that out for myself." Gus continued to advance of the big, walk-in safe. "Oh, my," he announced a moment after entering. "If it wasn't your job to protect your depositors' valuables, I would be quite angry at you for lying," he informed Higgins. "As it is, I'll simply ask you to come help me fill up a few bags."

Higgins raised a hand that shook as though palsied. "I cannot. It would make me . . . culpable."

Jaeger's head appeared around the two-foot-thick brick wall of the vault. "That's a new word for me. What's it mean?"

"It means that if I help you, in the eyes of the law it would be as though I robbed my own bank."

Gus Jaeger smiled nastily. "I'm sure you would find some way of explaining it. Now get in here or I'll blow you clear to Kingdom Come."

Walter Higgins wanted to sob. Shoulders slumped, he got up on his high-button shoes and shambled to the opening. For a wild second he thought of slamming the vault door on the outlaw and thus trap him for the law. Then hope died as he realized that it took two men to close the door. Inside, Higgins meekly held the bags, while the robber scooped stacks of banded bills off the shelves. A sickening sensation spread from his middle. There had to be at least 25,000 dollars here. A vast fortune. And he would be held responsible. He wanted to speak out, to refuse. One look at those cold, hazel eyes convinced him not to. At last it was over. Three sheaves of five-dollar bills remained.

With a nasty smirk, the robber pointed to them. "I'll leave a little seed stock. Thank you for your contribution."

Back in the usually sane, silent, stable world of the bank

proper, the gathering up had been completed. A hard hand touched his suit coat from behind. He shrank from it. With a push, Jaeger urged Walter Higgins toward his chair.

"Take yer seat, Mr. Higgins. We'll be leaving now. Nobody poke a head out or make a sound for at least ten minutes. If you do, you'll be hurt . . . and badly."

After they left the bank, Walter Higgins folded his arms on his desk, lowered his head, and began to sob softly. Faintly, from the street, he heard the drum of many hooves. It did not make him feel any better.

Sheriff Atwater sipped coffee from a tin cup and leaned back on the back legs of his chair, tilted against the wall of his office. A growing commotion outside drew his attention. At last, Parker Evans, the bank guard, rushed through the doorway. Eyes wide, hair in disarray, Evans looked like he had seen the Devil himself.

Atwater, a calm easy going man, did not even lower his chair front to the floor. He merely gestured with the half-full cup and spoke in a lazy drawl. "What's got you all excited, Parker?"

"We've been robbed, Sheriff! The bank. Five men came in and took every last cent. They ordered us to stay inside, but the minute they rode off, I snuck out the side door and ran for here."

Now the chair banged to the floor. "Five men, you say?"

"Yep. But from the sound of the hooves, I'd judge they were twice that number."

"Go spread the word, Parker. I'll be getting a posse ready. We'll ride out at once with however many I can buttonhole. You follow with what more you find soon as you can. Oh, by the way, you're deputized."

Sheriff Atwater followed Evans out the door. He headed directly to the eatery on the corner where he knew his three duty deputies would be. He rounded them up, and

seven others in for their dinner. They went next to the feed
and grain store and acquired five more men. The last stop,
at the livery stable, produced three more. A small boy with
black hair, cornflower blue eyes, and a dusting of freckles
ran up with a message from the bank guard.

"Mr. Evans says he has fifteen men rounded up and they
will be ready in ten minutes. He says that the ones you're
after left town to the north."

"Thank you, Tommy," Atwater replied as he swung up to
the saddle after swearing in the volunteers. "Well boys, we
know where to go now."

He turned the head of his horse and led the way out of
town.

The only northern pass out of the Uinta Mountains narrowed some fifteen miles out of Dutch John to a
steep-walled canyon. Three waterfalls, spaced from two to
five miles apart, thundered in silver streams from high overhead, curtains of mist around their bases. Crystal clear
water, icy cold to the touch, ran from these spectacular dis-
plays of nature. Aspen, cottonwood, hickory, and cedars
put splashes of green in the crags of the ochre gorge.

In the midst of this spectacular scenery, Victor Spectre
chose to set up his ambush. Out of sight around a curve, he
put a team of outlaws to falling trees, while others dug out
at the base of boulders, to roll them onto the trail. Satisfied
when he saw that project showing progress, he turned to
the inactive hard cases.

"Pick yourselves a good location on the slopes beyond
the barricade. Dig yourselves in. Then fix a place for at
least one other man who is working on the road. We have
no way of knowing how many will be coming after us. This
could be a desperate battle. One we cannot afford to lose.
We must turn them back decisively. I have every confidence in you."

"Sounds jist lak a gen'ral don't he?" Farlee Huntoon said in a not-too-quiet aside to Dorcus Carpenter.

"You got any complaint with what money we've made so far?" Carpenter asked acidly.

Huntoon had to think about that a while. "No. Now you put it lak that, none at all, at all."

Believing it important to appear entirely in control, Victor Spectre chose to ignore the babbling of the hillbilly. "They will be here before you know it, so you had better get started. Make sure you have plenty ammunition. Then, remember how hard those Mormons hit us outside Grand Canyon and hit this posse twice as hard."

Thus inspired, the hard cases went to it with a will. They dug out shallow pits and tamped piles of dirt and rocks in front for a firing platform, then some of the more enterprising among the usually lazy criminals concealed their efforts with cut branches. From a distance of twenty yards the leaves nicely hid the raw earth.

An hour later, everything lay in readiness. A lookout posted back down the trail rounded the curve at a brisk canter. He had his hat in his hand, waving it above his head. "They're comin'! They're right behind me."

He slowed and angled his mount beyond the barricade, then disappeared into the low-hanging branches of a big cedar. Moments later, the sound of drumming hoofbeats reached the ears of the waiting outlaws. In the blink of an eye, Sheriff Atwater and two others rounded the bend and rendezvoused with history.

Twenty-three rifles crashed, but only three slugs plucked at the loose woolen jacket worn by the lawman. Behind him, his deputies likewise went unscathed, with only damaged clothing. By then the rest of the posse crowded onto them from behind and the fight became a wild melee.

Sheriff Atwater looked on in helpless dismay while some members of his posse dismounted and sought shelter among the boulders and from behind the overhanging lip of the creek bank. At last he found voice for his worry.

"Don't dismount! Stay on your horses, men. We've got to pull back."

"They can't shoot through rocks," a haberdashery clerk shouted up from behind a huge granite mound.

"Why pull back?" another greenhorn at the lawman game asked. "We got 'em trapped."

"It's more like we're the ones trapped," Atwater muttered to himself.

At least, more slugs on both sides passed through air than flesh, he observed gratefully. That gave them an even chance, or would have if the suspected ten outlaws had not turned into a regular army of them. From the relative safety of halfway around the curve, he counted enemy muzzle flashes. Atwater came up with twenty-eight, which meant ten more shooters than he had. The way they all consumed ammunition, the sheriff reasoned, they would soon be down to knives and fists.

That speculation proved wasted effort five minutes later when the second half of the posse arrived in a cloud of dust. Townsmen and local ranchers shouted and milled in confusion until the presence of more men banished the fear in the timid and a decision was made to attack the hard cases behind the barricade. When they did, all hell broke loose.

9

Victor Spectre watched the arrival of the second posse with considerable apprehension. When their dash toward the barricade his men had erected turned to milling confusion, it raised his spirits a good deal. He clapped his partners, Ralph Tinsdale and Olin Buckner, on their shoulders and nodded toward the quandary below.

"Looks like they are doing our job for us," he stated heartily.

Tinsdale studied the disorganization a moment. "Can't we take advantage of this?"

Spectre thought about that. "Yes. Have the men slow their rate of fire and take careful aim. A few bodies falling off of horses should do wonders for that posse."

His words went out quickly. The steady crackle of rifles and six-guns dwindled gradually, until individual shots could be counted. That's when the bank guard, Parker Evans, decided to have his contingent charge.

"By God, they're coming at us again," Buckner blurted.

Spectre remained calm. "All the better, Olin. They have to slow down to get around the barrier. Our men can slaughter them."

All three escaped convicts looked on in astonishment as six of the more adventurous among the possemen raced directly at the barricade, guns blazing, to jump the obstruction. They cleared it with hooves dragging, and surprisingly, shot their way clear of the gathered outlaws, to win safety on the far side. The rest of the posse stalled out against the mass of dirt, rocks, and tree trunks.

"I don't believe that," Ralph Tinsdale gasped. "How could anyone have missed them?"

Gus Jaeger joined the trio at their vantage point on a small knob. "Simple, we weren't expecting it. We'll be ready the next time."

Having the charge broken finally allowed Sheriff Atwater to gain the attention of the entire posse. He stood on a rock partway up the slope of the canyon wall on the right-hand side and raised his arms over his head to signal for quiet.

"This isn't over by a long way. We haven't even hurt them, but they haven't beaten us either. We're going to have to do some thinking on this."

"Wish I'd have brought some dynamite," the owner of the General Mercantile grumbled.

Atwater looked at him with disdain. "What, and have us all deafened? No, boys, that's not the way. What I want is for about ten of you to ride back to the nearest ford across this creek. Then walk your horses up this way under cover of the near bank. From what I've seen of it, the overhang will give you cover up past where those robbers are holed out. We've got six fellers over there already. When you get up with them, position yourselves so that any stray shots from us won't hit you. Then fire a shot to signal us. We'll attack them together."

Several heads nodded in understanding and agreement. "That should work." Parker Evans spoke for them all.

Not one for rousing speeches, Sheriff Atwater looked hard at the posse and gestured with one pointed finger to the downhill ford. "All right, then, let's get to it."

Parker Evans picked ten men who had come with him and set out for the water crossing. Sheriff Atwater watched them out of sight, and then muttered softly to himself, "I sure hope this works."

Parker Evans and his picked crew found the bullet-riddled body of a stranger floating in the stream at the ford. At least one of the outlaws had been hit, he thought with grim satisfaction. Too bad it could not be more. He walked his horse into the shallow water and turned uphill. Silently, the others followed him.

A quarter of a mile from the ambush site, shelving sandbars formed a dry shelf on which to walk. It also ended the noisy splash of eleven horses walking. Cattails grew in profusion on the silt-covered higher portions of the sandbank. The sharp-edged leaves of the water plants cut at exposed hands and one slashed the cheek of Roger Latimer. He grunted and dabbed at the incision with one hand. When it came away covered in blood, he pulled a kerchief from his pocket and held it to the wound. Evans suddenly signaled for a halt.

The faint sound of voices rode the air above the gurgle of running water. Evans signed for the others to hold fast and eased forward. He rounded the bend where the barricade had been constructed and came face-to-face with one of Spectre's hard cases. Fortunately for the volunteer deputy, he had his six-gun in one hand. Unfortunately for any hope of sneaking past the outlaws undetected, he fired it into the chest of the scruffy, long-haired thug.

"What's going on?" a voice demanded. Three shots followed.

Parker Evans fired twice to cover his retreat, then turned tail. The rest of the crew wore expressions of disappointment when he rejoined them. Roger Latimer put their feelings into words. "What did you go an' do that for?"

In his defense Evans spoke what he had been thinking. "I didn't plan on it. I just came upon this feller with the robbers. They have men down here on this side of the roadblock."

"They sneakin' up on us, do you suppose?" asked one not-too-bright shop clerk.

"No, stupid, but it's plain we can't sneak by them now," Latimer complained.

Evans shrugged. "Yeah, we might as well turn back."

The pop-eyed, sandy-haired clerk belabored the obvious. "The sheriff ain't gonna like this."

Parker Evans had no intention of allowing that to be the last word. "Could be. But he'd like it even less if I got you all killed, don't you think?" Then another thought struck him. "Nope. We're not turning back. You," he pointed to Latimer, "ride back alone and tell the sheriff that I suggest he get the posse ready to attack from the front again. When the shootin' starts, we'll come on 'em from the crick."

"It's better than goin' back with our tails between our legs," Latimer agreed.

Evans tried for enthusiasm in his words. "And it'll work, too."

Suddenly the air of the canyon turned into a hailstorm of hot lead. The posse came back at them with guns blasting into the positions prepared by the outlaws. At first, Victor Spectre could not believe it. When a twig snapped off the tree he sat under and dropped on his shoulder, he lost all doubt.

"Pour it on, men!" he shouted. "Give them a taste of hell."

If they could turn them once more, really hurt them and break the charge again, then they stood a chance to bring an end to it. At least for now, Victor amended his thoughts. Pursuit would be inevitable. But it wasn't too far to the territorial boundary. That was definitely in their favor. Firing began from the six lawmen behind them, adding to the confusion. He saw two men fly from their horses as though yanked by ropes. Another dropped his weapon and howled, though the voice could not be heard above the bedlam of the fighting. The charge faltered.

These weren't professional lawmen, paid to risk their lives, Victor reasoned. Store keepers and clerks had too much else to worry about. Spectre brightened as the lead rank of the posse turned aside, to circle the upper end of the barrier. Another man took a bullet and turned away. Then, suddenly, a fresh salvo erupted from the creek bank. Men in overalls and business suits streamed upward, effectively flanking his forces, Victor Spectre saw. Their near-victory could become a terrible defeat.

Parker Evans surged upward over the lip of the creek bank. The front shoulders of his mount surged with power as they gained purchase on the more level ground above. To left and right he saw confused, frightened faces. Then the six men who had ridden beyond the gang charged downhill. Several outlaws actually broke and ran. This just might be it, he thought exaltedly.

Then a heavy .45 caliber slug ripped through his brain and ended the banking career of Parker Evans. Dead before he hit the ground, Evans lay atop one hard case he had killed only a second before.

When the townspeople with him saw Evans die their resolve disappeared in a whiff of powder smoke. Reining in sharply, they turned the heads of their horses toward the creek and dashed to safety. Suddenly without support, the six in the rear also swerved toward the shelter of the water. Half a hundred bullets followed them. One among the fleeing possemen uttered a piercing scream and did a back-roll off the rump of his mount.

Out in front of the wall of wood and dirt, the charge faltered, then reversed in a panicked scramble to the protection beyond the far side of the curve. Several of the less experienced among the gang raised a cheer. Pride even swelled in Victor Spectre for a moment, and prompted him to mount up and ride down among the entrenched gunmen.

"We did it, men. I told you we would."

Even the most cynical among them looked upon Victor Spectre with renewed respect. Several among the outlaws rushed forward to urge immediate action.

"Let's go after them," one suggested.

"Right. Run them to ground and finish off the lot."

"No." Victor dashed their expectations after brief thought. "We'll wait a while, see if they come back."

"We could be well along the trail if we leave now," Ralph Tinsdale implied.

Spectre considered that a moment. "Very well. We'll wait fifteen minutes and then send someone forward to find out what they are doing."

"That does it," Sheriff Atwater spat, as he tasted the bitterness of defeat. "We'll have to turn back."

"But they've got our money," Roger Latimer protested.

Sheriff Atwater had to answer that and fast. "We'll get it back. Here's how. We will pull back a ways from this bend. Regroup beyond the ford and find out what we have to work with. While we do, I'll send two of you back to find the Militia and ask them to join in. I know," he hastened to add to forestall the protest he knew would come. "Not all of us are Mormons, but they had money in that bank, too. They'll come. When we have soldiers here, we can crush these vermin like stink bugs."

"What if they don't wait? What if they come after us, or pull out?"

"If they do, Roger, while the militia is on the way, we'll fight them, give ground slowly. Or follow along if they run. One way or the other we have to finish this before they reach the border."

* * *

Nate Miller and Fin Brock returned after an absence of only five minutes. "They ain't there, Mr. Spectre," Miller reported. "We looked as far as the last ford and there's not a sign of them. Looks like they turned tail."

"That's fine, just fine," Spectre beamed. He turned to the eager faces of the gang. "Well, men, I think we can leave all of this behind us. We haven't far to go to be rid of the threat at any count. We will be in Wyoming within less than a day. Mount up and let's go."

Swollen with prideful success, the gang went to their horses. Encouraged by the high spirits of the men, Spectre allowed himself to expand a bit more on the theme as they walked their horses to the notch that led them to the high country of Bridger Basin.

"We're headed for a town, men," Spectre said loudly enough to let it echo back along the ranks. "And when we get there, we will send for Smoke Jensen."

Always the malcontent, Farlee Huntoon asked, "Mr. Spectre, how can you be so sure he will come?"

Eyes sparkling, Victor Spectre produced a broad, knowing smile. So confident was he of success that he did not even bother to insult the lout from West Virginia. "Oh, I'll think of something," he answered archly.

Smoke Jensen had a definite location in mind. It had been some time since he had visited Jackson's Hole. He reckoned that the high peaks around this spectacular basin would be ideal for him to work his way around whoever came along with Spectre, Tinsdale, and Buckner. He could clearly visualize a nice little cove in the Snake River where the sand washed almost snow white and the grass grew lush and thick. It smelled of sweet pine and wild daisies and the breeze blew softly with only a few days' exception. He would settle in there and then scout out the country around the basin.

Surrounded as it was by 13- and 14,000-foot peaks, the small "hole" served as the southern gateway to the Yellowstone country, the "Land of Smokes," as the Blackfeet, Crow, and Cheyenne called it. Beyond it, "civilization" had begun to encroach. Three towns now existed on land that had only a few years ago been covered red-black with the backs of millions of bison. Of all of these settlements, the only one Smoke considered deserving of existence was Dubois.

A quite, peaceful town, Dubois had an honest lawman, a church, and a school long before any such had existed anywhere else in Wyoming. They welcomed any among the law-abiding, with zero tolerance for beggars, criminals or trash. The reason? Smoke Jensen had helped make it that way. When Smoke's time came at last to leave, the townspeople threw a three-day fandango. Colorful bunting and Chinese lanterns decorated the main intersection. There was feasting—trestle tables groaned under the weight of food, kegs of beer, and bottles of whiskey—dancing long into the night, and games for the children. Narry a feminine eye, from eight to eighty, was dry when Smoke finally rode out.

Maybe he would visit Dubois on this trip and let the word get out from there that he had come back to Jackson's Hole. Then he would return to the Hole and begin to construct some unpleasant surprises for Spectre and the gang he would bring with him. It would be necessary, he knew, because the three of them would not come alone. Even together, they did not have the courage it would take to face him. Now, halfway across the Great Divide Basin, he called an early halt for the day.

He spent two hours of the remaining daylight to check his back-trail. Smoke found it reassuringly empty. Next he turned his attention to making camp. While he worked, his mind turned back to how he first encountered and dealt with Victor Spectre, Ralph Tinsdale, and Olin Buckner. . . .

Olin Buckner had dreams of building an empire in central Montana. He and two like-minded associates had worked over a few years to acquire ownership of Twin Pines, a small settlement in a lush valley that contained only four ranches. Two of them belonged to the consortium of Buckner and his friends. One of these had actually been obtained through legal means. Not so the business establishments of Twin Pines. The three saloons, two eating establishments, the hotel, and the feed and grain outlet had been acquired by the simple means of brute force. Only one business, the general store, held out. It was there that Smoke Jensen learned of the methods employed by Buckner's hired guns. Smoke had come in for supplies and had nearly completed his transaction when four of Buckner's bully-boys swaggered into the mercantile.

"Yer not sellin' anything to him," the self-appointed leader brayed, a stubby finger pointed at Smoke. "He's workin' for that Luscomb woman." He knew that much, but he didn't know who Smoke was.

The proprietor bristled. "I'll sell to whomever I please."

"Not anymore." The reply crackled in the suddenly tense atmosphere of the room. "Y'see, that's what I came to tell you. Mr. Buckner has decided this has gone on long enough. He's buying you out as of today. I brung over the papers, all legal and such. All you gotta do is sign." Grinning, he shoved forward the papers.

Reflexively the store keeper took them and began to read aloud. "*For the sum of one dollar, and other valuable considerations, I, Howard Leach, do agree to sell and convey all interest and claim to the property, building and contents thereof . . .*' One dollar! I wouldn't sell for ten thousand times that sum. And I would never sell to Olin Buckner and those scum he associates with. Now, get out of here, Tyson."

Swiftly, the grin on the face of Zeke Tyson turned to a

thunderous scowl. "I even brought you your dollar. You'll take it, if you know what's smart."

No question remained in the mind of Smoke Jensen as to how he would side in this matter. He eased away from the counter and faced off with the thug. "The man said he didn't want to sell."

Snarling, the hard case reached out and began to tap the chest of Smoke Jensen with one stubby finger. He made a big mistake. "Keep yourself shut of this, saddle trash. Best you get out of here and hit the road."

"Please."

"Please what?"

"Please get out. And *please* hit the road."

Pushed beyond the extremely low threshold of his temper, the dull-witted Tyson exploded with rage. "You five-and-dime tinhorn." He looked Smoke up and down with utter disdain, noting the low-slung righthand rig, with the .44 Colt Model '60, and the other one, worn slant-wise, at belt level on the left hip, butt outward. "You fancy yourself a gunfighter, eh? You're just about to find out what that word means."

"Please, Tyson, take it outside," Howard Leach appealed.

Frothing at the mouth, the thug whirled on the merchant. "All right, Howie, we'll do just that. Then, when I'm done, I'm gonna come back in here and get your signature on that paper or spread it with your brains."

Tyson led the way out into the street. Two of his henchmen followed. They spread out, with one hard case leaning on a rain barrel across the main drag, the other some twenty feet east of Zeke Tyson. Smoke Jensen came next, with the last thug behind him. Smoke made note that the lout remained at his back. It troubled him somewhat, though not a great deal. Tyson spread thick, trunklike legs, and stood flat-footed in the center of the avenue.

His words came in a jeering bray. "Any time yer ready, tinhorn."

Smoke raised a hand in a halting gesture and took a

quick sidestep to his left. "You're the one who wanted this, not I. If you want to make a play, go ahead. But get this scumsucker out from behind me first."

"Tally likes it right where he is. Don't ya, Tally?"

"Sure enough, Zeke," came the mocking reply from behind Smoke Jensen.

"Well, then, in that case, if you haven't anything more to puke out of that overworked mouth of yours, I suppose it is up to me to open this dance."

So saying, Smoke spun and dropped to one knee. His righthand Colt appeared in his hand in a blur and he shot Tally dead-center in the chest. Tally thrust himself backward and slammed into the front wall of the mercantile. Pain blurred his vision and he waggled the Merwin and Hulbert .44 in his left hand uncertainly, in search of a target.

Only Smoke Jensen had moved the moment his six-gun recoiled in his grip. He did a shoulder roll that put him ten feet from where he had started and well out of the line of fire from either Tally or Tyson. Unfortunately for Tally, the move had been made too swiftly. Zeke Tyson had fisted his own six-gun and let roar. The slug cut through air where Smoke Jensen had been and slammed into the bulging stomach of Buck Tally.

"Oh, God, Zeke, you done kilt me," Tally panted out. Gut-shot, his words came out coated in crimson. He slid to a sitting position with a mighty groan. His boot heels drummed on the planks of the boardwalk and he stiffened suddenly. A great gout of blood vomited explosively from his distorted lips and he fell over dead.

"Jesus, nobody can shoot that fast," one of the remaining toughs with Zeke Tyson babbled as he stared at the fallen gunman.

"Get him, goddamnit!" Tyson shouted. "What are you two good for?"

From his place in the center of the street, one quickly showed that he was good for dying. He tracked his already-drawn six-gun toward Smoke Jensen, who ducked below the rim of a horse trough and hugged the ground a moment. When slugs punched through the spongy wood of the opposite side and began to spill water onto the ground, Smoke popped up, sighted quickly, and blasted a lead messenger of death into the heart of the hapless hard case.

Staggered, he discharged his weapon in the general direction of Smoke Jensen and dropped to both knees. Smoke felt the heat of the bullet as it cracked past his right ear. His fourth round struck solid bone in the skull of the wounded gunman and put him into the next world. Smoke moved the instant after he fired.

Desperately, Zeke Tyson made his try for Smoke Jensen. In all his short life, Zeke had never seen anyone so fast and so accurate as this saddle tramp. His own slug cut through emptiness where the dauntless gunfighter had been a moment before. Then it was his turn to look down the muzzle of a leveled .44. He immediately did what any red-blooded, first-rate gunfighter would do. He ran like hell for the safety of a nearby alleyway.

Smoke Jensen turned his attention to the remaining henchman. Thoroughly cowed by the speed and deadliness of their intended victim, he had ducked behind the flimsy cover of the rain barrel. To his regret, it had not rained in twenty-seven days and the level in the barrel had dropped to only a couple of inches. He shot around its bulging middle and drew greatly unwanted return fire.

With the ease of a bar of lead dropped in a mud hole, Smoke's slugs cut through the oak staves of the intervening cylinder and out the other side to lodge in the chest of the crouching gunhand. Without a sound, he spread out on his back on the boardwalk. Smoke Jensen waited a moment, then approached cautiously.

Only a dwindling light remained in the eyes of the dying man. Pink foam bubbled from the holes in his chest and a spreading pool of red surrounded his shoulders. Concentrating his energy, he formed breathy words.

"Who . . . who are . . . you . . . mister?"

"They call me Smoke Jensen."

Understanding bloomed in those dead man's eyes. "I . . . I should . . . have . . . known. I'm . . . I'm dead, ain't I?"

No reason to hide the truth, Smoke reasoned. "You soon will be."

"Gawd, it . . . don't hurt any less."

"What doesn't?"

"Gettin' . . . done in . . . by the—the . . . best." Then he gave a mighty convulsive heave and died.

That's the moment Zeke Tyson chose to fire a shot from ambush. The bullet whipped by close enough to cut the hat from the head of Smoke Jensen. Smoke turned and drew his second Colt from its high holster. The muzzle tracked right and he fired into the puffball of powder smoke that lingered at the corner of the alley. It struck nothing and Smoke heard the thud of retreating boots. Prudence cautioned him that it would be foolish to go in and dig out the man. Instead, he crossed the street.

In the doorway, the merchant stood with an expression of awe on his face. "Lawsie, you did for them right sudden like. Mister Jensen, your custom is welcome in my establishment any time."

Smoke gazed on him with a hard eye. "Will it still be when I come after Olin Buckner?"

"Yes, sir. You can count on it."

When Smoke Jensen returned to town at the head of a large band of gunfighter friends and a number of oldtimer mountain man acquaintances from his days with Preacher, the store keeper stood true to his word. Although by that time, he wore one arm in a sling, the result of a savage beating he had taken from Buckner's henchmen.

Smoke had personally cleaned the plows of those responsible and they presently inhabited the hilltop cemetery west of town. In retaliation, Buckner had hired an army of gunfighters, put a bounty on the head of Smoke Jensen, and sat back to enjoy the results. That consequence soon bankrupted Olin Buckner and cleared the way for the final showdown.

After some judicious whittling away of the odds, Smoke and his rugged band closed in on the Crystal Cage Saloon, Buckner's headquarters. The fighting grew fierce and, at one point, it looked as though Smoke Jensen and his allies might go down in defeat. Two men had gained the roof of the bank across the street from the general store positioning themselves to shoot Smoke Jensen in the back. That was when the steadfast merchant took a hand in the game. He burst through the doors to his business, his trusty shotgun in hand and shouted to Smoke.

"Smoke! Look out! On top the bank."

Smoke had started to whirl around when the shotgun boomed and the store keeper blew one of the hard cases off his feet. Smoke settled with the other a second later. Smoke waved his six-gun at the man and quickly set to reloading.

"Thanks, I owe you one," the famous gunfighter told the merchant.

"Way I figure it, I still owe you a couple, Mr. Jensen," he responded, beaming.

Balance quickly shifted in the fighting. When he finally closed with Buckner, Smoke Jensen administered a thorough thrashing with iron hard fists. Bleeding and broken, Buckner lay slumped in defeat in a corner of a room above the saloon. But only for a moment. From an inside coat pocket, Buckner produced a two-shot, .50 caliber derringer. Racking back the hammer of the short-barreled, underpowered weapon, Buckner fought to get enough air to rail at his enemy.

"Goddamn you, Smoke Jensen. You'll pay for ruining me."

His first shot slammed into the thick, wide leather cartridge belt at the small of Smoke's back. It failed to penetrate, though it staggered the gunfighter. Yet, Smoke managed to turn and face his assailant. Buckner's second bullet cut a hole, front to rear, through the fleshy part of Smoke's right side. Its impact coincided with the discharge of the Colt in the hand of Smoke Jensen.

Put well off course, the slug went low and smashed the right hip joint of Olin Buckner. Dizzied by earlier wounds, Smoke Jensen stumbled across the room and kicked the now-useless pistol from the hand of its owner. Then he sat heavily in a chair, blood streaming from his side, and waited for someone to come.

10

It was the same when he faced Ralph Tinsdale. . . . Smoke Jensen had been a friend of Harrison Tate for over twenty years when he received a telegram at the Sugarloaf from Harrison's wife, Martha. Had Smoke dwelled in one of the glittery cities of the East, or even in Denver, his message would have come with a black border. Harrison had died three days earlier, ridden down by a runaway carriage. The driver had not been caught. Saddened by the loss of a good friend, Smoke and Sally Jensen made ready at once to take the train from Big Rock to Denver to attend the funeral.

When they arrived, Smoke found the circumstances relating to the death of Harry Tate a bit like over-ripe fish. He also became embroiled in a minor scuffle after the funeral, at the grave-side service. A scruffy-looking individual approached Martha, demanding to speak with her immediately. He was, he claimed, an attorney, representing a client who absolutely insisted that Martha sell some property to him.

Rude to the point of disgust, the lawyer kept a bland expression as he pushed his cause. Boorishly, he shoved the papers into the face of the grieving widow. Only the heavy veil that covered her face prevented him from actually striking her. Sally Jensen put one arm protectively around the shoulders of Martha Tate.

"You do not understand, madam. Women cannot inherit property in their own right. You have no children, so you may retain possession of your husband's property for so long as it takes to dispose of it. The sooner, the better."

His untimely and unseemly intrusion sent flashes of memory through Smoke Jensen. In an instant he recalled the pressure brought against the merchant in Montana. This sounded too much like that to ignore. Smoke moved forward as the cad shoved the papers forward again.

Smoke planted a big, hard hand on the nearest shoulder of the shyster and bore down with hard fingers. "Back off, buster," the lawyer said from the side of his mouth.

Smoke swung him with such force his hat spun away and his longish hair swung in the breeze. Smoke planted his other fist solidly against the still-flapping lips, painfully stilling them, and depositing the lout on his butt in the rain-wet grass. Smoke spoke softly, yet each word bore the weight of menace. "Now that I have your attention, listen good. The lady has just buried her husband. Kindly have the decency to allow a proper period of mourning. And, while we're at it, kindly haul your despicable carcass out of here this instant."

Shaken, the attorney cut his eyes from Smoke to the widow, then back again. "I don't know who you think you are. . . ." he began to bluster.

"Oh, I know quite well who I am. My name is Smoke Jensen."

Instantly the lawyer turned the ashen color of the already dead, a greenish tinge ringed his fat, greedy, now-trembling lips. *Everyone* had heard of Smoke Jensen. Shakily, he scrambled to the soles of his patent leather button shoes and made a hasty retreat, frequently pausing to glance nervously behind him. A fresh shower slanted through the limbless trees and cold fall rain made a damp ruin of the papers clutched in one of his hands. Later he was to find out that his client Ralph Tinsdale had not heard of Smoke Jensen, and didn't care to be advised about the subject. They both lived to regret that.

Over the next five days, Ralph Tinsdale resorted to other, more vicious means of enforcing his will on the Widow Tate. Tinsdale absolutely had to gain title to a choice, highly valuable square block in the center of downtown Denver. He desperately needed it to complete a land development scheme which would make him unbelievably wealthy, with more money than he could spend in three lifetimes. Two nights later, the carriage house behind the Tate mansion on Nob Hill caught afire. Two horses died, and a third was so badly burned that it had to be put down. The next day, Martha Tate found her beloved pet cat poisoned on the back porch. Crushed anew by this added grief, Martha retreated to her sitting room, to be consoled by Sally, while Smoke attended to affairs.

At the local police precinct, Smoke quickly found that the captain and most of his men resided solidly in the hip pocket of the as-yet unnamed speculator. The reception Smoke received when he went to file a complaint on Martha's behalf was cool enough to form frost.

"Accidents do happen, Mr. Jensen," the captain said airily. Then his obvious envy turned his coolness to arctic ice. "Even to the filthy rich."

Smoke could not believe what he had heard. "Are you saying that you are not even going to investigate this?"

"I see no real need."

Ire bubbled up in Smoke Jensen as he rose and leaned menacingly over the captain's desk. "*I do,*" he growled harshly. "If you are going to ignore this, then I'm sure not. I'll look into it on my own."

Steel glinted in the flinty gray eyes of the lawman. "You do and I'll have you behind bars for obstructing justice, interfering in a police investigation, and everything short of mopery."

"How could my investigation interfere with something that is obviously being so ill-served? Suppose you tell me, how can I interfere with an investigation that is not being made?" Smoke stopped suddenly, recalled an offer that had been made to him a year ago by another better lawman than this travesty. "I'll be back here, right enough. Only not to go to jail, but to watch you eat a large helping of crow." With that he swarmed out of the office.

Two hours later, a sheepish desk sergeant knocked on the door to the captain's office. "Uh—Boss, there's a United States Marshal out here, wants to talk to you. He's—ah—been here before."

"Oh, hell, I was about to leave for the day and head for Lulu's place. Send him in," he concluded, sighing.

Smoke Jensen entered the office and the captain's jaw sagged. "Deputy United States Marshal, Kirby Jensen, Captain. I'm here to advise you that I will be conducting an investigation into the cause of death of Harrison Tate, and the attempted extortion and intimidation of a widowed woman by the name of Martha Tate. Neither you nor your men will be required to participate. But I will expect your complete cooperation. Which boils down to this," Smoke added with a blooming smile. "Keep the hell out of my way."

Smoke had left the precinct station and gone directly to the office of the district U.S. Marshal in Denver. An old friend, Marshal Slator, had first offered Smoke Jensen a permanent deputy's badge some five years earlier when Smoke had aided the lawman in clearing out a nest of highwaymen who had plagued the gold fields and storage houses of Colorado. Smoke declined at the time. Slator made the offer again a year gone by. Smoke soon found that it didn't take more than ten words to find the silver circle pinned on his vest under his suit coat. Grinning, he then returned to the police station.

Shaken, the captain began to babble. "How—where— what in the name of God did you do to get that badge?"

"Accepted an old offer from a friend," Smoke answered factually. "Now, can we begin again? I want the names of any known arsonists believed to operate in this district. Also the names of animal haters. I also want a trace put on the carriage that ran down Harrison Tate. Where did it go? Who owns it? Where is it now? Who drove it the day Harry was killed?"

"You sure want a whole lot for a man who was in here not two hours ago begging me to look into some old lady's cat being poisoned."

Smoke gave him a nasty smile. "Why, Captain, I've only begun."

That night, three window panes were shot out of the second-floor front of the Tate mansion. That proved an immediate mistake. Smoke Jensen seemed to appear out of nowhere while the two, laughing, drunken men who had fired the shots staggered off down the flagstone walk. Each felt a light touch on one side of their heads an instant before their noggins were painfully slammed together.

Although dazed, one of them had the forethought to go for his six-gun, only to feel the muzzle of a .45 Colt Peacemaker, jammed into his stomach, and fired. The hot gasses blew through his intestines and did more damage than the slug. It reduced him to a writhing ball of misery. Beside him, his stunned companion gaped.

"Aw, God, Petey—Petey," he croaked brokenly. "What happened to you?"

A hard, square-jawed face swam into his view. "*I* happened to him," Smoke Jensen informed the piece of riffraff. "If you are not ready for some of the same, you'll be quick about answering some questions."

"Li—like what?"

"Who hired you to shoot up that house back there?"

"I don't know what you're talking about," the suddenly white-faced punk blurted.

Smoke Jensen showed the drunken lout the blood-spattered muzzle of his Peacemaker and tapped him on his belly. "Yes, you do."

Eyes grown wide and white, the words tumbled out. "I don't know. Some feller we ran into down at Mulrooney's."

"If you don't have a name, what did he look like?"

Eyes fixed on the threatening barrel of Smoke's revolver, the thug gave a description through trembling lips. It matched that of the discourteous lawyer at the funeral. Then he concluded with, "He offered a lot of money. A whole hundred dollars."

"Did he pay you in advance?"

"No. He said to look him u-up!"

"So you have an address. Give it."

Twenty minutes later, Smoke Jensen had the punk locked up and the corpse on the way to the morgue. With that out of the way, he summoned a horse-drawn cab and returned to the Tate mansion. In the morning he would pay a visit at the address he had obtained.

Ten minutes past nine, the next morning, Smoke Jensen let himself into the reception area of an elegant office suite in a five-story brick building on Boyle Street. The view from the top-floor windows gave out onto San Francisco Bay. The calm waters, Smoke noticed, wore a plethora of steam ships, their funnels belching black streams, moved majestically through the gaggle of white dots from sail craft of varying size. Smoke knew that there existed rules of the road, so to speak, for vessels on the water, but to him all that bustle appeared to be some sort of mystical dance. At a desk, set behind a dividing rail and forbidding, low gate, sat a prim, pinched-faced young man.

He wore a high, celluloid collar, and an expression of disdain. He had removed his coat, to reveal a snowy shirt, off-set by a florid cravat that seemed to bloom up under his chin. The fellow peered at Smoke through the lenses of a pince-nez and further pursed his already puckered lips. A brass nameplate on the leading edge of the desk declared the individual to be Jerome Wimple.

"May I help you, sir?"

"Yes," Smoke answered bluntly. "Who or what is Tinsdale Properties, Limited?" Smoke had obtained the name from the gold leaf letters on the frosted glass of the outer door.

The priggish secretary glanced around the outer room, at the potted plants, long burgundy drapes, dark wainscotting, and starkly white painted walls, as though to determine the answer to that question for himself. He sighed, as though loath to speak, and raised a narrow hand, with long, pallid fingers in a gesture of dismissal.

"We deal in real estate. Do you wish to list a property with us or are you looking to buy?"

"Neither one. I'm looking for a man who is supposed to work here."

Wimple's expression indicated that he had immediately lost interest, yet his position compelled him to continue this profitless course. "I am familiar with all of our employees. If you can give me his name, I'll be able to direct you to him."

Smoke hesitated a moment. "I don't have a name. Only what he looks like. He's about my height, heavier, maybe two hundred pounds, thick, black hair, a scar under his right eye, sort of red-faced, like a drinking man. Wears a large mustache, which he waxes and curves up the ends."

Oh, dear heavens, Brian Trask! Jerome Wimple blanched for only a fraction of a second, duly recorded by Smoke Jensen.

"I can think of no one of that description working for Tinsdale Limited."

Smoke Jensen took a menacing step toward the desk. "Oh, really? If I were to bounce you off a couple of walls, do you think it would improve your memory?"

Panic put a squeak in Wimple's voice. "You can't do that! Please leave or I shall be compelled to summon the police."

Smoke had reached the desk. With one big, hard hand,

he bunched the front of the starched white shirt of Wimple and yanked him off his swivel chair. With the other he delved into his coat pocket and produced the U.S. Marshal's badge.

"I *am* the police. United States Marshal. If I cannot get any satisfaction out of you, I'll speak to Mr. Tinsdale."

"M-Mr. Tinsdale is no—not in at the present time," Wimple stammered, consumed with sudden fright. *What would Bruce say about this?* he wondered. This would never do. Jerome Wimple found himself suddenly released. His rump hit the seat of his chair with a soft splat.

"Then I'll be back." Smoke Jensen turned on one boot heel and stalked from the office.

Down on the ground floor, Smoke started out the tall front double doors when a man entering brushed him rudely aside and passed on for the stairs. Smoke caught only a quick glance. About his size, florid complexion, bulbous nose, black hair, a surly sneer on his face. Smoke had walked across the small stoop and down the five marble steps to street level before he realized who he had just seen.

At once, he swung about and started back into the tall, brick structure. Smoke took the stairs up to the fifth landing two at a time. Quickly, he strode down the carpeted hallway to the door of Tinsdale Properties, Limited. Without a pause, he yanked open the door and stormed down on the startled Jerome Wimple.

"Where is he?" Smoke demanded.

"Where is who—er—whom?" Wimple bleated.

Smoke Jensen bent closer. "The man I just described to you passed me in the lobby downstairs. He had to be coming here. I want to see him now."

"You must be mistaken, Marshal. There's no one come in here since you left."

"If you are lying to me, you'll find yourself in a cell with some mighty tough customers. I guarantee you that you'll not like it."

Smoke Jensen let himself through the swinging gate and

advanced on the closed doors of offices along an intersecting hallway. Colt fisted, he threw open each portal, one by
one. The result turned out the same at each entry. At the far
end, he found an outside exit. The panel stood open a
crack. Beyond it, Smoke found an exterior iron stairway, a
fire escape. From far below he heard the steady ring of
leather boot soles on the metal treads. His anger mounting,
he returned to the office.

His hot, stinging words lashed into Jerome Wimple. "You
miserable piece of pond scum, you warned him off, didn't
you?"

"I don't know what you mean."

"Oh, but you do. Here's a little message for you, and for
your boss. I'll be back, and when I come, I will use whatever
force is necessary to get straight answers."

With that he stomped out of the office. It had been a mistake to show the badge. As a lawman, he was duty-bound
not to use undue force or to beat suspects. At least not in
public. Smoke Jensen consoled himself with one thing. He
had not been kidding about returning.

Over the next three days, Smoke Jensen followed a twisting trail that led at last to a large, lavishly appointed brothel.
His man, Smoke had been informed, would be spending
the evening and night there. Smoke also had a name
now—Brian Trask. From the dregs of Denver society,
Smoke had learned that Trask and a crew of henchmen
carried out the wishes of their boss, one Ralph Tinsdale.
The same Tinsdale who dealt in real estate.

Smoke had questioned Martha Tate about the offers she
had received. They had come through a lawyer, she insisted. But not the one at Harrison's service, she added.
The first before her husband's unfortunate accident. Although the police had not been exactly forthcoming with
information, Smoke privately believed that Harrison Tate's

death had not been an accident. Tonight he intended to verify that belief.

Brian Trask showed up at the parlor house a little after seven that evening. He was as loud and boisterous as he was crude. Smoke wondered how he had ever obtained a membership in one of the Bay Area's most exclusive bordellos. The parlor houses, unlike the vulgar cribs and doss houses of the waterfront, boasted private membership, elite clientele and the most discreet of parties and private arrangements. It cost a considerable amount to join, and applicants usually underwent intensive scrutiny. Smoke reasoned, correctly, that someone had bought Trask's membership for him. Smoke had shamelessly used a club card he found in the wallet of Harrison Tate, suitably altered to read "Junior," to gain admission. He spent the next two hours observing his target.

Seated in a red leather banquette, with a lovely, young hoyden under one arm, Smoke Jensen watched while Brian Trask teased and fondled several of the inmates of the establishment, and drank prodigiously. Then he consumed a mountainous meal of boiled pig's knuckles and ox tails, with a mound of sauerkraut, mashed potatoes, fried parsnips, and apple sauce. He downed it all with long quaffs of rich, amber beer. Afterward, Trask washed his fingers in a finger bowl as daintily as any Nob Hill fop. Then he took his pick from among the girls.

Smoke leaned toward the doxie he held in one arm and murmured into her ear. "The auburn-haired one there, what is her name?"

His hostess, who said her name was Vivian, peered across the room to where Smoke had nodded and saw Trask and the girl at the foot of a large, curving staircase. "Oh, that's Danielle."

"A lovely girl. But not so delightful as you." Disliking himself for what he was about to do, Smoke Jensen ordered a bottle of champagne and two glasses be brought to a room upstairs and suggested to the sweet young Vivian, who had all but crawled into his lap, that they adjourn to above floors. The bartender and waiter knew which room she used, so the champagne was there, waiting, when they climbed the stairs to the third floor. Even though the wine was brought up by rope-pull dumbwaiter, a human one was there ahead of them, hand out for a gratuity.

Smoke tipped him a three-dollar gold piece and saw him to the door, every bit the ardent lover. He kept control of his desire by thinking of his beloved Sally, while Vivian removed her outer clothing and paraded before him in her foundation garment. It was a dangerous pink, trimmed in black lace, with long garter belts that suspended black, net stockings. *It might be all hoity-toity downstairs, but in the privacy of a room,* Smoke thought, *a whore is a whore.* He watched her with feigned appreciation—well, not all that feigned—and then turned away from her to pour the wine. Before popping the cork, he deposited in Vivian's glass the powdered contents of a small envelope he had obtained from the doctor tending Martha Tate. The powerful, tasteless, odorless opiate derivative would induce sleep quickly.

He filled the glasses and watched the powder dissolve, then turned back and handed one to Vivian. They toasted a "night of bliss," and drank deeply. Smoke poured more champagne and again they drank it off. Smoke removed his coat, unfastened the buttons of his vest and removed it. Then he stepped behind the willing young thing and untied the laces of her undergarment. Over her shoulder he kept close watch as Vivian's eyelids began to droop.

"Your friend, Danielle? Which is her room?" he asked softly.

Vivian blinked sleepily. She could not understand why she was getting so drowsy so early in the evening. His question puzzled her also. "Wh-why do you want to know?"

"More champagne?"

"Ummm. I just want some happy times, Junior."

They all knew Harrison Tate, whom they considered a harmless old roue, who came for the food and drinks and the chance to gaze upon lovely young flesh. The arrival of Tate, Junior had them all excited. Vivian considered herself to have made a fortunate catch. She smiled languidly at him, inviting him to the bed.

"Champagne makes for happy times," Smoke Jensen suggested.

"'Jis' a little bit. I feel fun—funny."

"Then laugh and enjoy. We have the whole night ahead of us."

Smoke poured and asked his question again. Through dimming awareness, Vivian dredged up the required answer. "She's in two-oh-seven. Tha's right, two—uh—oh—seven. Why d'you want to know?"

"I thought . . ." Smoke told her, inventing, "that when her friend left, we could slip down and get happy together."

"Really?" Vivian's eyes rolled up and her lids closed over the exposed whites.

Smoke helped her to the edge of the bed, removed her clothes and put her under a sheet. He would give it an hour, then head for the room that held Brian Trask.

Brian Trask lay sprawled naked in the satin sheets of a thoroughly mussed bed. In his usual manner, he had rapidly thrust and ground his way to explosive release twice in one hour and promptly rolled onto one side and gone into a deep sleep. As instructed, Danielle had refreshed herself, dressed, and left the room. She had no need to extract her fee from the slumbering man's pocket; such vulgar matters were handled on the members' monthly billing. She had barely swayed her way to the stairs leading to the ground floor when Smoke Jensen appeared on the flight above her. He froze immediately and she went her way ignorant of his presence.

When Smoke reached Room 207, he crouched and tried the knob. The door was locked. From his boot top, Smoke took a slim-bladed knife and attacked the bolt. After a couple of tries, it slid back and the thin panel swung inward. Smoke went with it.

Moonlight filtered through the open window, and the curtains billowed inward on a light breeze. The zephyr smelled of sea tang and fog. Smoke Jensen crossed the floor silently to the large, four-poster bed. Silently, he looked down on the naked man who slept there. Silver shafts dappled the pale body, revealing slashes and circles of pink that denoted old wound scars. A tough, dangerous man, Smoke surmised. He turned away, went to the door, and relocked it.

Might as well get on with it, he thought as he returned to the bed. He bent down and roughly shook Brian Trask by one shoulder. The satiated man grunted and batted at Smoke's arm as though at a fly. Smoke shook him harder.

"You want more, honey?" Trask muttered.

"Wake up, Trask."

Smoke Jensen's bass rumble shocked Brian Trask to muddled wakefulness. "Wha—who—how'd you get in here?"

"Say I am a magician," Smoke told him. Trask reached for the sheet to cover himself. "No. Leave it."

"A man's got a right to his dignity," Trask growled resentfully.

"Not in this case. I've found that a feller in your present condition is more inclined to cooperate."

"I'm not cooperating with nobody," a truculent Brian growled.

"Oh, I think you will be. I want to know where I can find Tinsdale, your boss. Remember him?"

"I don't know nothing."

Smoke jammed a stiff thumb into a sensitive nerve ganglia in the man's armpit. Trask squealed like a stuck hog. "Again. Where is Tinsdale?"

Trask had drawn up into a tight ball. "I don't know. He's out of town."

"Where out of town? You are his chief enforcer, aren't you?"

"So what?" Brian asked after he stopped gagging. Smoke had put that same hard thumb to a nerve center under his right ear.

"So you know. Where is he?" A hard backhand to the exposed cheek of Brian Trask stung his eye and straightened him out.

"He'll kill me if I tell you anything," Trask babbled.

Smoke Jensen leaned in and dug the offending thumb into a complex of nerves an inch below the navel of Brian Trask. "I'll kill you if you don't."

When his squealing cut off, Brian Trask gasped and sobbed for air. "Yer a Marshal, you can't kill an unarmed, naked man."

"I've only been a marshal for a short while. I can easily forget about ever being one. Now, talk."

Brian Trask talked. Then Smoke forced the head gunhawk to dress and frog marched him out of the parlor house. When Smoke left the room, he not only knew who had killed his friend Harrison Tate—a gutter thug named Wally Quade—but also why. And what Tinsdale had in mind.

Ralph Tinsdale planned on capturing the entire center of Denver and exacting a fortune out of rentals. He also intended to do the same with every burgeoning city in the West. When Tinsdale met with resistance, he had the objecting land owner killed and dealt with the bereaved widow. Smoke had the name of the corrupt lawyer Tinsdale used and where to find him.

And where to find the criminal mastermind. Now, it was only a matter of time.

11

Baldwin & Fiske, Attorneys at Law, had offices in one of
Denver's most attractive and expensive office buildings. A
fashionable men's haberdashery store occupied the
ground floor. The impressive edifice had its own carbide
gas generating plant in the basement, along with a coal-
fired, steam radiator heating system. Even at night, the stark
whitish radiance of gas lights illuminated several windows
in the upper stories. In the rapidly growing, bustling metropolis, business went on around the clock. After booking
Brian Trask into jail as an accessory to murder, Smoke
Jensen went directly there. He had no difficulty setting foot
in the Babcock Building by the grand, polished granite-
faced main entrance.

At the rear of the lobby, Smoke found another modern
convenience. An elevator had been installed when the facility had been constructed. Operated during the day by an
attendant, who used a large rope pull to raise and lower the
open car, the device now stood vacant. Smoke Jensen studied the conveyance awhile and worked out how it
functioned. Baldwin and Fiske had offices on the fourth
floor. Smoke had fully expected to have to climb the stairs
to reach his immediate goal. Now he entered the cage of
the elevator and reached for the rope. He gave it a yank,

but the car did not move. He crossed to the opposite side of the open platform and pulled again. With a creak and groan, the floor rose under his feet.

A young man appeared suddenly from the lobby attendant's cubical and waved at Smoke. "Here, sir, let me do that for you."

"Thank you," Smoke replied with forced politeness, impatient to reach the office of the lawyers, and to do so unseen.

High-stepping to get onto the elevator, the muscular youth took up position and heaved on the three-inch rope. "We have a lot of tenants who work at night." He frowned slightly and paused before hauling again. "I don't recall seeing you here before, though."

Inventing rapidly, Smoke Jensen answered him calmly. "I was asked to come here tonight on a business transaction. To see one of your occupants on the third floor."

That information erased the frown. "Oh, yes. That would be Henning Mining. Old Mr. Harvey came in not an hour ago."

"Yes, that's it. But Mr. Harvey asked that our meeting be kept in strictest confidence."

Pausing in his attention to the rope, the young man laid an open palm on the center of his chest. "I assure you, I am the soul of discretion."

"Thank you, my man," Smoke responded with a heartiness he did not feel.

On the third floor, Smoke Jensen tipped the operator handsomely, stepped off the elevator, and turned in the direction indicated by an arrow on a directory. He walked along the hallway toward Henning Mining until out of sight of the elevator. Then he waited until it started down and headed for the stairs. He climbed slowly, careful not to make any betraying sound.

Up on the next level, he located the offices of Baldwin and Fiske. Smoke paused outside the door, listening. A light shone through the pebbly, frosted glass pane in the main entrance. No sound came from within. Cautiously, Smoke tried the knob. It turned, but did not release the latch. Again, Smoke resorted to the thin-bladed knife in his boot. The bolt gave on the third try. Smoke entered and relocked the door behind himself. Now all he had to do was wait.

While he went about that, Smoke decided, he might as well learn what he could from the files. A quick search of the outer office proved fruitless. No reference to Ralph Tinsdale or Tinsdale Properties, Ltd. Halfway down a corridor, brass lettering on a stout oak door announced the office of Lawrence Baldwin, Esq. Typical of lawyers—who were suspicious of everything, including their own shadow—it was locked.

Smoke Jensen forced entry and went to a rank of three head-high file drawers. He soon found them to also be locked. To his surprise, it took even more effort to slip the latch on the first set and slide open the drawer. He found the "T" section, but no file for Tinsdale. The second down yielded nothing also. Smoke began to suspect that he had been lied to. In the third drawer, he came across his first nugget of gold. A thick file bore the label *Tinsdale Properties, Limited.* It consisted mostly of real estate contracts, with a small bit of correspondence as well. Not wishing to advertise his presence, Smoke took the letters out to the reception area and read them under the night light.

To his disappointment, they provided nothing useful. He returned to the office and replaced everything as it had been. The search continued. Smoke drew blanks on the last two drawers. He closed the files and smiled to himself at the click that sounded when the sprung lock snapped back into place. On to the next.

Nothing, until the fourth drawer. There, under a warning label in bold-faced red letters that read: **MOST CONFIDENTIAL,** he found his reward. *Tinsdale Correspondence,* it was labeled. Smoke took the whole file out into the light. What he learned at first amazed, then angered him. No question that Tinsdale and Baldwin were in cahoots in the land swindles. Tinsdale wrote candidly of using intimidation, extortion, and murder to acquire parcels of land in the heart of Denver. On one, dated the day after the death of Harrison Tate, Smoke found the most damning evidence.

"Lawrence," the letter read. "A man named Quade will be coming by later today to see you. You are to give him five hundred dollars out of the Special account, and arrange a chair car ticket on the first train out of Denver, headed west. San Francisco would do fine. As always," and it was signed *Ralph*. There was a postscript that washed cold fury through the veins of Smoke Jensen. Wally Quade had been the name given him by Brian Trask the night before.

"P.S. I am sure the Tate property will be available soon. You might send Trask around to see the widow about it, eh?"

Smoke removed that from the file and dutifully read through the remainder. Nothing else came so close to sealing the fate of Ralph Tinsdale. Routinely, he searched the remaining file drawers, found nothing significant and settled in to wait for the arrival of the crooked lawyer.

He had prudently stopped off at a small street-front eatery on the edge of Chinatown and stocked up on an assortment of dim sum, bite-sized, portable foods that could be eaten as enjoyably cold as hot. They were in a woven sea-grass bag Smoke had carried into the building. He sat now behind the desk of Lawrence Baldwin, boots propped on the unmarked mahogany surface and reached in for a sample of the Chinese appetizers. Baldwin would be in about eight the next morning, Smoke estimated. Then he could remove another link in the chain.

Lawrence Baldwin, Esquire, respected and admired member of the Colorado Bar, confidant of the mayor of Denver, member of the Pioneers Club—an exclusive residence club for charter residents, who had come to Colorado before it became a state, and their male descendants, provided they all had and maintained enough money to be eligible—had a routine day in mind when he entered the outer reception area of his offices. He surely did not expect anything untoward today, and certainly did not have in mind what he discovered when he opened the door to his inner sanctum.

"What are you doing here?" The man to whom Lawrence Baldwin addressed that question looked large and dangerous. "How—how did you get in here?"

"Shut up and close that door," the darkly scowling stranger demanded.

In spite of his inclination to the contrary, Lawrence Baldwin found himself doing as told. Once the heavy oak panel clicked into place, he leaned back on it for support, his knees suddenly weak, his bluster vanished. It had at last registered upon him that the unknown visitor had backed up his commands with the ugly black muzzle of a very large Colt revolver. It had been pointed at his minute lawyer's heart. Fear sweat popped out on his brow and upper lip, oily and cold.

"Come over here and sit down," came the order from behind Baldwin's desk.

Lawrence Baldwin started his habitual route that took him to the place the stranger now occupied. He cut himself short and took one of the large, leather clients' chairs. His growing apprehension caused him to sag into it. With considerable effort, Baldwin found his voice again.

"Now, could you possibly tell me who you are and what you are doing at my desk?"

"It's Judgment Day, Mr. Lawyer Baldwin," Smoke Jensen told him in sepulchral tones.

Baldwin really began to sweat now. "What do you mean? What are you talking about?"

"Tinsdale Properties, Limited. Ralph Tinsdale. A man named Brian Trask, and another named Wally Quade. That's what I'm talking about."

Ghost-white in an instant, Lawrence Baldwin swallowed hard and fought the urge to bolt and run. He drew a deep breath, held it, let it out slowly. Took another. "Ralph Tinsdale is a client of mine. And I do represent his company. What business is that of yours?"

"Are you also his bag-man, to pay his hired killers?"

Had it been possible for Lawrence Baldwin to turn any whiter, he would have done so. "I won't dignify that with an answer. It's impertinent of you. There is a thing called lawyer-client confidentiality, you know."

"No, I didn't. But it doesn't matter in this case. I don't think this case will be going to trial anyway."

That didn't sound good, for several reasons. "What . . . case?"

"The People of Colorado versus Ralph Tinsdale, Lawrence Baldwin, Brian Trask, Wally Quade, et al. The charges: murder, conspiracy to commit murder, extortion, fraud, coercion, conspiracy and any others I can think up."

"What gives you the authority to make any charges?"

Smoke Jensen reached into his vest pocket and took out his U.S. Marshal's badge. He tossed it casually toward Lawrence Baldwin. It fell short, onto the top of the desk, and cut a long, deep gouge in the pristine surface as it skidded to a stop. Baldwin winced.

"I am a United States Marshal. And I have proof of your criminal activity in collusion with Ralph Tinsdale."

The lawyer in Baldwin took flame. "Whatever evidence you have has been gained illegally. You have no case."

Smoke shrugged. "Like I said, I don't think this case will go to trial. Now, tell me, where is Ralph Tinsdale?"

Baldwin correctly read the meaning of those words in the eyes of his visitor. Lips quivering, he tried once more to bluff his way out of it. "It won't go to trial because you obtained your evidence without a warrant."

"No. It's because of the most obvious reason a case cannot come to trial. A dead man cannot be tried for any crime." When Smoke said that, Baldwin shuddered. "Of course, if you give evidence for the prosecution, testify against the others, I'm sure something can be worked out."

For all his earlier pomposity, Lawrence Baldwin deflated rapidly. "All right, all right, what is it you want to know?"

"I have the general idea already. What I want is where I can find Ralph Tinsdale."

Baldwin swallowed with obvious effort, shook his head. "I'm not positive, understand? He—he's trying to expand his land empire. He's gone out to Dry Gulch Canyon. He wants to gain claim to as many working gold finds as possible. He'll be some—somewhere in there."

That verified what Trask and Quade had told him. Smoke gave him a nasty smile. "See? That wasn't too hard, was it?"

Baldwin hung his head, features bland and pallid. "I feel dirty."

"As well you should, considering what you've done. Now, let's get out of here."

"Wh-where are we going?"

"To jail."

"But you said . . ."

Smoke smiled nastily. "You underestimate me. I'm not so stupid as to let you run around free, knowing what I know about your operation with Tinsdale."

Baldwin's mouth fell open, yet before he could frame a reply, Smoke Jensen came around the desk in a swift, fluid motion, yanked the corrupt lawyer to the soles of his shoes and gave him a rough shove toward the door.

Dry Gulch Canyon, famous a few years ago for a fabulous gold rush, lay to the west of Denver. In the high mountain country, it could not be seen from any point except directly from above on the peaks surrounding it. Tons of ore had been mined and more tons of stream bed run through sluice boxes, producing hundreds of thousands of dollars in gold. Now only half a dozen mining companies operated here.

Modern and efficient, they each yielded better than 300,000 dollars a year. Ralph Tinsdale, in his dreams of empire, wanted to own it all. He had been advised against it by Lawrence Baldwin. The intricacies of mine ownership made impossible Tinsdale's usual tactic of killing off those who refused and coercing their heirs into selling out. Tinsdale, bloated with success, would hear nothing of it. He had been in the canyon only three days and already he had learned only how correct his lawyer had been. He sat in a dreary drizzle of rainfall, crouched over a ground-cloth-sheltered fire, in a side canyon. Three of his lackluster underlings were with him.

So despondent had he become that he did not hear the clop of a horse's hooves as a newcomer splashed through the puddles into the campsite. He barely looked up when the rider halted ten feet from him. Slowly he blinked when he recognized Wally Quade.

"What are you doing here? I thought you had been sent out of town."

"I didn't want to go. And then I got arrested, Mr. Tinsdale. For killing that old codger who wouldn't sell to you. Some U.S. Marshal. Name of Jensen. Captain Yardley let me out this morning. Trask, too. And your lawyer."

Stunned, Tinsdale could only gape and stammer. "Th-th-this can't be. How—how could he know who to go after?"

Quade shrugged his shoulders. "The thing is, it happened. Lawyer Baldwin said this marshal was comin' after you next. You best make ready. That Jensen is meaner than a wildcat with his bung sewed shut."

Galvanized into action, Tinsdale came to his boots. "You hear that, men? We've got a lawman coming after us. We'll make it his last manhunt." Tinsdale spun around on one heel, looked over their camp, the terrain to all sides. His decision made, he gave quick instructions. "Chances are he will come right before nightfall, or first thing of a morning.

Only we won't be here. Fix up your bedrolls to look like there is someone in them, then pick a spot where you can cover all the open ground. We'll let him get in here, thinking he's right among us, then cut him down."

Smoke Jensen arrived in Dry Gulch Canyon two hours before sundown. It took him less than half an hour to track the horse he had followed onto the soft bottom soil of the gorge. It led straight to a small, narrow side canyon. Smoke reined in and dismounted. He took a ground anchor from his saddlebag and screwed it into the turf. He tied off the reins of his horse and patted the animal on the neck.

"Stay here, Thunder. I'll be back shortly." Drawing his Winchester from the saddle boot, he started off to scout the ground ahead.

Well-trained by Preacher, his skills honed over years of practice, Smoke Jensen drifted through the trees on the inner gorge walls as invisible as the air itself. He quickly located the hiding places of two men. A ways farther into the canyon, he found another. He came upon two more near the dead end of the box canyon.

Carefully, with all the stealth he could muster, he worked his way back to the first man. His target lay prone, eyes fixed on a campsite where it appeared four men lay rolled up in their blankets, sound asleep. Smoke Jensen stepped out from behind a big, resinous pine and tapped the sole of the man's boot with his own.

"Waitin' for someone?" he asked quietly.

The hard case jerked with surprise and tried to whirl rapidly. Smoke drove the butt of his Winchester downward and smashed it into the outlaw's exposed head. The steel butt-plate made a mushy sound when it made contact. The thug twitched spastically and went still. Smoke disarmed him, tied him up, and moved on.

His second target sat with his back to a boulder. He chewed methodically on a slab of fatback in a biscuit and watched the opening of the gorge indifferently. Smoke slid the tomahawk from his belt and reached around the huge chuck of granite. With a swift, powerful blow he rapped the lout on the side of the head with the flat of the blade. On to the next.

Smoke found him like he had left him, squatted behind a bush, his knees up under his chin. A rifle lay at his side. When Smoke started his quick final approach, a hidden twig betrayed him. Its crackle sounded like a collapsing building to Smoke's hypersensitive ears. The hard case heard it too, only much less intense, so he reacted slowly. Smoke fell on him, rapidly bent him forward and rammed his face into the ground.

Mouth filled with dirt, the outlaw's shout of alarm came out a muffled grunt. Desperately, the gunhawk clawed at the butt of a six-gun in his right-hand holster. Smoke lifted him and slammed his head to the ground again. And again. The six-gun came clear. Swiftly, Smoke reached for his knife and buried its blade to the hilt in the right kidney of the thug.

Wheezing, the rascal sucked air and dirt into his lungs. His body spasmed and he forgot about his revolver. Smoke reversed the Greenriver knife and drove the pommel into the base of his target's skull. The lights went out, he stiffened into a rigid parody of a scarecrow and dropped from Smoke's grasp. He would probably bleed to death internally before he regained consciousness, Smoke considered, but at least he would not feel the pain. Stealthily, he moved on to the next.

Wally Quade lay near to where Ralph Tinsdale had hidden himself in a depression in the slope of the rear canyon wall. Smoke Jensen studied his location carefully for three long minutes. At last he had to concede that no way existed for him to approach unseen. He could get close, but in the last critical seconds, he would be exposed. Nothing else for it, so he began to glide through the trees.

When Smoke reached the tree line, Quade stiffened. He

couldn't believe what he had seen. How could he be here so soon? Why hadn't the others seen him and given a warning? The answer came to him with sudden, painful certainty. *They couldn't give a warning!* Quickly he filled his lungs and opened his mouth to bellow.

"Hey, Mr. Tinsdale, he's here! He's right in front—"

A hot slug from Smoke's Winchester cut his shout off in mid-sentence. The report echoed off the sheer walls. Wally Quade flipped over backward. Squalling, he clawed at his holster. The Smith American came free and he fired wildly in the general direction of Smoke Jensen. Smoke took his time and ended the babble with a well-placed round between the eyes of the murderer Quade. Then he started for where he had last seen Ralph Tinsdale.

Paralyzed with fear, Ralph Tinsdale squeezed back into the loose rubble where he lay in ambush. Impossible. No man could move so swiftly, so quietly to take out all his hired guns without giving himself away. Could he? He saw movement down the slope and fired off a hasty round.

He saw dust kick up ten yards behind the man who now bore down on him. His failure spurred him to action. Rising, he started to sprint uphill. The talus slithered and broke free under his panicked shoes. He stumbled and fell forward. Fiery pain erupted in one soft palm when it collided forcefully with the rough stone. The backs of the fingers of his right hand bled freely also, though he did not lose his grip on his six-gun. Ever so slowly, the lip of the gorge grew closer. From behind he heard the rattle and clatter of more shale as the relentless lawman pursued him. What was the name Quade had given him? Jensen?

Tinsdale's heart thudded with increased terror. Oh, God, could it be *Smoke* Jensen? Another upward glance showed him blue sky ahead. He could make it after all. But then what? He would be afoot, without supplies or help. He would lay for Jensen, shoot him when he came over the top.

His breath burned raw and too short in his heaving chest. His legs began to quiver. They felt like lead. The sounds of pursuit came from closer behind. At last he saw grass and a horizon beyond.

With a cry of relief, Ralph Tinsdale hurled himself over the edge of the canyon wall and onto the plateau beyond. Without a pause he scrambled around on the ground and faced the lip. He cocked his revolver and held it as steady as possible under the circumstances. Then he waited. It wouldn't be long. Jensen was right behind him. Time sped by. Smoke Jensen did not come. Tinsdale waited longer. Still no Smoke Jensen.

"Give it up, Tinsdale. You're out of the real estate business."

Incredibly the voice came from behind him. Tinsdale whirled and raised the Colt in his hand. Hot, stupefying pain slammed into his belly. Then again. Reflexively his legs churned on the ground and launched him out over the edge of the canyon. He disappeared from sight before Smoke Jensen could fire again.

12

And Victor Spectre . . . Victor Spectre had lived for years off the proceeds of crime. Always a shadowy figure, his name was not known to many lawmen. Those in the St. Louis area who did know it kept his secret and quietly enjoyed the show he made. Those who did not looked upon him as a philanthropist, a benefactor of social projects that had a civilizing effect on the citizens of the area. He lived in luxury, in the splendorous penthouse of a fancy St. Louis hotel. Stunted trees grew in the rooftop garden along with a rainbow of vibrant flowers, rich shrubs, and leafy ferns.

It was from here that he directed the actions of an immense gang that preyed upon the banks, railroads, smelters, and industries of Missouri, Kansas, Nebraska, and Colorado. A widower, Victor Spectre lived openly and notoriously with his mistress. A flamboyant redhead with an angelic face, superb body, and long, long legs that she took special pride in displaying frequently, albeit to the consternation of the society matrons of St. Louis, she had been Victor's consort for the past five years. His household also consisted of his son, Trenton, a boy of eighteen, who had eagerly and willingly followed his father's footsteps into the criminal life. Father and son adored each other, the lad consumed with hero worship, the parent full-blown with pride. Trenton had his mother's features and coloring, though carved in a handsome, masculine style. From his father he had inherited his jet black hair and brows, and the icy green eyes.

Trenton Spectre had been educated by private tutors and did not look forward with enthusiasm to leaving his father's burgeoning criminal enterprises to attend the senior Spectre's *alma mater,* Yale. "Nonsense," his father had objected in jest. "Many great criminal minds have been influenced and honed in the hallowed halls of Yale." Spectre had the usual bevy of a butler, manservants for himself and Trenton, a cook, maids who came by day to "do for the house," and a driver and footman for his carriage. Such were the idyllic conditions in the Spectre household when Victor encountered Smoke Jensen.

Peace had fled the High Lonesome and three good men had died defending their herds of cattle from a gang of rustlers as large as the average Army patrol. The cattle, brought up to the lush, green mountain pastures, had disappeared. The outlaws swaggered about as though immune to arrest. Indeed, in some counties of Colorado they *were* immune. The local law in those places had been in the hip pocket of Victor Spectre for a long while. They seemed unstoppable. Only, the rustlers had made one big mistake. The dead men were all fellow ranchers and friends of Smoke Jensen.

Although three separate herds had been involved, Smoke suspected a common cause, and a common destination. All anyone had to do was read the sign and follow the miscreants to the delivery point. After a long, arduous journey, fraught with hail storms, a prairie fire, and a tornado, the trail Smoke Jensen followed led to the stock pens of the Santa Fe Railroad in Dodge City, Kansas. Two of the Chicago stockyard buyers gave matching descriptions of those who sold the beefs. Smoke set out to find them in the three block long "Combat Zone" of the Gomorrah of the Plains.

Even though Dodge City was a Dead Line town, the No-Guns ordinance enacted by the city council and enforced by the city marshal, William Barclay "Bat" Masterson, Smoke knew his Deputy U.S. Marshal's badge exempted him. He found the first three rustlers in the Long Branch.

"I'm looking for Cole Tyree," he declared as he entered through the ornate, stained glass-paneled double doors. Immediate silence followed his announcement.

Every eye cut to the double rig of six-guns worn by the rangy, broad-shouldered man in the doorway. From behind the bar, the apron raised an admonitory hand. "There's a Dead Line in this town, Mister. You gotta give up them guns."

Smoke reached with his left hand to flip aside the lapel of his fringed, buckskin jacket to reveal the badge pinned on his shirt. "United States Marshal out of Colorado. I want Cole Tyree."

Like all good, obedient outlaws, Cole Tyree and his two henchmen had secreted several weapons upon their persons, including at least one hide-out gun. They made an effort to put them into play the moment the words left the mouth of Smoke Jensen. And that's where they made their final mistake.

Ace Longbaugh had only the cylinder of his shortened-barrel Colt free of the waistband at the small of his back when Smoke Jensen unlimbered his .44 Colt Frontier and plunked a hot slug into the belly of the rustler. Ace grunted and blinked his eyes, fighting to retain control over his badly damaged body. Meanwhile, Smoke saw movement to his left and pivoted.

This time the fight for control ended before it began. Bruno Butler took the round in his heart. Dead before he could complete his draw, he went rubber-legged and fell across a green baize table, scattering a stack of coins and a few bills. The latter fluttered to the floor while three bar girls shrieked and hugged one another. With Bruno out of it, Smoke turned toward the main threat, the as yet un-harmed Cole Tyree.

By then, Cole had his six-gun out and the hammer back. Ho had juot ocen two of hio men cut down without even clearing their irons. Part of him rebelled at carrying this any further, yet he knew he must. Eyes blazing, sweat oiling his face, he drove the words out in a shout.

"Who the hell are you?"

"They call me Smoke Jensen," Smoke replied and then shot Tyree in the chest.

Slammed back against the bar, the outlaw leader dis-charged his weapon into the sawdust and floorboards six feet in front of him. Smoke saw movement from the first man he had shot and turned for a moment in that direction.

With terrible effort, Ace Longbaugh brought his six-gun to bear. His finger closed on the trigger a moment after Smoke Jensen again fired on him. Hit off-center in the left side of his chest, Longbaugh shot a hole in the ceiling of the Long Branch before he slammed back against the piano. It gave off a discordant jangle of notes and held fast. Ace Longbaugh did not.

He slithered down the side of the upright and sat in a pool of his own blood. Slowly, he gasped out the last of his life.

Two city policemen appeared suddenly behind Smoke Jensen.

"Hold it there, mister. You've just violated our no-guns ordinance." He looked beyond Smoke. "And killed three men. Hand that Colt over and come with us."

"Deputy U.S. Marshal out of Colorado," Smoke told the aggressive cop tightly. "These men were wanted for rustling cattle in Colorado and crossing the state line to sell them. There's about thirteen more in town, I'd wager. You'd best be looking for them."

It had been a long speech for Smoke Jensen, but served

to dispel some of the doubt in the policeman. "Let me see a badge."

"On my shirt front," Smoke told him.

The lawman took a quick peek around Smoke's shoulder and nodded a curt acknowledgment. "Okay, marshal. Who are these men?"

Smoke named those he had names for and described several. Working with the local law now, Smoke Jensen quickly rounded up the remaining outlaws. Only five of them were foolish enough to resist. Smoke killed three of those. The shotgun accounted for the other pair. When questioned, the ranking member of the gang let slip a single name, one Smoke Jensen would come to hear often over the next few months: Victor Spectre.

Beginning that year in May, a series of bold bank robberies swept through the Rocky Mountains, culminating in Big Rock. Sheriff Monte Carson formed a large posse, split it into two, one half to be commanded by Smoke Jensen. Smoke readily agreed. He and Sally had a large portion of the assets of the Sugarloaf tied up in that bank. Not to recover so vast a sum could spell their ruin. Like many another deputation, the volunteer lawmen soon concluded they chased a whirlwind. Not so Smoke Jensen or Monte Carson. They drove the men under them, riding from first light to half an hour before sundown.

Night came swiftly in the High Lonesome. There was little time for an afterglow. The sun went behind the peaks to the west and the world turned black. Only those majestic pinnacles, mantled year round in snow, formed glowing silhouettes that projected streamers of orange, magenta, and gold. Smoke Jensen appreciated one such display far more than others of late. During the afternoon, he had come upon hoof prints of six horses. Two of them had distinctive marks he had also seen outside the bank in Big Rock. Their freshness indicated that by the next day, the posse would be in sight of at least some of the twelve-man gang who had robbed them of their investment money and life savings.

That set well with Smoke Jensen. The strength of these marauding bands, the rustlers numbering twenty-four, and now a dozen bank heisters, put a niggling suspicion in the back of Smoke's mind that the same man, Victor Spectre, was behind it all. He went to sleep under a blanket of diamond points ruminating on that.

Around mid-morning the next day, one of the two men Smoke had sent to scout ahead rode back to the posse on a lathered, blown horse. His face radiated excitement. "They're up there. Not three miles ahead. Walkin' their horses. Lucky for us we spotted them from inside the tree line, or we could have ran right down on them. There's six of them all right."

Smoke considered a moment. Given the direction they were headed, southeast out of the mountains toward the high plain that ran from eastern Colorado into Nebraska, the other six must be close at hand. He had eighteen men with him. Three-to-one odds on the six they had located. Better than two-to-one if all twelve joined up somewhere before they could catch them.

"Oh, and another thing," the scout reported. "The one I'd judge is leadin' them is dressed right odd. He's got on a ol', high, black, stovepipe hat, with a long feather stickin' out to the back. An he's wearin' a blue soldier coat, brass buttons an' all."

"A shell jacket?" Smoke asked.

"Naw. One like an officer wears."

That settled it for Smoke. They would hit these six fast and find out, if they could, where and when the other outlaws were to meet them. Then, with himself disguised in that outlandish outfit, at least six of the posse could get right in close, while the rest would fall on the robbers' flanks from ambush.

"Here's what we'll do." Smoke spoke suddenly, then

outlined his rudimentary plan. Twenty minutes later, they put the first phase in operation.

Smoke found himself well pleased with the way the posse spread out when he gave the signal. They came to a gallop and charged down on the unsuspecting hard cases. When the outlaws discovered their peril, they greeted the lawmen with a hail of wild firing that hit nothing. At a range of fifty yards, Smoke Jensen signaled for a halt.

Eighteen horses set their hind quarters and skidded to a stop. Eighteen rifles came to shoulders and fired a ragged volley. Four of the six scum died at once in a blizzard of hot lead. The other two, one wounded, threw up their hands in surrender. Smoke Jensen rode forward, his Colt Frontier keeping them covered.

Smoke put his cold gaze hard on the man in the blue coat, whom he had instructed be left unharmed. "Where and when are you to meet up with the rest of the gang?"

Equally icy, the leader tried to bluff it out. "I don't know what you're talkin' about, mister. All I know is that you are murderers. You cut these men down in cold blood."

"Only after we were fired on," Smoke countered. "And I reckon you've been around enough to know your blood's not so cold at a time like that."

"Maybe so, but I got nothin' to say to you."

Smoke cut his eyes to two of the posse. "Get him off that horse."

Roughly they dragged the man from his mount. At Smoke's direction they threw him on the ground and spread-eagled him, with the help of two more. Smoke dismounted and, as he did so, took a tomahawk from one saddlebag. He approached the man, testing the edge of the axelike weapon with one thumb. He hunkered down so his face was poised only inches from that of the other man. Smoke smelled the sour odor of fear, unwashed body and stale whiskey.

"Let me tell you something. I spent a lot of time around the Cheyenne while I was growing up. I learned me some right clever ways of makin' a feller hurt. The Cheyenne said I took to it right natural like. Thing is, I haven't lost my touch over the years."

"You're bluffin'. Yer a lawman. You can't do things like that."

Smoke cocked his head as though to say "Oh, really?" He spoke to the posse. "You fellers see anything going on here?" A couple of them guffawed, the rest shook their heads in the negative. "Well, now that *that's* settled, might as well get to work." He hefted the tomahawk. "How about I take off an ear? It'll be smooth, you won't even have a headache. 'Course if I slip, you'll never have a headache again."

Fear rapidly escalated to panic. His voice increasing by octaves, he pleaded for his life. "Goddamnit, you can't do this to me!"

Grinning, Smoke reached out and plucked the top hat from the ground beyond the man's head and put it on his own. "You won't be needing this. Oh. And boys, skin him out of that coat. It would be a shame to have it messed up with a lot of blood." Smoke raised the tomahawk.

Screaming in a banshee wail, the thug lost consciousness. Smoke turned his attention to the wounded hard case. One look at his unconscious comrade loosened his tongue readily.

"Look, I don't know everything. Not where we're gonna meet. Only that it is to be tomorrow. Clyde an' the others have the money. We're to take it to a bank in North Platte."

"What happens to it there?"

The thug looked at Smoke Jensen with growing terror. "I don't know. If—if Joe's still alive, you'll have to ask him." He nodded toward the supine hard case.

"He's alive." Smoke rose and went to where Thunder stood, munching grass. He took his canteen and stepped over the insensible man. He unscrewed the cap and poured a stream down into the slack face.

For a moment, nothing happened. Then Joe coughed,

spluttered and jerked back into the real world. His first conscious act was to reach up frantically and feel both ears. Without giving the man pause to enjoy his relief, Smoke Jensen came at him again.

"Where are you meeting Clyde tomorrow and what are you going to do with the money in North Platte?"

Defeat washed away the relief on Joe's face. "If you know that much, there's no way I can keep you from learnin' the rest. We're gonna hook up with Clyde outside Julesburg. On this side. The money from all the bank robberies is to be put in a special account."

"Whose name is on that account?" Smoke leaned menacingly closer, the tomahawk raised and ready.

"I can't tell you."

"Can't or won't? The tomahawk caressed the craven's cheek.

"I'll be killed if I tell you."

"No, you won't. You'll be a long way from there, safe in jail."

That's when he saw the light. Eyes fixed on the marshal's badge on Smoke's shirt, he spoke softly. "Someone named Victor Spectre."

Satisfied he had the right trail, Smoke and his posse went on to kill or capture the other band of outlaws. With the bank robbers jailed and more than $80,000 returned to the banks from which it had been taken, Smoke decided to look into the background of this mystery man, Victor Spectre.

Smoke Jensen sent inquiries through the network of friendly lawmen he had developed over the years. The answers that came back were disturbing to say the least. From the U.S. Marshal's offices in Kansas City, Missouri, and Fort Smith, Arkansas, he learned that Victor Spectre was considered an independently wealthy socialite in St. Louis. A philanthropist, he had endowed a library and had built a school in a downtrodden neighborhood of the Mississippi River metropolis. The Chief of Police in St. Louis had been even more effusive.

"It is my delight to state unequivocally that Mr. Victor Spectre is a veritable paragon of civil virtue," the mayor had written. "It has been my pleasure to frequently entertain him in my official residence. He is the champion of many charitable causes, makes an annual donation to a boy's home for waterfront waifs that is, to say the least, stupendous in size. Without him, our fair city would be much, much the poorer."

So, Smoke concluded at once, he would have to go after Spectre in a very different way than that with which he was accustomed. It would require that he make somewhat of a splash himself, so he continued planning. And it would be necessary to leave his beloved High Lonesome. Sally found out about his plan when she discovered him inspecting his dress clothes and several suits he had purchased over the years.

"Where are we going, dear?" she asked, hopeful he would say they would go back to visit her parents.

"Not 'we,' dear. I have to make a business trip to St. Louis."

Her entire adult life spent with Smoke Jensen, Sally had long ago learned how to skillfully hide her disappointment. She employed that talent now. "Cattle? Or horses?"

The Sugarloaf had only recently begun the process of changing over from a cattle ranch to a horse farm. Smoke had acquired a herd of twenty-five top quality brood mares and several stallions of impeccable lineage. Now, this conversion gave Smoke a moment of worry that his ploy had created more problems than it had solved. He had to think fast.

"Cattle. I think it is time we sold out the entire herd and I decided to try for the highest market, at a packing house that sells south, directly to New Orleans."

"And they are in St. Louis. Yes, it sounds good. I was

beginning to think we would never be free of those stupid, woolly-faced creatures. Go with my blessing. Though . . . I would like the opportunity to browse the fashionable shops in St. Louis. They have the latest styles from New York and Paris."

Smoke made a face and responded with mock irritation. "If you did that, we would need to have ten, rather than a thousand head. I'll miss you."

"And I, you." Sally smiled and patted his check. "When do you leave?"

"Tomorrow."

"Be careful. Don't get yourself hurt."

"Oh, I will. I've nothing to worry about in such a *civilized* place." Only Smoke Jensen did not believe that for a moment.

Through a banker affiliated with Sally Jensen's father, Smoke Jensen found the doors to the salons of high society open to him throughout St. Louis. He got his first look at Victor Spectre on his third nightly outing with the cream of the social whirl. It was a benefit dinner—at $50 a plate—for the campaign chests of several state politicians.

After the dessert—*crepes à la flambé*—which Smoke found overly sweet and lacking in substance, like the long-winded speeches that followed, Victor Spectre made a lavish presentation of a large check to the party's candidate for Governor. He was rewarded by abundant applause and flattering words. Smoke Jensen took an immediate dislike to Victor Spectre. Even if he had not known of Spectre's secret life, it would have been the same. Oily men, with too much money, which they used to buy politicians, rubbed his hair the wrong way. Wisely, he avoided direct contact with the criminal mastermind. That would come later.

Smoke Jensen spent a day at a saloon across the street from the hotel where Victor Spectre lived and conducted his clandestine business. Saloons seemed never to close in

St. Louis, there being only an hour or two respite when the swampers could clean the establishments and restock the bars. It made frontier drinking parlors seem downright tame. Reputed for their wildness, most closed their doors by midnight. Seated at a table by a front window, Smoke made mental note of those entering and leaving the hotel, who had the furtive outlaw look about them. If asked to put that description into words, Smoke would have been hard pressed to do so. It was more a feel, a sixth sense sort of thing, acquired over years of being around the breed. Any good lawman had it.

One peace officer, who was rapidly building a reputation for himself, Billy Tilghman, put it an interesting way. "You can dress a pig in a silk suit, but you still know it's a pig."

To his surprise, among those visiting the hotel, and presumably Victor Spectre, Smoke Jensen recognized the faces of three men. He had last seen their likenesses on wanted posters in the office of Monty Carson. The first came shortly before noon. He had been accompanied by a short, ferret-faced man with oiled, slicked back hair and equally shiny patent leather shoes. He smelled of lawyer to Smoke. The other two came together, late in the afternoon, after the clang, hiss, and chug of a slowing locomotive had announced the arrival of the East-bound local at the depot two blocks away.

The trio must represent the brains of Spectre's operation in Colorado, Smoke surmised, since the first man and his slimy companion had not left as yet. At least not from the front door. Smoke would have given anything to be able to overhear their conversation. Not given to flights of fancy, he dismissed all such longing and ordered another beer. It would be his sixth for the afternoon. And he had consumed a lot of coffee during the morning hours. He was in dire need of a visit to the chiksale, only he did not want to give up his vigil until the three wanted men reappeared.

His bladder had reached the aching point by the time that was accomplished. They came out together, along with the unctuous attorney, who spoke to them animatedly, gesturing emphatically with both hands. Smoke had settled his tab a short while before. Now he watched them out of sight around the corner, then hurried out into the street and followed. First to break off was the lawyer. He entered the tiled lobby of a run-down office building, its facade grimed by coal smoke and dust. Smoke made a note of the address and continued after the three hard cases.

They led him to a tall, narrow building, sandwiched between two huge brick warehouses on the riverfront. Piers extended out into the vastness of the mighty Mississippi. The area smelled of damp mud, rotting vegetation, and fish. Smoke gave them a few minutes before entering himself. In the time he waited, his sensitive sense of smell uncovered cooking odors as well. When he passed through the doorway into a large public room, he saw the reason why.

Expensively decorated with rich wall-hangings, lighted by crystal chandeliers that depended from a high, arched ceiling at the second-floor level, the establishment turned out to be an elaborate restaurant. Two tiers of balcony ran completely around the room, a mezzanine, and the second-floor level. A huge, horseshoe-shaped bar occupied the center of the ground floor. Thick waves of tobacco smoke, raucous chatter, and laughter rose up the walls all around. Not until he crossed an arched, oriental-style bridge did Smoke Jensen realize that the first floor had been offset and the cellar had been given over for a ruder trade. Bargemen and tugboat crews more than likely, he suspected.

White tablecloths, linen napkins, and real silver decorated the intimate settings for two, four, or six. Each table also held a crystal vase with a single red rose. Apparently Victor Spectre must be as generous with his underlings as he was in his show of being a social lion, Smoke mused. That, or these fellows were skimming off some of the cream. He spotted the men he had followed and gave the head waiter a generous tip to be seated at a table close by.

On impulse, Smoke ordered a Sazarac cocktail and then headed for the men's room.

Inside plumbing was still a novelty west of the Mississippi, even in this large city nestled on its banks. Several male patrons, out of sight of their contemporaries in the brightly lighted facility, remarked to one another on the oddity of relieving themselves inside a building. *Idiots,* Smoke thought with a flash of contempt. *Don't they know an outhouse is a* building? Back at his table, Smoke Jensen concentrated on attuning his ear to the conversation of the three outlaw leaders.

"So now it's an Army payroll," one declared. "I'm not so sure I like the risk."

"Not just a *payroll,* Gage. It's *the payroll* for Fort Leavenworth, Fort Riley, Hays, and Fort Dodge. Victor says it will come to more than three hundred thousand dollars, what with two months' back-pay thrown in."

Ice slid down the spine of Smoke Jensen. If Victor Spectre got his hands on that much money he would have the power to be untouchable. When a hundred dollars could buy a favorable decision from certain circuit judges, think what ten thousand could produce with even a federal district judge. He had to stop this train robbery, for that was what it surely would be, and bring down Victor Spectre before the payroll was taken by the gang. To do that he first had to learn more. That required that he listen to more of their conversation and endure a meal. To walk out now would raise suspicions.

Smoke ordered the standing rib roast, with creamed new potatoes and peas, and asparagus, while the one called Gage talked about telegraphing to bring in the number of guns they would need for the job. Then he expressed concern about the Army and the Pinkertons knowing who had pulled the robbery.

"No, not as long as we do like Victor said. Have some of the men call you Jesse and me Frank. It'll be blamed on the James-Younger gang."

When his food came, the roast carved at the table, it was the most attractive and succulent Smoke Jensen had ever experienced. The meat was dark pink in the middle, the outer edge a crusty brown, and surprisingly tender. The asparagus could also be cut with a fork. The potatoes and peas so sweet as to make one think they had come from a home kitchen garden. Smoke hardly tasted a bite. It appeared the outlaw trio intended to make a night of it here, so Smoke ate as quickly as possible without attracting attention, paid his bill—a little steep, he thought, at ten dollars—and departed unnoticed.

He knew where he could get the fine details of this robbery. Firmly fixed in his mind was the face of the smooth shyster with the greasy hair.

13

Railford Blumquist had offices on the third floor of the building Smoke Jensen had noted before. When Smoke arrived, he found to his good fortune that a light burned behind the windows which had gold leaf letters, outlined in black, that spelled out: ATTORNEY AT LAW. He entered and took the flight of stairs to the second floor two at a time. They creaked terribly, so he slowed and climbed the second ascent close to the wall to avoid unwanted noise.

Outside the door to Blumquist's office, Smoke prepared himself and then reached for the knob. His hand had not closed on it when it turned suddenly and the portal flew open. Smoke found himself face-to-face with Railford Blumquist.

Smoke recovered first. "Lawyer Blumquist, I presume." He stepped forward, forcing Blumquist to retreat into his office.

"Why, yes, yes, I am." The attorney frowned and looked upward at his unexpected caller. "May I ask what you wish? It's hardly business hours."

"I came for some information."

Blumquist screwed his mouth into a moue of disapproval. "Why don't you try the library? Tomorrow. When it's open. Now, I must go. I'm entirely too long overdue for a dinner party at my home."

Smoke took another menacing step, which compelled Blumquist to backpedal or lose balance. "Dinner will have to wait. I'm here about Victor Spectre and three lowlife scum wanted for a variety of crimes in Colorado."

For a second, Blumquist blanched, but covered it nicely. Face blank, eyes flat brown mirrors, he spoke with courtroom primness. "I do not know who you are talking about."

"Yes, you do. You and one of the outlaws paid a visit today on Victor Spectre at the hotel where he lives. And you left with all three."

Although swiftly plunged into a state bordering on terror, Blumquist continued to rely on bluster. "You've been following me. I'll have you arrested for that."

"I think not." Smoke's words had the consistency of iron. "Come on, Blumquist, you're an officer of the court and so am I. Only I happen to be a Deputy United States Marshal, investigating a crime that is about to be committed. A federal crime. And I have reason to believe you know the fine details of that crime. If you expect to get out of this with your life, if not your license, intact, you had better tell me all about it."

Although frightened, Railford Blumquist still managed to examine his persecutor with cold contempt. "You're nothing, Marshal. A badge with legs. And, like most lawmen, poor as a church mouse, I'm sure. Victor Spectre will crush you like a bug under foot."

"Then you admit knowing him?" Smoke probed.

"Let's say I know . . . of him. Come now, Marshal. Every man has his price. I'm sure I could contact Mr. Spectre and arrange for yours to be paid to you for forgetting all about this unfortunate situation." Smoke Jensen held up his left hand, fingers spread. Blumquist seized upon it. "Five hundred, is it?" He considered Smoke's silence. "Five thousand? Not even a drain on Spectre's petty cash."

Smoke produced a nasty smile. "No. Five knuckles," he

declared before he closed the fingers into a fist and hit Blumquist flush in the mouth.

Slammed backward, Railford Blumquist backpedaled until he slammed into the desk of his absent law clerk. The edge bit painfully into the small of his back. Smoke Jensen followed him up. Hard blows smashed into his chest and stomach. Agony radiated out to Railford's fingertips and toes. His head swam. Pain had always terrified him. As a child he had shrunk from the usual schoolyard and street conflicts. He lived every moment looking over his shoulder, expecting an attack.

He howled as he found himself picked off the floor and hurled through the air. His back made tormenting contact with the wall behind him.

The punishing blows began again. Tears sprang hot and stinging in his eyes. His lips mashed under the brutal knuckles and the pent-up water spilled from under closed lids. Once more Smoke picked up Railford and slammed him off a wall. Fighting for a modicum of control, the lawyer raised his hands in a pleading gesture.

"No. Please, no more. Don't hit me anymore."

Smoke stopped, hovered over the cringing, sorry excuse for a man. "Tell me about the payroll robbery. Every detail."

Half an hour later, Smoke Jensen had every last bit of information Railford Blumquist possessed. He knew where and when. He also knew where the loot was to be taken, and that Victor Spectre and his son, Trenton, would be there to receive it. All he had left to do was take Blumquist to jail, get to Jefferson Barracks, let the Army know about the robbery, and take care of the Spectres himself.

Victor and Trenton Spectre waited in the large, low barn on the abandoned farm where they were to meet the eight-man escort for the wagon-loads of gold and silver coin and bales of greenback currency that would soon arrive. They had no way of knowing that the train they expected the gang to loot bristled with guns. The stock cars did not haul cattle, hogs, and sheep to Kansas City to the slaughterhouses. Rather, they held twenty saddled horses each and a troop of cavalry.

Added to that, all of the men and some of the "women" in the parlor cars and Pullmans behind were Pinkerton agents. Victor Spectre's plan called for half of the gang to board at various stations across Missouri and at the right spot, take control of the locomotive and force the engineer to stop where the remainder waited with blasting powder to open the express cars and wagons to haul off the money.

Doomed to failure by the quick action of Smoke Jensen, the raid would end in bloody slaughter for the outlaws. In anticipation of that, Smoke moved in on the anxiously expectant father and son. He approached the barn from behind, careful not to reveal his presence. When he reached his goal, he worked his way silently along one side, his ears tuned to the low conversation from inside.

"Father," an adenoidal voice of a youth spoke as Smoke ducked to avoid a window. "This is more money than any other of our enterprises has yielded."

"Yes. It will be more than enough to purchase a large, steam-screw vessel." Victor Spectre laughed lightly, his voice warm with self-pride. "The owner's stateroom will be quite lavish, I promise you. You will travel in it, to oversee our enterprises in Mexico. It is a turbulent land, I grant you. And I sometimes succumb to a father's weakness. I worry about you going there alone."

"I won't be alone, Father. I have engaged the services of ten good men. True, they are young and filled with the prospect of adventure. But they are fast, and good with their guns. But I'm faster and the best. Besides, you're sending along five of your most trusted underlings."

"The Mexican bandits can come at you with more than a hundred men, Trenton."

"Not to worry, Father. Not with that Gatling gun." Trenton paused and frowned a moment. "We should have had more money for this expansion. What are you going to do to recover our losses in Colorado?"

Righteous anger clouded the face of Victor Spectre. "Try again. Perhaps in New Mexico or Nebraska. Even Kansas. I hear the sod-busters there have banks fat and ripe for the plucking. What burns deep inside me is that our setbacks in Colorado are the doing of but a single man. I find that hard to believe, but all of the evidence and the accounts of the survivors agree."

"Who is that, Father?"

"That goddamned Smoke Jensen. May his soul rot in the vilest pit of hell."

Suddenly the smaller door, inset in the tall, wide portals of the barn, flew open and a man stood framed by the jamb. He wore a fringed buckskin shirt, with trousers and moccasins of the same material. Slung low on his right hip, the butt of a Colt Peacemaker protruded from its holster. High on his left, canted at an angle, the butt of a second revolver showed in another scabbard.

"I believe someone has just used my name in vain."

Choked with rage, Victor Spectre could barely form words. "You—you're Smoke Jensen?"

"Well, I'm not God."

"What are you doing here?"

"I've come to arrest the both of you. Your gang is being taken care of by the Army and the Pinkertons."

Victor Spectre sputtered and his face turned scarlet. "Goddamn you to hell, Smoke Jensen." So saying, Victor went for his gun. Likewise, so did his son.

Trenton Spectre proved that more lay behind his words than teenage braggadoccio. He was fast and he was good. He had the muzzle of his weapon clear of leather before Smoke Jensen even reached for his righthand Colt. The .44 in Trenton's hand began an upward arc when Smoke drew with blinding, precise speed. Smoke had accurately judged that the boy would be quicker and surer than his father.

The hammer fell on Smoke's .45 Peacemaker an instant before Trenton lined up the barrel of his six-gun.

A bullet from Smoke's revolver punched a hole two fingers' width below Trenton's rib cage. It staggered the stout, broad-shouldered boy and threw his shot off. The slug sent up a shower of fine bits of straw and dust from the dirt floor of the barn halfway between himself and Smoke Jensen. Smoke pivoted to confront Victor.

Slowed by age, and hampered by the long cut of his suit coat, Victor Spectre had barely freed his Smith American from its shoulder holster when Smoke Jensen fired at him. Enormous pain erupted in the right side of Victor's chest and he dropped to his knees. The revolver fell from his grasp and thudded on the hard-packed ground. Smoke had no time to waste on him.

Youth totaled the balance in the unended contest between Smoke Jensen and Trenton Spectre. Trenton managed to maintain his grip on his .44 Colt and brought it up while Smoke fired at the boy's father. Now he blinked rapidly in an effort to fight off his blurred vision and raised the long barrel of the Frontier Model Colt. Beyond the blade front sight, the figure of Smoke Jensen jumped in and out of focus. Frantically he tried with a sweat-slicked thumb to draw back the hammer. He saw a flash of yellow orange and felt a terrible impact in his heart.

Then Trenton Spectre felt nothing at all. Dead before he hit the floor of the barn, Trenton Spectre still held tightly onto his six-gun. A scream of paternal anguish tore out of Victor Spectre's throat. He grabbed wildly at his .44 Smith and launched himself at Smoke Jensen.

"You bastard!" he howled.

Smoke fired hastily. His slug cut a deep trough along the head of Victor Spectre from temple to rear lobe along the left side. The wound released a halo of blood drops and knocked the criminal mastermind unconscious. Still charged for battle, Smoke Jensen had to force himself to hesitate and take stock. In an eyeblink he realized that the fight had ended.

A month went by before Victor Spectre could be brought to trial. Smoke Jensen attended, much put out at having to leave the High Lonesome to attend court in St. Louis. The first thing he noticed when the bailiffs brought Victor Spectre to the defense table was the ugly wound he had given the man. It had healed into a mass of scar tissue, from which sprouted short, totally white hairs that contrasted with the black of the remainder like the pattern on the pelt of a skunk. Fitting, Smoke had thought at the time. . . .

That had been nearly seven years ago. Now, Smoke Jensen had to allow that instead of preparing himself for a new, reformed life, Victor Spectre had spent his years in prison honing a sharper hatred and desire for revenge. Something, Smoke knew, would have to be done about it, and soon.

With dawn still a silver-gray promise on the horizon, Smoke Jensen broke camp the next morning. He had packed away everything and had only a skillet, coffee pot, trestle, and iron tripod to cool and stow in a parfleche before swinging into the saddle. He aimed Thunder's nose into the northwest and advanced into the tall, barely undulating, green sea that covered the Great Divide Basin.

Without any wind to fight, particularly a sharp one out of the northwest, Smoke made good headway. He had his first destination firmly in mind: the Arapaho and Shoshoni encampments of the Wind River Reservation, near Riverton, on the Bighorn River. He had only the ramparts of the Green Mountains, now a low, dark line that protruded above the curvature of the earth, between himself and his old friends among the Arapaho and Shoshoni. Smoke had a notion, reinforced by his recollection of the determination and implacable evil of Spectre, Tinsdale, and Buckner, that he might have need to call upon his Indian friends sometime in the near future.

For the time being, though, he remained content to let the horses eat the miles and leave him to his thoughts. Not for an instant had he harbored any regrets for killing Trenton Spectre. The boy was just shy of eighteen, and corrupt enough to be ripe for harvest by the Grim Reaper. It troubled him far more that he had not finished off Victor Spectre. Although justice remained swift and sure in most cases, three men he had spared had cheated the hangman and now required retribution from himself. Too much money, all of it ill-gotten, had bought a special kind of justice for them. A small thing perhaps, though another chink in the armor of the rule of law. *Stop it,* Smoke admonished himself. Such hankie-twisting philosophizing was a mental crutch for the weak and the cowardly.

He didn't lack for money or the things it would buy. Only a hypocrite would criticize and condemn the wealthy while he, himself, was rich. Provided, of course, his mind mocked him, it was money honestly earned. He quickly dismissed the conundrum a moment later when he saw the figures of three mounted men across his path.

"Howdy, a feller don't see many people out this way," the one in the middle remarked when Smoke Jensen had ridden up.

Smoke gave his reins a turn around the saddlehorn and tipped up the brim of his Stetson left-handed. "Now, that's a fact. You gents headed for Colorado?"

A thick, walrus mustache twitched in a mirthless smile. "Actually, it's Nebraska. Not to pry, mister, but where might you be directed?"

Smoke took notice of the way the trio eyed his 'Palouse stallion, expensive saddle, and the heavy-laden Debbie, his packhorse. "Thought I might set a spell in Riverton."

The talkative one shook his head regretfully. "That's a sort of unwelcoming place. Bein' all that close to an Injun reservation makes folks a mite edgy."

"True, I've been there before, know a few of the folks."

"Yep. That could make a difference. Any of 'em know you're comin'?"

Smoke smelled the danger plain as if someone had set fire to an outhouse. He decided to play it out. "No. Didn't write ahead or anything."

The spokesman cut his eyes to his companions before he replied to Smoke. "That's a might nice saddle, all silver-chased and such."

"Thanks." *Any time now,* Smoke cautioned himself.

Pale, gray eyes suddenly hardened to iron. "Much too nice for a saddle tramp like you." A gloved hand reached for the plow-handled grip of a Frontier Colt. "We'll jist relieve you of it."

Smoke Jensen sighed regretfully in the split-second it took for his long, strong fingers to curl around the butt-grip of his Colt Peacemaker. He and the highwayman drew almost as one. *This fellow is good,* Smoke acknowledged as the sear notches on his hammer clicked past. His attacker had the muzzle of his .44 clear of leather at the moment when Smoke Jensen dropped the hammer on a primer.

Bucking in Smoke's hand, the big .45 sent a hot slug flying into the chest of the would-be thief. An expression of disbelief and wonder washed one of intense pain off the face of the robber. His own weapon discharged downward and grazed the right front shoulder of his mount. The horse shrieked, reared, and threw its rider. Amazed that he still held his six-gun, the bandit hit with a spine-wrenching jar.

Fighting back pain, he raised his Colt and tried to ear back the hammer. Smoke Jensen had changed his point of aim in the short time the horse panicked. He deliberately put a round in the right shoulder of the man to his right front. Then brought his attention back to the first gunhawk. The Colt in the hand of Smoke Jensen spat a long spear of flame as it expelled another bullet.

This one popped a neat, black-rimmed hole in the forehead of Smoke's assailant, exploding messily out the back of his head, which showered the third highwayman with gore. Convinced by this display of speed and accuracy, he let the English Webley drop back into his holster and raised his hands with alacrity. His horse did a nervous little dance and that caused his eyes to widen and fear to paint his face.

"I ain't doin' nothin'. I give up."

"I gathered as much. Control your mount, then reach across with your left hand, and pull that iron from its pocket."

With that accomplished, the youthful thief looked at Smoke Jensen. "What are we gonna do now, mister?"

"We're going to play a little Indian game of trust. You are going to load your dead friends on their horses and then take them to the nearest town and turn yourself in to the sheriff for tryin' to rob and kill me. If there's any money on your heads, tell the sheriff to hold it for me."

"Wh—who are you? Who should I say?"

"Smoke Jensen."

"Oh, sweet Christ. I never knew."

"Well, now you do."

A new idea came to the rattled gunman. "What if I don't do like you say an' turn them an' myself in?"

"Then I'll hunt you down and kill you," Smoke spoke simply.

Instantly ghostly pale, the youth worked his lips a moment before any sound would come. "I believe you. By God, I believe you would. I swear it'll go jist like you say, Mr. Jensen."

Smoke gave him a bleak smile. "Somehow, I believe you're telling the truth."

Monte Carson laid the three telegraph message forms on his desk, his eyes fixed beyond the open door to the sheriff's office in Big Rock, Colorado. The first report came from the warden at Yuma Prison, detailing the depredations committed by the escapees in Arizona. *Brutal bastards,* Monte allowed. The other two came from Utah. Swollen to a gang now, the murders and robberies grew larger in scope. The third had included the information that the gang had last been seen headed for Wyoming.

That gave him pause to think. Frowning, he rose with an anguished creak from his chair and poured coffee. Seated again, he ground his teeth in a chewing motion and once more stared far off into the dark sea of pines on the distant slopes. At last he came to his conclusion. He smacked his lips and slapped an open palm on his desk. The loud report caused the jailer, Monte's friend of years, to jump.

"Abner," Monte announced in his best snake oil sales-man voice, "I think this is a good time for that little vacation I've been promising myself. Get in a little fishin', spoil myself with fancy food in Denver, visit friends."

Abner cocked a shaggy, gray eyebrow. "Like Smoke Jensen, for instance?"

Monte pulled a contrite expression. "Am I that trans-parent?"

A grin revealed long, yellowed teeth, and Abner nodded. "With them telegraphs on yer desk, an' Smoke headed into the same country, don't take a locomotive de-signer to know what's in your head."

"Right you are," Monte admitted. "Smoke's bound for the Yellowstone country. And he's the most valuable friend I've got."

Abner studied his boss. "You figger to go all alone?"

Monte pushed back and came to his boots. "I reckoned Hank Evans might make good company. If I push it, I might catch up before this mob of killers finds Smoke."

Spectre, his partners, and their gang—thirty-eight strong now—entered Wyoming by way of Flaming Gorge. Every-where they could look, beauty surrounded them. The delicate, pastel greens of aspen and cottonwood set the air to shimmering as their foliage quaked in the steady breeze. Earth tones ranged from black loam, to yellow, white, ochre, burnt umber, and red-orange, in strata of rock and soil that undulated along the raw faces of the eroded canyon walls. A cheery, blue stream burbled along over water-smoothed pebbles. Wildflowers nodded and bobbed in a riot of yellow buttercups, blue violets, bright red ladies slipper, and fields of white petaled daises. Birds twittered and trilled their mating calls from every point of the compass.

Sadly, all of nature's splendor went unnoticed by the grim-faced riders, who kept their heads straight ahead, eyes on the trail. Dorcus Carpenter and Farlee Huntoon vociferously ran it down, maintaining that their own mountains of West Virginia were much prettier, worth more as farm land, and produced the best white lightning in the whole United States. Gus Jaeger growled to them to shut up.

Only the scout, half a mile ahead on point, observed and appreciated this peaceful environment. For a moment, it profoundly touched his inner self. Sighing, his eyes misted slightly, he even gave thought to putting spurs to his mount and riding the hell away from this nest of vipers he had joined. Then the reality of the huge amount of money they had been offered reined in his conscience and he went about his job as expected. At half-past eleven he picked their nooning site and began to gather firewood.

After putting away a tin plate of warmed-over sow belly and beans, Victor Spectre selected seven hard-faced, humorless outlaws and called them together out of hearing of the rest of the gang.

"I have a special job for you men," Spectre informed them. "While we ride on into Wyoming, I want you to take supplies enough for eight days and head southeast into Colorado. There, you will grab a certain woman and bring her back to the little town of Dubois. Think you can do that without any problems?"

Nate Miller drew himself up, thumbs hooked behind the buckle of his cartridge belt. "Sure, Mr. Spectre. Nothin' to it. Where is it we're going?"

"Your target is the Sugarloaf. That's the ranch owned by Smoke Jensen."

14

Soft breezes, heavily perfumed, sighed across the rippling grass on the northern slope of the Green Mountains. Smoke Jensen had located a low pass, hardly more than a gentle incline to a sway-back saddle and, beyond the notch, a rolling scarp, carpeted in rich green buffalo grass that had already grown belly-high on Thunder. In the distance, beyond the last rampart, Smoke noted a thin, gray column of woodsmoke. If Smoke recalled correctly, that would be the digs of Muleshoe Granger, an oldtimer who clung to the ways of the trappers, regardless of little or no market for pelts. Granger had a Shoshoni wife and—had it been four?—kids the last time Smoke had been through. Smiling, Smoke altered course to put him in line with the cookfire's stream.

Halting some fifty yards from the log-fronted building dug into the hillside, Smoke raised an empty right hand and hailed the bent, bow-legged figure who had paused to study his approach. "Hello, the cabin. Is that you, Muleshoe? I'm Smoke Jensen. May I ride on in?"

Delayed by distance, Granger's words reached Smoke a bit muffled. "Why, shore. C'mon in." When Smoke reached the dooryard, Granger continued. "We's fixin' to take a bite to eat. Step down and join us."

Smiling, Smoke did just that. "I'd be obliged."

Muleshoe's family had grown to seven, Smoke noted. Those under twelve were buck naked, sun-browned like berries. The youngest was a mere toddler, who clung shyly to the skirt of his mother's elk-skin dress, and peeped around her ample hips at the stranger. While they ate, Muleshoe Granger gave Smoke Jensen a fish-eye from time to time, then smacked his lips, licked the gravy from an elk stew off his fingers and gave a curt nod.

"Seems as how I should know you. As I recall, we met long whiles back. Ain't you ol' Preacher's young sidekick?"

"That I am. And I've been through these parts several times on my own."

Muleshoe blinked. "That a fact? Well, they say the first thing goes is the memory."

Smoke gave a low chuckle, and a nod toward the younger children. "It must be true. At least it's not something else."

"What you gettin' at, Smoke?"

"Last time I visited your digs was about ten years ago. You had only four children then, as I recall."

Muleshoe laughed out loud and slapped a hard-muscled thigh. "Nope, it was three. But, by jing, you've got the right of it there. Plenty lead in the old pencil. Moon Raven's carryin' another in the oven right now."

Shyness overcome by an empty belly, the toddler had come forward. His sister, a girl of seven or so, helped him to a bowl of stew. All the while, he stared fixedly at Smoke Jensen. Smoke pointed to the youngsters with his chin.

"That's good to hear. You know, you two bake up some mighty fine-lookin' younguns."

Muleshoe beamed. "The pride of Granger Valley."

Smoke looked around. "You've named the place, then?"

"Yep. Had to. Folks is movin' in faster than fleas. Why, I've got me a neighbor all crowded up to me, cheek by jowl. He's not more'n ten miles over to the east. I had to file with the territorial government to hold what's mine."

"Civilization spoils everything, doesn't it," Smoke observed.

Muleshoe nodded. "Yep. There's powerful truth in those words. Now, are you real pressed for time? Or do you figger to stay the night? The youngins would love to hear some tales about Preacher," he coaxed.

"I'm not in that great a hurry. If you'll put up with me, I'd be pleased to spend the night."

Muleshoe gave him a thoughtful look. "That's good. Bein' as who you are and where, it might be best. From what I hear, you might be ridin' into some real danger."

"How's that?" Smoke asked.

"A friend rode through the day before yesterday, told me about a whole passel of men ridin' grim and hard in the saddle to the west of us. Says they come up outta Utah."

Smoke nodded his understanding. "That fits with what I've been hearing. You can be sure I've caught wind of them from time to time. But, tell me, have you seen anything of Three Finger Jack lately?"

With evening coming on, Victor Spectre, Ralph Tinsdale, and Olin Buckner had settled in camp stools at the front of one of the three Sibley tents they had acquired along the way. A decanter of whiskey gave off long, amber shafts of brightness in the flicker of firelight, as it passed from hand to hand. For all the outward appearance of conviviality, tension fairly crackled from one man to the next. Buckner's tone became quarrelsome as he vented his impatience.

"This protracted journey across the wilderness is becoming burdensome, Victor. I have never been much of a horseman. My rump and thighs still ache after each day's ride."

"You'll toughen up soon enough," Victor told him unsympathetically.

"I agree with Olin," Ralph Tinsdale injected. "If our purpose remains the same, to revenge ourselves on Smoke

Jensen, then why don't we simply head to the Sugarloaf and kill him in his own yard?"

Victor Spectre shook his head in resignation. Small wonder these two had been taken by Jensen so easily. Then he made a final effort to explain. "For one thing, it would be too quick and too easy. I want Smoke Jensen to die slowly and hurt a great deal while doing it. Then there's the fact that Colorado is quite civilized now. There are trains and the telegraph, thousands of residents, and competent lawmen." He did not go quite so far as to admit he feared being trapped in the more populous country around the Sugarloaf. Not by the law, but rather by Smoke Jensen. Gus Jaeger approached, his face even more horselike than ever.

"Mr. Spectre, the men are getting down-right antsy. They want for the walls of a saloon around them, some good whiskey, and some wimmin to tussle with. When are we going to get around city lights again?"

Spectre sighed. "In due time. What's wrong with the liquor we've provided for them? Isn't it good enough?"

"Nothin' wrong, really. Only that they'd like someone to share it with." Gus snickered. "What's up ahead?"

"An Indian reservation. A rather large one. Which reminds me. In light of what you've said, make it clear to the men that they are not, I repeat *are not*, under any circumstances, to attempt to bed any of the squaws. Indians are quite strange in their attitude toward women. If you are their friend and a guest, they will offer you a daughter or a wife to warm your bed, and think nothing of it. But if you lay eyes, let alone a hand, on any woman not offered to you, your scalp will decorate their shield. Make certain the men are aware of this. Tell them, also, that if any of them do pester the Indian women, I'll personally kill them before the bucks have a chance to."

Jaeger frowned. "That's mighty cold . . . sir."

"It's meant to be. Now, go on and cool their ardor with a little whiskey." After Gus Jaeger departed, Victor Spectre returned to the subject of Smoke Jensen.

"This little town up north, Dubois, is ideal for what we want to do. Not so large as to be difficult to take over, yet not so small that we cannot house this little army of ours within the city limits. And, from others I've met in prison, Smoke Jensen has a soft spot in his heart for the people of Dubois. All we need do is take it over and send word. Smoke Jensen will come to us. Further, if my other little project bears fruit, we'll have a most attractive bait to dangle in front of him."

Two days later, Smoke reached the lodge of Chief Thomas Brokenhorn of the Shoshoni at midday. Small children ran naked and shrieking among the Shoshoni brush summer lodges. Cookfires sent up their columns of white, while savory odors emanated from the pots supported over them by tripods. Warriors gathered from their homes to form a silent column, along which Smoke rode to the central lodge. He could not shake the feeling that their formation exactly mimicked that of the punishment gauntlet. He banished the unease when he saw the broad grin on the face of his old friend, Brokenhorn, who stood before his lodge with arms folded over a barrel chest.

"You have come far, old friend," Chief Brokenhorn declared by way of greeting.

"So have you," Smoke responded, meaning the older man's elevation to Civil Chief. "You were only leader of the Otter Society when I last saw you."

"Thank you, Swift Firestick. Dismount and make my lodge your own. We will eat, smoke, and talk of old times."

"It would be a pleasure, friend Thomas. Although it is recent times I am most interested in."

Brokenhorn nodded curtly. "Yes. Some very bad men rode through here yesterday. You must be seeking them." A kindliness lighted his eyes. "They are many. Come, take of the food of my woman, first, burn a pipeful, then we talk of these matters."

* * *

Monte Carson received a warm welcome from Morgan Crosby. Traveling light and fast, the lawman had made it that far in only four days. He filled his belly with some of Morgan's good cooking and settled back with a pipe he had taken to smoking of late.

Morgan broke one of their frequent long, silent spells. "I reckon you'd be interested in hearin' anything about Smoke Jensen?"

Monte took a long pull on the pipe. "I didn't come all this way for exercise. He's been here?"

"Yep. Five—six days ago. Had some right unpleasant fellers on his trail, though."

"What did Smoke do about that?"

"It's what we did, you should be sayin'."

Monte let a thin stream of white trickle from his lips. "All right, what did you two do about it?"

Morgan chuckled throatily before answering. "Mind now, I'd never seen Smoke Jensen in action before. He's 'bout as smooth as a well-oiled locomotive. Betwixt us, we convinced those fellers it were a bad idea to try takin' Smoke in with no more than five of 'em on their side."

A grunt came from Monte. "All right, where's the bodies buried?"

An expression of childlike innocence lighted the face of Morgan Crosby. "There ain't no bodies buried." He paused, slapped his thigh and cackled. "After Smoke rode out, I drug 'em off to feed the coyotes and buzzards. One of them got away. Though he be carrin' about six of my double-aught buck. Big feller he was, else he woulda been critter bait, too." Then he went on to describe the fight.

Monte Carson considered this. No doubt in his mind that Smoke Jensen could have handled all five by himself. Better than even odds when they split up like that. And Smoke not getting a scratch. Typical. Monte finished his bowl, knocked out the dottle, and ground the tobacco embers under one boot sole. He stretched and came upright.

"Which way did Smoke head?"

"That-away," Morgan told him, a finger pointed to the northwest. "Up Yellowstone way."

Monte nodded. "That fits with what he told me."

"Which is?"

"Smoke's bound for Jackson's Hole."

"A feller could take on a small army if he knew his way around there," Morgan opined. "An' I reckon that's what's after him from what I've learned."

"Smoke knows the place well enough. Ol' Preacher taught him every nook and cranny." Monte turned to face Morgan, still seated on the porch. He extended his hand. "Much obliged for the vittles. Sure sets nice in the belly. There's still a lot of daylight to be used so I reckon I'll head on out. Plenty ground between here and the Hole."

"Come by any time, Sheriff Carson."

"Please, Monte."

Crosby beamed. "Make it Morgan, then. Be proud to have you stop by and stay a while. An' bring your friend with you."

"I'll try. Believe me, I will. Good day to you, Morgan."

"An' to you, Monte."

Five minutes later, Monte Carson rode out of sight of the snug, though bullet-scarred cabin.

A large, whole ribcage of elk had been properly demolished, along with stewed squash, mixed with nuts, wild onions, and berries. With signs and rudimentary Shoshoni, Smoke Jensen related the story of the Great Elk Hunt he had gone on when only a slight bit older than his attentive audience. Some twenty children from the village had gathered around Chief Brokenhorn's fire to gawk at the tall, lean white man and hear his exciting stories.

"It was a hard ride for me," Smoke recounted. "I was still

little enough my legs stuck out from the sides of my pony. Some of you must ride the same way, right?" Giggles and whispered accusations rippled through the cluster of Indian youngsters. Smoke waited them out and went on. "Preacher and I joined with a whole lot of other trappers for this hunt. It would be the biggest ever. Five hands of men, in my language, twenty-five, came from all parts of the mountains. Preacher, of course, was the best hunter of them all. He was first to find the herd, first to kill a bull elk. I got to dress it out." More giggles and knowing nods.

"That arrangement didn't last long. By the third day, Preacher let me pick an elk out of the herd and take it as my own. 'First,' he told me, 'say a little prayer to the bull's High Self, askin' permission to take its life. Say that you have hunger and will be even more hungry in the long winter to come. Ask that the animal's spirit be born as the biggest elk of all.' That made my chest swell and I thought I was really something. Preacher told me he learned to pray like that from the Shoshoni."

"That's right," Tom Brokenhorn injected. "He did. In the time of my grandfather. And I remember that hunt. I was no bigger than Chusha over there." He indicated a boy of seven or so, squatted as close as he could get to Smoke Jensen. "Many of us joined in on that hunt and we all ate well the whole of winter."

Smoke went on to describe the surrounds each day and the shooting of elk with rifles and bow and arrow. He concluded, "Preacher told me later that three hundred bull elk and fifty young elk were taken in that hunt. We made meat for a week after."

"Tell us something more," Chusha pleaded.

Smoke stretched and forced a yawn. "Four stories is enough for one night. Your fathers will be wondering where you have gone. And your mothers will worry. Go on. I'll have another story in the morning before I leave."

After the last, reluctant boy had walked off among the lodges, Smoke realized he actually was sleepy. He roused himself and headed for the lodge that had been prepared for him. Tomorrow he would head to the Arapaho camp.

Seven hard-faced men rode onto the Sugarloaf early the next morning. They made no effort to conceal their approach from the headquarters buildings. Earlier, one of them had watched a large contingent of hands ride off to the horse pastures. By his count, only half a dozen remained to work around the barns and blacksmithy. Well and good, Nate Miller thought. When the Sugarloaf hands had gotten well out of sight and sound of the main ranch buildings, he ordered his crew forward.

Riding slouched in the saddle, Nate led the outlaws up the steep two mile lane from the gate to the ranch yard. He and his men made only slight nods and grunted responses when hailed by the first man to discover them. Looking neither left nor right, they rode on. Stumpy Granger looked up from the anvil, which still rang from the blows he had given a particularly stubborn horseshoe. He made them right away as gunfighters.

With most of the hands gone for the day, that did not bode well for those left behind, Stumpy considered. He wiped a black-smudged hand across his brow to eliminate the sheet of sweat that covered it, and watched silently, eyes slitted, as the hard cases walked their horses up to the tie-rail outside the kitchen door. There they dismounted. Still no one challenged them. Although they had been in several scrapes with Smoke Jensen, the ranch hands were hardly seasoned gunmen. They held back as the strangers started for the door.

They soon found they had backed off too long when two of the human debris pushed into the kitchen. At last, the six wranglers began to gather around the outlaws.

"What's yer business on the Sugarloaf?" one of the bolder hands asked.

"If it was any of your business, you'd have been told,"

growled a rat-faced individual, his right hand on the smooth butt of his .45 Colt.

Stumpy took up the challenge. "Mayhap you didn't hear too well. This here is the Sugarloaf. Smoke Jensen's ranch. Bein' as how we belong here and you don't, that makes it our business. What are you here for? An' who sent you?"

"Oldtimer, you really don't want to know."

A forge hammer in his left hand, Stumpy menaced the five men he faced. He was about to speak again when a loud crash came from inside the house. Wood splintered and a man yelped.

Sally Jensen looked up as the kitchen door swung open. Surprise washed over her face when she faced two unfamiliar men. "What are you doing here?" she demanded.

A lean, lanky one, who she would later learn was named Nate Miller, asked, "Are you Sally Jensen?"

"Yes, I am."

Miller guffawed. "We've come to take you on a little visit."

"I think not. I have no plans to go anywhere," Sally retorted defiantly. "Especially with the likes of you. Get out of my kitchen."

"When we go, we're takin' you with us."

Her purse lay in the middle of the table. Sally made a quick grab for it and produced her .38 Colt Lightning. She had already begun her squeeze through on the double-action rig when she spoke again. "Get . . . out . . . of . . . my . . . kitchen."

"Look out! She's got a gun," the man with Miller yelped.

Sally came out of her chair with enough force to knock it over. One leg splintered when it struck the floor. Already, Miller had moved to the side. The other thug started to dive through the open doorway. Sally fired then. The slug cracked past close enough to the outlaw that he felt the hot wind. Sally started to squeeze off another round when Nate Miller dived at her from her blind side.

Fingers like iron slats closed around her wrist. "Gimme that, bitch," Miller spat.

She fought like a Fury. Sally's nails clawed Nate's cheek. He yowled, and clapped a hand over the quartet of flowing red lines. He managed to get the web of his other hand between the hammer and the rear of the receiver of Sally's Colt Lightning. The sharp little firing pin bit deeply into his skin. Sally stomped on his arch and then brought a knee up toward his groin. Only because he moved his right thigh did she fail to do him severe damage. Ignoring the deep gouges on his cheek, he used his bloody hand to shake her violently.

"Let go of that gun," he growled as he slammed her head into the point of his shoulder. Sally bit him on the arm. Miller grunted out his pain and punched her on the side of her head. Sally saw a wild burst of stars behind her eyes and her knees sagged. It relaxed her grip on the revolver and it clattered loudly to the floor.

Miller howled with pain as he shook his hand free of the firing pin and the weapon dropped away. Quickly he spun Sally around and took hold of both her shoulders. He shook her like one would an errant child.

"Listen to me," Miller spat furiously, flecks of foam flying with his whiskey breath. "You're coming with us. Either over my shoulder or on your own two feet, you're coming. I don't much care which it is. Bart, give me a hand."

Bart turned away from the door with alacrity and crossed the room to where Nate held the dark-haired woman. Each man took an arm and frog-marched her to the door. Nate Miller turned sideways and led the way out, dragging Sally behind him. When she appeared as a captive, the hands at last reacted. As one, they went for their guns.

When he saw Miss Sally in the clutches of the two hard cases, Stumpy Granger let fly with the hammer. Driven by the power of a blacksmith's muscular arm, the heavy object slammed into the forehead of the rat-faced thug. He went down like a slaughterhouse steer. Stumpy cackled with glee.

Already reaching for his six-gun, Stumpy chortled, "Right betwixt the runnin' lights."

A swift exchange of lead followed. One bullet cracked by close enough to cut the knot on the headband Stumpy wore. Momentarily the sodden cloth fell over his eyes. It caused his shot to go wild, to slam into the wall of the house. One of the saddle trash shrieked in pain, gut-shot by two ranch hands at the same time. Blood bubbled up his throat and formed a pink froth on his lips. He shuddered mightily and fell face first into the dirt, dead from a perforated stomach and blasted liver before he hit the ground.

"Stumpy, I'm hit," a young voice called from the blacksmith's right.

Granger yanked the cloth band free and looked that way. Young Clell Eilert knelt in the dust, his Colt held limply in his left hand. "Git down, boy. Get clear of this now," Stumpy commanded. He fired a round at the man who must have shot Eilert, and noted with satisfaction when the slug tore into the right side of the outlaw's chest. Another hand lay dead in a welter of gore. Nate Miller waved a six-gun over his head and called to his men.

"Mount up, boys. Git the hell out of here."

He roughly threw Sally onto the saddle of the dead hard case and led the way at a fast trot down the lane toward safety. Quickly his underlings broke off and followed suit. In less than two swirling minutes, the fight ended. Stumpy counted up the toll.

"One of them dead, and one of ours," he glumly reported to anyone interested in hearing. "At least two of them wounded, three of ours. What's worse, though, is they got Miss Sally. There's gonna be hell to pay for that."

* * *

"There's gonna be hell to pay for that," Ike Mitchell echoed Stumpy Granger when the hands returned, after being summoned by a shaken Sugarloaf worker.

"Damn straight," Stump muttered agreement.

Ike surveyed the scene. "Get everyone who is able gathered up, Stumpy. We'll pick a skeleton crew to maintain things here, the rest will ride after those bastards."

"Jist what I had in mind," Stumpy offered.

When everyone collected around Ike Mitchell, he outlined his plans. At once the hands who would accompany him went about making ready. It did not take long for Ike to see Bobby lead his mount to the corral rails and climb up to tie on his bedroll. Ike crossed to him.

"I'm sorry, Bobby, you're not going along."

"Yes . . . I . . . am," Bobby insisted as he tightly jerked down on a pair of latigo strings. "It's my fault anyway. I shoulda gone with Smoke. We could have stopped those guys long before now."

Taken aback by the boy's vehemence, Ike could only shake his head. "That's not realistic, Bobby. Smoke is miles from here, and these fellers came from who knows where. You cannot come with us. Smoke and Miss Sally would never forgive me."

Torment twisted Bobby's features. His words came out heavy and torn with anguish. "I've gotta go. Don't you see? *She's my mother!*"

Something ripped inside Ike Mitchell. Buried memories flared up of himself as a boy of twelve, standing over the grave of his mother, killed by Indians." All right, Bobby. Bring that little carbine of yours, and your six-gun. We leave in ten minutes."

15

Smoke Jensen bid farewell to Chief Brokenhorn early that morning. The Chief clasped Smoke's forearm and nodded toward the northwest.

"Go carefully, old friend. I will keep braves to watch the evil ones. I promise you that when you need them, warriors will come to help you."

"That could get you in a lot of trouble for leaving the reservation armed and without an army escort."

Thomas Brokenhorn gave him a fleeting, bitter smile and shrugged. "We are no strangers to the white man's trouble. Ride in peace and send word when men are needed."

"Thank you, old friend. May your lodge always have ample food."

A twinkle filled the eyes of Brokenhorn. "You go now to those snakes in the grass?"

"What a thing to call the Arapaho," Smoke said in mock chastisement.

"Old ways die hard. Old enemies even harder."

"Yes, I'm going to talk with Blackrobe. I'll give him your best."

"What does this 'best' mean?"

Smoke chuckled. "Better you didn't know." With that,

Smoke Jensen swung into the saddle and rode off toward the Arapaho encampment.

At the head of the column of vengeful ranch hands, Ike Mitchell soon noted that the trail of the kidnappers led roughly in the same direction Smoke Jensen said he would be taking. He said nothing of it at the time, content to be assured they quickly closed ground. Sally Jensen was a plucky lady. He felt confident she would do anything she could to slow down her abductors.

Bobby Harris kept up well, Ike also observed. Not once did the boy complain of the fast pace or the ache that must be in full bloom in his thighs and crotch. They rode on through the afternoon. Twenty minutes out of each hour they walked their horses to keep them from becoming blown. If the outlaws failed to do the same, the chances of coming on them soon increased considerably. The western sky turned magenta and they had not yet made contact.

Reluctantly, Ike called a halt for the day. While the hands went about the setup of camp, Ike took Bobby aside. They chewed on cold biscuits while the man tried to make his most important point with the boy.

"Bobby, I want you to promise me one thing. When the shooting starts, you hold back. I want you out of the mix-up as far as you can be. Oh, you'll have a chance to get in your licks. I want you to pick a spot from which you can watch and see any of the outlaws try to escape. If they do, pot 'em."

The boy nodded thoughtfully. "Yeah, yeah, I can do that."

"Good boy." Ike resisted the impulse to pat Bobby on the head and nodded instead. He strode back to the cookfire and poured coffee.

When the last of the red-eye gravy had been sopped up with the last biscuit, and the final bit of ham had been munched contentedly, Ike Mitchell called the hands together around the fire. He informed them of the likelihood that the outlaws were headed for the same place as Smoke Jensen. He also advised that they had a good chance of catching up the next day. When the wranglers of the Sugarloaf had digested that, he asked for suggestions about what to do when they caught the kidnappers in the open.

Handy Barker had the wildest idea. "I say we rope 'em by the ankles and drag those bastards to death." Oddly enough, several hands agreed.

"We oughta get the law in on this, don't you think, Mr. Mitchell?" Perk Toller, the youngest, newest hand offered.

Fred Grimes, an oldtimer, had a sobering thought. "Remember one thing. Those fellers have Miss Sally with them. We will have to be mighty careful with any shooting we do. Best thing I think we can do is find 'em, then get around them and set up an ambush. Two of us could make a grab for Miss Sally while the rest of the outlaws are tryin' to escape the ambush."

Ike thought that the most reasonable, if a bit timid. Yet, Bobby Harris summed up their general attitude with his quiet, simple statement. "I say we kill 'em all."

Deep, rhythmic throbbing came from the big, "singing" drum of the Arapaho village. Four men sat at it, each with his padded beater, pounding out the notes of a hunt song. Shoulders hunched forward, their heads thrown back to the star-milked sky, they chanted the words of the favored piece. A huge fire burned nearby, with the chiefs and elders seated before it with their honored guest.

Smoke Jensen leaned back on a porcupine quill-decorated backrest and gnawed on a rib bone. The meat was sweet and rich. In the chill of the high plains night, smaller fires flickered in every lodge, making of themselves a vast display of huge, skin lanterns. When the gunfighter licked his fingers to signal he was through eating, Chief Blackrobe produced a pipe, lighted it with a coal from the fire, and made the six points. Then he passed the calumet to Smoke Jensen, who did the same as his host, took a long draw for himself and began to speak of his reason for being there.

"A moon ago, three bad men escaped from Yuma Prison in far off Arizona. They have taken a vow to hunt and kill me. I do not fear them. They are only three. But, they have taken a gang to themselves, dangerous men, made all the more so because they are not the best at what they do. They number many times two hands." Smoke paused to let that sink in.

"It is said that these men have ridden into this country," Smoke continued. "Though why they come here I do not know."

Silence followed for a while, during which Smoke passed the pipe on. At last Blackrobe spoke. "We have seen such men. As you say, they number many. They rode through here two suns ago. I did not like their looks, though in truth, they did no harm. So I sent young warriors to watch over their progress. I would believe that they are the same men of which you speak. If so, you could use some help. I promise to take this up with the Council. If approved, men can be sent whenever you need them. Now, let us talk of other things and drink some of the coffee you have brought with you."

Bound hand and foot, Sally Jensen sat on a rock, apart from the scruffy band of thugs who had taken her captive. She was cold, hungry, and miserable, though determined not to let her captors know that. With only a faint orange glow on the horizon, one of the hard cases separated from the rest and came toward her. He carried a tin plate and a spoon.

"I have some grub here. Brung you some water, too. I'll untie your hands so you can eat, if you promise not to make a fuss."

Sally thought it wise to remain assertive. "I doubt I could keep down anything cooked by the likes of any of you."

A low chuckle sounded in the shadows. "You'd be surprised. Ol' Hank's a fair to middlin' cook. If you aim to live through this, you'll need to eat to keep up yer strength."

She recognized the truth to that. "I suppose you are right. I promise not to try to escape while my hands are free."

"I'm sure you won't. Because I'm gonna sit right here and watch you."

"Where are you taking me?" Sally asked once her hands had been freed and she held the plate.

He saw no reason not to respond. "North. To a little town name of Dubois. The boss says that yer husband will come there to get you free."

Sally frowned and iron edged her words. "If he does, you can be sure you will all regret the day it happens."

Again that irritating, superior chuckle. "I doubt that. Lady, there's thirty-eight of us. More'n enough to face down Smoke Jensen."

"Are you sure? What do you really know about my husband?"

Considering that a moment, the outlaw spoke softly. "I ain't never seen him, ma'am. But, I hear he's one ring-tail heller when he's riled."

Sally smiled to herself, pleased with this response. "That's true enough. He and three others took on more than fifty men one time. Smoke was shot twice, but he killed or wounded twenty of them by himself."

"Lord God, ma'am, if you'll excuse my cussin'. He's a bit more than most of these fellers are expectin'. Some of us is purty good, but not *that* good."

"Another time, he took on thirteen men in the middle of a street by himself. Five of them died, the other eight received one or more wounds. Smoke took a crease across the top of his left shoulder," she added sweetly.

"That's powerful good shootin', ma'am."

Sally used all her feminine wiles to sell her message. "I thought you ought to know. Perhaps it would be wise for you to make the others aware of these things?"

Thoughtful silence followed. "Ummm. Yes, I do think you're right."

A rustle of brush and crunch of a stone underfoot announced the arrival of another of the outlaws. A hulking brute, he smelled of tobacco smoke, stale whiskey, and unwashed body. A broken-toothed grin shined yellowish in the reflected firelight. Fists on hips, he took a long, slow look at Sally Jensen. Abruptly, he reached out and chucked her under the chin, his thick thumb and forefinger squeezing painfully.

"Well, now, I reckon it's time for us to get a little relief, don't you, Sam?" With his other hand he massaged his crotch suggestively.

Sally's confidant, Sam, bristled immediately. "You heard what Nate said, an' Mr. Spectre, too. She ain't to be touched." He sounded as though he meant it.

Menace bristled in the lout's words. "You callin' me out, Sam?"

"I reckon, if needs be."

Nate Miller appeared out of nowhere. He gave the surly thug a hard shove. "Get back where you belong. You, too, Sam. Once Miz Jensen is fed, anyway." He tipped his hat to Sally. "Sorry, ma'am, if Ogilvey upset you. He knows better. Or he at least should. I'll have Sam here rig you a safe place to sleep."

Icily, Sally answered him. "Thank you, you are so kind."

Silently, she hatched plan after plan on how to escape. And rejected them all. The time would come, she kept telling himself. It surely would.

Ike Mitchell sat his horse, his face a mask of dejection. The trail they had followed so far had completely disappeared. He pointed to the multiple tracks that led into a swiftly flowing stream. Early that morning they had ridden hard and fast to the north to get around the outlaws. An ideal spot had been picked for an ambush, and the Sugarloaf hands had settled in to wait.

When the kidnappers had not appeared by noon, Ike had to conclude that they had taken a new trail. He set three men southeast along the way by which he had expected the outlaws to approach. They found the camp, and a trail that led off due west. Hastily, one returned to inform Ike. He immediately started off in pursuit of the new route. Fogging along the new path, they eventually came to this fast-flowing mountain stream. The horses they sought had entered it right enough.

Only they did not come out on the other side. Fifty-fifty chance for up or down stream. Ike considered it a while, then consulted the others. "You boys have tracked enough horses in your time. What do you say? Did they go up or down?"

Stumpy had his ideas. "I say up. It's in keeping with they goin' to Wyoming."

That did it for Ike. "I agree. Three of you trail south, downstream, for about four miles. If you don't cut any sign, turn around and join up with us as soon as you can." He eyed the gathered hands. "All of you keep a sharp eye. They can't stay in that water for long. We'll ride both sides of the banks. Make better time that way."

Monte Carson sweated bullets. Hot sun beat down on the waving sea of grass in the Great Divide Basin. He felt gratitude that Hank Evans had come along. Never complaining, that big smile plastered on his freckled face even in this heat, Hank rode at Monte's side. Bare-headed, Hank's carroty hair could be a flaming torch. They had covered considerable ground in the past two days since leaving the cabin of Morgan Crosby. Only today's ride and they would be in the Green Mountains. If all went well, they would negotiate them by the end of the next day.

Monte chafed at any delay in catching up to Smoke. Even if he only got word of the gunfighter's passage he would feel better. *Thirty-five to forty men in the Spectre gang.* The words haunted him. Monte honestly doubted that the three of them could go against such numbers and come out of it alive. At least not all of them. Would it be Hank who got it? Or would he cash in his chips at long last?

Never once did Monte consider that Smoke Jensen might be sent off to meet his Maker. Smoke was the stuff legends are made of. He was as close to being immortal as any man could hope to be. Self-consciously, Monte forced himself off this path of introspection. Last thing he needed before going into a shoot-out was to worry about the outcome. Years as a fast gun, and more as a lawman, had taught him that. He turned to look at his chief deputy as Hank shouted over the rumble of hooves.

"What say I go off and find us something for supper?"

Monte shook his head. "Wait until we're in the mountains."

Hank patted his belly. "I hear there's some pigs that gone wild up there in the Greens. Mighty tasty."

Monte laughed. "Exactly what I was thinking. Roast one of them whole and bring along what we don't eat for tomorrow."

"A young porker would be real fine," Hank agreed.

Half an hour later, they came upon a pair of scruffy road agents who had stopped off to rob a hapless family of four who had a broken wagon wheel. Monte spotted them first, the man and woman frightened witless, hands in the air, while the human trash rifled their clothing for valuables. Two sobbing children were cowering behind the jacked up wheel. Monte had his six-gun out of leather before thinking about it.

So engrossed were the thieves that they failed to notice the approach of the lawmen. Monte got within twenty yards of the pinched-faced one before the bit of crud raised a sallow, startled face to stare at the threat of a .45 Colt. Unable to shoot because of the proximity of the victims, Monte anticipated that the outlaw would not be so inhibited.

He jinked to the right a moment before the craven robber fired. The bullet cracked past and the shooter jumped to one side to get a clearer shot at his intended target. Monte seized on the change of position to get off a round. His slug flew straight and true.

It struck the miscreant in the center of his chest, punched through a lung and severed the aorta. The thug literally bled to death before he realized he was dying. His legs went out from under him and he flopped on the ground. His partner exchanged shots with Hank and dived for the protection of the damaged wagon. Hank sent more lead after him. The slug cut chips from the wagon's sideboard. Meanwhile, Monte Carson edged his horse to the off side of the buckboard and stood in place to meet the brigand when he rounded the harnessed team.

"What th' hell?" the snaggle-toothed outlaw blurted.

"Throw it down," Monte commanded.

"Hell no!" the bandit shouted defiantly.

Monte's horse shied in the instant when he fired. His bullet went wide and low, to gouge deeply into the road agent's hip. With a yelp of pain, the hoodlum dropped to his good knee. His Colt bucked and snorted fire. The slug cut a hot line along Monte's ribcage. Then his own Peacemaker barked and the highwayman flipped over backward. Monte and Hank reined in, checked the dead men and turned back to the startled pilgrims.

"Praise the Lord!" the blonde woman declared, hands clasped and upraised.

"You saved us, mister. We're much obliged."

Monte had his dander aroused. "No thanks to the both of you. Folks should know better not to be out here unarmed, or without an escort."

Icily, the woman answered him in self-righteousness. "We do not believe in guns, mister. They're the work of the devil."

"Maudy's right, mister. We don't hold by guns and violent ways." He cut his eyes to inspect the aftermath, then added ruefully, "At least, she don't. After what happened, I've sorta changed my mind."

"*Richard!*" Maude bleated.

He rounded on her. "I mean it, Maudy. They might have done who knows what to you and the girls, after they robbed us, that is. You saw what a man, properly armed, could do to end their evil ways."

Still unswayed, Maude answered testily. "Such matters are best left in the hands of God and the law."

His own ire aroused, Richard narrowed his eyes and spoke hotly. "And just how long do you expect it might have taken for God to take a hand? Or the law to get here? We'd all be dead and turned back to dust before we could count on any help from them quarters. An' I don't mean to blaspheme by that. God's got other things to look after, an' the nearest law must be a hunnerd miles away."

Monte Carson cleared his throat in embarrassment. "As it happens, the law is right here. Monte Carson, sheriff of Price County, Colorado. This is my chief deputy."

Richard looked startled. "We still in Colorado?"

"Nope. This is Wyoming, right enough. We're looking for a man."

"An outlaw?" Richard prompted.

Monte shook his head. "No. A friend. Tall man, lean, with broad shoulders, clean shaven. Far-off lookin' hazel eyes, red-brown hair." He described Smoke Jensen.

Richard cut his eyes to his wife. They both shook their heads. "We've not seen anyone like that," the man answered.

"Don't reckon you will, then. He should be ahead of us a ways. Can we give you a hand with that wheel?"

"I'd be right grateful. Got a spare lashed to the under-side."

Within twenty minutes the new wheel had been fixed in place. Monte wiped axle grease off his hands and turned to his horse. Richard interrupted him with effusive thanks and a question. "What's to be done with those two?"

"No doubt they have a price on their heads. If you can put up with the stink, take them along and turn them in at the next town."

"Not on your life," husband and wife agreed.

Monte mounted, laughing, and gave a friendly wave. Then he and Hank rode off in search of Smoke Jensen.

16

Seen from a long, ragged bluff, the town of Dubois looked even more unimpressive than the description given of it by Victor Spectre. Three days of hard riding, from first light to last, had brought them to this point. The gang sat their mounts near the rim that dropped off sharply to a talus slope three hundred feet below. A beatific smile lighted the face of Victor Spectre. He made a sweeping gesture with a black-gloved hand.

"There it is, gentlemen. We have arrived. We will divide into four groups. Three of them to be led by myself and my associates, the fourth by Augustus Jaeger. We will then approach the town from all sides and take it by storm. The key is to minimize the amount of violence it requires to assert our control. Paramount is the disarming of the populace."

Farlee Huntoon looked blankly at Dorcus Carpenter. "What th' hell he say?"

Dorcus translated. "He says first we take away all their guns."

Spectre continued as though the interruption had never occurred. "Second is to make certain that only a selected few escape to carry word of conditions in Dubois. I would suggest no more than two or three, and separately. Lastly, is to secure all means of communication to the outside world.

After that, you are at liberty to despoil the community and its citizens to your hearts' content. Mind you, that is to be in moderation, we do not want the town burned down around our feet."

Several guffaws answered this. Then, Fin Brock chortled, "Rustlin' petticoats never started no fires, Mr. Spectre. I reckon to keep my 'despoiling' to the ladies of Dubois, an' that's a fact."

Spectre gave him a cold smile. "Fine, Mr. Brock. One final admonition. You are not all to celebrate at the same time. An endless orgy is not in my plans. You must all get proper rest and sleep. We also need men on the alert to keep watch. Augustus Jaeger and Reese Judson will be in charge of a system of lookouts. Because, when he gets word, Smoke Jensen will come. And when he does, it will be as though all the Furies rode with him. Enough for now. Let us divide and prepare to conquer."

"Jeez, he talks like one of them play-actors," Farlee complained to his constant companion, Dorcus.

Carpenter nodded agreement. "I'd be a mite bit more comfortable with plain speakin', myself. Best if we be with the bunch comin' from this side. Less ridin' that way."

Farlee Huntoon laughed at that, a sort of gulping, slobbering sound. "I gotcha there, pardner."

In ten minutes it had been accomplished. Their spirits high, the gang of ruffians and deadly rabble set off to capture a city.

Irving Spaun had opened his bank in Dubois the year before a horde of outlaws had descended upon the town. Two months after their arrival, Smoke Jensen came to Dubois. After a lot of bloody fighting, the outlaws, at least those left alive, fled. Irving had proudly aided in their expulsion. He still prided himself at being good with a shotgun.

Even though he had reached the age of 55 and had a pot

belly, he still got out and hunted prairie chickens, doves, and Canada geese. Many a winter afternoon, after the bank had closed, he would arrive at home with a pair of plump rabbits. It had been two years now since anyone had tried to rob the bank. On that occasion, the unlucky bandit had been blasted into eternity by Irving's trusty Parker. At the bank he loaded 00 buckshot. On this bright, sunny day, as Irving stepped outside to lock the door for the noontime recess, he felt confident that all was, and would remain, well with his world. Ten minutes later, he discovered how sadly wrong he had been.

Seated at his usual table at Molly Vincent's Home Kettle, he awaited a savory plate of corned beef and cabbage, with potatoes, onions, and carrots. Suddenly, the double front doors flew open with enough force to shatter the etched-edged glass in one panel. Three men stood in the opening and menaced everyone inside with huge six-guns in gloved fists.

"Nobody make a sound," the one in charge commanded. "Jist sit still and don't make trouble. My friends here are going to come around and relieve all you gents of any weapons you may have. Then, I'm gonna name some people I want to stand up and come with us."

"You can't get away with this," the fat, male cook and owner, Mollson, who was called Molly by everyone, blurted.

An amused, sneering smile appeared on the leader's face. "I don't see anything around here that could get in our way. Now, don't even twitch an eyelid. Go clean 'em out, boys."

Quickly the outlaws complied. They came up with five cartridge belt and holster rigs, two pocket pistols, and a derringer—owned by Vera Pritchard, who operated Miss Pritchard's Residence for Refined Young Ladies, the local sporting house. Six other men, who had been taking their noon meal, including Irving Spaun, had been unarmed. Irving thought longingly of his shotgun, at rest beside his desk in the bank.

Molly Mollson continued to protest. "There ain't enough money in this place to make it worth robbing. The risk is too big."

Eyes wide and rolling, the leader informed all in general, "Oh, we ain't here only to rob you. We've decided to settle down a while. Sort of become your neighbors."

"This is preposterous," Hiram Firks, who had bought out the general mercantile, blustered. "Why, the army would come, gather you all up and hang you."

Another sneer. "Not if we lived right in among you, in your houses."

"You can't do that, it's against the law."

That brought a belly-laugh from the trio. "So's robbin' you of ever'thing you've got. An' that's exactly what we aim to do. Right after we kill Smoke Jensen."

"Who?" Molly bluffed. "Never heard of anyone by that name."

A runty thug with squinty eyes, set too close together, pointed a crooked finger at the storekeeper. "Then you cain't read an' yer ears is stuffed full of wax. Ain't anybody don't know Smoke Jensen."

"That's enough, Farlee. Though he's right. Jensen's supposed to be the big hero around here, saved your town, ain't that right?"

Farlee Huntoon nodded idiotically. "Yeah, ain't it?"

Irving Spaun sighed resignedly. "Yes, that's entirely correct. And may I add that if he were here, you sorry trash would be running for your lives or on your way to the cemetery. Now kindly leave us to our meal."

"Sorry, can't do that," the leader contradicted. "I want the following folks to stand up. The banker, the saddle-maker, the general store owner, the lady that runs that fancy whooer house, the feed and grain store owner, the harberdasher—did I forget anybody? Oh, yeah, the sawbones whose shingle is hanging out over the ladies' wear shop, an' the lawyer."

"This is outrageous," Reginald Barclay, the only attorney

in private practice in Dubois, objected. "What do you intend doing with us?"

Cold gray eyes pinned Barclay to the wall. "Killing you if you don't do as we say."

From outside came an irregular spatter of gunfire. It made the fact abundantly clear, even to dull-witted Huntoon, that the take-over did not go as peacefully elsewhere.

Hand working frantically to stuff fresh shells into the open breech of his Greener double-barrel, Percy Latimer, the Dubois barber, kept his eyes fixed on the two hard cases sprawled in the street. Terrible damage had been done by the loads of double-aught buckshot he had fired into their midsections. Large, thick pools of blood had formed around them while they lay gaping at the sky with unseeing eyes. From across the street, two of the outlaws' companions continued to trash the windows of Percy's tonsorial parlor.

Fragments of glass, painted in a red-white-and-green diamond pattern, lay on the floor all around Percy. It would cost a pretty penny to replace that, he considered. He seated the final cartridge, eased shut the breech and checked the release lever to make certain it had caught properly. A figure moved behind a water barrel. Percy cocked the Greener. Exposing only part of his head and one shoulder, Percy swung up the shotgun and squeezed off a round.

A shriek came from one man, who took a pair of pellets in his right arm. "Damn it, Jake, he got my gun arm."

"Shoot left-handed," came the reply from the recessed doorway to a saloon.

"I can't hit a blessed thing that way."

"But you can keep that bastard's head down while I rush him."

"Oh . . . I never thought of tha—"

"You never thought no-how, Louie. Now, git ready."

Louie sent rounds flying wildly into the barber shop. The huge, bevel-edged mirror turned into a thousand slivers of quicksilver. Percy's favorite shaving mug disintegrated in a shower of crockery. Percy winced and cursed under his breath, then rose up swiftly and caught sight of a shadowy figure. Bent low, the hard case ran along the front of the saloon. Percy brought the Greener into line and fired another load.

Buckshot from the ten gauge took out the bandit and a large portion of a window behind him. The glass bowed inward, then erupted in a wild shower. Jake went ass-over-teakettle into the Thirsty Man Saloon, slammed by ten pellets of burning lead. Percy pushed the catch and opened the breechloader. Spent brass casings popped up and he pulled them free. Humming to himself, he replaced them with fresh ones.

Percy swung the shotgun into line again and saw a shower of sparks spray from the long barrels of the goose gun. A fraction of a second later, intense, white pain exploded in his skull and his head snapped backward. The Greener clattered uselessly to the boardwalk outside.

Glee colored the words Louie shouted. "I got him, Jake. I sure's hell got him. Jake? Where are you, Jake?"

Bert, the bartender, and six customers in the Yellow Gulch Saloon found themselves confronted by eight armed men. Fortunately, depending on how one looked at it, three of the customers had reputations for being good with their guns. In an instant, even before any demand for money could be made, the air filled with lead. Bullets flew from both sides. Even with their disadvantage of first having to draw, the customers put slugs into a pair of outlaws and forced the others to retreat.

Hands gripped tightly on the forestock of a short-barreled ten-gauge Wells Fargo shotgun, Bert called encouragement to his assistants. "Drinks on the house to anyone who kills one of them devils."

"For how many and how long?" one of the young gunfighters inquired.

"A whole day. From opening to closing time. An' for the one who gets the job done."

"How about his friends?"

Bert thought a moment, during which a shower of bullets cracked through the batwings. "Yeah, an' them too."

Their doom came home to them a moment later when a voice called from outside. "Come out with your hands high, or we'll throw in a stick of dynamite."

"Dynamite? Stick-up men don't carry dynamite," another of the defenders observed. "Where could they have gotten that?"

"I don't think I want to stick around and find out," the younger one declared.

"If we go out there, we're dead men, you know that," Bert reminded them. "You boys killed two of their partners."

"Last chance. Come out or die there."

An older man, a rancher, gave that some thought. "I'd rather die here, fightin' like a man, rather than go out there and be shot down like a dog."

Bert slammed the shotgun to his shoulder as he saw a dark figure rushing at the swinging doors. He fired in an eyeblink. The outlaw flew back into a tie-rail and spun a flip over it. Something sputtering a stream of sparks dropped between his legs.

"Get down!" Bert shouted.

A moment later, the front of the saloon blew in on top of them. Shock and sound waves bulged the walls on the sides and the windows blew out, sashes and all, before the glass could break. Bert felt himself lifted off his feet, his boots still rooted to the floor, and hurled against the back-bar. His ten-gauge spun off into the cloud of debris that rose from the plaster walls and sawdust-covered floor. His last conscious thought was: "My God, I'm dead."

All of the others suffered similar experiences. They and Bert found out after the furor ended that they had not expired in the blast. Hard hands dragged them clear of the wreckage and roughly shoved them into the street. Gus Jaeger stood in the center of the block, legs wide-spread, arms folded over his chest.

"Bring them here," he commanded. "Put them on their knees." When they had the seven men positioned as Jaeger wanted, the outlaw leader glowered down at the helpless bartender and his customers. In the prolonged silence, the youngest gunhawk began to whimper.

"So you killed three of my men," Jaeger charged them. "Which ones of you did it?" When only their silence answered them, it irritated Gus mightily. He drew his Colt and put the muzzle an inch from the back of the head of a bar fly. Slowly he cocked the weapon.

"Tell me. Who did the shooting?"

Again they all remained silent. Gus Jaeger squeezed the trigger and blew the face of the town drunk all over the street. Still, he received no reply. He shot another of the customers. Then another. Suddenly bored and disgusted, he turned to his underlings.

"Give me a hand, boys. "We'll just kill them all."

Four more shots soon echoed off the walls of the standing buildings.

Within half an hour, a totally unsatisfactory time for Victor Spectre, all resistance had been crushed. Spectre rode in splendor to the central intersection of the community. There a windmill and storage tank provided water for the entire town. A bandstand stood there, also. Spectre dismounted before it and climbed the steep flight of steps. He faced the frightened people, gathered there and took the report from Gus Jaeger.

"All who resisted us have been killed. The rest are here. We lost seven men killed, nine wounded. Most of the injured will be up and around by tomorrow."

"Too many," Spectre stated curtly. "This was supposed to be quiet and easy."

"I'd say these folks were not aware of that," Ralph Tinsdale remarked as he joined them.

Victor Spectre shot him a hard, hot stare. "You are not funny, Ralph. Where do you suppose we will find men to replace those lost?"

Tinsdale frowned. "Smoke Jensen is only one man, Victor."

"But he will come with an army. We need ours intact to face him." He paused and turned away to study the confused and terrified people. "I have something to tell these people."

From his position in the front row, Irving Spaun got a good look at the man who must be the leader of The Enemy. That's how he looked at these invaders—The Enemy. In his mind's eye, Irving even saw the capital letters. He had noted earlier, after opening his bank to the outlaw scum, that Dr. Fred, Frederick Barbour, had been pressed into service to tend the wounded. Not the injured townsfolk, but The Enemy wounded. Irving silently hoped that Dr. Fred would hurry a few of them on to meet their judgment.

Unfortunately, Barbour was a dedicated healer. He could no more harm a patient than take his own life. Irving closely watched the exchange between the—for want of a better word, he called him the foreman—and the boss. Then the man in charge turned to face the assembled townspeople. He raised his arms to signal for silence and, when the gathering stilled, he revealed the most astonishing ideas that Irving had ever heard.

"Good afternoon. My name is Victor Spectre. I have

come here for a cause that needn't concern you. Shortly, some of my men will escort you to your place of business and your homes. The purpose of their visit is to obtain every firearm you possess. And all of the ammunition."

A burly, retired rancher interrupted in an angry bluster. "We got a right to own guns."

Spectre shook his head sadly, as though faced with a truculent, but dim-witted child. "Not when they might endanger some of my men. Believe me, it is for your own good. Some of your friends and neighbors have already died because they chose to resist us. From now, until we leave this town, we are in charge. You will obey us without question or hesitation."

"Like hell we will," the outraged rancher snarled.

Spectre turned to his foreman and spoke quite casually. "Augustus, shoot him."

Faster than any man Irving had even seen, except Smoke Jensen, this Augustus fellow drew his six-gun and fired. The bullet entered the open mouth of the rancher and exited low in the back of his neck. He went down loosely, an unstrung marionette. Two women screamed and another fainted dead away. Smiling pleasantly, Spectre turned his attention back to his horrified audience.

"I will repeat. You will obey without hesitation or question. Now, another matter. Singly or by twos my men will be divided off and you will provide for them in your homes. They will have a room to themselves, and you will cook for them. In return, they will leave you strictly alone. This is to be merely a board and room situation. They are under orders to take their . . . pleasures elsewhere. Such will remain the case, unless some of you become obstreperous. In which case, my men will be free to exact recompense in any manner they see fit. Do we understand one another?" Several low mutters rippled through the people of Dubois. "I can't hear you." More replies now, some in normal speaking tones. Victor Spectre nodded meaningfully to Gus Jaeger. *"I can't hear you."*

More joined in, all cowed, unwilling to be loud enough

to draw attention. To Irving's disgust his fellow citizens seemed mesmerized by this petty dictator. Their timidity had the reverse effect.

"I STILL CAN'T HEAR YOU," Spectre bellowed.

"Yes, we understand!" came a shouted reply.

"That's better. You will answer loudly, promptly, and truthfully any and all questions asked by myself, my associates, or my men. From here on, until our departure, of which I told you, this is our town."

Quickly then, Gus Jaeger designated men to take the residents to their stores and homes. Thorough searches were made. The outlaw foreman took three men along with him when they went to search the mercantile. Shortly after entering, two of the trash emerged with wheelbarrows heaped high with cases of ammunition, armloads of rifles, and half a dozen handguns. When the search ended, Jaeger escorted Irwin to the bank.

There he surveyed the vault and two free-standing safes. Satisfied, he nodded. "This seems secure enough. We'll keep the money here until we're ready to leave town. Now you take me to your home. We'll have a little look there. No doubt the mayor has the nicest house in town. Victor and his partners will stay there. As no doubt the next richest man in town, you will have the pleasure of hosting me."

"Oy veh! I am flattered and honored at the privilege," Irving replied sarcastically.

Jaeger glowered and raised his hand menacingly. "Any more smart-mouthing will earn you a fat lip."

"My wife keeps a kosher kitchen," Irving cautioned.

"I don't care what she calls it, Mr. Banker, so long as it's clean and there's plenty of grub."

Irving sought to educate this lout. *"Kosher* means 'pure—clean.'"

"Fine. Now, I want ham and eggs and biscuits for every breakfast."

Irving made bold to interrupt. "We do not eat ham or any pork."

Gus cocked an eyebrow. He'd never heard such nonsense. "Well, she'll fix it for me. You don't have to eat it if you don't want to."

"You don't understand. If my wife cooks pork in our kitchen it is no longer kosher. It will be contaminated."

Growing angry, Gus growled at the banker. "I don't give a damn about that. So long as there's not cockroaches crawlin' everywhere and moldy food laying around, I'll eat what I want and you can do the same."

Horrified at the image of filth and vermin in his home, Irving gathered the last of his reserves and spoke with defiance. "She will cook for you in the washhouse. I will not allow my kitchen to be tainted."

To Irving Spaun's surprise, Gus Jaeger began to laugh. "By God, you're a feisty son, aren't you? All right, Mister— er—?"

"Spaun. Irving Spaun."

"Mr. Spaun, have it your way. Just so long as I have my ham and eggs, biscuits, and some fried potatoes would be nice. Do you odd folks eat—ah—beef?"

"Yes, of course."

"Well, then, have the missus pick up a nice roast at the meat market for tonight."

"How is this food of yours to be paid for?"

Gus gave him a smile. "The usual way you pay for anything you buy, with your own money." With that they left for the house.

Once all of the arms and ammunition had been confiscated, Olin Buckner came to where Victor Spectre stood beside the great pile of munitions. "This has gone nicely. Men who are unable to resist must obey."

Victor nodded agreement, well satisfied. "Before long, the poor fools will find themselves totally dependent upon you, me, and Ralph for the barest necessities for survival."

"That's how it should be," Buckner replied contentedly.

"The best and the brightest should rule and lesser mortals submit."

"The next thing is to pair up the men whose homes we've searched with their wives and children and place them in their houses under guard. Those who are involved in providing services in the stores, saloons, the bank, the hotel, and cafe are to be sent to their tasks."

"What about any single men?" Buckner asked.

Spectre made a show of considering it, though he had his mind made up long before entering the town. "They could provide a constant risk. We'll have some of the more hardened among our men take them off a few at a time. We can offer them the chance to join us. If they refuse, they can dig their own graves before being shot."

17

When the last of the single males refused the offer to join the gang, and had been mercilessly shot down, Victor Spectre turned his attention to the single women. Those he had kept in the central square while the killing went on. Now he summoned all of his men. Back on the bandstand, he gestured to the frightened, weeping women.

"You men have all fought well. There are some among you who conducted yourselves with outstanding bravery. It is my intention to reward you suitably for this outstanding service." He named the ones cited to him by Gus Jaeger. "Your compensation awaits," he went on with a gesture to the women. "You will each have a private room at the hotel for tonight. And you will be free to take your pick of these lovely maidens to keep company with you."

Their loud cheers drowned out the rest of what Spectre had to say. When the designated men had made their selections and hauled off the frightened, protesting women, Spectre held his hand up to silence the other men. "For the rest of you, deserving as you are of some prize, you may pleasure yourselves with the remainder of the feminine pulchritude of Dubois for the balance of the afternoon. Have at them, good fellows!"

"Hot dang! That's for me," Dirk Jensen yelled gleefully,

his long, greasy blond hair swinging freely around his shoulders. He exposed his crooked yellow teeth in a lustful leer and headed for the nearest single woman, a girl of around fourteen.

Shrill screams began to rise moments later as the raping began.

Early on the morning of the second day in Dubois, Gus Jaeger stepped out on the porch of the home of Irving Spaun and rolled a cigarette with papers and tobacco from the pouch of Bull Durham in his shirt pocket. He lighted it and drew the smoke deeply into his chest, held it a while. Then he sighed it out with satisfaction. His belly was full of the sweetest ham he had ever tasted, four eggs, home fries with onions, and a platter of biscuits. Pleased with himself, he ankled down the steps and headed for the carriage house at the back of the lot.

There he saddled his horse and led it out into the alley. Leather creaked as he swung into the saddle. At a gentle walk, Gus headed toward the mayor's house, where he was to meet with Victor Spectre and his partners. He found them still at the breakfast table.

"Pour him a cup of coffee," Victor commanded the maid standing in attendance on the table. "Did you sleep well?" he asked Gus.

"Yes, thank you. That Mrs. Spaun is a great cook. I've never had beef so tender and juicy. We had roast last night," he clarified with a chuckle. "With braised potatoes and something she called asper—aspergrass?"

"Asparagus," Victor corrected. "A meal fit for a king. Well, we have a lot to do today. Wait in the drawing room, I'll join you in a minute."

Victor Spectre and Ralph Tinsdale came into the small room, made to look larger by a bay window. Spectre settled on a Louie Quinze chair, a cup and saucer in one hand. "Now then, I want you to select six men to act as messengers. I will send them out with flyers I am having printed today." His cordial smile turned bleak. "I am putting a price of twenty thousand dollars on the head of Smoke Jensen. The posters will advise anyone interested in trying for the reward to come here to Dubois. I am also offering excellent pay, board, and room until Jensen is captured and brought to me to kill."

"That's mighty generous, Mr. Spectre. Are our men eligible for that bonus?"

"Of course, Augustus. I conceived of this idea last night. It is a splendid way to fill our ranks. Maybe tenfold of our losses. Also, it serves as insurance in the event my primary ploy to draw Jensen to us fails."

Rather than share Spectre's elation, Gus frowned. "You'll have every proddy son of a bitch in three territories crowdin' in here. Half of them won't even be able to use a gun. We'll have one hell of a time keepin' control."

"Not to worry. That's what your veterans are for. They took this town. They should have pride enough in it to keep down the rowdy element."

Gus smiled at this. "You know people rather well, don't you, Mr. Spectre?" It was more statement than question.

Victor's chest swelled and he all but patted himself. "I pride myself on that, Augustus. Now, make sure that business is conducted as usual. See that those quartered with the merchants and businessmen get their charges out and about. We can't entirely prevent people from coming into town. If we isolate ourselves, it would attract too much attention. So, I want you to arrange to have any damage covered up, make that unfortunate situation with the saloon look like a fire, and clean up the spilled blood."

Rising from the velvet loveseat he occupied, Gus Jaeger started for the door. "I'll see to it right away."

Victor Spectre allowed himself a moment to gloat as he stared out the three-sided opening of the bay window. Then he sighed out softly, "Smoke Jensen, your hours are surely numbered."

Unaware of the conquest of Dubois, Smoke Jensen dropped down from Togwatee Pass into Jackson's Hole two days after the town fell to Victor Spectre and his outlaw army. The tension that had swelled within him over the past week soothed away when he gazed upon the sheltered basin. For as far as the eye could see, lush, tall grass waved in a gentle breeze. Sunlight sparkled off the rippled water of the Snake River as it meandered through the middle of the declivity. White stones, as fine as crushed gravel, lined the watercourse. Pines and tall Douglas firs perfumed the air.

Smoke breathed deeply of the crisp, clean air, made thin and precious by the altitude. All of nature was alive with animal and bird sounds, which reached Smoke's ears in pleasant waves of tweets and warbles, the scrabble of claws, and grunts or snorts of larger creatures. Relaxing further, Smoke soaked up the peaceful feel of it all. Unbidden, his mind wandered back to the first time Preacher had brought him here to trap beaver and hunt elk. . . .

It had been a crisp early spring. Deep drifts of snow lay along the shaded western slopes of the surrounding mountains. A thin wafer of clear ice clung to the bank and exposed pebbles in the Snake River. Preacher's usually guarded expression eased into serenity as they rode lower onto the floor of the basin. Preacher waved a hand in a sweeping gesture.

"Ol' Jackson was one smart hombre, Smoke. Look at this place. The last real corner of Paradise in the High Lonesome, or anywhere else for that matter. Pure, untouched. We won't build a cabin here. Nawsir, we're gonna fix us a stone lodge. Build out of rocks is what."

"How'er we goin' to put a roof on it?" Jensen asked.

Preacher frowned. "We'll have to cut a couple of trees, I

allow for that. An' when we're through with it, come next spring, we're gonna tear it all down."

All these years later, Smoke Jensen found the Hole still well-populated with elk. Huge piles of antlers had been erected by earlier visitors, and the soft ground held numerous hoof impressions. He caught sight of several dozen of the magnificent animals as he ambled his way to the southeast, in search of a campsite. Shortly he came upon the right place.

Located far enough from the Snake so that its waters burbling over smoothed rocks would not hide the sound of any approach, the small clearing would serve well for his first several night's stay. Smoke strung a short picket line, with the halters of his horses rigged so they could walk along and graze. Then he unsaddled Thunder and Debbie. Stretching out the kinks of a long day's ride, he drew a deep, rich breath and set off to locate windfall for a cookfire.

Hunger made itself known while Smoke assembled a stone ring on a bare circle of earth which he had cleared with a folding shovel. He completed the task and padded to the rack that held one of his parfleche panniers. From that he took a stout Cheyenne hunting bow and quiver of arrows. Then he added a coil of rope and a folded layer of cheesecloth. Anticipating the flavor of fresh roasted meat, he strode off to hunt for his supper. When he came abreast of the horses, he spoke softly to the 'Palouse stallion.

"Let me know if someone comes by, Thunder."

Raised around animals, Smoke had no delusion that the critters understood his words in a literal sense. Yet, like most men alone in the wilderness, Smoke found himself talking to his horses. He kept his eyes to the ground, searching for an animal trail. He soon found one. A narrow path, most likely made by deer. Hoofprints verified that, along with small, still moist droppings. The slightly rounded points of the front of the impressions pointed to the river.

When he drew close enough to hear the gurgle of the clear, swift water, he selected an arrow and nocked it to the string. Creeping now, he made a slow approach to the opening. Ahead he identified the spotted, buff side of a young deer. The graceful little creature had its neck bent, mouth in the chill water. A tiny flag of brown and white flickered as a dragonfly buzzed its hind quarters. Cautiously, Smoke moved to one side and searched for any larger hind.

He found one at once. A yearling, weighing about 125 pounds. Perfect. Exercising immense care, Smoke raised the bow and drew back the sinew string, while he appealed to the animal's spirit for understanding. The ball of his thumb touched his cheekbone and he took aim. His release was smooth. The keen-edged metal head entered flesh right behind the front leg and the shaft plunged inward to the fletching. Pierced through the heart, the year-ling uttered a shrill bleat and reared, then fell, mortally wounded.

Momentarily saddened by the necessity of having to take the creature's life, Smoke nevertheless looked on grimly until the end. The fawn had sprinted away at the cry of alarm and pain. Walking carefully, Smoke stepped out onto the riverbank. Quickly he dragged the deer to a low limb and tied the forelegs together. He swung the short length of rope over the branch and pulled the creature upright.

With swift, sure strokes, he field-dressed the deer. He set aside the heart and liver, which he washed in the stream and wrapped in cheesecloth. Then he scooped out a hollow and buried the intestines. Lowering the carcass, he cleansed it in the Snake, and washed his arms. Grunting, he hefted the meat over his shoulders and started back to camp. He would eat the liver raw, while a rack of ribs and a front haunch roasted. The heart would be for breakfast. The rest, he decided, he would smoke in a rock smoker he would build tomorrow. He would hang the meat high in a tree. The hind quarters could cure for a few days, until he would be ready.

* * *

Using carefully graduated sizes of smooth, flattened rocks from the riverbed, Smoke Jensen started on his stone smoker early the next morning, after a breakfast of fried venison heart and cottage fries with wild onion. There were camus bulbs and wild turnips in the basin, he knew. He could look forward to a rich venison stew. Far from being a gourmand, nothing prevented Smoke from the appreciation of good food when he had it. Smoke had reached the fifth tier, the rocks meticulously fitted together, when he noticed a thin column of gray-white rising above the trees at some distance to the northeast.

Pilgrims. It had to be. No one who knew anything about the habits and wandering nature of Indians would be that careless. Unless, of course, the party was large enough not to worry. Dismissing it, he worked on until he had used the last of the stones he had retrieved from the water. When he waded, barefoot, into the Snake to pluck more rocks from the shallows, he noticed a barely perceptible blur in the air at a considerable stretch in the opposite direction of the column of smoke. Someone knew what they were doing, he surmised. They had built their fire under the wide spread of tree limbs, which would diffuse the smoke. Mountain men, or some like himself, who had been raised by that hearty, savvy breed. Smoke cut his eyes back to his work project.

"Well," he said aloud. "I've made my feet ache enough for one day."

He climbed out of the water, dried his feet and shoved them into boots. After he saddled Thunder, he mounted and rode out on a circuitous route around these curious signs of other humans.

After a careful search of the area around the well-tended fire, Smoke Jensen moved in close enough to see the men seated under the wide-spread limbs of an ancient pine, its branches thick with long, silken needles. At once, he recognized two oldtimers. Zeke Duncan and Ezra

Sampson had been fur-trapping partners for the better part of fifty years. So adapted had they become to life in the High Lonesome, not even advanced age could separate them from it. Their hat-sized fire gave off smoke for only one reason.

Drops of liquefied fat dripped into the coals from the six squirrels they had set to slow-broiling over it. A lattice of green willow branches supported the carcasses of the tree-dwelling rodents. Although he had eaten no more than three hours earlier, the aroma of the cooking meat smelled delightful to Smoke. Quietly he edged back deeper into the underbrush and crawled a hundred yards before standing and walking to where he had ground-reined Thunder.

Mounted, Smoke Jensen rode out a ways, then turned back, angled toward the camp and howdied them loudly when he came within view. A cheery answer came back to him. "Ride on in and set a spell."

Then, when he had ridden close enough to be recognized, Zeke did a little dance step, beaded and quilled moccasins twinkling in the sunlight and called out with delight. "Why, you be that ring-tailed rattler, Smoke Jensen. So, you're the one snuck up on us a while back. That's right, you be Preacher's little friend."

They still never miss a thing, Smoke thought with respect.

"Not so little anymore, Zeke," Ezra advised. "Yer welcome, Smoke." Eyes sparkling, he gave Smoke a wink. "Be a whole lot more welcome if you've got a jug of Who-Shot-John along."

"Not with me. I have a crock along for medicinal purposes back at camp."

"Where might that be?" Zeke asked.

"Over yonder a ways," Smoke told him, pointing in the general direction.

Ezra cocked a snow-white eyebrow. "It ain't over where them dummies have got that signal fire a-goin', would it be?"

Zeke butted in. "Not likely, Ez. Preacher would have taught him right. But, say, how come you knowed we was here?"

Smoke told them simply. "Same way I knew those others were around. From your smoke smudge."

"Naw," Ezra objected. "We've been real careful."

Smoke nodded to the fire. "Those squirrels are dripping fat onto the fire. It made a cloud in the branches of this pine."

"They're almost ready, too," Zeke advised. "You'll sit a spell and share a couple with us, won't you? There's coffee hot in the pot now."

"That's kind of you, Zeke. I'll take that coffee. And I'll eat some squirrel. I have some biscuits left over from breakfast."

"Couldn't be better," Ezra enthused.

Smoke cut his eyes to take in the whole of their camp. "Tell me, why is it fellers as smart as you are camped under the tallest tree around?"

Zeke grinned. "It ain't thunderstorm season yet. Otherwise you wouldn't find us nowhere near this giant. Now, put some daylight in that saddle and let's swap a few lies."

Smoke and the old mountain men sat cross-legged and drank coffee and told tales about Preacher for half an hour. At which time, Ezra pronounced the squirrels ready to eat. While they tore at the succulent, tender flesh, and gnawed on biscuits and wild onion bulbs, Zeke gestured to Smoke with a hind leg of squirrel.

"D'you know yer a wanted man again?"

Smoke thought on that a moment. "No. What's the story?"

"There's word out for gunhands to gather and hunt you down, Smoke. Big reward for your hide. Twenty thousand dollars. Alive, that is."

Smoke whistled soundlessly. "Who has that sort of money?"

Zeke continued his tale. "There's this feller, Victor Spectre he calls hisself. He an' a whole passel of rowdies tooken over the town of Dubois."

"What!" Smoke blurted. "When did this happen?"

Ezra got in his two bits' worth. "Couple—three days ago now. From what we've heard fellers driftin' through here say, there was some powerful killin' done. Folks they spared are kept prisoner in their own homes."

His jaw seriously torqued by this news, Smoke abandoned caution. "Damn that filthy slime. This fight's between him and me. The people of Dubois are special to me."

Both of the oldtimers nodded eagerly. Zeke summed up their thoughts. "Reckon this Spectre feller knew that."

Recovered slightly, Smoke conquered his rampant emotions. "Nothing can be done about that now. He would have to have a regular army to take the town. Thank you for the warning. I appreciate it. And, thanks for the food, which was good, and the company, which was even better. I think I'll move along, see who those others are."

Zeke gave Smoke a knowing wink. "They're noisy and they smell bad. Could be you're walking into a hornet nest."

18

Having been warned over and over, Smoke Jensen needed no further urging to make a wide, slow, careful approach to the other camp in the basin. Two small, conical peaks stood between him and the unknown visitors. Smoke took advantage of that to advance undetected to within three hundred yards. The column of smoke continued to rise into the morning sky. A shower of sparks formed an ascending ball around it as someone threw something rather heavy on the fire.

Fools, Smoke thought in disgust. If there had been a war party of Blackfeet or Cheyenne in the area, or any other tribe, these idiots would already have their hair curing on scalp stretchers. Might as well advertise their presence with a brass band. He dismounted and tied off Thunder in a grove of cottonwoods. Then he wormed his way through the thicket of young trees, taking thirty minutes to do so, until he could clearly distinguish sounds from the camp. A cast-iron skillet gave off a musical ring, metal utensils clattered and the men talked volubly. Smoke made a quick count of seven different voices.

Their topic of conversation riveted Smoke's attention. "You know what I'm gonna do with the money for catchin' Smoke Jensen?"

"Naw, Polk, but I'm sure you're gonna tell us."

"Right you are, my friend. I'm gonna get me a room in the fanciest hotel in San Francisco, rent me a pair of the purtiest ladies of the night, and give the room service manager a thousand dollars and tell him to keep the champagne and food coming until it's gone. Then I'm gonna give him another thousand and get two different girls."

"Awh, you won't be able to keep it up that long, Polk."

"Tell me about it, Curruthers. What is it the gals down in Dallas call you? Ol' False Start Carruthers, right?"

A tin cup bounced noisily off the thick trunk of a pine. "Damn you, Polk, that ain't true. I don't care what that Lill told anyone who'd listen. It ain't so. I was jist a little drunk is what. An hour's rest and I sure showed her where Johnny hid the garden hoe."

Another voice joined the banter. "Curruthers, Polk, ain't either one of you with any sense when it comes to money and wimmin. I been talkin' with Yancy and Rand. They're talkin' about poolin' their shares an' buyin' land. Run a few hunnard head of cattle an' even hire men to work them. I sort of thought it would be an idee to throw in with them. Three shares buys a whole lot of cows and other people's sweat."

Curruthers sneered. "Gonna become big-shot ranchers, huh? Fat chance."

Polk sniggered. "You do, Hooper, an' we'll come rustle them beeves."

Hooper grew serious. "They hang rustlers down in Texas, Polk."

Suddenly defensive, Polk bleated in an effort to forestall any confrontation. "Hey—hey, I was only funnin'. I'd never rob from a partner. Ain't honorable." He added a shrill giggle. "Besides, I'll be in San Francisco gettin' my ashes hauled."

Another voice, silent so far, rumbled with a dash of cold water on their plans. "You heard what they did in Dubois.

If we ride in an' throw our hat in the ring with them boys, and we do get Smoke Jensen, you'd best use your share to find a deep hole to crawl into and pull it after you. There'll be U.S. Marshals an' the Army, and who knows who else huntin' us down. They took a *town,* boys. They pestered the single women and killed a lot of folks. Ain't gonna be likely forgotten."

Polk jeered at him. "Ballard, yer gettin' yeller in your old age."

"Hell, he ain't thirty."

Polk's voice sobered. "For some folks, that's old."

At last, the seventh man, who had listened to all this with interest, contributed his idea. "I'll tell you what we should do, if we're smart. I say we ought to find this Smoke Jensen all on our own and bring him in. Collect our reward and ride the hell out of there. Sure's my name is Liam Quinn."

Smoke Jensen had heard enough. He also noticed that for all their big talk, none of them seemed eager to move on to Dubois. Carefully, he selected several landmarks to pinpoint their locations in the dark, and moved on.

We've crossed over into Wyoming, Sally Jensen thought. She judged they had done so some two days ago, based on the change of terrain to high plains prairie. The mountains, though some were tall and rangy, had a smooth, rounded-over appearance. And, for miles one could see waving seas of grass, patches of it golden-brown remnants from last year's growth. She had yet to learn where they were going.

"We're takin' you to the man in charge," or "You'll meet yer husband up ahead a piece," was all she could get out of Nate Miller, the outlaw leading this band of ruffians. Sally had gone beyond worry or fear. Instead, a cold, hard anger built within her, one tempered by caution and experience, but deadly in nature all the same. She no longer sought a means of escape along the trail.

That would come later. Most likely when Smoke was

near. She would bide her time, reinforce her anger and loathing of these unwashed border trash, and make herself ready physically and mentally. To do the latter, she reviewed incidents in which she had been involved with Smoke, or because of him. One occurrence hardened her more than the others.

It had been the time when she had been beaten, shot, and left for dead by unsavory louts who belonged to the Masters gang. She had gone to her father's home in New England to recuperate and the gang had followed to get retribution on Smoke Jensen. They had died there, in New Hampshire, and she had given birth to the twins. Louis Longmont and Jeff York had lent Smoke a hand and had been proud godfathers for the newest additions to the Jensen clan. Now, she drew on memories of the pain, the despair she had felt, her fear for the babies she carried. It forged the malleable metal of her present outrage into a white hot bar of steel.

To maintain her physical condition, she found little she could do. She ate every scrap they allowed her, of course. And, when left unattended to take care of nature's demands, she lifted heavy rocks to maintain the strength in her arms. She walked about the camp furiously whenever untied. And she moved with snakelike sinuosity in the saddle as they rode, to tone her torso. It wasn't much, she acknowledged, but it helped. The time *would* come, and she *would* be ready to act.

Only a sliver of moon hung over Jackson's Hole when Smoke Jensen eased into position outside the camp of the gunmen. A decided chill hung on the May night, the air damp and tingly, borne on a breeze that wafted over deep banks of rotting snow. To ward off the cold, the thugs had built a large, roaring fire. Anyone this careless and stupid deserved what they were about to get, Smoke thought in indignation.

Still, he had anticipated the gigantic bonfire and smiled in satisfaction as he considered the two sticks of dynamite he had brought along. They were already capped and fused when he shoved them down the front of his trousers, behind his cartridge belt. With everything in readiness, he drew his .45 Colt and fired a round over the heads of the hapless men gathered around the blaze. In an instant they all went to the ground as one.

Smoke Jensen called to them in harsh tones. "You men don't belong here and you've picked the wrong man to go after. Saddle up, put out that fire, and get out of here while you still have your lives."

One of the men stood up. "You're not scarin' us, mister." He sent a round into the dark, in the direction Smoke's voice had come from. Only Smoke had moved. Now he raised the Peacemaker and blasted the bold gunhawk to perdition with a slug through the heart. Immediately the clearing became a scene of panic.

Three of the saddle trash made a wild scramble for their mounts, while the other trio elected to fight back. They came to their knees and shot wildly into the surrounding blackness. Night vision ruined by the bright blaze, they had not the slightest chance of seeing Smoke Jensen.

Smoke howled like a wolf and moved to yet another position. He fired at the confused gunmen and moved as return rounds crashed into the underbrush where he had been. Now that he had the remaining six properly aroused, he heaved first one, then the second stick of dynamite into their fire.

Almost at once, the first exploded and knocked the defenders flat. Then threw flaming wood everywhere. The second followed a second later, the ground shaking underfoot even worse than before. Shock and blast extinguished what had been left of their fire. Smoke tracked muzzle flashes, noted that only four remained, and picked a target. The roar of his .45 drowned out the noise of the others'.

"Oh, my God, Liam, I'm shot," Polk wailed as the initial

shock of Smoke's bullet wore off and his chest flamed with agony.

At the camp of Zeke Duncan and Ezra Sampson, the two oldtimers listened to the sounds of confrontation in the distance. Zeke took a long, deep pull off the contents of a glazed, earthenware jug they had found at sundown, near the place they had taken to using on the riverbank, and passed it to Ezra.

"Well, Ez, it sounds like Smoke Jensen is paying a not-too-friendly visit to those young toughs over yonder."

Ezra cocked his head to one side, tilted up his chin and took a long swallow of the premium rye whiskey in the jug. "Does seem that way. I reckon that's why he left us off this jug, to keep us in camp. Wonder if they appreciate the call?"

They both cackled over this witticism for some moments, passed the crock around another time and grinned like conspirators when the noise abruptly ceased. The quiet grew louder. Zeke sipped again, belched and passed the container to his partner.

"Say, Zeke, you figger Smoke will swing by an' share this present he left with us?"

"Might be. You can never tell."

"I sure hope he does. I'd like to hear all about those boys who waste so much firewood." Cackling, Ezra extended the jug toward Zeke.

After he had reduced his opponents to two, he moved yet again. "You two, I have a message for Victor Spectre, Ralph Tinsdale, and Olin Buckner."

After a short, tense silence, a voice called out shakily. "We don't know anybody by them names."

Smoke's laughter mocked them. "Sure you do. You were talking about them earlier this afternoon." He fired another round toward the cringing Ballard and Quinn.

A longer silence followed, then a weak reply from Quinn. "All right—all right. What do you want us to tell them?"

"Tell them they can hire every two-bit gunhand in the territory, and beyond, but that I'm a lot harder to kill than the best of them. I think you have found that out for yourselves." Smoke chuckled loudly enough for them to hear him. "One last thing, so there's no mistake. Where is it, again, that you are to meet Victor Spectre?"

"In—in Dubois."

"Then I'll leave you to find your way there on your own."

Smoke had glided well out of earshot before the two badly shaken gunmen began to whisper to one another. Pleased with himself, Smoke faded into the night.

Monte Carson stood by the head of his horse, two fingers slipped behind the cheek-strap of the headstall. He gazed off thoughtfully toward the distant, sparkling waters of the Bighorn River. Between him and the wide, shallow stream lay the lodges of the Shoshoni of the Wind River Reservation. Three of the Indians rode in his direction, one held a lance, elaborately decorated with sprays of feathers. An official delegation, Monte thought, sure of that. He turned to Hank Evans.

"Company comin' will have at least one minor civil chief along. Might not be the one who presents himself as leader. So keep a sharp eye, Hank, and see if you can spot the real chief."

Hank Evans worked his cheeks and lips and spat out his used-up cud of Union Leader cut plug. A stream of tobacco juice followed. "You're gettin' crafty in yer old age, Monte."

Sheriff Carson chuckled. "Naw. It's just a little something I learned from Smoke Jensen a few years back. Injuns don't take a back seat to the white man when it comes to diplomatic tricks. Smoke pointed that out and explained that most times it is the fault of different language or different ways of seein' the same thing that makes a parlay go sour, or a treaty fail."

Hank studied the Shoshoni representatives as they rode nearer. "If you'd ask me now, I'd say it was that older feller with the lance. His mouth looks like it's used to givin' orders. And there's that hawk nose and them hard, bright eyes."

"Don't be in a rush. Take a little more time and be sure. It could be the difference between being welcomed or told to get the hell off their land."

"Or keepin' our hair," Hank added wryly.

Monte nodded. "There's that, too."

Close now, the riders reined in. Monte made the universal sign for peace and it was returned. Then he signed that they had coffee, sugar, biscuits, and molasses. Grinning, the Shoshoni dismounted. Before they did, the one dressed as a chief cut his eyes to his lance-bearer and received an almost imperceptible nod.

Hank Evans took note of that as he dismounted. He prepared a clear space for a fire and set out the makings for a quick brew. Water came from his canteen, coffee from a cloth sack, as did the biscuits. A small, screw-top jar held blackstrap molasses. The Indians settled on their horse blankets and Monte sat with them, cross-legged. While Hank prepared their snack, Monte signed that he was looking for a man.

"What man is this?" the lance-bearer asked in fair, though accented and lilting, English. His eyes locked with Monte's.

"Smoke Jensen."

"Ah, Swift Firestick."

Monte blinked at the thick-shouldered younger man. "Is that a serious name?"

Chief Tom Brokenhorn, in his guise as the lance-bearer of a civil chief, smiled. "No. It is a joke that Smoke Jensen shares with me." He rose and changed places with the even younger man in the middle, while Hank distributed tin cups of coffee and biscuits slathered with molasses. "From the description he gave to me, you must be Monte Carson. I am Chief Brokenhorn."

Monte cut his eyes to Hank, who gave him an "I-told-you-didn't-I?" grin. "Smoke speaks highly of you, Chief Brokenhorn."

Brokenhorn spread his full lips in a wide, white smile. "So he does of you, Monte Carson." He made the name sound like one word.

"Please, call me Monte."

"I am Tom."

"Are you Christian, then, Tom?"

A dry chuckle came from Chief Brokenhorn. "In name only. My mother was attracted to the words of the Black-robes from the Queen-Mother land before I was born. She had the sacred water sprinkled on her. And, she gave me one of your white men's names. For a while, the Black-robes kept a mission among our people. When I was little, I went to school there, taught by the Fathers. I learned *Français* and English. Also a little of the tongue called Latin. The Fathers wanted me to become the first red man priest. But I knew I was not made to be a medicine man, I was to be chief."

Monte grinned at him. "Funny the grand ideas a feller has when he's a little boy. I always wanted to be a lawman . . . or a famous outlaw."

Brokenhorn nodded. "And we both had our dreams become real, Monte."

Nodding, Monte agreed with him. "So we did. Though I never became a *famous* outlaw, Tom. No stomach for it."

Chief Brokenhorn laughed aloud. "That is why I am a civil chief. I have taken the war trail many times in the past, was head man of my warrior society, but I never liked the stealing and killing."

"You are a wise man, Tom. Now, tell me about Smoke."

"He came through here five suns ago. Bad men came before him. Nearly eight hands—er—forty of them. I suspect that our friend, Smoke Jensen, hunted them. And I also think that they hunted him."

Monte nodded. "You're right there, Tom. That's why Hank there and me came after him."

"I have warriors keeping watch. The bad men are in the white village of Dubois." He pronounced the town's name in the French manner, as *Du-bwoah.*

A grim expression darkened Monte's face. "Then Smoke will be goin' there before long."

"Monte, Smoke told me he would be going to the basin the white trapper, Jackson, found many years ago."

"Yes. He told me the same, Tom. I'll go there first."

"I will send warriors with you, men to replace the watchers. First, though, you must stay with us a while, rest your horses and let them grow fat again. It is not known if there are more bad men coming, but our neighbors, the Arapaho," he made the name sound unclean, "say that some do, by two or three in a group. We must learn what we can before you go."

Monte nodded. "I agree. Looks like Smoke's stumbled into another hornet's nest," he added grimly.

A pot of beans bubbled over the small fire on the vast breast of the mountain slope. Nearby, the whole carcass of a young antelope turned on a green wooden spit. Ike Mitchell and the hands from the Sugarloaf had arrived on the southeastern face of the Rattlesnake Hills shortly before sundown. Without being bidden, Bobby Harris began to gather dry wood for the cookfire. The small stone ring radiated heat as the temperature dropped with the coming of night. Several of the men complained over the past few days about the food.

With good cause, Bobby thought as he sat on a flat-topped boulder, staring out across an ocean of grass. The hams they had brought along had run out two days earlier. That left a slab of bacon, already green around the edges and slickly white on the rind. It smelled sour while being cooked and tasted the same way. Until today they had not taken time to hunt and dress out game for the cook pot. This afternoon, when two men had upchucked their noon meal, and three others had refused to eat, necessity had forced it.

It slowed progress. Yet Ike reckoned they had closed a lot of ground and, since losing the trail of the kidnappers, they might catch up to Smoke within a few days. They had better, and before the army of outlaws did, Bobby thought in irritation and impatience. He had toughed a lot, the boy realized. No longer did his thighs and crotch ache through the night, keeping him awake. He slept so hard now that he did not even hear the snores of the tired hands. They just had to find Smoke. He'd know how to get Sally back. Bobby stirred and broke off his distant stare across the rolling steppe of Shoshoni Basin when Ike stopped beside him and gave his shoulder a firm squeeze.

"A nickel for your thoughts, Bobby."

Bobby forced a warm smile. It was hard not liking this strong, silent man. "The price has gone up," he observed cheerily. "I was . . . thinkin' about Sally an' where she is. And . . . about Smoke."

Ike nodded. "Ain't a man among us that has anything else on his mind. You worried we won't find her?"

Bobby drew a deep breath. "I'm worried we'll find her all alone and . . . too late." He shuddered, his thin shoulders heaving.

"No, Bobby. I can't let myself believe that could happen. She'll be all right. She's a tough lady. Smoke's taught her how to be a survivor."

"I hope she remembers what she learned," Bobby sighed. "And—and she's not young anymore."

Ike laughed softly. "Now, that depends on your point of view. There's men ridin' with us who'd see Miss Sally as a spry girl, compared to themselves. Thinkin' like that's for a small boy—rather than a growed-up member of a volunteer possee," he hastily added, lest Bobby explode again. "I come to tell you, grub's ready."

Bobby's blue eyes glowed in the firelight. "Yum. I can taste that antelope now."

"Over-growed goat, you ask me," Ike muttered as he led the way back to the cookfire. There still being some left, he thought, they might pop a buffalo out on the basin. Now that'd be some real eatin'.

When Buck Ballard and Liam Quinn reached Dubois, their spirits hung below their horses' fetlocks. Dirty, sweaty, faces powder-grimed, they presented a disreputable spectacle that Victor Spectre watched coldly as they paraded down the main street. They halted before the Full Bucket Saloon and asked directions to locate Spectre. When they entered the lobby of the hotel, they looked even more like whipped dogs.

"We're lookin' for Mr. Spectre," Liam Quinn mumbled.

"I am he," Spectre stated icily. "Who are you?"

"I'm Liam Quinn, an' this is Buck Ballard. We're what's left of seven men comin' to sign on to hunt Smoke Jensen."

"Where are the others?" Ralph Tinsdale demanded from beside Victor Spectre.

Quinn shrugged. "Back in Jackson's Hole, dead as far as I know."

Olin Buckner sniffed with distaste. "What happened?"

"It seems, we already ran into Smoke Jensen."

Victor Spectre retook the initiative. "How do you know that?"

Liam Quinn studied his boot toes. "He—ah—sent you a message, Mr. Spectre."

Face twisted in contempt for Smoke Jensen, Ralph Tinsdale snapped, "What possibly could he have to say to you, Victor?"

Quinn told them what Smoke had said. Buckner and Tinsdale exploded with outrage. Buckner swore blackly, hate blistering the air as he called Smoke everything but a man. Tinsdale took exception to Smoke's claim to be better than the best guns they could hire. He called the last mountain man a two-bit, tinhorn, has-been. They would have said more, had not Victor Spectre cut them off in mid-tirade.

"Relax. We still hold the reins. Let Jensen think he has us off balance, quivering in our boots, afraid of shadows." He turned to Ballard and Quinn. "Do you men still intend to join us?"

"Yes, sir," Quinn answered for them both.

Spectre sniffed the effluvium that emanated from them. "Then get yourselves cleaned up. You're disreputable." He turned on his partners. "Make no mistake, we are in control. When the men with Nate Miller get back from Colorado, Smoke Jensen will come crawling. And when he does, he will die."

19

Smoke Jensen came to Dubois much sooner than Victor Spectre expected. Two nights after Ballard and Quinn reached the captive town, Smoke joined a group of would-be hard cases drinking in the Watering Hole Saloon in Dubois. He stood alone at the darkened end of the bar and sipped a beer. None of the louts and trash had recognized him when he entered. He continued to taste his brew while they bragged about how ferocious they would be when they got their hands on Smoke Jensen.

Obviously amateurs, they began to amuse him. One fellow in particular: a florid-face, a fat-gut spilling over the buckle of his cartridge belt, a big, porous wart of a nose, a mouth too wide and thin-lipped, a regular toad of a man, who had a new opinion of what to do with every sloppy swallow from his schooner of beer. If only silly words counted in a gunfight, Smoke thought.

Unaware of the contempt of Smoke Jensen, the slob brayed on. "I say the first thing we do is hold him down and cut off his tallywhacker. That'll make him squirm."

Sweet fellow, Smoke Jensen thought. Another gulp and he was off again.

"Yah, then we feed it to him." That brought a lot of laughs.

"Naw, that wouldn't work," another lout contradicted.

"He'd bleed to death before we could hurt him more. Mr. Spectre wants him brought in alive. Speakin' of that, Prager, when are you goin' out after Jensen?"

The lard tub interrupted a swallow of suds to gape at his interrogator. "Me? Hell, Woodson, I ain't goin' anywhere until the free board and room and the beer run out. If Jensen wants to take me on, he can come to me."

In the silence that followed, Olin Buckner entered the saloon. He made a long sweep of the men arranged along the bar and came to an eye-bulging halt on the distant figure of Smoke Jensen. Instantly in shock, his mouth worked a second before he could sound words.

"He already has, you idiot!" he yelled at Harlan Prager, a trembling finger pointed at Smoke Jensen. "He's right down there." With tremendous will, he broke his paralysis and grabbed for the 1875 Smith and Wesson, Schofield, Wells Fargo Model .45 at his hip.

The first thing Smoke did was shoot Buckner. Then he shot out the lights. In the process of taking out the five kerosene lamps, he dived for the floor. Confusion broke out at once. Thugs slammed into one another shouting. Shots slammed the walls, echoed and re-echoed. His six-gun empty, Smoke reholstered it and drew the second. He crawled through the maze of churning legs, tables, and chairs toward the open end of the bar. Muzzle flashes continued to momentarily illuminate the scene of struggling men, all intent on reaching the corner of the bar where Smoke had stood. In a double flame brightness, Smoke found himself face-to-face with Harlan Prager. The lard-tub gaped and opened his mouth to shout to the others.

"B'god, here h—"

Smoke shot Prager in the gut. Moaning, the fat outlaw fumbled to draw his own weapon. He did, only much too late. Prager fired a round that smacked into the shoulder of a fellow hard case. Blood spouted, along with dust and bits of cloth. Prager's eyes went wide. He raised the six-gun again.

Smoke Jensen fired his second round. It bored a hole in

the chest of Harlan Prager. Thrown sideways, Prager fought to keep himself erect, while his knees sagged beneath his weight. He groaned loudly, feebly raised his long-barreled revolver, and died as Smoke Jensen expended a third round on him. In the confusion, Smoke moved on.

He soon found his goal.

A black void stretched behind the mahogany. Smoke crawled into it. Sure enough, as he had expected, he soon found a "priest's hole" in the outer wall of the saloon. It soon became obvious, because of its gaping openness, that the bartender had preceded him. Quickly, Smoke wedged his shoulders through the small doorway and out into the cool night. He found himself in a narrow alley that paralleled the long sidewall of the liquor emporium. Smoke sensed the presence of someone else in the passageway and had his Colt out and pressed into a yielding stomach before the barkeep whispered urgently.

"Don't shoot, Mr. Jensen. I live here an' I know you're an all right guy. I was here when you cleaned up the town. I want you to know I shot out the lamps at the ends of the bar." He breathed a gusty sigh of relief when the pressure of the six-gun eased off.

"Thank you for that."

"You'll need a way out of here. I'll show you where to go."

"My horse is out front," Smoke told him.

"I'll get him for you."

Smoke's soft chuckle sounded loud in the tense atmosphere. "He won't let you. I'll go get him. Wait here."

Thunder remained where Smoke had tied him off half a block from the saloon. Sounds of chaos still came from the darkened barroom. Smoke walked over, unmolested, and retrieved the 'Palouse stallion. In seconds he disappeared into the alley. While he accomplished this, a question occurred to him.

"Why did you wait for me in this alley?"

"I figured you might know about the priest's hole."

Smoke tipped back his hat while the barman led the way away from the saloon. "I'm flattered. What I want to know is why did you have one handy?"

"I'm a Catholic, so I knew about them from church history. You know, the persecutions in England and Holland a long time ago? So, I had one put in the Watering Hole when I bought it."

"Clever."

A half dozen twists and turns later, the bartender pointed down a long, dark residential street. "Keep goin' along there and you come to the edge of town. My name's O'Roarke and it's been an honor to assist you."

"Thank you, O'Roarke. I'll never forget a fellow student of history."

Smoke went on alone. He would be exiting on the south side of town, but he could easily swing west and then north, to head back toward the Absaroka Range and Togwatee Pass. The Hole lay just beyond.

Early the next morning, Spectre's army of riffraff and thugs forced the citizens of Dubois to assemble at gunpoint. The place where they gathered was before five houses on the downwind edge of town. After a long wait, Victor Spectre stepped up onto the porch of the middle structure and addressed the crowd.

"The reason we are here this morning is for you to witness an object lesson. This is in payment for the audacity of Smoke Jensen to actually enter this town and brazenly create a riot in a respectable saloon. To show you and him that we are serious about maintaining order in Dubois, we are going to burn these five houses to the ground."

An elderly, white-haired man, back bent with age and rheumatism, stumbled forward out of the press of people. "No, please. Don't do that. It cost me every cent I had to build that house. It's for my sunset years."

Victor Spectre stared icily at him. "It's too bad you picked such an unruly town in which to settle. Torch them, men."

Wails of anguish rose from the victims as the flames spread. Their neighbors consoled them as much as they could, being under the guns of the outlaws. When the flames reached the rooftops, Victor Spectre and Ralph Tinsdale moved away. Spectre caught the eye of Gus Jaeger and signaled him to join them.

When they had gathered off to one side, Spectre spoke quietly to them. "Until now, we have given no thought to going after Smoke Jensen. Now he has come to us without the bait even being in place. Furthermore, with Olin Buckner in bed, gut-shot and not expected to live, I think the insult is great enough that we should take the battle to him. Augustus, I want you to select a dozen men and send them after Jensen. Pick up his trail. It will be devious, but it can be done. I suspect he is hiding in Jackson's Hole. Have them pursue him relentlessly. I do not want a repeat of this sort of thing. Tell them to pin him to the ground and send word. We will come wherever they are and kill him there. If that is not possible, have him killed on the spot."

Anticipating pursuit, Smoke Jensen made it easy for the outlaws to find his trail and follow him. At least he did until mid-morning, the next day, when he reached the foothills that led to the sheer peaks of the Absaroka Range that buttressed Togwatee Pass. From there, the signs of his passage became few and far apart. It would, he felt assured, whet their appetite for finding him. Some two miles short of the summit of the Pass—which formed the transition from the Absarokas to the Gross Ventre Range, which surrounded Jackson's Hole—Smoke halted and explored a tangle of dead-fall and boulders located fifty yards up-slope from the pathway.

With his Winchester and ample ammunition in place, Smoke returned to the trail below, and created signs that led past his picked spot and on toward the notch. Then he left the traveled roadway and wiped out all indications of his presence. With that completed, he returned and settled in among the rocks and tree trunks. He had a long wait.

Smoke munched alternately on a cold biscuit and strip of jerky, the sun slanted far down in the west, when a trio of hard cases cantered into view over a down-curve in the trail. More quickly followed, until Smoke counted an even dozen. He let them get right in close, then sprang his ambush.

During the long, lonesome day, he had taken the time to rig a dead-fall, which he let fly first. Then he yanked out the three sticks that propped up a loose boulder, which rolled down with amazing speed on the surprised outlaws. The swinging tree trunk cleaned two riders from their saddles. Only one had time to yelp in pain and surprise. The huge granite stone jinked at the last moment and crushed to death three men who had abandoned their saddles, certain that their horses would be struck.

With five hard cases taken out of action, Smoke Jensen opened up with his Winchester. Another member of Victor Spectre's outlaw army threw up his arms and uttered a piti-ful shriek before he fell forward over the neck of his horse. Panicked by the unaccustomed weight and the smell of blood, the animal went berserk. Squalling, it crow-hopped and sun-fished until it dislodged the morbid burden, then sprinted off down the trail. It crashed into three mounted border trash. Their mounts reared and one man lost his seat. He hit the ground hard and bounced once.

By then, the human rubbish had recovered enough to return fire. Their slugs screeched and moaned off the mound of granite boulders. Smoke had shifted slightly and began to shove cartridges into the loading gate of his rifle. When he had filled the tubular magazine, he shouldered the weapon and began a rapid fire salvo that pinned the gunmen to the ground. Surprise had served him well enough at the outset. Now, the remaining seven men recovered enough to think through their situation.

Quickly they split up and began to move obliquely up the hill toward Smoke's position from different directions. Their rush caused Smoke to draw back to his secondary position in a jackstraw pile of down-fall, where he would make his final stand.

"By God, there must be a dozen of them up there," Farlee Huntoon yelled in confusion as he worked his way up the slope.

Liam Quinn, who knew from experience, answered him. "Nope. Just Smoke Jensen. Sure an' he's one heller with a gun."

"Cain't be," Farlee objected, unwilling to face the truth. "Any one man shoots that fast cain't hit nothin', nohow."

"Jensen can," Liam assured him, then ducked as another fusillade cut twigs from the brush beside his head. From behind him, Liam heard a man yelp and go down to thrash in a tangle of wild blackberry.

Farlee Huntoon groaned in fear. "Awh, gawdamnit, that's six of us he's kilt already an' we ain't even put a slug in him."

Liam Quinn, who knew only too well how efficient a killing machine was Smoke Jensen, mocked the frightened lout from West Virginia. "Well, why don't you just go up there and do something about that?"

Huntoon drew himself up, smarting from the contempt in the Irish outlaw's voice. "All right, I will."

He started forward when two others decided the same thing. One went down without a sound, the second fled for the protection of a pine trunk. Farlee Huntoon hugged the ground and shivered violently.

Smoke still held his own against the remaining five outlaws. A moment after he broke the charge of the incautious pair who had risen from the grass, he paused to feed fresh cartridges to his Winchester. When he did, one of the crew managed to flank him and knelt behind the trunk of a fallen pine. He rested his elbow on the rough bark on the top and took aim at the side of Smoke's head. Oblivious to the danger, Smoke remained ignorant of the gunman's proximity until he heard a meaty smack, followed a moment later by the flat report of an old, long-barreled Sharps buffalo rifle.

Smoke cut his eyes to the left, where the danger lay, in time to see a shower of hair, skin, blood, and bone as the sniper lost the back of his head. The shot had come from uphill. Everyone went motionless as they took in this new factor. Then another old Sharps opened up on the group on Smoke's right.

A big, .56 caliber slug took down another of the thugs. His piercing screams echoed through the pass as he writhed on the ground, gut-shot and dying. A second later, Smoke Jensen's Winchester barked and Farlee Huntoon flooded his trousers as he desperately tried to sink into the turf. The hidden marksmen with their Sharps rifles knocked over two more hard cases and the resolve of the remainder vanished.

Three of the rabble turned back to form a rear guard. They died at almost the same instant, as Smoke and his unseen allies fired nearly as one. With Farlee Huntoon far in the lead, Liam Quinn and Dorcus Carpenter fled.

Smoke sent a .44-40 slug after them, then came out into the open. Shading his eyes with his hand—his hat had been knocked off by a close bullet—he stared up-slope toward the positions of his rescuers. With the exception of the one who had tried to blind-side him, he could have handled the twelve men easily. That did not diminish the depth of the gratitude he felt for his helpers. While his gaze roved over the rising ground, two figures rose from the underbrush, Sharps rifles held over their heads in a sign of victory.

Zeke Duncan and Ezra Sampson long-legged it down to

where Smoke waited for them. Zeke began cackling while still fifty yards away. "Them fellers musta filled their britches 'fore they could get out of here."

"Most likely they did," Ezra agreed, sniffing the air.

"I owe you two," Smoke announced as they came up to him. "I owe you big."

Zeke worked his whiskered mouth a moment before replying. "Well, we was enjoyin' it mightily, watchin' you clean their plows, but then that dirty little sneak tried to pop you from the side. So we figgered it best to take a hand."

Smoke nodded shortly. "Glad you did. I'd be dead as these fellers." Smoke made a sweeping gesture.

One of the supposed corpses groaned. "I ain't dead yet, you bastard."

Ezra Sampson reached him in three swift strides. He roughly jammed the muzzle of his Sharps under the thug's nose. "Don't you think you oughtta call him Mr. Jensen, before he comes over and finishes the job?"

Herman Ogilvey tried to brazen it out. "Go ahead, shoot me, you old fart."

BANG!

Ezra Sampson gave him what he wanted.

Smoke Jensen winced, but spared no more sympathy for the dead man. Instead, he asked the question that had been at the forefront of his mind since he first had an inkling of who had come to his aid. "What brought you two out here?"

Zeke and Ezra exchanged embarrassed glances, two school boys caught by the school marm peeping in the girls' side of the outhouse. Zeke studied the toes of his boots. "Thing is, we came over to thank you for the jug of the other night and found yer camp empty. We sorta figgered what you had in mind, so we decided to tag along and see how it all worked out."

"We also wanted to thank you for the hind-quarter of venison you gave us," Ezra added, as though that had anything to do with it.

Smoke broke out in a genuine grin. "You two old frauds.

You reckoned I'd need some help. And as it turned out, I did. For which I shall always be grateful. Now, let's gather up these weapons and get on back to the Hole."

Shortly before sundown, the self-appointed posse of Sugarloaf riders reached the Wind River Reservation to find Monte Carson already there. Ike grinned sheepishly when he shook the hand of the lawman.

"Seems we had the same idea, Monte. When did you leave?"

"About two days before you, I'd judge, Ike," Monte answered with a chuckle.

Tom Brokenhorn escorted them to places by the Council fire. "We are meeting to decide what to do," he explained. "You will not understand our words, so I will tell you what we discuss. I am worried that our friend, Smoke Jensen, is in more trouble now than even he can be aware of. I have asked the Council to reach a consensus on sending a war party to give what help we can." He paused and gave a fleeting smile. "I have only two more to win over."

A protracted debate followed, in the musical Shoshoni language, ripe with its Athapaskan root origins. At last, the single hold-out lowered his eagle-wing fan and gave a curt nod. Smiling, the chief turned back to his white visitors. "It is done. I will immediately select a war chief and he will gather men to ride north to the Snake Basin. You may go with them, if you wish."

Monte nodded thoughtfully. "I think that would be good. Especially if the army stumbled on your braves. As a lawman, if I accompany them, I can give lawful reason for their being off the reservation."

"It is as though Smoke Jensen spoke those words. Thank you, Lawman Carson." To the Sugarloaf hands, he added, "I will give you a beaded belt as safe passage through my people scattered on the reservation. I wish you all well."

20

Nate Miller and his motley crew rode into Dubois half an hour before sundown. Word had not yet reached the town about the defeat of the gunmen sent after Smoke Jensen. Many of the hard cases hooted and called insults to Sally Jensen as the rabble gathered to gawk. Nate Miller pushed his way through the mob, to clear a path for Sally to follow. Her protector on the journey, Sam Hutchins, took her gently by one elbow and escorted her beyond the slobbering louts.

"Pay them no mind, ma'am, they're nothin' but trash."

And what are you? Sally asked herself silently, then gave him a brief smile. "Thank you, Sam. And, thanks for the support. I'm afraid I'm a little stiff after being tied to my horse all this time."

"It'll go away. I heard Mr. Spectre tell Nate jist now that he'll put you up in the hotel. A room to yourself."

Sally could not resist a flash of sarcasm. "How very thoughtful." Then she relented on Sam's behalf. He had been respectful, even kind, during the long trek. "What do you know about this monster who so cavalierly orders men to kidnap a woman and bring her to him?"

Sam frowned. "I wouldn't call him a monster, ma'am. He's a good leader. Has this whole thing thought out real clever. Why, look at this town. Don't look like a shot was fired when they took it over."

Sally seized on that at once. "What sort of man would want to take a town away from the people who rightfully own it, its residents?"

A big smile grew on Sam's face. "You ever hear of politicians, ma'am?"

Blushing at being outsmarted so easily, Sally put on a good front. "Besides them, then, if you will."

"Now you have me there, ma'am. All I know is he said it was necessary in order to get your husband to come at him."

Sally smiled sweetly. "I thought that was why I was kidnapped."

Sam looked glum. "Yeah. There's that, too."

Stopping abruptly, Sally stamped a foot. "Doesn't he realize that whether I am here or whether he has the town or not, Smoke will come after him?"

With an effort of mental gymnastics Sam rejected the truth of what she said. He chose to change the subject. "Come along, ma'am, I'll see you to the hotel."

Victor Spectre waited for Sally Jensen in the lobby. Ignoring her foreknowledge, Sally hotly demanded to know for what reason she had been brought there. Smirking, Spectre allowed as how it surprised him that she had not figured it out already.

"You have a special role in my immediate future. You are my cheese."

"Cheese?"

"Yes, dear lady, cheese. As in mousetrap. In this case, the mouse is your husband, Smoke Jensen."

Thinking it wise, Smoke Jensen moved his camp south to a smaller portion of the basin. Double Peak thrust up due east of him. Once he had set up, he sighed regretfully over the duplicated work he faced to rebuild his smoker. And he needed to get another deer.

He hunted with a bow again, disturbing little in nature with his kill. A larger animal this time. Smoke dressed it and hung it in a tree, then set about the thankless task of building a new smoker. He had no idea how much longer he would be there, and any meat he had left over, he could give to Zeke and Ezra. Sundown caught up to him and he fried some of the liver. He would finish tomorrow.

Near noon the next day, Smoke stretched to his full height after lighting a smudgy, green wood, hickory fire in the chamber to one side of his smoker. He froze at the faint crackle of a stepped-on twig nearby. It took only one stride to retrieve his Winchester. He held it cradled loosely in his left arm when a man's head appeared over the tops of some low, new-growth aspen. The stranger held his rifle up by the stock, a white cloth tied to the barrel. Smoke surmised it might be a napkin.

"Hello, the camp. You be Smoke Jensen?"

"I am."

"I'm comin' in under a flag of truce. Will you honor that?"

"I will. Ride on in."

From the looks of the man, up close, Smoke wondered how he had ever been able to find the camp. He wore a derby hat, cocked jauntily to one side, a striped suit, with a collarless shirt, made gaudy by wide, vertical red stripes, separated by thin white ones, and carriage boots, with the cuffs of his pants stuffed in. A city dude, Smoke put him as being.

"I have something to show you, Jensen," he declared.

Smoke motioned him to the picket line. "Tie off and I'll take a look."

After the citified thug dismounted and secured his horse, he came forward with his saddlebags over one shoulder. He opened the buckles on one side and delved within. He came out with a fine gold chain, from which hung a cameo. It was one Smoke Jensen knew only too well. Next came the .38 Colt Lightning Smoke had purchased for her when they had first become available in Denver. It took every bit of Smoke's will to keep his face impassive. When the gunsel reached into the bag for something else, Smoke raised a hand to halt him.

"I've seen enough. Where is Sally?"

Over-confident, the rogue made a stupid decision to taunt Smoke. "Who?"

An instant later he found his shirt-front bunched in one powerful fist of Smoke Jensen, his feet off the ground, dangling. "Where . . . is . . . my wife?"

"All right—all right, leggo me. I'll tell you what I was told to say." When Smoke released him, the suddenly nervous, smaller man fussily adjusted his clothing in an effort to regain his composure and get the quaver out of his voice.

"Make it good. And make it fast," Smoke growled.

"I was told by Mr. Spectre to tell you that if you want your wife to live, you will ride into Dubois within two days. You are to come alone and unarmed. If you bring help, she will be killed on the spot. Remember, two days. Come in by then, or on the third day, your Sally dies."

Without a word, Smoke took Sally's possessions from the messenger, spun him around and roughly shoved him toward his horse. "Get out of here, you outhouse rat, and don't look back."

After the messenger departed, Smoke reviewed the brief, fateful message. Fat chance of either of them surviving if he believed any of that, he considered. He would have to get Sally out of there on his own, then bring in help to deal with Victor Spectre. To do that, he needed a better look at Dubois.

In camp, outside Togwatee Pass, Bobby Harris sat apart from the hands who had treated him like an equal for more than a year. On their journey northward, his pose of manhood had slipped as time wore on. The boy had been buoyed up by a spirit of adventure alone for the last two days. Now he rested an elbow on his knee, his chin cupped in an open hand. His lower lip protruded in a typical little-boy pout. Ike Mitchell found him there as long shafts of orange speared through the trees and the eastern sky turned blue to purple.

"You're looking sort of glum. Want to talk about it?"

Bobby looked up rapidly, his face an open bloom of hope. "Yes—er—no. Yes, I do, Ike," the boy concluded, his features crumpled into despair again.

"Well, then, where do you want to start?"

"At the beginning, I guess. I should have gone with Smoke."

Disappointment clouded Ike's eyes. "Don't start on that again."

Bobby darted out a hand and put it on the foreman's arm to stay further complaint. "No, please, Ike, let me tell it my way." At Ike's dubious nod, he went on. "I wanted to show Smoke and everyone that I was big enough to do a man's job. So, I should have gone, because afterward I got to feelin' like the other hands were laughing at me. That I was nothing but a little boy to them. Then, when those men took Sal—Mom, I couldn't stand it any longer. See, if I had gone with Smoke, we would have moved a lot slower than him alone. We could have been close enough to take after those bas—devils right away.

"They went the same way Smoke did, you said so. We might even have run into them on the way, fought it out, and they would never have taken m-my mother." He paused, eyes begging for understanding. "Anyway, I could have been more useful . . . than . . . I am now. And I'm worried about her. I'm afraid something bad will happen." Bobby's eyes filled and he sniffled softly in a fight to keep back the tears.

Reminded of his own turmoils at the threshold of puberty, Ike impulsively reached out and hugged Bobby to him. With rough compassion, he ruffled the straw-blond hair. "Smoke knows you are a big man now," he spoke reassuringly. "Smoke'll be almightily exercised over you coming along, but he'll know it was your worry over Miss Sally."

"He's got the right of that, boy," Monte Carson, who had come up quietly behind them during the painful exchange, said gruffly.

Setting aside the tin cup, Smoke Jensen praised the coffee, then turned to the real reason for his visit to the camp of Zeke and Ezra. "Could you two carry a message for me?"

"I don't know why not. Who's it go to?"

Smoke answered tightly, unsure how they would receive the news. "There's two people, really, Chief Tom Brokenhorn of the Shoshoni, and Chief Blackrobe of the Arapaho. They are camped on the Wind River Reservation. I'll write it out for you and you can leave in the morning."

Zeke cocked an eyebrow, pursed lips. "Kin they read writin'?"

"Tom Brokenhorn can. You'll have to tell Blackrobe."

"All right. What's this gonna say, this message?" Zeke accepted.

"That they are to send as many warriors as possible right away. They are to meet me to the east of Togwatee Pass, on the plain, ten miles from Dubois."

Ezra puckered his lips, which made his mustache waggle like a furry snake. "We—ah—sorta reckoned to get in on that affair."

"You still can. Ride back here with the Indians and you'll be in plenty of time."

Zeke asked for both of them. "What are you fixin' to do now?"

"I leave this afternoon to get another look at Dubois."

Ezra whistled softly. "Sounds to me like you're a sucker for danger."

A cold, bleak look filled Smoke's yellow-brown eyes. "Could be *I'm* the danger."

Smoke Jensen left the eastern grade to Togwatee Pass shortly after the moon rose. Its pale, silver light washed the land with enough brightness to see. He would be close to Dubois before mid-morning, Smoke estimated. Thunder trotted along the well-used trail, which ran five miles north of the camp where Monte Carson and Ike Mitchell slept through the night, eager to reach Smoke's camp in Jackson's Hole the next day. Neither the ex-mountain man nor the posse knew of the others' presence.

And Smoke could have used them, had he but known.

Over the past three days, fourteen more gunfighters and bounty hunters had drifted into Dubois, which brought the total to well above fifty-five. They dozed late into the mornings, and lounged in the saloons through the afternoons and each night. With the town in the hands of the man who had hired them, most had not known such peace and security since childhood.

Much to the disgust of Tim O'Roarke, most of the outlaw horde made the Watering Hole a sort of headquarters. Fully three dozen lounged in the saloon on a lazy, warm afternoon. Half a dozen more had gone upstairs with some of the soiled doves. Most of them would be down before long, Tim knew. For all their bragging about what bad actors they were, and what gifts they were to womanhood, they were actually more like little boys with short fuses. How different they were from Smoke Jensen.

That thought gave O'Roarke pause. He wondered where Smoke was right then, what he was doing.

* * *

Nestled down into a depression outside Dubois, a pair of field glasses to his eyes. Smoke Jensen slowly swept the lenses along the buildings nearest to him. For two blocks they were residences. All of them had two things in common, Smoke observed. No one worked in the flower beds, the gardens, or went to and from the stables at the rear of the lots. Only two had lank washing, which fluttered listlessly in an indifferent breeze, on lines in backyards. Yet each house had a scruffy-looking hard case propped back in a chair on the porch. He went back over them again, then a third time.

The people who live there are prisoners in their own homes, Smoke realized as he looked on. Then he changed his point of focus to the first of the commercial buildings. He at once noted a greater density of outlaws among the people on the street he viewed now. They swaggered through the vanquished residents, who scurried away with furtive backward glances. Smoke spotted several faces he recognized from earlier encounters with Spectre's minions. He would have to move to sweep the main street.

Fortunately a shallow ravine ran parallel with the face of the town where Smoke observed. After he satisfied his curiosity enough, Smoke shifted into the fissure and worked north along it until he reached a culvert where the main roadway crossed it. There he removed his hat and raised up enough to scan the main street with ease. What he saw deeply troubled him. In the same heartbeat it relieved him of an earlier anxiety. At least now he knew where Spectre held Sally.

Heavily armed outlaws, in roving patrols of two and three, alertly prowled around the hotel. More sat in chairs on the balcony and under its canopy on the boardwalk. The saloons received good play also, he perceived. Small wonder. A collection of this sort, used to some space between themselves and others, needed an outlet for the tension their closeness would surely create. Easing down, Smoke took out a sheet of paper and began to sketch in the location of each nest of hard cases with a stub of pencil. With that accomplished, he moved again.

Throughout the remainder of the day, Smoke timed the movements of the outlaws, entered the positions of lookout posts and the length of the watch duty. No doubt Spectre thought their presence would keep him from getting rough when he made his move to save Sally.

"How little he knows," Smoke said wryly to himself.

When he withdrew, well into the night, he had an idea of where every lookout had been placed, where Spectre himself spent the night, and how many men could be expected in the saloons. With however many guns he had at his disposal, Smoke decided he would go in after Sally at the time specified. That would provide time for the warriors to get here. Once he had her clear of town, Spectre and his gang would be swept out of town in a way that would give nightmares for the rest of their lives to any who survived, Smoke vowed silently to himself.

Without warning, the door to the room where Sally Jensen sat staring at her lamp-lit reflection in the windowpanes made mirrors by the blackness outside. She tensed slightly, back unconsciously arching in preparation for a spring to flee or to attack. She was convinced that these rabble could sink to the lowest, vilest of crimes, given only the slightest provocation. Slowly, she turned her head to see who her faithful guard, Sam, had let enter.

It turned out to be Victor Spectre. In one hand he held a tray with covered dishes. "I thought I would bring you your dinner. I brought a plate for myself, as well." He started for a small, sturdy, drop-leaf oak table.

"Thank you, but I am not hungry," Sally replied absently.

Brushing aside her rejection, Spectre began laying out the plates. "You must eat to keep up your strength, my dear. It's roast loin of pork, with potatoes and gravy, some garden greens, and even a slice of cherry pie. The cherries are locally grown and put up by my temporary host, the mayor's cook. I've brought an appropriate bottle of wine, and there will be coffee after."

Sally put ice into her voice. *"I said I am not hungry."* A sharp pang in her stomach put the lie to that. Reluctantly, she had to admit the accuracy of his words. "Although I suppose you are right. I must maintain my strength in order to fight you vermin."

She went to the chair he held out for her. After seating her, Victor Spectre fussed about the table like a prissy waiter in a French restaurant. At last, he took his place and raised knife and fork. Then he hesitated.

"Ah—perhaps you would prefer to give a blessing first?"

Sally Jensen pulled a wry face. "Considering the circumstances, I hardly think I can be thankful for this food."

"Uh—yes, I follow you. Well and good, then. You might as well commence, we do not want it getting cold."

Hesitantly, Sally began to eat. Throughout the meal, she noticed that Spectre seemed oddly fascinated with her. He eyed her askance for the most part, yet occasionally Sally would look up from cutting a piece of meat to find him staring. She held her peace through most of the meal, determined not to make this a pleasant occasion for her captor. His continued behavior finally broke her silence.

"Tell me, Mr. Spectre—"

"Victor. Please, call me Victor."

"Very well, Victor. Tell me, has it been a while since you shared the company of a lady?"

Spectre's school-boy fascination faded into a scowl. "Your husband saw to that. I have been forced into the close company of only men for the past five and a half years."

"Didn't your wife visit?"

Sadness replaced the bitterness. "My wife—my wife passed on the year our son was nine." Suddenly the anger flared again, and Spectre let it all spill out. "That's why I'm here. That's why I am doing this. Smoke Jensen murdered Trenton. He killed my son."

Sally could not hide her expression of shocked disbelief. "Surely that can't be so. There has to be something you are not telling me, perhaps something you don't even remember about the—incident?"

"No, nothing. I was there. I witnessed it. The boy was already wounded, could not offer further resistance. Then your husband turned on me. His shot went high. . . ." Unconsciously, Victor Spectre raised fingers to the white streak in his hair. "I was knocked unconscious. When I awakened, days later, Trenton had already been buried."

Sally touched her napkin to her lips, mind searching for something with which to mitigate the indictment against Smoke. "Couldn't the shock of being shot, and knocked unconscious, have distorted your recollection of how events transpired?"

Oddly impacted by this unconventional suggestion, the turmoil it created could be clearly read on the face of Victor Spectre. He considered it a moment, then hardened his features again. "Not at all. I know what I saw. That is why I have shown such fascination with you. You are so refined, such a lady, that I wonder how you can live with so notorious a murderer as Smoke Jensen?"

Sally's compassion for this tormented man vanished. Icily, she responded to him. "Smoke Jensen is not a murderer, and I do love and live with him quite nicely, thank you."

"Sorry, you don't understand. What I want to know is what Smoke Jensen is like as a husband?"

"Don't be impertinent," Sally snapped.

Spectre forced a grin. "It is not idle curiosity, and I did not intend it to intrude on a husband and wife's conjugal privicy. Yet, the fact remains," he went on to add sneeringly, "you will be a widow soon, and all you will have is memories of Smoke Jensen. When that is the case, you will find that you have certain needs that—yes—that I will be more than able to fulfill."

Sally Jensen sprang to her feet and snatched up the tray and its unfinished meal, which she hurled at Victor Spectre. Then she slapped his face with a resounding smack.

21

Well satisfied with his survey of Dubois, Smoke Jensen returned to his temporary camp in a hidden canyon five miles from the town. To his surprise, he found fifteen Shoshoni warriors waiting there. Running Snake, their war leader, turned out to be a grandson to Chief Tom Brokenhorn and spoke English well.

"We have been watching the bad men who camp in the white village. When that happen, I send message to my grandfather to have warriors come if you need."

Smoke found it hard to see Brokenhorn as a grandfather, yet he was already one as well. "I will probably need, right enough. When did you send for warriors?"

"On the day we see White Wolf sneak into town," Running Snake said with a grin.

That meant Zeke and Ezra would run upon them on the trail, Smoke reasoned. The Shoshoni's next words surprised him and brought to mind a question he had for a long while.

"I also have word that some worthless dogs of the Arapaho are a hand's span of sun behind us. They will be here in the morning."

Given that the two tribes had been traditional enemies for centuries, Smoke could never figure out why the government, in its infinite wisdom, had put them together on the same reservation. Maybe the land-greedy politicians hoped they would wipe out one another? He gave off worrying it to make his guests coffee, with lots of sugar, then put meat on the cookfire.

"We will have coffee and talk," he told Running Snake in Shoshoni. "Then we eat."

"It is good. When you last visited our camp, I was not yet born. There are many things I would like to know."

Smoke Jensen cut his sharp gaze to Running Snake. "Like what got these fellers riled up at me enough to tear into that village?"

Running Snake nodded. "Yes, there is that . . . and other things."

Morning brought the aroma of brewing coffee and frying bacon. It also brought twenty-eight Arapaho warriors, Zeke and Ezra along with them. That surprised Smoke, who made quick to ask about it. A grinning Zeke explained.

"We ran into these fellers just south of the pass. They tole us that they had been following a large party of Shoshoni and white men for two days. So Ez an' me figgered ever'-body what was up for this tussel were already accounted for. We rode along."

Ezra took up the tale. "Then, when we got to the pass, we cut sign of Injuns an' whites ridin' together. We left a stone cairn tellin' them where to come. Should be here some time today."

That gave him a larger force than Smoke had hoped for. Even so, he frowned. "I don't have any more days to spare. Today's the deadline. I have to show myself in Dubois or Sally will be killed tomorrow."

Zeke questioned that. "You don't really think that feller would make good on his threat, do you? Why, he'd lose his advantage."

"You and I know that, and so does he. But, I'm afraid the one in charge is unable to think clearly right now. He might consider it just desserts for me, even though he would die in the process."

Ezra spoke encouragingly. "I make it a good sixteen white men, and about thirty Shoshonis."

Smoke sounded grim. "He'll die then, no matter what happens to Sally."

What jolted Smoke even more came when the mixed band arrived shortly after noon. Smoke almost blew the head off his foreman when Ike Mitchell and the Sugarloaf hands sprinted ahead of the approaching Shoshoni warriors into the box canyon. He received yet another surprise when he saw Monte Carson and Hank Evans along. He vigorously shook his old friend's hand and led him to the cookfire.

"I have to leave soon, Monte, but there's time for a cup of coffee."

"Leave? For where?"

"Dubois. Victor Spectre has given me two days to turn myself in to save Sally's life. This is the second day."

Monte had heard about Sally's kidnapping from Ike. He had cursed and kicked rocks and slammed a fist into a pine trunk at the time. Now he let go a low, rumbling swear word and fire lighted his eyes. "You're not going alone?"

"That's what he expects, but I don't think so. This many people on hand calls for a change of plan."

Monte and Ike looked wary. Ike was first to take up the burden. "There's one person along you may want to cook up some special plans for, Smoke."

"Who's that?"

"Bobby."

Smoke exploded upward to land hard on his boot soles. "What the bloody blue hell did you let him come along for?"

Ike gritted his teeth, knowing the ire of his boss to be justified. "I—ah—didn't exactly 'let' him come along. He insisted. The kidnapping of Sally was sort of the last straw for him."

Before Smoke could hunt down the boy and unload on him, Ike took him aside and told him of his conversation with Bobby. It cooled the anger Smoke had built. Carefully he thought over what he would say while he sought out the lad, who had wisely decided to avoid Smoke's notice. Smoke found Bobby at the picket line, industriously brushing out his horse.

"Bobby, I am not happy with this. You can be sure of that. Although I think I understand why you came along."

"Yes, sir. You're going to send me back."

Smoke softened his expression with a fleeting smile. "No. You may stay. But you'll have to stay behind in this camp until the fighting's over. Having Sally's life in danger is enough, too much in fact. The risk of putting you in harm's way is more than I could bear. I—well, at first I thought of you as a nuisance. Since then, I—I've come to love you every bit as much as my own natural sons." *There, I've said it,* Smoke's expression declared.

Bobby's eyes went wide and round. "You do? You really do? I thought—I thought you looked at me as nothing but a little boy, someone to take fishing and teach about ranching."

Impulsively, they found themselves in a tight embrace. Smoke seemed reluctant to end it, pride in Bobby's indomitable spirit filling him. At last he let the boy go. "I have to do some planning with Monte, Ike, and the war chiefs."

"Then what, Smoke?"

"I'm going to Dubois to get Sally."

With Zeke's admonition that Spectre would not be crazy enough to eliminate his one insurance policy by killing Sally the next day fresh in his mind, and in light of the large number of men on hand, Smoke made drastic changes in his plans. If he did not show up by the deadline, it would put them further off balance, he reasoned. Smoke figured that a little havoc in Dubois might also have a beneficial effect. Shortly before dusk, he and Zeke rode out of the canyon mouth and started for Dubois. Already confused by Smoke's failure to appear in town, Spectre and his underlings would not be in good shape for a dawn attack after a sleepless night. They reached a spot from which they could observe everything going on along the main street. Patiently they waited out the long hours until alertness slackened.

Then they made their move. Smoke had earlier pointed out to Zeke several sentries who dozed off. Silently, moccasins replacing boots, Smoke and Zeke ghosted in on a pair of these. Solid blows, with the flat of tomahawk blades, quickly rendered the thugs unconscious. Smoke and Zeke each dragged their man off into the grass, to bind and gag them. Then they set off after another group of laggards.

"Over there," Smoke whispered in Zeke's ear. "There's two of them."

At a creeping pace, Smoke and Zeke closed in. When they came within ten yards, they could hear muffled conversation.

"By dang, I'm gettin' sick and tired of this. Who'er we watchin' out for?"

"Smoke Jensen, of course."

"Would you know him to see him? I don't blame him for not comin' in today. A man'd have to be a fool to ride into a town bristlin' with guns like this one." He laughed softly. "I'd kinda like to come face-to-face with him. Shake his hand and tell him how smart I think he is for keepin' outta Spectre's clutches."

A voice answered him from out of the darkness. "You kin, if you want to, Yonker. He's standin' right in front of you." Zeke chuckled softly a moment before he clonked the other outlaw over the head with his tomahawk.

Galvanized by this disclosure the first gunhawk came to his boots. "You are? Smoke Jensen? Where are you?"

"Right here," Smoke told him as he slapped the lout alongside the head with his 'hawk. Abruptly rubber-legged, the gunman went down in a heap.

Again, they dragged the senseless burdens out into the tall grass and tied them securely. Zeke edged over to Smoke. "I reckon that's enough, don't you?"

Smoke's breathy chortle lightened his words. "Yeah. On this side. We need to take a few more."

By two o'clock in the morning, they had taken out seven more lookouts. Then Smoke and Zeke split up and moved to positions on opposite sides of the town. Late hangers-on in the saloons soon found themselves listening to a timber wolf chorus. The eerie wails echoed off buildings and floated in the streets in such a way that no one could pinpoint their place of origin.

Judson Reese, deep in his cups, summed the experience up best. "They seem to come from everywhere at once, and entirely too close."

None of the dolts, who had been reduced to blurry vision and stagger-legged stumbles, volunteered to go out and find the wolves. When one of the cries changed from wolf to the cough and yowl of a mountain lion, several tough hombres paled noticeably and slunk away to upstairs rooms in the saloon for the night. Suddenly a shout of alarm came from one of the still-conscious sentries outside.

"Fire! There's a shed afire on the edge of the town."

Tongue thick with whiskey, Farlee Huntoon voiced the question many wanted an answer for. "Gol-dang, what caused that?"

Nate Miller gave him a cold gaze. "Smoke Jensen. What else could it be?"

Guffawing at the quandary of the lawless trash, Smoke Jensen and Zeke Duncan pulled back into the darkness to get some sleep before the big attack. Behind them, the abandoned, tumble-down shack continued to burn until first light.

From her confinement in the hotel, Sally Jensen had heard the commotion outside. It cheered her more than anything had in a week. When the animal calls began, she rushed to the small barred window of the jail from the chair in which she had been sitting. She had been brought to the cell-block at sundown, when Smoke failed to appear. Now she knew why Smoke had not come in earlier.

Smoke was out there now. Sally knew that as certainly as she knew her heart still beat. He hadn't given up, and he would not make some useless sacrifice of himself to save her. The time would come soon. She had to be ready to act. Yet, in the back of her head, she worried for Smoke's safety.

Her worry increased when Victor Spectre burst into the marshal's office and stormed into the cell-block. He ordered her cell unlocked and entered in a barely contained fury. Roughly he shot out an arm and grabbed her elbow in a steel grip.

"This is all your fault," he accused irrationally. "Smoke Jensen is on a rampage out there and it is all because you are here."

Sally glared at him stonily. "And who is it that had me brought here?"

Coldly, Victor Spectre ignored her. "Your husband is being a nuisance and has to be taught a lesson. It is a pity that you have to be a part of that lesson. I had decided to give him more time," Spectre lied smoothly. "Now, that is not possible. Tomorrow morning, at eight o'clock precisely, you will be taken out on the balcony of the hotel and shot to death."

Dawn's light had not yet turned pink from gray when Smoke Jensen and his volunteers approached Dubois. At his suggestion, the Shoshonis and Arapahos kept well out of sight, spreading out on the north and south flanks of the town. From a distance, Smoke swept the streets with field glasses. He spotted a few sleepy hard cases on the streets. All drooped from lack of rest. All looked in a low state of readiness. Smoke made a quick decision to attack at once.

"We won't have a better time," he told Monte Carson. "Surprise is still ours. We'll swing through this group of houses and take the main business section in a wide sweep. If it will make you feel better, Monte, we'll call out to them to surrender. At the least sign of resistance, we kill them where they stand."

"What about Sally?" Monte asked seriously.

"I'll find her. As a matter of fact, I have the notion Spectre will bring her to me."

Monte checked the face of his turnip watch. "Time to be doing it."

"I agree. Hank knows what to do?"

Monte nodded. "He'll attack from the far side when he hears the first shot."

That first discharge did not take long. Three hard cases came on the run from houses along a neat, tree-lined street. One of them, who had seen Smoke before, yelled to the others.

"By God, that's Smoke Jensen! Get him."

In the lead, Smoke took a hurried shot. His slug went a bit wide, to punch through the shoulder of one outlaw before the gunman could clear leather. Another appeared to trip over an invisible rope and sprawl in the gravel of the road, blood spewing from a gaping wound in his back. The third brigand, the one who had given the alarm, hastily re-holstered his six-gun and threw his hands in the air. Those in the lead went on by him. Someone at the rear would gather him in. From the far side of town, Smoke could hear gunfire.

Hank Evans and the remainder of the Sugarloaf hands would be streaming through to the business district. Another block and those on this side would join them. Then they would see. Smoke could only trust that it went the way he had planned it. Ahead he could see the balcony of the hotel. Three small figures stood on it. The one in the middle was that of a woman. Ice abruptly filled Smoke's stomach.

Another half block and the features became identifiable. Much as he wished otherwise, the woman was Sally. Smoke recognized Victor Spectre to one side. He held the muzzle of a Smith and Wesson American to her temple. At once, Smoke gave the signal to halt.

"Take it easy, Spectre. I came to see my wife was safe."

Spectre snickered. "Why wouldn't she be?"

"You said that if I did not come in within two days, you would kill her the third."

Feigning astonishment, Spectre spoke mockingly. "Why, I believe you are right. But, now you are here. If you are prepared to gave yourself up, we can discuss the release of your wife."

"If I believed that, you could also sell me the Washington Monument. Release her now and we can talk about my surrender."

"No, Smoke," Sally blurted.

"She is right. The answer is no. Whether you cannot count, or you are arrogant, I made up my mind. I decided that she dies at eight o'clock this morning. Now that you are here, the situation has changed again. That gives you . . ." Spectre fished his watch from a vest pocket while his henchman held Sally. "An hour and forty minutes. You have that time to pull back your men and give up to me, or she dies as scheduled."

Smoke Jensen led the way out of Dubois. To Monte's urgent questions, Smoke said only to wait and see. Smoke met first with the Shoshoni and Arapaho leaders. Running Snake listened to Smoke with interest, made a couple of suggestions and then asked how Smoke expected to make it work.

"It all depends on getting Zeke and Ezra into position to cover the hotel. From there on, we'll have to play it by their lead. All you need worry about is to be ready when I get Sally away from Spectre."

At ten minutes prior to the appointed time, Smoke Jensen walked Thunder down the wide main street of Dubois. An eerie silence held over the town. Residents looked away as Smoke rode by, ashamed in their helplessness. That would change, he reflected, if all went the way he intended.

Smoke had instructed Ike to have the men take all surplus arms and ammunition and provide them to the populace as the hands fought their way through the residences of Dubois. The citizens had fought to recover their homes once before, he had little doubt they had changed in only a few years. This time they had the added impetus of having the outlaws quartered among them. No one would like that sort of thing, Smoke reasoned.

And they would be given an opportunity to even the score. When he reached a block's distance, Smoke saw Sally once again on the balcony. This time two hard cases held her arms, well away from her body or the reach of a well-aimed foot. Smoke saw that two of those responsible for this situation had chosen to gather on the covered porch of the saloon, before the double bat-wing doors. No doubt they had come to gloat and claim his head, he surmised. As promised, Smoke appeared to be unarmed, his holsters empty. Victor Spectre stepped forward as Smoke Jensen reached the corner of the intersection.

"There has been another change of plans, I regret to say," Spectre declared, a nasty smile on his face. "We thought it to be too delicious an irony to overlook. This bright morning, you are going to get to witness your

wife being shot to death. Then, you shall be killed with
the same weapon. Only slowly, with each of us placing
bullets at likely places. Your ankles, wrists, knees, elbows,
hips, shoulder joints, your abdomen, the right side of
your chest, then the left, and last, your head. By then,
several days will have passed, during which we shall
enjoy ourselves enormously. You recall my associate, I
am sure. Ralph Tinsdale. Unfortunately, you shot Olin
Buckner. He is looking on from his sickbed in the hotel
above. We are three men whom you have terribly
wronged. And, for that wronging, you must now pay."

Smoke Jensen tensed as he edged even closer. Through
tight, thinned lips he made his response to Spectre. "Get
on with it, you windbag son of a bitch."

According to his plan, Smoke had drawn near enough to
the balcony for Sally to easily jump to the rump of Thunder. Smoke cut his eyes to those of his wife in a meaningful
glance a moment before two meaty smacks sounded in the
strained silence of the intersection. Instantly, Sally jerked
free of her suddenly lessened restraint and darted toward
the rail as the reports of two distant Sharps buffalo rifles rippled through the heated air. The two outlaws fell dead on
the balcony floor. In a blur, then, she vaulted the railing and
dropped to the skirt of the saddle on Thunder's back.

"Stop them!" Victor Spectre shouted, though not before
Sally Jensen yanked her .38 Colt Lightning free from the
rear waistband of her husband and fired on him.

Victor Spectre and Ralph Tinsdale sprawled in an undig-
nified manner on the worn boards of the porch. By then,
Smoke had freed the .45 Colt, which had also been concealed at the small of his back. He fired in a blur of speed.
His first slug cut the hat from the head of an astounded
Victor Spectre. Every thug present went for his gun. Hot
lead began to crack and snap close to the two Jensens. Sally
held onto Smoke with one hand and gamely discharged
two rounds that quickly wrote an end to the checkered
career of Fin Brock. Then the Arapaho and Shoshoni war-

riors whooped and hollered to create a diversion that allowed Smoke Jensen to take advantage of an opening in the gathered ranks of criminal slime and bolt through.

Arrows moaned their distinctive melody to strike flesh in the chests, stomachs, and throats of many a hardened rogue. They went down screaming as Thunder gained momentum and drew a wider gap between the human garbage and the priceless cargo the 'Paloose stallion bore. More gunshots crackled as the Sugarloaf hands invaded the residences of Dubois and shot down the toughs who had elected not to watch the destruction of the wife of Smoke Jensen. For all their villainous ways, they had retained their respect for women. It did them little good, as the vengeance-hungry ranch hands poured round after round into their hastily assembled ranks. Some broke and ran, escape a higher priority than any reward they might receive.

In all this confusion, Smoke and Sally quickly rode to safety. The entire confrontation had taken less than three minutes, Smoke discovered when they cantered across the small bridge at the west end of Dubois. Not bad at all. Behind him the volunteer fighters pulled back to make ready for the final assault. Not a one of the three responsible for this encounter would escape alive, Smoke Jensen had decreed.

22

Victor Spectre raved in fury at this debacle. He refused to look at it as a setback, let alone a defeat. When Ralph Tinsdale offered some platitude about their still holding the town, and that Smoke Jensen would be compelled to come to them, if he intended to do anything about it, Victor Spectre rounded on him, face carmine with rage.

"That is exactly the point. Smoke Jensen will absolutely come after us now. His wife is safe, he has those damned Indian allies and nothing to lose."

Tinsdale tried to calm the outraged Victor Spectre. "Quite the contrary, I would think. Taken from Smoke Jensen's viewpoint, why do anything more? He has his wife, safe and sound, why not simply pack up and go home?"

A malevolent glow burned in Spectre's eyes. "Because Smoke Jensen does not play live and let live. *He will come.* He has a large enough force and we have taken losses. He knows that. When he came after me, he had no way of knowing Trenton and I would be alone in that barn. Yet, Jensen came without a single other man."

Peevishly, Tinsdale snapped his opinion. "We should have killed that woman when we had the chance."

"No, Ralph," Victor Spectre answered, more calmed now. "Then we would have had a furious man on our hands to deal with. One who would not have stopped at burning down the entire town, if necessary, to get to us. What we should have done was to have Smoke Jensen back-shot and not stand around to gloat. The fact remains, Jensen will be coming. I want you to have the men ready for an attack at any time. And see that Olin is made as comfortable as possible. If he is up to it, give him a rifle he can use from his sickbed. We need every gun we can muster."

"Mom! *Oh, Mom!*" Bobby ran to Sally Jensen with outstretched arms, his light, blond hair flopping on a round head, hat spilled off in his excited discovery of his adoptive mother among those who returned from town. Mother and son hugged delightedly and shed copious tears. Then Sally broke the embrace and stood the boy before her.

"You disobeyed Smoke and myself alike. I'm disappointed, Bobby. No, that isn't true. I'm truly delighted to see you. For a while there, I didn't—didn't think I would ever see you again."

Smoke walked over and cleared his throat gruffly. "We're going to have to stop meeting like this, my dear. People will begin to talk."

Sally feigned anger. "Is that all you have to say to me? Not hello? Or glad to see you?"

"No, it's not all," Smoke said through a grin. "If you'd had the muzzle of that Lightning any closer to my head when you popped off three rounds at the Lammer brothers, we wouldn't be having this conversation." Then he grabbed her and gave her a mighty hug that lifted Sally's feet off the ground. "It's so good to have you here. For a while there, I actually worried that it wouldn't work."

"What? The famous Smoke Jensen worried about a little thing like that?" Sally teased. For a moment her eyes swam with more tears. "Oooh, Smoke Jensen, I love you so. I never lost hope that you would come for me."

Smoke was serious this time. "Coming for you is one

thing. Getting you out unscratched is quite another. I've heard about it from Ike and the hands, but tell me, how did it really happen? How did you let it?"

Sally made a pained expression. "Darn it, they caught me at the sink, away from my purse and gun. If they would have come twenty minutes earlier, while I was shelling peas, there isn't one of them would have left there alive. As it is, a couple of them didn't. And there's one I owe a lot of gratitude to. His name's Sam something-or-other. If you can spare him, do so." She described Sam Hutchins and told Smoke how he served as her protector when the others wanted to have their way with her. Smoke agreed that he deserved to live if possible. Then he excused himself and joined the other leaders for a short conference on how they would finish the remainder of the outlaw army.

"I don't need to tell you that we have to hit them hard. And all at once. First the sentries on the edges of town. Then we close off the only streets that lead out and move in on the center of the business district." He went on to give various assignments of specific buildings to the Indians and ranch hands. Zeke and Ezra he again positioned where they could bring long-range covering fire on the hotel. With that accomplished, and satisfied that the outcome would be in their favor, Smoke called for a good, hot meal before they went back to Dubois.

Running Snake looked across the expanse of tall grass to the village of the white men. He had grown up longing to do what he would in a minute be doing. As a small child, he had sat at the feet of the elders listening to their exciting tales of sweeping raids through villages: Arapaho villages, Absaroka villages, Sioux villages, and even white villages. They sang songs of the far off Tishmunga, Assinaboine, Modoc, and Hurons, who burned to the ground many settlements, villages, and even towns of the whites. The descriptions of flames leaping high thrilled him. Even with the admonition from Smoke Jensen to leave the people and their wood lodges alone and fight only the outlaws did not detract from Running Snake's expectations.

This day, he vowed, would be sung about for many seasons to come. He waited only the signal to attack. The men had painted for war, their ponies wore feathers and ribbons braided in their tails and manes. Hand prints, circles, and lightning streaks in warpaint protected the animals from the bullets of the enemy. When the signal at last came, they would all know greatness.

And then it came!

Five shots blasted across from them. Running Snake raised his lance above his head and threw back his head. Mouth open wide, he uttered a chilling war cry and heeled his pony in the ribs. With a snort and grunt, the close-coupled mount sprang forward. Behind him twenty-eight warriors shrilled their own challenges and urged their horses to a gallop. Ahead, gaping residents of Dubois pulled back into their houses and ducked low, or flattened out on the floors.

To their utter amazement, the charging Indians rode on past without firing a shot. At least not until a handful of outlaws offered resistance. Then, bows twanged and arrows moaned. Old trade rifles barked. Ancient percussion revolvers, their brass fittings worn thin, snapped in anger and put balls from .36 to .44 calibers into the chests and faces of the enemy. Three of Spectre's vermin died in the first hail of lead. Another took an arrow in the thigh and dropped to one knee. Before he could raise his .45 Colt to fire again, Running Snake drove the long, leaf-bladed head of his lance through the vulnerable chest. The flint point burst out the dying thug's back, a foot of the shaft with it. The force of the powerful arm of Running Snake and the galloping pony rammed the tip into the ground and pinned the writhing ruffian, an insect specimen on a display card.

Abandoning the spear, Running Snake waved his arms to direct warriors into intersecting streets. Before he knew

it, the Shoshoni leader found himself at the edge of the
business district. Outlaws swarmed in confusion. Dust rose
to obscure everything. Powder smoke wafted heavily on
an indifferent breeze. Quickly he dismounted and brought
his Spencer carbine to his shoulder. When the angry, shouting face of an armed white man came into the sights,
Running Snake squeezed off a round.

It blew away the lower jaw of the outlaw and sent him
reeling away down the street. Another quickly filled the
empty space, face contorted by rage, who charged toward
Running Snake with flame spitting from a six-gun, while
the Shoshoni worked the lever action to open the breech
and insert another paper cartridge in the breech. With too
little time, Running Snake tried to bring up his weapon as
a club, only to not have a need.

Smashed down by a tomahawk in the hand of Bright Sky,
the thug splashed the roof post of the saddlery shop with
his blood and brains. Running Snake completed loading,
added a percussion cap to the nipple and looked around.
To his surprise he saw they had advanced half a block. It
would not take long now.

White Beaver could hardly contain his Arapaho brothers. Several curvetted their ponies in nervous circles. He
vaguely believed it to not be right to have to wait for the
white men to start the fighting. Especially two times. White
Beaver was unaware that his thoughts echoed those of Running Snake. It would be so easy to race through these white
lodges and burn everything. Why kill only some of those in
the village? And why fight as ally to the Shoshoni? A spatter
of gunfire lifted the restraint on his warriors and they
streamed into town from the north.

To the right of White Beaver, one outlaw gaped in astonishment and shouted the news to his friends. "M'God, it's
Injuns! We're bein' attacked by Injuns."

White Beaver swung his right hand and arm across his

body and shot the outlaw with an old Dragoon pistol that had belonged to his father. The .44 ball smacked loudly into the left side of the thug's chest and tore its way through both lungs. Constantly advancing, White Beaver did not see him fall. Nor did he see a local resident dash out behind the line of Indians to retrieve the weapons of the human trash. Instead, he snapped his arm right and upward to aim at a man in the second floor window of a house.

For an instant, his eyes locked with those of the gunhawk. White Beaver read fear there. Then the white renegade's face washed into an expression of deep regret as he saw his death coming. The hammer fell on the Colt Dragoon in the hand of White Beaver. To the surprise of the Arapaho, the man was propelled forward by an unseen person to crash into the glass a moment before the bullet struck him in the neck. A voice followed.

"That'll learn ya not to pester my littlest girl." Quickly followed by, "Oh my God! That Injun shot him."

More surprise awaited White Beaver as the dying outlaw fell through the air, his trousers around his knees. He hit the ground hard and did not move. The Arapaho war leader rode on. Another block and he signaled his warriors to break off and enter other streets, to close off the center of the village.

Victor Spectre, or someone working for him, learned quickly from mistakes, Smoke Jensen observed. Several marksmen with long-range rifles had been stationed on the roofs of two-story buildings in the downtown area. From there they could make things uncomfortable for those closing in on the outlaw band.

At least until one got careless and exposed himself to the still-keen eyesight of Ezra Sampson. Dust puffed up from the vest of the hard case and his head snapped back. Only a fraction of a second later, Smoke heard the report of Ezra's Sharps. Immediately, two of the sharpshooters turned their attention toward the old mountain man.

Ezra's next shot went far wide of the mark and Smoke knew he had been nicked at the least. No such condition afflicted Zeke Duncan, who promptly accounted for another of the roof-top shooters. The man's back arched and he flopped face-first on a slate roof, to slide down to the edge and off. He landed on the ground with a loud plop. Four of the gunmen turned their fire on Ezra's position. Ezra gave them a taste of the same with a .56 caliber ball that took off the back of the head on one outlaw. Then Smoke heard a faint cry from Ezra.

"Dangit, you done hulled my shoulder."

Emboldened by this, the remaining marksmen incautiously showed themselves to jeer at the injured men. They quickly learned, much to their regret, that it took more than a scratch or a hole in a shoulder to stop one of the mountain breed. Two balls dropped as many men and the remainder scurried for cover.

A third suddenly yowled and went down with a Shoshoni arrow in his thigh. Smoke gave a slight nod of appreciation and moved to another vantage point, where he could study the ever-narrowing area where Spectre and his henchmen could still find shelter. Two thugs broke cover from inside the Watering Hole Saloon. With Smoke Jensen looking on, Ike Mitchell spun around the alley-side of the general mercantile and shot one rogue through the breastbone.

"Over here," Smoke shouted at the other when Ike's six-gun cylinder hung up on a backed-out primer.

Obediently, the fast-gun turned toward the sound of Smoke's voice. His eyes widened when he recognized Smoke Jensen. Smoke also registered an eye-squint of surprise when he saw the features of Whitewater Bill Longbaugh. No slouch as a gunfighter, Longbaugh had been rumored to have gone into the land swindle game and left gun-slinging behind. Perhaps the amount of the price on Smoke's head, or the chance to up his sagging reputation by claiming that head had been too tempting for Whitewater Bill.

Whatever the case, it became instantly obvious that Longbaugh lamented his decision. He crouched low, knees bent and torso leaned forward, as though already gutshot, and his face took on a pained expression. His thick lips worked and his voice came out cramped and weak.

"Awh, shit!" Then Longbaugh added in a whine, "Uh—Smoke, we don't have to do this."

"It's you came here lookin' for me. Now it's time you started the dance."

"There's no other way?" Whitewater Bill pleaded.

At the negative shake of Smoke Jensen's head, Whitewater Bill Longbaugh made a desperate grab for iron. He almost made it. He had his sweat-slicked fingers on the fancy pearl grips of his Smith and Wesson Scofield when Smoke cleared leather. Longbaugh gave a yank and the grips slid free of his insecure grasp. Instantly an expression of wild alarm washed over his face as he corrected and made another try.

Smoke had his barrel leveled and the hammer back when Longbaugh managed to draw the cylinder clear of his soft pouch holster. The barrel came out as Smoke's hammer fell. A powerful blow struck Whitewater Bill in the gut as he looped his thumb over the hammer. Staggered by the impact of the bullet fired by Smoke Jensen, he wobbled into the middle of the intersection. With great effort, he raised his wheel-gun again and fired a round. It turned out to be the closest to good luck Longbaugh had since he had encountered Smoke.

Fire erupted along the side of Smoke's left shoulder. The shallow wound had no effect on the outcome, since Smoke Jensen already had a second slug on its way to bury itself in the chest of Bill Longbaugh. Bright lights exploded behind the eyes of Longbaugh on impact. Quickly the shower of sparks faded into the eternity of blackness he would endure. Without regret, Smoke turned away to seek

out another of Spectre's henchmen. He had no trouble
finding one. One that came at him from behind.

Slobbering as usual, Farlee Huntoon rushed through the
bat-wings of the Watering Hole. "I gotcha, Jensen, by God,
I do," he chortled.

Smoke had barely started to turn when Huntoon raised
his Merwin and Hulbert .44 to make a back-shot. Even
with this head start, Smoke beat Huntoon to the first
round fired. The fat .45 slug sped from the muzzle of
Smoke's Colt and slammed into the protruding gut of the
hillbilly outlaw. Huntoon's mouth and eyes went wide and
round. Enormous pain erupted among his organs. In spite
of that, he managed to trigger his weapon.

Huntoon's bullet entered the side of Smoke's whipcord
jacket and bit into flesh, to form a short tunnel right below
the skin. Fire radiated through the body of Smoke Jensen
and he took a single, staggered step before he eared back
the hammer again and put another deadly projectile into
Farlee Huntoon. This time the hot lead destroyed the lower
lobe of Farlee's right lung. Choking on his own blood, the
West Virginia trash triggered yet a third cartridge.

With a shower of splinters, the slug buried itself in the
boardwalk, between the widespread boots of Smoke Jensen.
A black scrim, harbinger of things to come, settled over
Farlee's vision. He worked numb lips and tried to gulp back
a fountain of sanguine fluid that threatened to erupt out of
his mouth. He partly succeeded and panted out a few
words from a body rapidly weakening.

"I . . . think . . . I've . . . died."

Smoke Jensen watched the Merwin and Hulbert drop
from fingers no longer able to hold it, stepped in close and
spoke with whimsical assurance. "Not yet, but you will."

A flurry of shots from the general mercantile drew
Smoke's attention. Leaving the dying Huntoon behind, he
headed that way. Six Sugarloaf hands had some of Spectre's

minions pinned down inside the store. Before Smoke could reach the establishment and size up how to drive them out, Stumpy Granger let out a yowl and began to hop on one foot, holding the other in a gnarled hand.

"Bastit in there shot off a couple of my toes," he yelped to anyone who wanted to hear. Then he dropped the injured foot to the ground, took aim and fired at a wisp of dark shadow that crossed behind the shot-out display window. The heavy crash of a body striking the floor told the result. Stumpy cackled and reloaded his shotgun.

Smoke made a quick assessment and spoke to his hands. "There's seven of us now. Three of you take the alley. Go this way, there's no windows along that side, and head around back. Stumpy can stay here and lay down covering fire on the front. Perk, Buford, Handy, when you've had time to get in place, fire a shot and we'll charge them together."

"I like it, Mr. Jensen," Handy Barker spoke up.

Five minutes went by, during which Smoke wondered if the hands had run into a silent ambush, when he heard a muffled shot from the back of the building. Stumpy opened up with his shotgun, alternated with rounds from a six-gun, while Smoke Jensen, Jules Thibedeaux, and Mort Oliver rushed the storefront.

It became a mad scramble for the outlaws inside. Nine hard cases tripped over one another, fired blind shots into ceiling and floor and tried to force their way out the rear. Hot lead from the Sugarloaf hands met them. They recoiled and sought the wider, sliding door entrance on the loading dock. That only served to expose them more. Then Smoke and the two men with him entered the front with six-guns blazing.

Three of the trapped thugs tried to resist. They died before the eyes of their comrades in a swift, deadly duel. One gunhawk, smarter than most of them, laid his Colt on a counter and raised his hands. He spoke sage advice.

"There ain't gonna be any big pay-off for us. Me, I'm quittin' right now. Don't shoot, I give up."

In three minutes it had ended. Stumpy Granger took charge of the prisoners while Smoke had a look around the unnaturally quiet town. He soon discovered that all of the gunmen had either been killed, captured, or had fled. Except for a few, Smoke reasoned, who would hang close to Spectre, Tinsdale, and Buckner. That left Smoke Jensen with only one thing to do: hunt down the three responsible for all this destruction, misery, and death.

23

Their attention centered on the Watering Hole Saloon. While Smoke Jensen made preparations to storm the building from its blind side entrance and the rear, using his Indian allies to pour a withering fire into the front, a stout, florid-faced man with a shock of white hair and thin mustache, and a large shotgun, approached in a dignified manner.

"Mr. Jensen. You remember me, don't you?" At Smoke's hesitation, he went on, "I'm Issac Spaun, the banker. I helped you the last time you had to do this."

"Oh, yes. You did well, as I recall. It looks like you put in a hand this time, too."

Beaming, Spaun nodded vigorously. "That I did. And I came to offer more help if needed. I have fifteen men from town, all well-armed, who want to be in on putting an end to this terrible affair."

"There's not much to do, Mr. Spaun. We're going after the three responsible right now. They and a handful of gunmen are in the saloon over there."

"Well, we came to help. I suppose we could keep an eye on the second floor windows. And there's a door up there on the side."

Smoke gave him a warm smile. "Thank you, I appreciate you doing this. Pick your spots and we'll get started."

Four minutes later the Arapaho and Shoshoni warriors began to whoop and caterwaul, while they sent a shower of arrows in through the shattered casements. Some of the outlaws showed themselves in the window of the upper story, only to be shot away from their vantage points by the townsmen. Smoke Jensen let the softening-up go on for a full ten minutes. Then he ordered the ranch hands forward as the outside firing dwindled to nothing. Smoke personally led the assault on the side door.

Hank Evans used his burly shoulder to smash through the thin, poorly secured portal. Smoke rushed in at once and skidded to a halt. He found himself face-to-face with Ralph Tinsdale, who held a shot-barreled ten-gauge shotgun, pointed directly at Smoke's chest.

Smoke Jensen reacted automatically and instantly. He put a bullet between the eyes of Ralph Tinsdale. The shotgun in Tinsdale's hands discharged into the pebbly, pressed tin ceiling as he went over backward. Smoke swung to his right to confront Gus Jaeger and felt a powerful blow in his lower right side. His shot went wide of the mark, only nicking the Prussian gunfighter in his left upper arm. A quick glance showed Victor Spectre on the landing, a smoking revolver in one hand.

At the present, Smoke had no time for Spectre, who had tried to shoot him in the back. He returned his attention to Jaeger, who unlimbered two shots at Smoke, both of which missed. On the floor, Tinsdale shuddered his last and expired in a welter of blood. Smoke fired again, aiming at the center of mass on the chest of Gus Jaeger. The bullet went home and shattered the breastbone of the gang foreman.

Gus Jaeger took two unsteady steps backward and abruptly sat in a sturdy oak captain's chair. He looked down foolishly at his .44 Colt Frontier, as though he did not know its function. Then, remembering, he raised it to aim at Smoke Jensen. From the other parts of the saloon, Smoke heard scattered exchanges of gunfire. He had the position and time advantage over Jaeger and used it fully.

Smoke's bullet slammed into the face of Gus Jaeger to make an exclamation point of the gunhawk's long, patrician nose. The chair went over backward and Gus Jaeger sprawled in the clutches of Father Death. Sudden movement drew Smoke's attention to the stairwell. Victor Spectre had disappeared onto the second floor.

Favoring the wound in his side, and the stinging from arm and back, Smoke limped slightly as he followed after Spectre.

Every nerve screamed caution as Smoke Jensen climbed the stairway. Near the top, he bent as low as his injuries would allow and presented the least silhouette possible when he edged over the second floor landing. When no bellow of gunfire challenged him, Smoke came upright and stepped into the hallway. To add to his irritation, he found every door closed to him. However he chose to proceed he had the sinking sensation that he would select the wrong one. A quick glance to the rear showed him a narrow, steep stairway now covered by hands from the Sugarloaf. That decided him.

Smoke turned to his right and went to the front of the building. There he began a game of cat-and-mouse, seeking the villainous man behind so much misery. The first door he opened yielded up only three corpses. At the second, the hinges squealed loudly when he flung back the panel. One dead man there. Smoke moved to the next.

He felt resistance. The lock had been set against him. He stepped to the side, raised his left foot and readied himself. With all the force he could put behind it, he drove his boot into the portal beside the cast-iron lock mechanism. Metal shrieked, wood splintered and the door flew inward. From the bed, a thoroughly frightened soiled dove stared at him while she clutched a sheet to her bosom and made little squeaking sounds.

Smoke tipped his hat. "Sorry, wrong room. Are there any more of you up here?"

Mute at first, the lady of the evening eventually found her voice. "Y-yes. Two or three . . . I think."

"Thank you. I hope I don't bother them as much."

Banishing the vision of rounded silken shoulders, Smoke went on with his search. He found the next two rooms empty, then got a look at a pair of scarlet sisters in bloomers and shifts, who hugged each other in the middle of the room and wailed like banshees. Once again he apologized and moved on. Room after room proved to be empty. Smoke had taken only three strides past the last one he had inspected when the door to it silently swung open on well-oiled hinges.

His boots removed, Victor Spectre stepped out into the hallway on silent, stockinged feet. He held at the ready a Smith and Wesson .44, which he raised slightly to make a perfect back shot on Smoke Jensen. How much he would have liked to make Jensen suffer, but everything was in a shambles and he believed it best to simply get it over and escape. Carefully he lined up the sights.

That flicker of motion, reflected in the glass chimney of a kerosene lamp, alerted Smoke Jensen to the danger. Instantly, Smoke dropped to one knee, his Colt Peacemaker on the rise as he turned toward his would-be assassin. His .45 bullet reached Victor Spectre before the latter's left the barrel. Slammed into the wall, Spectre's slug went wild down the hall. He fought back pain and cocked his weapon again.

Fortune deserted Victor Spectre entirely then. Again, Smoke Jensen's round reached its target before his could be discharged. Shoved back through the open door, Victor went to all fours, and struggled dimly to stay alive. *Smoke Jensen had to die!* He told himself that in a litany of desperation. Obligingly, Smoke presented himself again. Victor was waiting for him and fired a shot that cut meat from the muscular underside of Smoke's left armpit. Then, suddenly, the world of Victor Spectre washed a brilliant red.

Scarlet changed to dazzling white, and then blackness. Shot through the head, Victor Spectre died without ever recognizing the error of his ways.

Not satisfied with the death of his enemy, Smoke Jensen continued to search the upper floor. Alarmed voices called to him from below. He recognized one as that of Monte Carson. Over his shoulder he called to his friend.

"Come on up, Monte. I just killed Victor Spectre. We have to find what else is up here."

Footsteps pounded on the stairs as Smoke went to the next room. Monte joined him after he had checked it. They headed to the last room at the head of the hall. Smoke stood to one side of the door, .45 at the ready. Monte turned the knob and flung the panel inward. Smoke spun around the jamb and into the room. There, a feeble Olin Buckner tried to raise a Winchester and fire at Smoke Jensen. A Shoshoni arrow protruded from his left shoulder and hampered his effort. Smoke crossed the room to the bed and yanked the rifle out of Buckner's weak grasp.

"I haven't seen you for a while, Buckner," Smoke gibed at the wounded man. "Can't say you're looking better than ever."

"You bastard," Buckner panted breathily.

Smoke examined the man. The local doctor had done a good job. Outside of the arrow, it appeared that the bullet wound Smoke had given him was healing well. It showed not a sign of angry red swelling that would indicate infection. That pleased Smoke Jensen mightily. He told Olin Buckner why.

"It looks like you will most likely live to meet the hangman, Buckner. If it's any consolation, I won't enjoy watching that. Public executions have never been my idea of having fun."

"A lot of good that does me," Buckner grumbled.

"I'm sure it doesn't overjoy you. Now, where's the loot your gang accumulated?"

"To hell with you. If that damned Indian had not shot me, I would have killed you the moment you came through the door."

Smoke's eyes narrowed. "You're not good enough. Never mind, we'll find it, and we'll do it before bringing the doctor to deal with that arrow."

Buckner paled. "You can't do that! I'm your prisoner," he squealed like a pinched pig. One look at the stern, unrelenting expression of Smoke Jensen, and his appeal died. "There's a door on the—on the balcony. It's locked. We put everything in there."

"Whoo-eee! Lookie there," Zeke Duncan howled gleefully when the door had been forced on the improvised strong room. "Must be a fortune here. Naw, three fortunes."

A shaft of light through the doorway gave a soft glow to stacks of gold and silver ingots. Bags of coin, and neat rows of paper currency, filled tables jammed tightly together. Enough money to boggle the minds of nearly anyone.

Nursing his wounded shoulder, Ezra peered over the shoulder of his partner. "Ya ask me, I allow as how it's all Smoke's now."

Smoke Jensen surprised and disappointed a number of people with his response. "No. It has to go back to the places they undoubtedly robbed on the way here. The banks, and stores, and stage lines can be identified and what remains divided among them. Which reminds me. Whatever money we find on these trash has to be the wages Spectre was paying them, so we can round that up and add it to this."

Zeke looked genuinely pained. "Sure is a shame to get hands on so much gold and have to give it back," he mourned.

At that moment, Sally joined the cluster on the balcony, accompanied by her bodyguard of Shoshoni warriors and ranch hands. She extended her hands to take one of each aged mountain man. "At least you got to rescue a lady in distress." Then she impulsively came forward and kissed each of them on the forehead.

Crimson rose from the collarless necks of their shirts to the roots of their thinning gray hair. Zeke began to shuffle his moccasins, while beside him Ezra dragged out a huge, paisley kerchief and mopped at his face to hide his blush and rubbed the toe of one boot with the other.

"Awh, gosh, ma'am, we was only doin' what's right," Zeke muttered softly.

Ezra shifted his cud of tobacco. "That's right, ma'am. We was only helpin' a friend. 'Twern't anything special."

"Well, I love you both for it," Sally declared with a sunny smile.

Tension eased and Smoke Jensen took the opportunity to make an announcement. "We'll rest up here a few days, then make ready to return to the Sugarloaf."

"So soon?" Banker Spaun objected. "You've hardly gotten here. We have to celebrate this great victory."

Smoke sighed, indicating his regret. "Sorry, but there's the spring branding to tend to and the herd needs culling for sale. Horses don't wait for people."

Spaun looked hurt, then brightened. Nodding toward the heavily blood-stained clothing of Smoke Jensen, he spoke with renewed encouragement. "Shot up the way you are, you won't be going anywhere for a while. We'll still have a few days to whoop it up."

Smoke Jensen cut his eyes to those of his wife. He saw the anticipatory gleam there and read it correctly. "Yes, I'm sure we will."

ORDEAL OF THE
MOUNTAIN MAN

1

Dust rose like a brown shroud around the rumps of a long string of shiny coated horses as they trotted, tails high, away from the lush pastures of Sugarloaf, Smoke Jensen's ranch. Smoke and a dozen hands, including Utah Jack Grubbs, Jerry Harkness and Luke Britton, had set out to drive a herd of two hundred remounts north to Fort Custer on the Crow Indian Reservation in Montana. It would turn out to be a much longer and harder journey than Smoke would have believed, becoming a grueling ordeal for Jensen and every man with him.

At the lower pasture fence, Sally and young Bobby Jensen sat their mounts and waved at the departing backs. Sally thought uneasily of the many times Smoke had ridden away on far more dangerous missions. Over the nearly ten years they had been married, after Smoke's first wife and son were brutally murdered, Smoke had strapped on six-guns, and frequently a badge, and had gone off to right the wrongs done to himself, or more often to others, even strangers. Smoke didn't see himself as any sort of Robin Hood, though he had read the legends as a youth, learning from the old mountain man, Preacher, what he had abandoned when he strayed from his parents' wagon as a half-grown child. The family had been bound for the Northwest Territory when he got lost in the wilderness.

Sally had first seen Smoke Jensen as a ruffian, a barbarian a *gunfighter.* She was teaching school at the time. Smoke came to town and cleaned out a gang of gun trash and saddle tramps, leaving a wide wake of bodies along the way. At first, his blood-thirsty conduct disgusted and frightened her. She had soon learned better, when he rescued her from the clutches of the gang boss. After that, she knew him as a tall, handsome man with longish, reddish brown hair and a ready smile. Now, she brushed aside such reflections and thought about the three hands who rode with him.

Jerry Harkness had been with Smoke, ever since he changed from cattle ranching to raising blooded horses. Jerry knew more about horses and their ailments than most veterinarians. He had grown up on a Thoroughbred farm in Kentucky. Lean and tall, Jerry was in his mid-twenties, with the bowed legs of a jockey, his muscles bunched and corded. He was, as their cook, Zeke Thackery, put it, smack-bang loyal. Jerry rode for the brand and would die for it if need be.

Another cut from the same mold was Luke Britton. A year or two younger than Jerry, he was an easy-going, even-tempered young man with a high school education, which was an exception for the times. Barrel-chested and broad-shouldered, he was frequently mistaken for a bare-knuckle boxer. Which he wasn't, but he could hold his own, much to the regret of many a proddy drifter who challenged him. Luke was a man to ride the river with.

Jack Grubbs was a short, bow-legged, salty horse expert with a checkered past. When the Sugarloaf foreman had interviewed him only three months earlier, he had been troubled enough by what he learned to turn Jack over to Smoke to question. Later, after he had hired Grubbs, Smoke told Sally that Jack had been in prison. A streak of wildness in his youth, Utah Jack had explained, which he had outgrown. Recalling his own past, Smoke had said that all Jack needed was a chance to redeem himself. For some reason, that now came back to give her a cold shiver along her spine. She shook it off and turned to their adopted son.

"Come on, Bobby. We might as well ride back to the house. We won't see them for two months," she added with a sigh. How she would miss her beloved Smoke, she thought as she brushed a lock of black hair back behind an ear.

Bobby wrinkled his freckled, pug nose and put words to her thoughts. "I'm gonna miss Smoke awfully." His fourteen-year-old's voice croaked with the awkwardness of change. "I hope nothing happens to them."

With Luke and Utah Jack on swing, Pop Walker on drag, Smoke Jensen rode at the front of the trail herd with Jerry Harkness. They headed for Wyoming in a lighthearted mood. Jerry cracked a constant string of Indian and-Politician jokes.

"D'you hear the one about the politician who went out to explain to the Sioux chiefs about the new treaty? He got out here with an interpreter who translated his words. After each sentence had been put in Lakota, the chiefs would grunt and say, 'Unkce!' He told them how they would be restricted to reservations from now on, and again they said, 'Unkce!'" Smoke was surprised that Jerry pronounced the word correctly: *Oon-K'CHAY.* "So this goes on until the end, when the chiefs all tapped their open palms with their eagle wing fans and shouted it three times.

"Then one chief got up and made a short speech. The interpreter told the politician that the chiefs thanked him for his good words and wanted to know if he wished to see some of Sioux life. The politician said that yes, he did. He had always wanted to see a buffalo hunt. It was arranged, and hunters rode out to find the bison while the chiefs and the politician started walking out on the prairie where the buffalo roamed. All of a sudden, the interpreter reached out and grabbed the politician's arm and stopped him from stepping in a big pile of buffalo bull plop, and said, 'Be careful not to step in the *unkœ*.'"

Smoke groaned and held his side; he had heard it before. "Jerry, don't you have anything better to amuse yourself?"

"Oh, sure. Did you hear about the Indian, the settler, and the politician who all died and wound up outside the Pearly Gates?"

"Spare me!" Smoke wailed in mock agony.

Four days later, six pair of eyes watched while the herd crossed the border from Colorado into the Wyoming Territory. One of the men in the small party, Yancy Osburn, turned to the others.

"That's them, all right. Burk, you ride north and let Hub Volker know they're on the way."

Ainsley Burk nodded, then asked, "What are the rest of you gonna do?"

Osburn pointed to the sleek remounts. "We'll follow along, send back reports on their movement."

"Good enough. I'll tell Mr. Volker that." Burk walked his horse away from his companions in order not to draw the attention of the drovers.

Once out of ear-shot, Yancy turned to the others with a nasty grin. "Well, boys, now that we've got Mr. Rule Book out of our hair, I've got me an idea how to pass our time while those nags move north."

"What's that?" two chorused.

Yancy gave them a wide wink. "I know of a nice little stagecoach we can rob."

Fifty miles northwest, Owen Curtis sat in his saddle, his left leg cocked up around the pommel, eyes fixed on the brown humps of his prize Herefords. He had paid a pretty penny for the first bull and three cows that formed the base of his herd. Over the years, he had added new blood, and his stock increased by nature's decree. Although the bevy was still small, Owen modestly counted himself as a rich man.

By the lights of many who struggled against the hostilities of Wyoming Territory, the severe winter weather, summer drought, and of course always the Indians, Curtis was indeed a wealthy, successful man. The rumble of distant hooves drew his attention to the head of the grazing beefs. Three of his hands kept them in a loose gather, allowing them to move slowly through the grassy meadow, eating their fill, while subtly leading them toward water. Seven riders appeared abruptly over the ridge of the basin, riding hard toward the cattle.

Owen Curtis looked on helplessly, stunned by the sight, as puffs of white smoke blossomed from the muzzles of the rifles the intruders held to their shoulders. Two of his men went down as Owen swung his leg into the stirrup and slid his Winchester from its scabbard. More gunshots crackled through the basin, and the cattle bolted and began to run wildly across the meadow. A half dozen more rustlers jolted down the side slopes of the bowllike pasture and began to turn the cattle back on their frightened fellows.

Curtis took aim and knocked one outlaw from his saddle with a bullet through the chest. He worked the lever action of the Model '73 and sought another target. The only problem was that he had attracted the attention of the thieves. Three cut their horses in his direction and bore down on the rancher. One of them raised a rifle and fired.

A bright, hot pain erupted in Owen Curtis' chest. Debilitating numbness swiftly followed. Owen groaned and tried to line up his sights on the man who had shot him. The other two fired then, and he dimly heard a bullet crack past his head. Sheer whiteness washed through his skull an instant later, and he sagged in the saddle, lost his grip with his knees, and slid to the ground.

Immediately, Hubble Volker snapped an order. "Get these snuffies under control and take 'em out of here."

"Where to, Mr. Volker?"

"Take 'em up to Bent Rock Canyon, Garth. There's plenty pines up there to build a holding corral."

Garth Evans reacted, predictably, at once. "You mean *work?* Get blisters on our hands?"

Hubble Volker laughed. "Ain't what you had in mind when you joined the Reno Jim gang, is it? Well, when you're countin' your share of the take, you'll forget the broke blisters an' sore muscles." He turned and shouted across the rumble of hooves to the others. "Get 'em under control. Head 'em up and slow 'em down."

With an anticipatory twinkle in his eye, Yancy Osburn watched the steady approach of the stage to Laramie. The heads of the six-up team bobbed rhythmically, and their powerful shoulders churned to draw the heavily laden vehicle forward. It had taken Osburn and his cohorts a day's ride to get in position. Yancy figured the herd of remounts would stay to the main trail, there being plenty of Indians roaming out there if they did not. Now they were about to relieve the Wells Fargo company of a good deal of loot. Osburn made curt gestures, directing his men to position.

He and Smiling Dave Winters remained in the center of the road, a fleshy barricade. The coach disappeared into a dip, and each of the outlaws raised a bandanna to cover his face. Weapons at the ready, they waited for the stage to reappear a scant thirty yards from them.

Pounding hooves, a jingle of harness and the creak of leather springs announced the arrival of the Laramie stage. The heads of the lead pair surged above the draw and gained the level. Quickly the rest appeared, and Yancy made out the driver and shotgun guard. He raised his Winchester and killed the guard before the driver could react to their presence in the road.

With only his six-gun for defense, the grizzled teamster hauled on the reins and applied the brake. The coach swayed to a dusty stop. Immediately the masked outlaws moved in.

Ansel Wharton had driven stages for Wells Fargo for nine years. In that time he had been robbed eleven times. He knew exactly what to do when he saw the masked bandits strung out along the road and blocking it ahead. Especially when the shotgun guard jolted backward and toppled over the side of the driver's seat. Meekly, all the while fuming inside, he hauled on the reins and brought the coach to a stop. The masked ones, like these, rarely killed everyone, he consoled himself.

"Afternoon," called the big one in the middle of the road. And Ansel could tell the sneer that had to be under the bandanna by the tone of voice. "We'll relieve you of the strongbox, if you please."

"What if I told you we don't have one?" He had to do that, company orders.

The bullet-headed outlaw in charge shook his head. "Then your wife would be a widow."

"Ain't got a wife. She died of the cholera back a ways. Now, let me see, was it in sixty-an'-four, or seventy-two?"

Anger rang in the snarled response. "Quit stallin' and hand it over."

Facing defeat and knowing it, Ansel shrugged. "I'd be obliged if you let me step down an' you had a couple of your friends remove it. It's a heavy sucker this trip."

Instantly the outlaw's mood changed. He laughed delightedly. "Mighty nice to hear. Good enough, old man, climb on down. Mind, keep yer hand clear of that hogleg yer packin'."

"Oh, I been robbed before. An' I know what to do, otherwise I wouldn't be here."

"There's some of you do learn, I do declare."

The Jovial Bandit, Ansel named him mentally. He'd remember the voice. The size, too. This one was a brute, a huge bruiser with broad shoulders, a hefty girth, thick arms and wrists. Looked like he could take on three men at once and not raise a sweat. He worked his way down the small, round, cast-iron mounting steps and walked to the head-stall of the lead horse.

"Keep him from spookin', don't ya see?" he explained to the highwaymen.

Yancy Osburn raised a ham hand to the brim of his hat and pushed it back. "Now there's a smart man. Good idee. Keep 'em calm while we relieve you of everything else and ask the passengers for a contribution."

Ansel hastened to give advise. "There ain't but one strongbox." He carefully omitted the shipment of gold bars under the backward-facing bench seat inside.

"All right, everybody out of the coach. We forgot to bring any fancy steps, so you'll have to jump down."

An angry voice of defiance came from an imprudent drummer inside the coach. "You're not going to get away with this."

His sample case cost a fortune, and he had no intention of losing it. His pudgy hand darted inside his pinstripe suit coat and came out with a nickle-plated Baby Smith .38. Hastily he fired a shot that grazed the shoulder of one of the outlaws to the side of the coach.

A roar of gunfire immediately answered him. Riddled by five bullets, the salesman slumped back in the leather of the seat and bled all over the coach and other passengers. Two women began to shriek and hug one another. Unfazed by the disturbance, Yancy Osburn motioned to the door again with his rifle barrel.

"Everyone out."

In short time, the passengers had been relieved of their valuables and herded back inside the vehicle. Osburn set two men to unharnessing the horses. Before they left, the outlaws scattered the team. Galloping off

with their considerable loot—the gold undiscovered—
they cast not a glance at the stranded occupants of
the stage.

"We'll have to hunt down them horses," Ansel told the
two male passengers. "One of you stay with the ladies and
see that they are all right. This is going to be a long day," he
predicted with considerable accuracy.

Reno Jim Yurian looked down from a long slope that
formed one wall of a box gorge known as Bent Rock
Canyon. A satisfied smile formed under the pencil-line
black mustache that adorned his thin upper lip. Not a sign
of the stolen cattle could be seen. His flat, gray eyes took on
an inner glow.

"We can keep them here until we have the horses as well.
Then take them all in to sell. There's a livestock broker I
know who doesn't look too close at brands."

"You mean your partner, Mr. Kel—" At an upraised hand
from Jim Yurian, the not-too-bright Hubble Volker cut off
his words before saying the name.

Always the dapper dresser, Reno Jim preferred red silk-
lined, black morning coats, with matching trousers,
brocaded vests and frilly, white shirts, with spills of lace at
front, collar and cuff. He adjusted the latter now as he
stared down his talkative second in command from under
the wide brim of the flat-crown, black Stetson he habitually
wore cocked at a rakish angle.

"Never mind who. The point is he will buy anything we
bring him. I want you to take over here for now and wait for
word on the horses. I'm going on up to Muddy Gap to see
that everything is ready for their arrival."

Another branch of the Reno Jim Yurian gang had grown
bored waiting for the fabled horse herd to come to them.
Like Yancy Osburn's men, they chose to engage in some

casual criminal activity to pass the time. The Bighorn and Laramie Line coach to Muddy Gap lumbered right up to them before the shotgun guard realized they had ridden into trouble.

"Stand and deliver!" demanded a swaggering, barrel-shaped highwayman with a gaudy ostrich plume in his floppy, chocolate brown hat.

"Like hell," roared Rupe, the shotgun guard, as he brought down his 10 gauge L.C. Smith and let go a load of 00 buckshot.

His shot column took the hat from the arrogant bandit and pulped his face with thirteen of the seventeen pellets. Immediately three of the holdup men leveled their six-guns and slip thumbed through a trio of rounds each, which shot Rupe to doll rags. Beside him, the driver slapped the wheelers' rumps with his reins to no avail as he took one of the shots intended for Rupe in his left forearm.

Muscles and tendons, strong and rangy from years of working a six-horse team, contracted and drove the broken ulna bone out of the driver's arm. He yowled and sat help-lessly while two robbers caught the headstalls of the leaders and stopped the coach.

"Everybody out. Show us what you've got."

A cawing voice of censure came from inside the coach. "Young man, that's a disgusting, vulgar thought. Shame on you."

Laughing outlaws surrounded the vehicle. "You must have been a schoolmarm, 'm I right?"

Guffawing, a freckle-faced, redheaded bandit touched the brim of his hat to the descending dowager. "It's been my experience that schoolmarms are most familiar with that famous challenge of the youngens, ma'am. You know? 'You show me yours and I'll show you mine' It was a lot of fun doin' that, as I rec'lect."

Examining him with cold, blue marble eyes from above jowls made enormous by excessive, snowy facial powder and carmine rouge, she snapped in tightly controlled outrage. "You are a most disagreeable young man."

"I reckon I am. After all, I do rob stages for a livin'. Hardly a recommend to the better element of society, 'm I right?"

Looking as though she might faint dead away, she fanned herself with a black-gloved hand. "Spare me from such depraved trash."

Anger flushed what could be seen of the outlaw's face. "I ain't trash. You get that straight, you old bat."

To emphasize what he had said, the redheaded bandit stepped in close and popped her in the chops. That proved too much for one of the male passengers. He leaped forward and drove a hard right into the gut of the impudent thug, who bent double and gasped for air. The defender of womanhood followed with a clout behind the ear, which dropped the young highwayman at the feet of the woman he had assaulted. Immediately a shot cracked over the heads of the passengers and the would-be rescuer fell dead on the spot.

Sobbing, the woman turned away. The bandits worked quickly after that. They relieved the passengers of all valuables and took the strongbox, missing the shipment of bullion the stage carried. Like the Wells Fargo team, the horses were run off when the highwaymen left.

2

A thin, white spiral of smoke came from the chimney of the Iron Kettle, the best eatery in Muddy Gap, Wyoming Territory. That it was the only public eating house in town, outside the hotel, the proud city fathers preferred not to acknowledge. Along the ambitiously wide main street, several prosperous business establishments had hung out their shingles. The raw wooden side walls and fresh paint of the building facades testified to the newness of this thriving community.

Among them were Harbinson's General Mercantile, the Territorial Bank of Muddy Gap, the only stone building in town, Walker's Saddlery, Hope's Apothecary and Sundries, Thelma Blackmun's Ladies' Fashions, Tiemeier's Butcher Shop, a blacksmith, the feed and grain store, and four saloons. At the north end of town stood a small, white, clapboard church. To the south, an equally miniscule schoolhouse.

Inside the school, class had been in session since eight that morning. The younger students, with the shorter attention spans, had become restless, eager for recess. The older grades, three through eight, laboriously attacked their assignments. Virginia Parkins, the schoolteacher, was listening to the sixth grade read aloud when the door slammed open against the inner wall and three large, loutish youths swaggered inside. Although she had two fourteen-year-olds and one fifteen in the seventh and eighth grades, Virginia recognized these ruffians as being considerably older, the youngest not under sixteen. She looked on them with a frown of irritation.

With expressions of blended contempt and disgust, the bullies strutted up the aisle and stopped beside the desk of young James Finch. One of them, a pig-faced boy named Brandon Kelso, spoke from the advantage of his height.

"Git outta that desk, Jimmy. You ain't got no business wastin' yer time here."

Eleven-year-old Jimmy Finch cut his eyes away from the imposing figure standing over him. He swallowed hard and spoke in a near whisper. "I gotta read next."

"What's that?" Brandon reached down with a large hand and yanked the slight, big-eyed boy out of his desk. "Your daddy needs you to help work stock. Now get yer butt outta this dump and do as you're told."

Beside Brandon, Willie Finch, Jimmy's older brother, sniggered. "That's right, Jimmy-Wimmy, Paw sent me to fetch you. Git yer skinny little ass movin'."

Thoroughly frightened, the small boy started moving his feet before Brandon Kelso lowered him to the floor. Outrage at this invasion overrode the usual quiet, nonaggressive demeanor of Virginia Parkins. She came to her feet so abruptly that her tall, backless stool toppled over and the book in her lap hit the floor with a loud bang.

All eyes turned her way. "Enough of your crude vulgarities, Brandon Kelso. You and these other louts need your mouths washed out with soap. Now, leave the children alone and get out of my classroom."

Brandon took a cocky step toward her. "Who's gonna make us, *Teacher*?" He sneered the last word.

Fat, porcine lips curled in contempt, Brandon Kelso studied the outraged young woman before him. She might make a good poke, he thought to himself, though he lacked any experience in such encounters. Couldn't be much older than himself. Those green eyes and the auburn hair, her wide, pouty-lookin' mouth, made his groin swell and ache just lookin' at her. Never thought she had any fire in her.

He had quit school four years ago, before *she* had come here. He got tired of doing the sixth grade a third time at the age of thirteen. Now, if she had been here, he might not have quit. She would have given him something to fill his . . . mind . . . with when he was sittin' in the outhouse. He made kissing motions with his lips. Her unexpected reaction surprised him.

Virginia turned sharply away and walked directly to one corner by the blackboard. She came back with a stout willow switch about four feet long. Before its purpose registered on Brandon Kelso, she began to lay about the hips and thighs of the three bullies. The limber switch made a nasty whir and sharp smack with each stroke.

When they all joined in a yelping chorus, she reached out and took the ear of the smallest in a firm grip and gave it a hard twist. Squealing, Danny Collins did a fancy dance step all the way to the door. Driving the others before her with the switch, Virginia hustled all three out onto the low stoop and hurried them down the steps. From the safety of the school yard, Brandon Kelso turned back to throw a final, ominous taunt.

"You know my father is on the school board. If you want to keep your job, you'd better watch what you do to me an' my friends."

Fists on hips, she called after them. "I'll risk that. Now, git. And don't come back."

That task completed, she returned to the schoolroom. Her expression calmed from its earlier outrage, she spoke in a soothing, quiet voice. "You may return to your desk, Jimmy. You will read next."

***

Riding his handsome, chestnut roan, Thoroughbred stallion down the center of the main street of Muddy Gap, Reno Jim Yurian sat tall in the saddle. He looked neither left nor right. With the schooled knees of a trained equestrian, he controlled his mount past the yapping of dogs, the shrill yells of children racing barefoot through the street and the bustle and whirl of wagons, horsemen and pedestrians. A light hand on the reins, he guided Walker's Kentucky Pride toward the tie rail in front of the Territorial Bank of Muddy Gap.

There the well-mannered horse stopped primly on a dime and waited without even an ear twitch while Jim Yurian dismounted. He looped the reins over the crossbar and removed his black leather gloves. Reno Jim used them to flick the spots of trail dust from his trouser legs and the sleeves of his immaculate swallowtail morning coat, then stepped regally up onto the boardwalk. Without a glance in the direction of the bank lobby, he walked to an extension of the plank sidewalk that ran along one side of the building into an alley.

At its end, he began to ascend a flight of stairs that ended on a small platform outside a door that gave access to the second floor. Halfway down the well-scrubbed and highly polished hall, he paused a moment before the frosted glass pane that occupied the upper half of a closed door. Taking a deep breath, he reached out and turned the knob.

He shouldered past the gilt-edged letters that spelled out in bold face:

BOYNE KELSO
GRAIN AND LIVESTOCK BROKER

He entered and flashed a winning smile at a willowy man in his early twenties, seated at the desk in the outer office.

"Good morning, Mr. Masters."

"Good morning, Mr. Yurian. Mr. Kelso is expecting you. Go right in."

"Thank you."

Robbie Masters looked after the visitor and sighed deeply. *Oh, God, he's soooo handsome,* he thought. Then he quickly busied himself with the stack of papers on his desk. Thus occupied, he did not see the sudden, hard expression of contempt on the face of Jim Yurian. Reno Jim opened the dividing panel and stepped into the sanctum of Boyne Kelso.

"I have good news, Boyne." When he closed the door securely behind him, he went on. "That herd of remounts on their way to Fort Custer will soon be ours."

Kelso revealed his surprise. "They really exist, then?"

"Yes. Some of my men watched them cross over from Colorado. Just short of three weeks, they should be on the Crow Reservation. That is, they would be, if we didn't have other plans for them."

Beaming, Kelso rubbed pudgy hands together. "Excellent, excellent. This calls for a mild celebration. I recommend the saloon-bar in the Wilber House Hotel. They pour a fine bourbon."

Reno Jim smiled back. "That sounds fine to me."

Together, they left the office and strode out onto the main boardwalk. They talked of inconsequentials as they strolled toward the hotel. Every man who passed respectfully touched the brim of his hat in salute to Boyne Kelso. A woman in a wide, gray, voluminous dress and white-edged bonnet of the same material nodded politely.

"Afternoon, Deacon Kelso."

"Good afternoon, Amanda," Kelso responded grandly.

Reno Jim smiled behind his hand. He knew that Kelso, born to a Protestant family in the north of Ireland, was considered a pillar of the community. Throughout Wyoming Territory, his rectitude was legend. No one questioned his scales, or the quality of seed grain he sold. Considered a loving husband and father, with charming, well-mannered children, Kelso was frequently held up as a paragon of societal excellence.

What would those fine, well-meaning people think if they knew the truth of Kelso's nature? Reno Jim mused.

Most likely they'd fill their fancy drawers. Well, they needed those well-intentioned souls. Without them, they could never survive in the business of robbing and rustling. Nor could they profit any longer from the land swindles handled by their trusty underling in the land office. When the good folk lost their meekness, terrible things happened. He shivered when he recalled what had occurred recently in Cripple Creek.

Somehow, the good people of that area had found out they were being bilked, cheated, robbed and even murdered by minions in the employ of Reno Jim Yurian. They had organized a Vigilance Committee. He suppressed a shudder as he visualized eleven of his best men dangling from ropes over the limbs of brooding oak trees, so much gruesome fruit. And his own ignominious route from Cripple Creek, tarred, feathered and slung over a pole. Reno Jim quickly banished the horrible visions as they reached the hotel.

Inside, seated at a rich cherrywood table, Reno Jim eyed the softly glowing brass lamps and fittings, the dark, lustrous sheen of the mahogany bar, the muted nature of the flocked, red velvet wallpaper, and sighed in contentment. This was the sort of world he preferred to live in. A coatless bartender, in sleeve garters and a blue, pinstripe, collarless shirt, brought them a crystal decanter of premium bourbon and two matching glasses. After he poured and departed, Kelso made quiet inquiry of Reno Jim.

"How soon will your men be coming here?"

"Some time next week. Certainly before the horses get here. I want to take them farther north."

"Good. I'll be busy over the weekend with the church council."

That brought a low chuckle from Reno Jim. "You had better keep your nose clean if you want to hold on to your fine reputation. But your plans are no problem. I'll also be busy over the weekend."

They talked on for a while. During their third glass of the smoothest, sweetest bourbon Reno Jim had ever tasted, a sudden commotion rose in the street outside. Shouts to the effect the stage had been robbed brought both men to their boots. They shouldered their way through the room and out the batwings into the lobby.

A crowd had gathered in front of the Bighorn and Laramie Stage Line office by the time Boyne Kelso and Reno Jim Yurian reached there. Men in overalls and flannel shirts, ranch hands in long-sleeved yoke shirts and jeans, merchants and their clerks in wool suit trousers, collarless shirts and aprons shouted questions.

"How many of 'em was it, Sam?"

Jaws at work on a cud of cut plug, the driver replied offhandedly. "Reckon there was nigh onto ten of them."

Over their entreaties, Boyne Kelso spoke loudly. "How much did they get, Sam? The bank had a shipment on there, you know."

Conscious of the need for secrecy in transactions, especially of bullion, Sam glowered at the big broker. "Didn't touch that. Never mind, Mr. Kelso, that's between the company and the bank. What's got me riled is that they killed Rupe."

"That's an outrage," Kelso thundered. "I certainly hope your company has enough compassion to arrange for some church ladies to go along when his widow is given the news. And I say now that these depredations must cease. To that end, I am offering a reward of five hundred dollars, dead or alive, for those responsible. Any idea who, Sam?"

Sam shook his head. "Nope. They all wore masks. Didn't give me a name, like that Black Bart feller out in Californey a while back. Jist took the money, and these folks' valuables, and rode off. We'd have been in sooner if they hadn't chased off our horses."

Kelso wrung his hands and cut his eyes from one man to another. "This is deplorable. We cannot tolerate this any longer. Where's the sheriff? Why hasn't he sent out a posse?" He turned back to the coach. "You folks who were on the stage, let me offer my condolences that this reprehensible deed was done so near to our fine community. If any of you are completely out of pocket, come see me. I have a grain and livestock brokerage above the bank. The name's Kelso."

With that, Kelso turned away and stalked toward the sheriff's office. Hiding his grin, Reno Jim Yurian went the opposite way to retrieve his horse from in front of the bank. In ten minutes he rode clear of town, headed to meet his gang and see what new profit had been gained in the holdup.

Across a dividing ridge, Smoke Jensen decided the time was right to take care of what had been bothering him for the past day and a half. He reined in and motioned Jerry Harkness to take the herd on. He sat his new 'Palouse stallion, Cougar, while the remounts legged their way past. His face set in concentration, Smoke seemed not to notice the dust that boiled up.

When Luke Britton, riding drag today, ambled by, Smoke gave him a light wave and dropped back down their trail. Near the crest of the ridge, he angled into a craggy gorge and reined up. Five minutes later, three seedy-looking characters, whom Smoke had seen several times trailing them, walked their mounts into view. At once, Smoke rode out and confronted them, Cougar crosswise on the trail.

Smoke kept his voice level as he addressed them. "I think it's time you fellers stopped trailin' us."

"Who says?" the one in the middle challenged.

"I do."

Face suddenly flushed with anger, the proddy one spat at Smoke. "That don't cut no slack with me."

Smoke cut his eyes to each in turn. "Then I'll give you a choice. You can turn around and light a shuck out of here, or you can tell me why you are following us."

Through a sneer, the mouthy thug posed a question. "What if I said we was lookin' for to hire on?"

Shaking his head as though saddened, Smoke said, "Then I'd have to call you a liar."

"That does it, by God. That surely does it," roared the aroused hard case as he dipped a hand swiftly toward his six-gun.

He had just cleared the cylinder of his Colt from leather when Smoke's .45 Peacemaker blasted the stillness of the rolling countryside. A slug spat from the muzzle and smacked solidly into the center of the chest of the saddle trash. His life shattered within him, the hard case reared sharply back against the cantle with enough force to snap the hat from his head. Then he went boneless and flopped onto the rump of his nervous, dancing horse.

By then, the other two had unlimbered their revolvers and now attempted to bring them up in line with this unnervingly fast stranger. They failed miserably in the attempt. Smoke's second round punched into the right side of the chest of the gunman nearest to him and shattered his shoulder blade. The thug's Smith American went flying in reflex to the pain that exploded in his body.

His companion thought better of further aggression. He turned his horse, spurred it to a gallop and sprinted for the top of the rise. As he disappeared over the crest, Smoke Jensen walked Cougar over close to the wounded man.

"Now, tell me. Who are you ridin' for?"

Groaning, the trash looked up at Smoke through a haze of pain. "We ain't workin' for nobody. We—we only figgered to cut out a few head and make a little money off 'em. That's all, mister."

Smoke's expression registered disappointment. "Why is

it I don't believe you? Well, in the event you all of a sudden remember who it is, you can tell him the reason you got shot up is that you ran into Smoke Jensen."

His shock-pale skin went even whiter. "Oh, Jesus."

"He can't help you. You ride on out of here while I pick up that six-gun. We've got a herd to deliver."

3

A great, bloated, orange sun hung on the eastern horizon over Muddy Gap. The smoke from wood-burning cookstoves streamed from stovepipes. Shrill voices of children, out to do their chores, could be heard in the backyards of their homes.

A small girl in a paisley dress called from the hen yard. "Chick—chick, here, chick-chick-chick!"

A boy, somewhat older than she, could be heard in a low barn. "Soo-oo, Bossy. Hold still. I gotta milk you."

From a spanking-new carriage house, another boy announced cheerily, "Here's your oats, Prince."

On a hillside overlooking the town, Hubble Volker sat his mount at the center of a crescent formed by the Yurian gang. Together, they gazed down on the scene of domesticity. Volker waved a hand in the direction of Muddy Gap.

"We'll give 'em a little more time. Let the shops open up, and the bank. Then we make our move. Too bad the boss couldn't come along. He'd have enjoyed this."

Hairy Joe spoke over the rumble of his stomach. "I smell biscuits bakin'. Sure could use some of them."

Volker gave him an amused look. "Maybe you can he'p yerself to some when we clean out the town."

Pleading sounded in Joe's voice. "But, I'm hongry now. What we gonna eat?"

"Air, if you didn't bring something along," Volker told him with a snort. "Me, I've got me some corn bread from last night, an' some fried fatback. Shore gonna taste good. You gotta plan ahead, Hairy Joe."

Hairy Joe appealed to a generosity that did not exist. "Least let me have shares in some of that, Hub."

"Nope. Ain't got enough. Ask the other boys. They only brung enough for theyselves, too."

Scowling, Hairy Joe subsided. He cut envy-filled eyes to the rest of the gang while they munched on their leftovers. Unappeased, his stomach continued to growl. For solace, he rolled a quirley and puffed it to life. The smoke wreathed his head.

Two hours later, the main street began to bustle with merchants and their employees. Doors opened and shades went up. A few early customers rolled into town on buckboards or on horseback. Hubble Volker looked on, weighing the right time. It would not be long, that much he knew.

Riding in twos, as directed by Yurian's second in command, the gang entered the main street of Muddy Gap from different directions. Each pair went to an assigned business front. Hub Volker and Garth Evans entered the bank. One teller looked up and peered at them from under a green eyeshade, a welcoming smile already forming on his lips. Then he saw the weapons in their hands and the masks over their faces.

"OHMYGOD!" he blurted.

Volker took immediate command. "That's right, folks, this is a holdup. Everybody put your hands over your heads. You tellers, fill moneybags with everything in your tills. You, Mister Banker"—he gestured with the muzzle of his Merwin and Hulbert revolver to the portly gentleman seated in a glass cubicle behind the tellers' cages—"you be so kind as to step over to the vault and empty it out."

Stammering, the banker refused to comply. "You can't get away with this. The marshal will come running, and the sheriff is back in town. I'll not help you steal from these good people."

"In that case, we don't have any more use for you," Volker told him.

Hub raised the Merwin and Hulbert, and it roared loudly in the confined space. Glass bulged inward and showered musically to the floor as the bullet passed through the dividing window and struck the banker in the forehead. He flew backward out of his padded, horse-hide swivel chair and crashed noisily against a file cabinet.

Three women customers began a chorus of shrieks and wails at the sight. Volker shoved through the swinging gate that divided the lobby from the working end of the bank and yanked a bug-eyed clerk from his desk. He shoved him toward the big safe. "You'll do. Get busy stuffin' these bags with money."

"We'd better work fast, Boss," Evans advised. "That shot's sure to bring the law."

Volker's bandanna masked his nasty smile. "Good. Then we won't have to waste time huntin' them down."

Muffled yet recognizable yells of alarm came from other businesses. A man in shirtsleeves ran from the haberdashery. "Help! I'm being robbed."

A second later, a sharp report ended his appeal for aid. The clothing merchant staggered in the middle of the street, went rubber-legged and fell in a heap. From the general mercantile came the cymbal crash of disturbed galvanized washtubs and buckets. Moments later, two masked men swaggered out onto the street. One clutched a fat cloth bag. Behind them, the proprietor appeared in the doorway, a shotgun in his hands.

Swiftly he brought the weapon to his shoulder and fired. He had been too hasty. Only three pellets entered the back of the robber with the loot. Most of the shot tore into the cloth sack. It erupted in shreds; coin and paper currency flew in all directions. Three of the gang, left to cover the street, turned their revolvers on the storekeeper and cut him down in a hail of lead. Most of the nasty work had been done by then. Two-thirds of the Yurian gang had gathered in the middle of the block, ready to ride out.

At last, Hub and his cohort stepped out of the bank, arms filled with canvas money satchels. "All right, boys, mount up," Hub called.

Belatedly the law showed up in the person of Sheriff Hutchins and two deputies. Hub slung the drawstrings of his money pouches over his saddle horn and turned to respond to the warning shot and the shouted demand to surrender.

Filling his hand with the Merwin and Hulbert, he triggered a round that nicked a nasty gouge along the point of the sheriff's shoulder. To his left, another member of the gang threw a hasty shot at one of the deputies. Then bullets flew from both sides. The sheriff took cover behind a rain barrel and fired around one side.

Gundersen, a chubby outlaw originally from Norway, grunted and clutched his belly. Hub shouted to the man closest to Gundersen. "Give him a hand getting mounted. We've got to get outta here."

In the next instant, Hub Volker saw his chance and raised the Merwin and Hulbert to sighting position. He squeezed off a shot and watched in satisfaction as the bullet struck the sheriff full in the mouth. A spray of blood, bone, hair and tissue erupted from the back of the lawman's head.

By then, the shock had worn off some of the townsmen. A new crackle of gunfire rippled down the street. One of those offering resistance was the mayor, Lester Norton. Determined to contain them until the law and volunteers could act, he alternately fired and ducked from obstruction to obstruction as he steadily advanced on the gang. He was in midstride when a bullet fired by Evans smashed into his right shoulder and knocked the Winchester from his hands. Wisely, he went down and played dead. The gang had had enough. Ducking low, the final few swung into their saddles.

Firing wildly, the outlaws put spurs to their horses and thundered along the main street while citizens ducked and shot blindly back. Two men from the Sorry Place Saloon ran to the side of the sheriff and knelt to give him aid. They soon saw that he needed none.

One of them immediately lost his breakfast. The other stood and cursed the outlaws as they stormed out of town. Only a scatter of stray shots pursued them. In a minute, except for a thin dust cloud, nothing marked their presence at all.

In the aftermath, while the wounded received care and the dead were carried off to the undertaking and used furniture parlor, Boyne Kelso sought out Mayor Norton. He found the mayor being patched up by Doc Vogt outside Harbinson's General Mercantile. Arranging his features into his best expression of concern and outrage, he took the mayor aside to the saloon-bar of the hotel. There, amid much hand wringing and gesticulating, he poured out his prepared spiel.

"Lester, I am deeply concerned by this. Why, only a handful of volunteers went out as a posse, led by our least experienced deputy. The sheriff is dead, and Grover Larsen is cowering at home, afraid the outlaws will come back. What I said about the stage robbery only last Friday goes double for this assault on our very homes."

Lester Norton cut his eyes to Boyne Kelso in a sideways glance. "You mean you'll put up a thousand dollar reward?"

Kelso mopped his brow and took a long pull on his cup of coffee. "Yes, of course. Two thousand if that is what it takes. I've talked to Ralph at the bank. He's president now, I suppose. They'll put up money for the reward also. Eb

Harbinson is still picking up cartwheels and gold eagles, but he offered a hundred. Got most of his back, even if they did kill his father. But the point is not that."

Norton took a swallow of coffee. "What is it?"

Kelso polished off the last in his cup and poured for both of them. "What is most important is that we must reinforce the law in this town. We have to find a replacement for Walt Hutchins immediately. We both know that Larsen is too old for his job. He's slow and the sound of gunfire frightens him. He needs to be replaced as well as the sheriff. Believe me, until we do, this town is terribly vulnerable." His warning was not lost on Mayor Norton.

Since early morning it had been building. Smoke Jensen kept a watchful eye on the towering clouds to the southwest. Slowly they progressed across the eastern downslopes of the Rocky Mountains and spread out across the high plains country. The storm had all the looks of a vicious, straight-line squall. Among land born storms, such a phenomenon ranked second only to a tornado in ferocity. Smoke had encountered only four in all his years in the High Lonesome. One of the old fraternity of mountain men had tried to explain it to him once.

"It happens when a whole passel of cold air spills down the face of the mountains to collide with warm, moist air slidin' up from hotter country in Texas and New Mexico and the desert of Chihuahua," Smoke had been told. "When they impact it births tre—men—dous thunderstorms, Wal, boy, hail, lightnin' an' goose-drowner rains roar across the prairie. Sometimes some of them form slightly concave straight-line winds of fearsome velocity." Old Spec Dawes had continued his description to a rapt Smoke Jensen. "Like their big brothers, the twisters, they can strip the roof off a building, lift a cow off its hooves and drive straws through a tree trunk.

"Anything movable, an' a lot that ain't," Smoke had been

told, "is driven ahead of the powerful blast rather than being lifted into the sky. Bowled over and rolled like a chile's ball, a man can easily be reduced to a pulpy bag of broken bones."

Memory of that description, and the storms he had actually experienced, made a tiny flicker of unease in Smoke's mind. It also kept him extra watchful.

Shortly before the nooning, the light zephyrs that had brushed the manes and tails of their horses dropped abruptly, then picked up as a stronger breeze from a slightly different quarter. Smoke frowned and again cut his eyes to the dust cloud. What he saw decided him to ride ahead a ways and look for a sheltered gully or basin where they could hold the remounts and wait out the storm. His search proved harder than he had expected.

Two miles ahead he found a ravine that was too small. Determined, he rode on. Cougar began to sense the change in the atmosphere. He rolled big, blue eyes and snorted, his ears twitched, his tail swished nervously, and his spotted rump writhed as though snakes crawled under it. Another mile went by without any likely spot. Smoke had about decided to turn back after covering what he estimated to be half a mile more. Then he saw it.

Sunlight cast stark shadows over a cut in a hill. A fold, eroded into the rising mound, lay behind. Perfect, Smoke saw when he entered. The high side of the bluff lay between the direction of the storm and the small, closed valley formed by rushing water in ancient days. At once he turned back to lead the horses there.

"There's shelter ahead that we can use," Smoke told Harkness when he returned to the gather of animals. He cast a precautionary gaze at the approaching storm. "If we have time, that is."

Over the next hour the dingy brown mass swirling in the air extended upward and out over the drovers as they worked Smoke's horses toward the sheltered valley. The stout breeze stiffened into a harsh wind, chill and turbulent. Uprooted sagebrush bounded along the ground. Small dust devils formed and raised dirt, leaves, and pebbles into the air, only to dissipate and spew their content across the faces of the men and the coats of their mounts.

Steadily the force increased. Invisible hands tugged at the sheepskin coat Smoke Jensen had shrugged into when the temperature had dropped drastically. The gale acquired a voice. Shrill and eerily mournful, it moaned around the ears of the ranch hands. Riderless, the remounts flicked their ears in agitation. It would not take much more to spook them, Smoke knew, and only a third of them had been driven into the narrow passage that led to the valley beyond.

Suddenly the western horizon washed a blinding white. Sheet lightning sizzled and crackled through the air, followed by a cataclysmic bellow of thunder. Caught in the strobing effect, the legs of the half-broken horses went all akimbo. For a second they appeared to skid in place. Then they broke in every direction. Panic reigned as the straight-line, cyclonic storm slammed into them. Rapidly the remounts ran before the punishing tumult. At once the men went after them.

With only a third of the two hundred horses headed into the little valley, the hands had no choice but to pursue. Battered by rain blown nearly horizontal, the Sugarloaf riders streamed helplessly after the frightened critters. Blinded by the huge, silver streaks that fell with sodden determination, they made poor headway against the vicious bursts of frigid air. Realizing the impossibility of it, Smoke Jensen shouted himself hoarse in an effort to call back his men.

Slowly they gave up, knowing that they would have an even harder time recovering the animals after the storm had blown beyond them. Together they sought shelter in the valley along with Smoke. Above their heads the sky turned an ominous black.

* * *

In half an hour the trailing edge of the storm spattered itself out on the leaves of cottonwoods that ringed the valley. With Caleb Noonan left behind to watch over the sixty horses that had not fled the storm, the rest set out to search for the scattered remounts. Smoke had no doubt that they had a long, hard task ahead of them.

"We'll spread out and work in circles," he suggested. "Bring them back as you find them."

After a fruitless afternoon of search, Smoke had a flash of inspiration. While the others speared chunks of fatback from tin plates and chewed glumly, he outlined his idea.

"Tomorrow morning we're going to try it another way. Luke, I want you to go back to that valley after you eat. Bring up a couple of mares. It would be best if you can bag at least one that is in season."

Grinning riders cut their eyes from Smoke to one another in knowing glances. So long as the wind held from the southwest, that would sure as shootin' work. Smoke came to his boots and went to the nearby stream to scrub his plate clean with sand. Luke Britton left with a good two hours' light remaining.

Later, with the sun only a pink memory on thin bands of purple clouds in the west, the tired hands rolled up to rest until morning. Smoke Jensen sat alone, smoking a cigar beyond the glow of dying coals. Lost in deep thought, his reverie was not disturbed even by the mournful hoot of an owl in a pine nearby.

Luke Britton considered himself lucky to find one mare in heat. He brought back three others, and wily horse experts, Jerry Harkness and Utah Jack Grubbs, offered advice on how to make the most advantage of this. What they came up with required a rather indelicate procedure involving some old cheesecloth from a side of bacon and a bit of messy work around the tail end of each mare. When they had finished, Smoke sent the dozen men out in groups of three.

Within half an hour, Jerry Harkness rode in with a dozen snorting, skittering young stallions in tow, led by ropes around their necks. He gave Smoke a cheery wave. "It worked, all right. What do we do with them now?"

"I'll hold them here. Go on back and find me some more. Ah—Jerry, you did good. Any more on the way?"

"Sure enough. Jeff is about twenty minutes behind me. He has a string of twenty."

Smoke brightened. "At this rate, we might be on the trail again by this time tomorrow."

Sunlight twinkled down on the puddles in the ranch yard thirty miles to the northeast of Muddy Gap. Elmer Godwin looked out from the barn, where he had been mucking out stalls. He liked working for Sven Olsen, an even-handed, fair-minded man who paid well and whose young wife set a good table. He also had a true friend in Sven's oldest son, Tommy. A gangling orphan in his late teens, Elmer had grown close to Tommy over the past nine months he had worked for the Olsens.

During that time, they had trapped for furs, and he had taken Tommy hunting, fishing, and even bare-bottom swimming in the coppery brown, shallow water of the Platte River. Still a kid at heart, Elmer had enjoyed it every bit as much as Tommy. His reflection ended when the subject of his thoughts called from inside the barn.

"Awh, c'mon, Elmer, I ain't gonna do this all alone."

Elmer turned back. "Jist catchin' a breather an' a cup of water from the pump."

Tommy Olsen appeared in the open barn door. Big for his age, he was a sturdy, stocky boy with a shock of auburn hair and a mask of freckles that covered both round cheeks. He examined Elmer with clear, blue eyes that twinkled with intelligence.

"We goin' swimmin' after this is done?"

Elmer grinned. "Sure are, Tommy. We'll take along a bar of soap, wash off this stink."

"Wheewu! You tellin' me. The pigs are worst. Be glad when that's over."

Before Elmer could make answer, he stiffened and cocked an ear to the distance. "Quiet," he cautioned. "Someone's coming."

Tommy's eyes went wide. "Is it Injuns?"

Turning his head to better hear, Elmer frowned. "Don't think so. Hoofbeats are too regular. Like soldiers riding." That reminded Elmer of something else. Over the last two months he had heard a lot of talk about bandit raids. "Tommy, let's go to the house. We have to tell your mother and sisters. Then you take a gun and go with them to the root cellar. I'll fetch your paw."

Reunited with his gang, Reno Jim Yurian led them up the lane to the Olsen ranch. When they reached the barn-yard, they spread out and advanced on the house. Reno Jim raised his hat with his left hand, his right on the pearl grip of his six-gun.

"Hello, the house. Your best chance is to come on out and not show any fight. Otherwise, someone is going to get hurt."

In answer, a rifle barrel slid through a firing loop in a thick wooden shutter that had been hastily closed. "Git off this place, mister, or it'll be you who is hurtin'."

It was a young voice, a boy not yet out of his teens, Jim Yurian correctly surmised. He had never met Elmer Godwin, yet he could clearly visualize him. Scrawny, scared out of his boots, perhaps his father gone for the day, his hands shaking so much he could not draw a good bead. With exaggerated slowness, Reno Jim drew his nickle-plated Merwin and Hulbert .44 and pointed it roughly in the direction of the window.

You've had your warning, boy. Now you and everyone else come out of there."

Fear pushed young Elmer to incautiousness. "You can go to hell!"

Reno Jim put a shot into the wooden shutter an inch above the rifle barrel. At once the other outlaws began to blaze away. Suddenly one of them gave a startled yell and pitched forward over the neck of his horse. The tight circle of hard cases blew apart.

Gunmen spun their mounts while others rode out to ring the house. Those who had turned saw a stocky man kneeling in the doorway of the barn, a rifle to his shoulder. He fired as his presence registered on the gang. Three of them threw shots at him, all of which missed. Sven Olsen did not.

His next round clipped the hat from the head of Prine Gephart and cut a bloody gouge along the crown of his scalp. Wavering in his saddle, Gephart let his mount amble him away from the line of fire. Dazed, he indistinctly saw the demise of the valiant rancher through a haze of red, as blood washed down his forehead and into his eyes.

Half a dozen more bullets crashed into the barn door. Two of them struck Sven Olsen in the chest and abdomen. Knocked from his kneeling position, he sprawled, his Winchester inches from his outstretched hand. A wave of dizziness swept over the rancher. He blinked and bit his lip against the pain in his belly. Gradually it numbed to a low throb. Dimly he saw the outlaws abandon him for already dead and turn back to the house. Elmer was in there alone, the dying man thought in desperation.

A rain of slugs battered the Olsen house. Chunks of wood splintered away from the shutters, and the rifle barrel withdrew. Only to reappear at another window. Impatient at this stubborn resistance, Reno Jim dismounted and gestured to three others to join him. They ran to the porch, where they were in under the field of fire from the window.

Reno Jim saw a sturdy bench against the outer wall and produced a grim smile. "Here we go, boys. Grab hold of this bench and we'll batter down that door."

With four strong men on the task, the portal rang and shuddered at each impact. After ten stout crashes, the crossbar began to yield. It splintered at first, then cracked loudly. Another push and the door flew inward.

Two outlaws, followed by Reno Jim, burst into the room. They caught movement to one side and swung their hot-barreled six-guns toward it. Reno Jim proved faster than any of his men. Coolly, he raised his .44 Merwin and Hulbert and shot Elmer Godwin through one lung and his heart.

Without another glance at the youth he had murdered, Reno Jim issued crisp orders. "All right. Clear out anything of value, then set this place afire." Out on the porch, he called to the remainder of the gang. "You boys round up all the stock and head 'em up. We'll drive them to Bent Rock Canyon with the rest."

4

Two days after the raid on the Olsen Ranch, Smoke Jensen and his hands rode into Muddy Gap. At first they did not understand the furtive, nervous, and downright suspicious glances afforded them by the residents. They got a clearer idea when they began to note bullet holes and scars on the building fronts, and above the town, on a knoll not yet fenced and consecrated for the purpose, fresh graves in what would be the town's cemetery.

Smoke Jensen passed on his observation to Utah Jack Grubbs. "Looks like these folks have run into some trouble of late."

"Injuns, do you think?" Utah Jack offered.

"From the looks of all the bullet holes and the scared way the folks have been looking at us, I'd say white men. Outlaws from one gang or another."

Utah Jack discounted that. "Surely they have some law in this town. That the place ain't shot up worse than it is, I'd say whoever it was, they got run out real fast."

Smoke shrugged. "You may be right, Utah. We'll find out soon enough." He nodded ahead in the street, to where half a dozen armed men stood resolutely, weapons at the ready. They formed a wedge that denied passage to anyone not at a full gallop. At the head stood a man with a bandaged right shoulder.

When Smoke and his hands came within twenty feet, that man raised his arm to signal a halt. "That's far enough, strangers. Who are you?" He shifted uneasily. "And what's your business in Muddy Gap?"

Smoke Jensen did not answer directly. "Looks like you had some trouble here lately."

A frown creased the mayor's brow. "And how do we know you're not the ones who caused it? Besides, you haven't answered my question."

Smoke went unfazed. "My fault. M'name's Jensen; I'm from the Sugarloaf horse ranch in Colorado. These are some of my hands. We're driving a herd of remounts to Fort Custer."

Mayor Norton's frown deepened to a scowl. "You're going on the Crow Reservation with only four men?"

A light smile brightened Smoke's face. "Nope. The rest are holding the herd outside town."

Norton cradled the shotgun in the crook of his right arm, winced at the pain in his shoulder, and scratched his head with his left hand. "Jensen, you say? Might you be any relation to a fellow named Smoke Jensen?"

"Might be and am. Folks have called me Smoke for a long time."

Hope flickered momentarily on the face of Lester Norton. He took a step forward, extended a hand. "Mayor Lester Norton. My pleasure. It's said that you have been a lawman for many years now. A U.S. marshal?"

"Deputy, yes."

"Are you still carrying a badge, Mr. Jensen?"

"Not at the moment."

A raucous bray came from one of the saloons. On top of it came a yelp of protest in a decidedly feminine voice. Smoke cut his eyes that direction for a moment. Mayor Norton looked that way also, his glower even more thunderous. He made an inviting gesture to Smoke Jensen.

"I would be obliged if you would accompany me to the Iron Kettle, Mr. Jensen. There is something important I wish to discuss with you over a cup of coffee."

Smoke shrugged. "Fine with me. We came in for supplies. That won't take a lot of time. You boys might as well come along," he told Jerry Harkness and his hands. "Load up on some real ghluffi ou iiii "

Walking their horses to a tie rail, the Sugarloaf party went with the mayor to the corner cafe. Once inside, Jerry and the other hands took a separate table. Smoke seated himself across from Mayor Norton. His gaze took in the blue-checkered, lace-trimmed curtains at the window, the row of shiny copper molds on a shelf above the back counter and a sturdy potbelly stove at the center of the rear wall. A serving window under the shelf gave a view of the kitchen beyond. A still-trim woman who might have been in her early thirties brought them coffee without being told. When she had served them and gone to take the orders of the ranch hands, the mayor leaned across the table and spoke with some urgency. Smoke could smell his pitch a mile off.

"We're in trouble here. Over the five days since those outlaws raided town, half the riffraff in the territory have drifted into town. It wouldn't take much of a spark, or a whole lot of smarts, on the part of some to make a move to take over the town. We need you, or someone like you, to clean the trash out of Muddy Gap."

"Why not have the sheriff take care of it?"

"Sheriff Hutchins was killed by the bandits. We buried him two days ago up on the hill out there."

"You have a town marshal, don't you?"

Mayor Norton looked Smoke Jensen square in the eye. "Marshal Grover Larsen is too busy hiding under his bed to help us against this glut of ne'er-do-wells."

"But, why me? I have a herd of horses to take care of. I have a contract and a deadline to meet."

"First off, because I have heard that you are a fair and

honest man, a top-notch lawman, regardless of the wanted posters and what they say. Secondly, you have acquired some notoriety as a gunfighter. Third, because you are here, we don't waste time we may not have sending for someone. Lastly, because the town can pay handsomely for your services. Can't your hands take care of the horses for a while, even a few days? Surely you can clean them out in less than a week."

"I could, given some help."

Lester Norton glowed with expectation. "Then you'll undertake to do it?"

Smoke drained the last of his coffee and came to his boots. Leaning toward the mayor, he made his decision. "I'm sorry, Mr. Mayor. I'm not your man. We can't be late at Fort Custer or the army will not pay for our horses."

Smoke Jensen started for the door when a choked, frightened cry for help came from outside. The voice was that of a woman.

After brooding for a week over his humiliation by that snotty twist of a schoolmarm, Brandon Kelso saw the opportunity to gain his revenge. In the aftermath of the bandit raid on Muddy Gap, as more and more frontier trash moseyed into town, the thought came that he and his friends could get away with just about anything.

Sheriff Hutchins was dead, his deputies out on the trail of the gang that had robbed every store in town, and Marshal Larsen had taken to bed, complaining of a terrible gripe. His chance came unexpectedly on the day Smoke Jensen rode into town. It being a Saturday, Prissy Missy Parkins had no duties around the school. Instead, she had come out of her small house and walked to the center of town to purchase her needs for the week to come. She entered Blackmun's Ladies' Fashions first. Brandon quickly summoned his two willing accomplices.

They watched from the mouth of an alley as Virginia

Parkins went from store to store. Her last stop, Harbinson's General Mercantile, coincided with the arrival of Smoke and his hands. Brandon Kelso paid scant attention to the strangers and the confrontation with the mayor. Intent on his prey, he had eyes only for Ginny Parkins.

When she came out of the general store, her arms filled with packages, Brandon and his two loutish friends stepped out onto the boardwalk and formed a semicircle around her. Ginny looked up startled.

Braying in self-generated contempt, Brandon leaned close to her. "Sorry you tried to make a fool out of me now, you dried up sow?"

Although caught off guard, Ginny's quick wit came to her aid. "I never tried to make a fool of you, Brandon. You do quite well at that all by yourself. Now, please get out of my way."

Emboldened, Brandon reached out and gave her a shove. "You ain't goin' nowhere, you bitch. Not until we say you can. What a sorry waste of a woman you are." He cocked a sarcastic pose, one eyebrow elevated. "Never had a man, have you?"

"You vulgar gutter snipe, that is none of your business," Ginny answered hotly.

Brandon chortled, then spoke through a sneer. "Yup. You ain't never had a man. Bet you're a shriveled prune . . . know what I mean?"

"You filthy animal. Your father will hear of this." Ginny wished she had a free hand. She would slap the face of this impudent, odious, degenerate around on the other side of his head. Then, remembering the switch she had used on them at the school, her higher, moral self sternly chided her. *Bite your tongue, girl. Violence never really settled anything.* Ginny had only a second to rethink her outburst.

Stepping forward the three brutes snatched the packages and string net bag from her arms. Laughing nastily, they hurled the parcels into the street. Hooting in derision, they stepped off the boardwalk and began to kick and stomp her purchases. Paper bags burst, to spray flour and salt. Eggs splattered and ran yellow out into the dust to be absorbed. Three onions went flying.

Enjoying himself immensely, Brandon hauled back a booted foot and kicked a head of cabbage with such force it went flying through a second-floor window of the Wilber House Hotel across the street. Ginny Parkins gathered herself and put hands to the sides of her mouth.

"Stop that! Please stop. Someone help me. Please help me."

By that time, three drunken pieces of human debris had come out of the Sorry Place Saloon to see what was going on. Brandon, carried away by his success so far, and seeking to impress the saddle tramps, spun back on one boot heel and snarled as he raised a hand as though to strike her. "Shut up, you bitch."

At that moment, Smoke Jensen stepped out onto the street. He instantly took in the tableau before him. His cold, gold-brown gaze fixed on Ginny as she cringed back and raised a hand defensively. Aroused by her helplessness, Brandon and his sidekicks took two quick steps toward her, the destruction of her groceries forgotten, and closed around her, their hands raised again. Laughing, the trio of worthless frontier rubbish joined them, and they began to push Ginny around the circle from one to another.

When she screamed again, Brandon brought up his ham hand to strike her in the face.

Suddenly an iron-hard grip encircled Brandon's wrist. His eyes bulged with the effort as he tried to move and found he could not.

It took Smoke Jensen only three long, swift strides to reach the scene of the shameful encounter. He lashed out with an arm and closed steely fingers around a thick wrist and squeezed. He encountered resistance and applied more pressure. At once, the hand of the punk he held in his grasp turned snowy, then began to swell and flush a dark red.

"Let go! Leggo me!" Brandon Kelso wailed two octaves above his normal register.

Smoke Jensen yanked him around and drove a hard right fist into the pouting lips of Brandon Kelso. Blood flew and a tooth cracked. Kelso went slack in the knees. Smoke indifferently pushed him aside. Brandon sprawled face-first into the dirt. Smoke faced the three riffraff.

"Leave, if you don't want to hurt for a long time," he advised. "Leave town if you don't want to stay here forever, out on that hill above us."

Two of them still possessed enough sobriety to actually glance over their shoulders at the mounds of bare earth that covered seven graves. "Oh, yeah?" the third, more inebriated one sneered. "Who do you think you are?"

Calmly, Smoke answered him. "Oh, I *know* who I am."

"Jist who is that?"

With a nasty, deadly smile, Smoke answered him. "Folks call me Smoke Jensen. I'm the new sheriff in Muddy Gap."

"Oh, God," one of the less intoxicated blurted.

White-faced with sudden terror, his partner gasped and gulped and staggered to the edge of the boardwalk, where he bent over the tie rail and gave up his burden of beer. Gripped by the certain presence of sure, swift death, he bleated miserably to his companions.

"C'mon fellas, let's get out of here."

Quickly they stumbled away. Behind them, Brandon Kelso dragged himself to his boots. He looked confused at the departing backs of the saddle trash. He raised appealing hands to them.

"Come back. What's so important about who this peckerwood happens to be?"

Over his shoulder, one of them answered him. "Because he is Smoke Jensen, that's why."

Brandon looked down at his hands, then cut his eyes to

Smoke. "That don't mean nothin' to me," he muttered and then charged.

Smoke Jensen squared off and met him with a solid left-right combination that rocked Brandon's head back, pink spittle flying from already split and bleeding lips. Brandon let go a wide, looping right, which Smoke blocked easily. Then the last mountain man stepped in and began a snare drum tattoo on the soft, pulpy belly of his opponent.

Brandon gulped and grunted. Eyes wild, pain flaming in them, he turned his head to appeal to his friends. "Wal, don't just stand there. Jump in an' help me."

Young Danny Collins held back, while Willie Finch, always in the sway of Brandon Kelso, and filled with false bravado, leaped forward to join the fray. Less than a second later, he began to regret it.

Smoke rapped Brandon in the mouth again and pivoted sideways to Willie, cocked back at the hips and drew up his right leg. When Willie Finch charged within range, Smoke unleashed that leg in a lightning strike. The flat of Smoke's boot sole caught Willie in the belly. Its force drove the boy back, doubled over, cheeks puffed out by the force of the wind knocked from him. Thin, green, bitter gorge rose up from his throat and spilled onto his shirt. Darkness danced before his eyes. Smoke turned back to young Kelso. Grinning, he made inviting gestures to draw the lout in closer.

"C'mon, you want more, don't you?"

"You bet your butt, mister. I ain't afraid of you."

"You ought to be," Smoke advised him.

"Oh, yeah? What for?"

Smoke shook his head sadly. "You just don't get it, do you? I've killed a hundred better men than you'll ever grow up to be. Now, get out of here, you little turd, before I break something serious."

"Like hell!"

By then, Willie Finch had recovered his courage and leaped on Smoke's back. Momentarily pinning Smoke's arms to his sides, he yelled in the gunfighter's ear. "I got him, Bran. I got him good."

Danny Collins found his nerve and waded in also. He landed two good blows to Smoke's side and belly; then Brandon was there. Before the leader of this collection of misfits could swing, he received one of Smoke's kicks. This one square in the crotch. With a shrug, Smoke broke Willie's hold and flung the thin boy away to slam into the front of the barbershop. With a soft groan, Willie slid down the clapboard wall of the tonsorial parlor.

Smoke turned at once to make a quick end of Danny Collins. He did it with a pair of swift, hard punches to the boy's face. Danny groaned and went down like he had been shot. Smoke gave his attention to Brandon Kelso.

Bent over, Brandon wheezed, gagged and moaned in blind agony. Knock-kneed with pain, he walked like a shackled duck toward escape across the far side of the street. Smoke Jensen stalked after him and closed in four swift strides. He put a hard hand on one shoulder and spun Brandon Kelso to face him.

Soft, deadly menace rang in Smoke's voice. "The lady is waiting for an apology."

"No"—sputter-wheeze—"way I'll do that."

"You want more, then?"

For the first time, Brandon's belligerence broke. He winced and cringed away from Smoke's intimidation. "No. No, man. But I ain't gonna apologize."

Smoke took Brandon's nose between his left index and middle finger and squeezed. With a good yank, he brought the lout along with him to where Virginia Parkins stood, hands over her eyes. Smoke tipped his hat and spoke politely.

"Ma'am, this pitiful piece of human garbage has something to say to you."

"No, I . . ." Smoke squeezed the nose. "Eeeh—eeeh! Yes-yes. I'm sure sorry we busted up your stuff, Miz Parkins."

"And you will pay for their replacement, right?"

Another tweak of the nose. "Yes. Yes, I will."

"Dig it out, then."

Brandon Kelso fought back tears as he reached into his pocket. He brought out a fistful of coins. Smoke looked up at Virginia Parkins and then cut his eyes to her ruined purchases. "How much did this cost you, ma'am?"

She told him, and Smoke plucked the proper amount from Brandon's open hand. He handed it to Ginny, then turned Brandon by his nose and planted a boot across the junior thug's buttocks and sent him on his way. He returned to the boardwalk and looked up to see the mayor standing, openmouthed, staring at him. Smoke reached out his hand.

"Well, Mr. Mayor, I think I'll take that badge you offered. Looks like you have a need here, right enough."

"Thank you, Mr. Jensen, thank you from the bottom of my heart. But—what about your herd?"

Smoke Jensen looked beyond the mayor to see his top hand standing there grinning. "Jerry, you take the herd on for a few days. I'll catch up before the end of the week."

"Right, boss. Say, you do good work, Smoke."

Mayor Norton led the way to the sheriff's office and jail. There he showed Smoke around and further explained the situation in Muddy Gap. In particular he apprised Smoke of the names of the local boys he had taken down a notch minutes earlier. While they talked, Boyne Kelso stormed into the room. Fury exploded out of him.

"Mayor, I demand that the man who beat up my son and robbed him be arrested at once." He cut his eyes from Norton to Smoke, noted the badge and jabbed a long finger at him. "Well? What are you waiting for? If you're the new lawman I've heard about, you had better start earning your keep. I want that saddle bum arrested and jailed."

Smoke provided him a sarcastic grin. 'I'm afraid that is impossible. You see, I'm that 'saddle bum.'"

Kelso's jaw sagged a moment, then he regained his self-righteous outrage. "Lester, I can't believe you've hired a thief to replace Sheriff Hutchins."

"I haven't," Mayor Norton told him blandly. "This is Smoke Jensen. He is a former deputy U.S. marshal. And your boy was tormenting Miss Ginny."

"I don't believe it. Brandon is a good boy. He would never do such a thing."

Smoke took it up. "You had better believe it, Mr. Kelso. He and two other oafs assaulted the schoolteacher, took her packages from her and destroyed the contents. When your brat made to strike her, I intervened. The money I took was to replace what they had destroyed."

Indignation filled Kelso. "You can't do this. I'm Boyne Kelso. And, my son is . . . my son."

Smoke's eyes narrowed dangerously. "Are you implying that you, too, assault women and ravage their property?"

Astounded, Kelso's mouth worked for a second before he could find words. "What impudence. I'm warning you . . ."

Smoke moved like a striking rattler. He crossed the short space between himself and Kelso with two strides and took the outraged man by the front of his shirt. With seemingly no effort, he shoved the portly body back against the closed door with enough force to knock the air from the blustering Kelso.

"No, Mr. Kelso, I'm warning you. If that misbegotten piece of garbage you call your son so much as spits on the boardwalk, I'll coldcock him with my Colt and drag him to jail. From here on, he—and you—will be on the best possible behavior. Now get out of here and let me do my job."

Once Smoke saw the horses on their way, he waded into cleaning up Muddy Gap. His first target was the saloon out of which the drunken trash had come to join in tormenting the attractive young schoolteacher. Word had preceded him, Smoke discovered the moment he entered the barroom.

"Well, what do we got here?" a truculent voice demanded as Smoke strode through the batwings.

"Looks like somebody who don't have any business here," a tall, burly saddle tramp gritted. "Why don't you jist turn around and git the hell out?"

Smoke centered on him. His left arm extended, he shot an accusatory finger at the pugnacious thug. "I want your name. Now!"

Grinning in anticipation of a good brawl, the lout answered. "Rafer Diggins. I'm the meanest, toughest, woolliest he-coon in these parts."

Blandly, Smoke told him, "I doubt that."

With that in the mix, Rafer Diggins let out a roar and charged Smoke Jensen.

5

Rafer Diggins saw himself as larger than life. A brawler since his early teens, he had never been bested since the day he walloped his brutal, drunken father and ran away from home. A man who stood a good three inches shorter and at least thirty pounds lighter would be an easy mark. Or so thought Rafer Diggins when he launched himself away from the bar.

A laughing companion shouted encouragement. "Go git him, Rafe."

Rafe puffed himself up on fighting rage and deep breaths as he closed on Smoke. The brawny barroom tough cocked a ham fist back by his ear, prepared to knock the lights out of this lawdog. Grinning, Smoke Jensen waited for it.

When the punch came, Smoke did not move his body. He jinked his head to the side, and the fist whistled past. Then he unloaded with a low, right uppercut. It buried to the wrist in the beer gut that leaned vulnerably toward him.

Diggins had time for one groan as his eyes bulged and the air gusted out of his lungs. Then Smoke laid a hard left to the side of the bigger man's jaw. Stars exploded before Rafe Diggins' eyes as his feet went out from under him and he landed on his axe-handle-broad rear. He did not stay there long.

With a diminished roar, he sprang to his boots and waded in again. Methodically, Smoke worked at cleaning his clock. A right-left combination halted Rafe's advance. His arms groped ineffectually to get his opponent in a bear hug. Failing that, Rafe threw wide, looping punches that Smoke slipped on the points of his shoulders.

Staggered, Rafe tried a kick. Smoke caught his boot and raised it while he twisted. Pain shot up Rafe's leg, he went off balance and toppled backward. His head made a loud noise as it struck the edge of the bar. Sighing softly, he slumped to the floor and lay with his cheek resting on the lip of a brass spittoon. Confident that it was over, Smoke turned to address the cluster of the remaining trash.

"I want the rest of you out of here and out of town. You have ten minutes."

Before Smoke could continue, Rafe Diggins recovered faster than expected. He bounded off the floor with an enraged bellow; a glint came off a knife he held low in his right hand. Smoke saw it at once and pivoted to evade a straight thrust. Diggins had every intention to gut him like a deer.

Trying a back slash, Diggins bore in with his deadly blade. Smoke considered the alternatives for a moment, then acted as common sense dictated. Quickly he scooped up the leg of a chair broken in the fight. When Diggins lunged again, Smoke brought it down on his right forearm. Bones cracked and Diggins howled in pain. The knife fell from his grasp. At once the experienced brawler went for his six-gun left-handed.

He barely had the barrel clear of leather when Smoke Jensen shot him in the shoulder. Jolted back, Diggins rammed his back into the bar. He stiffened, then sagged in defeat. Smoke reached him in four quick strides. Roughly he slammed the man around and searched him for more hide-out weapons. Then he began to frog-march Diggins out the door and off to jail.

Grumbling, the other frontier debris followed after. Out in the street, Rafe Diggins roused enough to overcome his pain and make one more try. From a leather pouch suspended by a cord down his back, he snatched a straight razor and snapped it open as he made a vicious slash at Smoke Jensen's throat.

Smoke did not even hesitate. The big .45 Colt Peacemaker filled his right hand, and his fingertip lightly tripped the trigger. Rafe Diggins jolted to a stop and looked down disbelievingly at the black hole in the center of his chest that began to leak red. His uninjured arm dropped to his side, and the razor fell from his numb grasp. His face went slack. Slowly he canted forward and began to fall. He landed on his face with a thud, in a viscous puddle of mud. Smoke Jensen stepped over and looked down coldly at the dead man, whose head was a welter of shattered gore. Then he turned his attention to the thoroughly cowed collection of rogues.

"Like I said, I'm posting you out of town. After ten minutes, if any of you are still here, I'll come after you. And, I'm warning you, I will shoot to kill."

In a mad scramble, they left in all directions, like a flock of pigeons with a fox in the barn.

Word of Smoke's accomplishment spread rapidly around town. Aaron Tucker, the owner and daytime bartender at the Sorry Place saloon rushed outside when Smoke passed by to wring his hand and offer praise.

"Let me tell you, Sheriff Jensen, you're doin' a marvelous job. There was some shanty trash hanging around my place. Nothing I did could get rid of them. When they heard of what happened at the Gold Boot, they cleared out without a word."

"Well—ah—thank you."

"I'm Aaron Tucker. I own this place. Anything you want, any time you come in, it's on the house."

"That's not necessary, Mr. Tucker."

"No. I know that. That's why I'm offering it."

"Thank you again."

When he completed his rounds, Smoke returned to the office to find another form of gratitude. A small rectangle of cream-colored note paper lay on his desk. He opened it and read the contents.

"Dear Sheriff Jensen," it read. "I fear that I failed terribly in expressing my gratitude for my rescue at your hand. Violence upsets me, and I had recently been subjected to such shocking indignities, that I quite forgot myself. Please let me make it up to you with an invitation to a late supper this evening. I will expect you at eight o'clock, if that is suitable." The invitation had been signed simply, "Virginia Parkins."

Smoke Jensen puckered his lips as he put the note aside. It would appear the schoolteacher knew her manners after all. What's more, he had always been a sucker for a home-cooked meal. Especially one prepared by such an attractive young woman. Yes, he would enjoy their supper. Images of his Sally, so far away, clouded his anticipation. Smoke looked up to see a small, freckle-faced boy standing expectantly in the open doorway.

His name, Smoke had learned, was Jimmy. He had come by earlier and informed Smoke that he had done odd jobs for the late sheriff. "Like sweep up when the deputies were out on a posse," he had illustrated. Smoke decided to make use of his services now.

"Just a minute, Jimmy. I have something for you to do." Smoke found paper and a worn, steel nib pen in the top drawer. Carefully he drew the letters of his acceptance in a fine copper plate script. He blotted it, folded the sheet in half and extended it to the boy.

"Take this to Miss Parkins, please."

Jimmy's eyes went wide. "Our teacher? What's it about?"

Smoke gave him a brief frown. "That's not for you to know. Here's a dime for your trouble."

He handed a silver coin to the lad, who scampered off on bare feet, puffs of dust left behind by his heels. Then Smoke leaned back to reflect on his progress. Considering he had seven in jail, at least fifteen run out of town, and another on his way to Boot Hill, plus an invitation to supper, Smoke thought he had made a good start at getting a handle on the undesirable element in Muddy Gap. He might be able to rejoin the herd within three days.

"Mr. Jensen, you saved my life, my job and my reputation. I can't thank you enough." Virginia Parkins blushed lightly as she spoke. "Only one thing . . ."

"Yes? And, please, call me Smoke."

"Very well, Smoke. My friends call me Ginny." She took a deep breath and launched into her favorite theme. "I suppose that, all considered, there was no other way of handling that awful situation this morning. It's just that I have devoted my life to ending the violence with which we, as a people, seem obsessed."

Smoke Jensen sat, somewhat ill at ease, on a delicate, velvet-upholstered chair in the parlor of Virginia's tiny house. The rich aroma of a roasting cut of beef came from the cast-iron cookstove in the kitchen. Mingled with it was the unmistakable aroma of a peach pie. Their supper might be late, but far from light. Conscious of the need not to offend her, he carefully weighed his reply.

"You are right about the first part, Ginny. Under the circumstances, the only thing those craven louts would properly respond to was superior force. Bullies like Brandon Kelso take any show of politeness or mild-mannered behavior as a sign of weakness. That's exactly what they feed upon. So, in order to get them to behave in a proper manner, I first had to get their attention."

A slight frown divided the space between her eyebrows

vertically. "You certainly did that. What if . . . what if one of them had produced a weapon?"

Smoke shrugged, trying to ease the bluntness his words described. "Then I would have had to shoot that one."

Ginny shivered. "May we speak of something else?"

"Certainly. Muddy Gap is a raw, new town. How many students does that afford you?"

"I have sixteen. From first to eighth grade."

"That's quite a few for a place on the edge of nowhere. My wife was a schoolteacher when I met her."

Again that small grimace of irritation. "Is that so? I'm surprised at her attraction to a lawman."

Smoke chuckled softly. "So was she."

That lightened Ginny's mood. "And were you?"

"Oh, no. I think I fell in love the first time I met Sally. She was, and is, so different than any other woman I had ever encountered. And beautiful, too."

"You are a lucky man, Smoke. To have wooed and won someone whom you feel so strongly about." She rose onto her high-button shoes. "I am sure that roast is ready now. Go on in to the table, I'll have everything on in a minute. All I need do is fix the gravy."

Smoke pulled a teasing expression of being highly impressed. "All that and gravy, too. I feel like a regular guest of honor. Don't tell me you have home-baked bread to sop with."

Ginny suppressed a giggle. "I certainly do."

"Then, let us begin."

Aaron Tucker was unaccustomed to being called back to the Sorry Place at night. His summons came from the night bartender, delivered by the old fellow who worked as a swamper. He showed up on the front porch of the Tucker house at eight-thirty that night.

"Fred says there's trouble brewin', Mr. Tucker. Some of

those gunhawks are gettin' drunk and makin' talk about ambushing the new sheriff."

Aaron pursed his lips. "They might find that harder to do than they expect." He sighed heavily. "All right, I'll come."

When they reached the saloon, Aaron Tucker found the situation worse than he had expected. Five surly men lined the bar. Four more sat around a table, cards spread before them for a game of five-card stud. Behind the mahogany, Fred Barnes wore a worried expression. The only friendly face in the saloon was that of Mayor Lester Norton. He nodded a curt greeting to Aaron and cut his eyes around the room.

Aaron saw what he meant. The usual local clientele had been run out, or had not come in at all. Aaron walked up to him. "What brings you out tonight, Les?"

Norton rolled his eyes. "My mother-in-law is visiting. 'Nuf said?"

With his establishment filled with heavily armed hard cases, Tucker had to force a chuckle. "How long is she going to be here?"

"A week. Or more. There's no telling with her, Aaron." Again he sighed. Then he broached the subject both of them feared. "I thought the new sheriff was working at clearing out this riffraff?"

"He is. Has to rest some time. And eat a meal." Aaron Tucker's admiration for Smoke Jensen had not diminished. "I hear the schoolmarm invited him to supper."

A chair went back with a loud bang when the back struck the floor. "Barkeep, these cards are greasy. You been storin' 'em with the free lunch?" growled one of the hard cases. "Bring us a new deck."

Fred Barnes shrugged and made a helpless gesture. "That is a new deck."

Aaron gave a nervous glance. "I think we need Sheriff Jensen. Les, will you—ah—will you go prevail upon him to come down here?"

Mayor Norton pushed away from the far end of the bar.

"Sure, Aaron. The sooner we rid our town of this sort, the better. It won't take long to get him."

Smoke Jensen and Virginia Parkins sat in her parlor, sipping coffee and letting their meal settle. Smoke felt a minor discomfort at her proximity. He should have brought someone along, maybe the mayor. Or, Ginny should have provided a third party. He felt a twinge of relief, then, when a knock sounded at the door. Ginny excused herself to answer. She came back with the mayor in tow.

Lester Norton did not waste a moment. "Mr. Jensen, it is certain that trouble is brewing at the Sorry Place. There are a number of ruffians gathered there. They've made talk of bushwhacking you."

Frowning, Smoke Jensen came to his boots. "They just lost their chance. Excuse me, Miss Ginny, it appears I have more to do before I can settle down at the jail."

Virginia came to him, put an admonitory hand on his forearm. "Be careful, Smoke. Surely they will be reasonable. Like those others who left town on their own?"

"I wouldn't . . ." Mayor Norton started to blurt, only to stop at the hard look on Smoke's face.

Smoke filled the gap. "What the mayor means is that he wouldn't worry if he were you." Then to Norton, "Shall we go? This shouldn't take long."

Virginia still looked concerned and unconvinced. "Please—let me know how it comes out."

Smoke smiled. "I'll stop by before making my last rounds." He started for the door.

"We'll have pie," Ginny called after him.

It had all been worked out while the mayor had been absent from the saloon. The four men who had been playing cards now stood at the rear of the room, their backs to the wall. The five hard cases who lined the bar had spread out. They eyed the batwing doors intently, marking the time. Aaron Turner had gone behind the bar. One hand hovered over a hefty bung starter.

Mayor Norton entered the saloon first, nearly precipitating a fusillade. Two of the gunmen at the rear actually unlimbered their six-guns. Smoke Jensen came in a moment behind the mayor, his .45 Colt leading the way. He shot first one, then the other man who had drawn their weapons. Deliberately aimed high, the heavy slugs slammed into their shoulders. Two Colt Frontier models thudded in the sawdust on the rough-hewn floor.

In the next second, Smoke Jensen roughly shoved Lester Norton to the floor, and the air rocked to the roar of eight blazing six-guns. Smoke shot one of the trash at the bar and dived into a roll that took him halfway across the room. He came up with bullets cutting the air to both sides and over his head. Another quick shot and a would-be ambusher went down screaming, his kneecap shattered. Smoke raised his six-gun and fired again.

A fifth saddle tramp groaned and left the fight, shot through the right side an inch above his hip bone. Smoke dived behind an overturned table and expended his last two rounds. Another man in the back of the room sprang backward and collided discordantly with the upright piano. Smoke's final slug destroyed half of the top octave. The strings pinged musically as the lead snapped them.

Smoke holstered his right-hand revolver and reached for his second Peacemaker, worn high on his left side, butt forward and slanted across his hard, flat stomach. A slug from one of the hard cases at the bar clipped the hat from his head. He returned the favor with a bullet that struck the face of the cylinder in the offending six-gun.

Hot needles of pain shot through the shooter's hand, and he let go of his damaged weapon. Another tried to work his way around to Smoke's blind side. He made three side steps along the bar and stopped suddenly when Aaron

Turner rapped him smartly on the top of his head with a bung starter. The gunhawk crashed to the floor with a meteor shower behind his eyes.

Alone in a reign of such fury, the remaining hard case chose wisdom over pain. He reversed the revolver and offered it to Smoke butt first. Far too wise in the ways of gunhandling, Smoke did not fall for that one. Instead he gestured toward the green baize top of a poker table.

"Lay it down there. Do it or I'll shoot you anyway." Smoke turned to where the mayor remained sprawled on the floor. "Now, Mr. Mayor, if you'd be so kind as to help me take this garbage out of here and lock them up."

"What's the charge?" complained the one with the red, swollen, throbbing hand.

"Assaulting a peace officer, for a start. Maybe the territorial attorney can make attempted murder stick."

Fear loosened the brigand's tongue. "No, man, I swear, no. We didn't intend to kill you, just bust you up a little and run you out of town. Nobody said a thing about killing. I swear it."

Coolly, Aaron Turner put in his contribution. "He lies." He nodded to the one Smoke had killed. "That one stood right here and said they would bury you come tomorrow. They all thought it a good idea. The mouthy one there said something about drilling you tonight and planting you in the morning."

Smoke Jensen stopped in his roundup of the casualties. "Say, I wanted to thank you for your timely assistance. You're pretty handy with that thing."

Turner looked down at the bung starter in his hand and back at Smoke. He smiled shyly, and his ears colored. "Oh, this. I get a lot of practice."

Smoke nodded. "Might be you won't have near as much for some while." With that he and the mayor started off with their prisoners.

* * *

Before making his last rounds of the business district of Muddy Gap, Smoke Jensen returned to the small house owned by Ginny Parkins. He found it dark. *Odd,* he thought. *She said we'd have pie when I returned.* He raised one hand and rapped knuckles lightly on the front door. Silence answered him. He knocked again, a bit louder.

A floor board creaked behind the closed portal and Smoke heard a rustling. "Ginny, is that you? Did I disturb you?"

"Go away."

"What? I thought . . ."

"I heard the gunshots. I heard it all. I know what that means for you to be here now. Someone else didn't survive. I'm sorry, Smoke. But violence, and those who cause it, are not a part of my life. Now, goodbye."

"Uh—ycah. I—ah—goodbye, Ginny. Thank you for a delicious supper."

Smoke trudged away, thinking gloomy thoughts about schoolteachers. His own dear Sally had had similar opinions when first they had met. At least this time, he had no one to woo and win.

6

Reno Jim Yurian and his gang sat around a large table in the office of what had once been a prosperous, if short-lived, mine. A good twenty years earlier, Arapaho warriors, angered at seeing the belly of their Earth Mother plundered, had attacked and killed the six men working the claim. Because the mine shaft was accessed from a small shed attached to the office, the Indians did not burn it down out of religious awe. Now a new wealth visited the abandoned structure. Each of the outlaws had a stack of coins and currency in front of him.

To the casual observer, they could have been preparing for a poker game. In fact, Reno Jim had only seconds before finished the distribution of each man's share of their most recent forays into the criminal life. It came to quite a tidy amount. As one, they began to count the total. Reno Jim waited until they had finished and he had their full attention.

"That's only a start, boys. We'll move the cattle and horses at the same time."

"Won't that cost a lot to feed the cattle so long, boss?" Prine Gephart asked.

Reno Jim bit the tip from a skinny, black cigar and lighted it before answering. "Not really. They're on graze and there's plenty of it. When we have the horses, we'll move them at once. First, though, there is the problem of this fast gun running the horse herd. If he wasn't bullin' Colin here." He clapped the wounded brigand on the shoulder, and Colin Fike winced. "We have a serious obstacle in our way. And his name is Smoke Jensen."

Early the next morning, Smoke Jensen left the sheriff's office and paid a brief breakfast call on the town marshal. Inside the Iron Kettle, Grover Larsen glared across the red-checked tablecloth at the badge adorning Smoke Jensen's chest. Somehow he could not manage to meet the amber-flecked eyes. His voice was surly, uncertain.

"What did you drag me down here for?"

"I need your cooperation, Marshal Larsen."

Suspicion and unease briefly lighted Larsen's flat, gray eyes. "'Cooperation'? What kind?"

"The Harbinsons have a printing press over at the general store, don't they?"

"Yes, they do. Why?"

"I want you to come over there with me. I intend to post guns out of town. It would help if I had your name and signature on the flyers also."

Grover Larsen considered this while he chewed a bite of ham. "That doesn't sound like too much to ask."

"Then you'll do it?" Smoke watched as Larsen shrugged slightly and speared another piece of ham.

Another shrug and the jaws worked methodically. Grover Larsen swallowed and spoke softly. "You bought me breakfast. I suppose it's the least I can do. Besides, it's my duty. Mind, though, I'm opposed to interfering with a man's right to carry a gun."

Smoke smiled, satisfied that there might be some grit left in the man after all. "So am I. I intend only to post against nonresidents. The citizens of Muddy Gap, and those known to be local folks, will not be affected by it." Then Smoke dropped the other boot that Larsen had been waiting for. "That's why I need your help in enforcing it. You know who belongs and who don't. Will you do it, Marshal?"

Larsen's worried frown turned to a deep scowl. "I didn't count on that. There's some rough characters out there."

"That's why I'll see you have someone to back your play. While you relieve any strangers of their guns, they can cover them."

Cocking his head to one side, Larsen mopped at an egg yolk with a fluffy biscuit. "Might work after all. Yep. Let's finish up and we'll go see young Eb Harbinson."

A black mourning band showed prominently on the sleeve of Eb Harbinson's shirt. He seemed reluctant to dig into the cast type and dirty the press to print so small a run. He listened to what Smoke wanted, nodded to show the ability of his equipment to do the job, and rubbed the palms of his hands on his trouser legs.

"We planned to start a newspaper. But there aren't enough people in town yet to justify the expense." He came to his feet from the chair in front of a rolltop desk. "I suppose printing these flyers is a better use of the press than gathering dust. But, if you want signatures, you'll either have to sign each one separately, or I'll have you do it on a blank plate and etch around them."

"How long will that take?" Smoke asked.

Eb rolled his eyes to the ceiling. "I'd say you could have them late tomorrow.

"Not soon enough. We'll sign them."

"How many do you want, Sheriff?"

Smoke calculated aloud. "I want one in each business in town, on the church and school, also. And two for each end of town. A few spares in case someone takes exception to them. Say twenty-five, thirty."

Eb nodded his understanding. "Fine, I can have them ready by ten o'clock this morning."

* * *

After leaving the general mercantile, Smoke Jensen started his rounds of the saloons, to hustle the unwanted element out of town. The first of the unsavory milieu he encountered were Bert Toller, Quint Cress, and Big Sam Piper. The trio of fair-to-middling gunfighters stood at the bar in the Golden Boot tormenting the swamper. The grayhaired, older man toiled to put down fresh sawdust after the previous night's cleanup and mopping.

"Hey, *boy*, yer hand's shakin' so much you got sawdust on my boots," Quint Cress complained.

"What you need is a drink, old-timer," Big Sam told him through a nasty chuckle.

Harvey Gates looked up with the eyes of a cornered animal. "No, sir. I done gave up drinkin'."

Cress twisted his face into a mean sneer. "Oh, yeah? When? After they invented the funnel?"

"Please, fellers, I've—I've got work to do."

Quint Cress crossed to the cowed man and yanked the bucket of sawdust from his grasp. "You get sawdust on my boots again an' they'll be plantin' you before sundown."

A steel-hard voice came from the doorway. "That's the last time you do that."

Cress whirled, a shower of yellowish wood chips flying from the rim of the bucket. "Oh, yeah? Who says so?"

"I do. Sheriff Jensen. Now, return the bucket to the man and let him get on with his work."

From farther down the bar, Big Sam spoke hesitantly. "Uh—Quint, I think that might be a good idea. This be Smoke Jensen."

A crazed glint shone in the eyes of Quint Cress. "You think I don't know? I don't care a damn, either. I say he's not as hot as he's put up to be." He dropped the bucket to the floor and started for the door. "I'll be waitin' for you outside, Jensen."

Smoke let him go. He turned to the remaining pair and

addressed Big Sam. "You seem to have more sense than your friend. This town is off limits to you and your kind. So, I'll ask you politely. Gather up whatever you brought with you, mount up and ride out. You have fifteen minutes."

Big Sam Peiper made a show of considering that for a moment; then his voice rang with new strength. "I don't mind you raggin' Quint some. He needs tooken down a notch. But, you jist asked something we can't do. Why, we'd be the laughing stock of the whole territory. No, sir, we ain't gonna go."

With that, he and Bert Toller, who had said nothing so far, dropped hands to the grips of their six-guns. Smoke let Sam Peiper, whom he figured more for a mouth than a shootist, get his long-barreled .44 Colt clear of leather, choosing instead to take on Toller first.

A good choice, he soon discovered as Toller moved with a blur, his six-gun snaked out and on the rise by the time Smoke snapped his elbow to his right side and leveled the .45 Peacemaker in his fist. The hammer fell, and a puff of cloth and dust flew from the front of Toller's shirt. A dark hole appeared some three inches above the belt Toller wore. A second hole popped into place directly above it a fraction of a second later, to form a perfect figure eight.

Immediately, Smoke swung the smoking barrel of his Colt to Big Sam Peiper. Big Sam stared at his partner and watched him die. Bert Toller had barely hit the floor when Sam let out a despairing shout and bolted for the door.

"No!" he screamed. "I ain't gonna die." Wildly he threw a shot at Smoke over his shoulder.

Smoke had dropped to a crouch when Big Sam started his direction, so the shot went high, to spang off the stovepipe and crack the plaster behind. Smoke fired his third round as Big Sam hit the batwing doors. Sam Peiper crashed through the swinging partitions and onto the boardwalk, as blood streamed down his thigh. Smoke Jensen came right behind him.

Limping, Big Sam Peiper headed toward Quint Cress. "Ga'damn, he shot me, Quint. It hurts real bad."

Cress looked surprised. "You ain't never been shot before? What kinda gunfighter are you?"

"Naw. Ain't been shot. I always was faster."

Quint Cress shook his head. "Sam, Sam, get out of the way, let me finish this amateur."

Big Sam staggered in a tight circle, raising his Smith American. "No. I'm gonna do it. Nobody puts a hole in Big Sam Peiper."

He faced Smoke Jensen now, who much to the consternation of Big Sam had an amused expression on his face. With careful deliberation, his own visage screwed into a grimace of pain, Big Sam raised his revolver. To his dying instant, he knew he had never seen Smoke Jensen draw his Colt. Yet, all of a sudden he saw the yellow-orange bloom and a thin trail of smoke start from its muzzle.

Then a bright white light dazzled him, and immense pain erupted inside his head. All feeling left his hands and feet. The alabaster radiance swelled and enveloped him. For a fraction of a second, Big Sam Peiper saw a tiny black dot form at the center of the sphere. Unfeeling, he toppled to the ground, the back of his head blown away, and in a twinkling, the blackness overwhelmed him.

Quint Cress stared in horror. No one could be that fast. Hell, Big Sam already had his six-gun cocked before this Smoke Jensen drew. For the first time, the bravado deserted Quint. Yet, he knew inexorably that the hand had to be played out to the end. He swallowed hard to remove the lump in his throat and dropped his hand to the grips of his Colt. Jensen, his head wreathed in powder smoke, could not possibly see him draw.

Wrong. Quint Cress had his Frontier Colt free of leather and on the way up when an invisible fist slammed into his stomach. He started to double over in reflex, only to be straightened up by another enormous pain in his chest. He wound up on his back, staring up at Smoke Jensen, who held his Peacemaker in a steady, level grasp.

Quint Cress used the last of his dying breath to ask his most pressing questions. "Wh-what are you, Jensen? Who are you?"

A tiny mocking smile lifted the corners of Smoke Jensen's mouth. "Some people have called me the gun-fighters' gunfighter."

And then, Quint Cress heard and saw only blackness.

Early that same morning Reno Jim Yurian and three of his men sat astride their mounts overlooking a long, narrow depression in the prairie, too shallow to be called a valley. A wide, deep ravine defined the western margin, with a large, round knob bordering the east. In its center ran the trail north through the Bighorn Mountains, and on toward Buffalo, Wyoming. From there, it led north into Montana and the Crow Reservation. Reno Jim tilted back the brim of his black, flat-crown Stetson and waved a gloved hand at the peaceful spread of terrain.

"There it is, boys. The perfect place to take that herd. I reckon it will be here in no more than a day, two at the most. Hub, I want you to set the boys up to preparing an ambush. Take your time and make it look natural. The last thing we want is them to get wise too soon. Also, make sure there's enough mounted men on both sides, beyond the rise, to take quick control of the herd."

"Right, boss. You gonna be here with us?"

Reno Jim produced a thin-lipped smile. "I wouldn't miss that for anything. For now, me and Smiling Dave are going to set up camp so you boys can have something hot to eat after you get done."

What he meant, of course, was that Smiling Dave Winters would do the work while he sat under a tree and practiced his card-dealing tricks. Naturally, no one mentioned it to Reno Jim. Under Hub Volker's direction, the men spread out to locate a good spot to establish a roadblock-style ambush. It took only a short while to accomplish that.

Garth Evans rode back from around a slight bend in the

trail with a cheery smile. "Hey, Hub, I've got the ideal place. That bend there"—he pointed behind him—"will mask it, an' there's some cottonwoods to form a barricade."

"Good work, Garth."

At once, Hub put men on cutting down the trees. Using hand axes was a sure invitation to blisters and sore hands, yet the outlaws set at it with a will. The sound of their chopping rang across the prairie. One by one the thigh-thick cottonwood trees tottered and fell with a crash. Dragged into place by horses, the logs were trimmed and made ready. Sets of post augers appeared from a chuck wagon, and the outlaw rabble groaned.

Hairy Joe cut his eyes to Prine Gephart as he plied a clamshell post-hole digger. "Doin' that corral for the cattle was bad enough. Now we gotta build a damn fort wall." He slammed the device into the hard ground again.

Prine cranked the long handle on his screw-type digger. "It ain't a fort, Joe. It's a sorta fence, like we're makin' the whole valley into a corral."

Hairy Joe groaned. "This is gonna take a week to close across the whole valley. From what I hear, we ain't got that much time."

"We'll get it done," Gephart assured him. "If Hub has to make us work all night."

"Oh, great. I can hardly wait."

Progress went quicker than Hairy Joe thought. By nightfall, all but a hundred yards at each side of the valley had been closed off. Tired far beyond their usual limits, they gathered quietly to eat plates of chili con carne Colorado, bowls of beans and corn bread with which to sop up both of them. Only four of them pulled bottles of whiskey from saddlebags to take long pulls before settling down like the rest into deep slumber.

Meanwhile, Smoke Jensen set about a quick, harsh cleanup of Muddy Gap. He picked up the posters at ten-fifteen. After putting one on the bulletin board outside the general store, he gave half to Marshal Larsen, and they set about posting the entire town. Their actions generated immediate reaction. Several merchants came onto the boardwalk to voice protest. It never failed to draw a crowd.

"Now, see here," the butcher, Tiemeier, declared in a loud bray. "You can't do this. I've got a right to carry a gun."

"You are not affected, Mr. Tiemeier," Smoke explained patiently. "Read it carefully. Only nonresidents are required to surrender their arms."

"Even so, you have no right to do this on your own."

"I'm not. You can see the city marshal's signature right there beside mine. And, this morning the mayor and city council met and passed the ordinance."

For half an hour, Smoke busied himself tacking up the edicts, ending with the two at the north end of town. He had finished the final nail when five specimens of range trash drifted up. Hats pulled down low on brows, they walked their mounts to the gate post where Smoke had affixed one of the flyers and read it with obvious difficulty. At last one of them turned to glower at Smoke.

"Who are you to try to make us do that?"

Smoke tapped the badge pinned to his vest with the hammer. "I'm the law."

Leaning forward, the mouthy one jabbed a thick forefinger at Smoke. "You're a fool if you think we're gonna give up our guns."

Smoke stepped closer to him. "You do or you don't cross the town line."

This time the belligerent one reached even farther and poked Smoke in the chest and emphasized each insult with a thrust. "You'll play hell stopping us, you two-bit, tin-star, yellow-belly—Yeeeiii!"

His scream came when Smoke dropped the hammer and reached up swiftly to snatch the offending finger and bend it backward until the bone snapped loudly. At once, Smoke let go and grabbed the front of the man's shirt.

With a solid yank, he jerked him clear of the saddle. Pivoting, Smoke slammed him to the ground hard enough to drive the air from his lungs.

He dropped on one knee to the loudmouth's belly and delivered a left-right-left combination to his face that left the man dizzy and gurgling. Immediately, the others went for their guns. Smoke came to his boots in an instant and hauled his Colt Peacemaker clear in a blur. The four thugs gaped at him.

"Now put your guns on the gate over there or pick up your friend here and get the hell out of town."

Cutting their eyes from one to another, the four stared in wonder. Not a one had half-drawn his revolver. One of them looked at their companion groaning on the ground. "Just who the devil are you, mister?"

"Smoke Jensen."

For all his misery, the one at Smoke's feet got up quickly and mounted his horse. All of them tried not to meet the hot eyes of Smoke Jensen, which bored into them. With submissive touches of their hands to the brims of their hats, they turned their horses and rode away.

Little Jimmy showed up at noon with a plate for Smoke from the Iron Kettle. It held fried chicken, gravy with boiled potatoes, and hominy. He also had an encouraging message.

Freckled face writhing with the energy of his delivery, Jimmy informed Smoke, "Fred Chase, one of your deputies, is back in town. He says he'll come out and relieve you after dinner," he squeaked. "Said he should be here about one-fifteen this afternoon."

"Thank you, Jimmy." Smoke dug in his pocket for a coin. Jimmy looked at him expectantly.

"Can I stay here until you finish? I'll take yer plate back. Okay?"

"It's may I, Jimmy," Smoke corrected, the image of Sally hovering in his mind. "And, yes, you may."

Jimmy's eyes glowed. "Oh, boy, maybe I'll get to see you wallop a few bad men."

Smoke frowned. "You had better hope you don't. Which reminds me. If anything turns rough out here while you are around, duck. I mean, crawl underground."

"Yesss, sir," the little lad replied in disappointment.

When Fred showed up and introduced himself, Smoke explained what was expected of him and what to watch out for. Then he walked back into the center of town with Jimmy at his side. He gave the boy another dime and sent him off to the Iron Kettle with the empty plate. Then he started for the first of two saloons he had on his list to clean out this afternoon.

When he shoved his way through the batwings, Smoke walked smack into a fist in the mouth.

7

Smoke Jensen rocked back on his boot heels, then low-ered his head and drove into the man who had hit him. Off balance, the tough back-pedaled until he struck a poker table and sprawled across it, scattering coins and chips.

"Hey, get off the table," one of the irate players com-plained.

From the bar, another added, "Yeah, Red, I thought you were gonna really fix the new sheriff. Looks like he's done fixed you."

Goaded by the taunt, Red Cramer sprang to his feat and made a dive for Smoke Jensen. Smoke waited for his charge. At the last second, he side-stepped and clipped Red behind the ear. Red flew sideways and crashed into yet an-other table. Beer gushed upward in amber geysers as schooners broke in showers of glass, and the table's occu-pants sprawled in disarray. Red wound up face-first across the collapsed table. Slower this time, he came to his boots.

Smoke stood there ready to meet him. Only this time, Red decided he'd had enough of bare-hand grappling. He dropped a hand to his holster and hauled on his hogleg. He should have known better.

Although superior to most of the thugs Smoke had faced since coming to Muddy Gap, Red Cramer managed to bring only the muzzle of his Colt to the top of the pocket before Smoke shot him in the chest.

Red's expression of surprise spoke volumes. For a moment he could simply not believe that he had been beaten. Especially by some nobody from Colorado. Then came the rush of certain knowledge. How could this be happening to him? Red Cramer went limp, and his Colt thudded on the floor. His eyes rolled up, and he sighed as though in regret for his short life and many sins. Then he died.

Smoke faced the remaining occupants of the Red Rooster saloon. "You men were already in town when I posted it. Though by this time, you have to have seen one or more notices on your way in here. So, I'll give you exactly thirty seconds to rid yourselves of every firearm you are carrying, and any knife with more than a three-inch blade. There are no exceptions," Smoke added as one of the toughs started to voice a protest. "Failure to comply will result in being escorted out of town, by way of a visit to the justice of the peace and a stay in jail."

A long, silent fifteen seconds clicked away on the octagonal face of the oak-cased Regulator wall clock above the piano. Then, grumbling lowly among one another, three of the riffraff began to deposit weapons on the bar. When the slender, black hand reached twenty seconds, four more began to divest themselves of six-guns and knives. The thirty-second deadline arrived in the Red Rooster, and Smoke Jensen cut his eyes from one to another of the three holdouts, then down at the corpse cooling on the floor.

"If you don't want to join him, I'd suggest you join your friends over there at the bar."

Two of them looked at Smoke as though he had spoken in tongues. The third scuttled to the bar and began to unburden his person of all arms. The pendulum of the Regulator ticked again, and the second hand advanced. One of the holdouts began to sweat profusely. His hand trembled visibly as he raised a finger to point at Smoke.

"I've heard of you, Jensen. They say you're fast."

Smoke nodded. "D'you reckon to be faster?"

"N-no—ah—no." His gaze fixed on his boot toes, his bravado deflated as he shuffled to join the others who had given up their weapons.

With a flicker of a smile, Smoke addressed the thoroughly cowed brigands. "Thank you, boys. When you are ready to leave town, you can pick those up at the sheriff's office." Then, to the bartender, "Herb, put the hardware behind the bar. Someone will be by to pick up all of it later." With that, he turned on his heel and left.

Shortly after noon, Smoke Jensen left the task of collecting firearms to his deputy, Fred Chase, and headed for the Sorry Place. There he ordered a schooner of beer and helped himself to the free lunch counter. He stood at the bar, munching on a sandwich he had made of ham, rare roast beef, and two cheeses, when four of the local merchants entered and walked purposefully toward him.

"Sheriff, we have to talk," Eb Harbinson, their spokesman, declared.

Smoke laid down his sandwich, took a bite of hard boiled egg and faced them calmly. "What's on your minds?"

"This scheme of yours might work well for you, Sheriff, but we believe you have gone too far."

"How is that? There are less hard cases in town, isn't that right?"

Momentarily at a loss for words, Eb Harbinson watched as Smoke bit into a fat dill pickle and chewed thoughtfully. Eb took a deep breath and went on. "What you say is true. Only there may be too few of them around."

Smoke remained terse. "Meaning what?"

Eb felt his surety draining from him. "Well, we've talked it over and we all agree. This posting has been bad for business. Sales are down all over town. You have to stop turning people away."

Shaking his head, Smoke tried to reason with them. "I am not turning people away. They have a choice. Surrender their guns or they don't come into town."

Eb looked pained. He started to speak, only to be interrupted by Tiemeier, the butcher. "The way we see this, it's the same thing. A lot of local ranchers have heard about it, and they're not coming in for their supplies. That hurts business all around."

Smoke looked hard at Tiemeier's blood-stained, leather apron. "Don't you think they butcher their own stock?"

Red-faced, Tiemeier snapped back. "Of course they do. If I don't sell them beef and pork, there's still hams and bacon. Folks don't build smokehouses around here, wrong kind of wood. Then, there's my friends here, the other merchants in town. They are really suffering. You have to let people come into town."

Smoke studied the protesters awhile, noted the expressions of urgency they all wore, then tore off a mouthful of sandwich and munched it. A flash of anger crossed Tiemeier's face at this. That was what Smoke had been waiting for. His eyes narrowed, and he swallowed to clear his mouth before speaking.

"What you are asking is not possible. The mayor prevailed on me to help rid your town of the trash. I'm doing exactly that. I do not need the people I'm supposed to be protecting to come whining about slow business. The last time I looked, there is not a cradle-to-grave assurance of being taken care of in this country. A man's got to carry his own weight here.

"It's not the job of government, whether city, territory or the stripe-pants boys in Washington, to guarantee you anything, let alone a right to success. That's up to you to do the very best you can. If you don't participate, and wait for someone else to do it all for you, you deserve to fail. I'd suggest you all give Eb here a little more business for that printing press. Do up some flyers of your own, explaining that not one local will be turned away, and you might even list a few specials in your shops. Then see that they are circulated among those living outside town. Now, I'd like to finish my—"

Ticmeier interrupted him. "By God, man, you can't be serious."

Smoke grew a scowl. "If you are going to bring God into this, Preacher always taught me that He helps those who help themselves. I'd suggest, gentlemen, that you abide by that rule." Smoke started to add more advice, only to be interrupted by a loud disturbance out in the street.

A pair of gunshots racketed off the building fronts. Glass tinkled in their wake. Raucous voices raised in curses mingled with laughter. Another window went in a shower of silver shards. A bullet cracked into the clapboard front of the Red Rooster saloon. The protesting merchants had grown quiet and now ducked with alacrity as another slug bit a gouge of splinters off the front of the liquor emporium.

"Hey, Drew, that's purty good shootin'. See if you can hit that lamp."

"Easy, Grant, watch me."

Hot lead spanged off metal, followed by the tinkle of broken glass. The odor of kerosene reached Smoke Jensen's nostrils. He looked around to find himself the only one standing. Quickly he strode out onto the boardwalk.

Two gangling, young louts stood unsteadily in the street, reeling from the effect of too much liquor. Their dirty-blond hair hung in long, greasy hanks that swayed with each drunken step they took. They could have been twins, except that one stood a good four inches shorter than the other and looked as though his face had yet to need a razor. The older wore a scraggly wisp of yellow hair on his chin. He also held Marshal Grover Larsen by the shirt collar. He spoke as Smoke came into the light.

"You done that right nice, Drew. But you got a ways to go to be good as me. Watch me shoot the 'o' outta the word 'Groceries' on that winder." Grant raised his six-gun and fired.

To the right of the door to the general store, the window collapsed in a cascade of shards. From beyond his back, Smoke heard a groan. He shot a hard glance over his shoulder to Eb Harbinson.

"Would you like to see your other window go? Or do you want me to do the job I was hired for?"

"Go. Go on," Eb moaned.

Smoke Jensen stepped off the boardwalk and took a stance in the dirt street. "That's enough, boys. Let Marshal Larsen go and give me those guns."

Grant Eckers and his younger brother Drew had ridden into Muddy Gap to get supplies for their father's ranch. They also intended on having a few drinks and maybe sporting some with the girls in the Gold Boot. Although only sixteen, Drew had been assured by his older brother that he would have no trouble getting whiskey.

"After all," Grant had assured Drew, "Paw darn near owns this town. Ain't nobody gonna refuse us."

They had ridden up to where Marshal Grover Larsen stood watch. Being locals, the lawman had passed them on through. Unfortunately for him, the brothers had been sucking on the dregs of a bottle supplied by Grant, and their liquor-fogged brains made them take exception to the prohibition signs. After reading the notice, Grant had grabbed the marshal by the scruff of his collar and forced him to run alongside the boy's horse as they trotted into town.

When they dismounted, Marshal Larsen tried to make good an escape. Grant proved too fast for him. In two strides the strong youth caught up and yanked Larsen back. He held the lawman by one arm while he and Drew pulled their six-guns and began to bang away at the building fronts.

"Serve them right, getting uppity like that," Grant pronounced sentence.

The whiskey had started to wear off when Grant heard the cold voice behind them, demanding they give up their guns. He turned with his captive, a laugh on his lips, expecting to see another worn-out old man like the marshal. Instead, he saw the hard, rangy body of Smoke Jensen and the icy light in those strangely colored eyes. Beside him, Drew stumbled around also, his six-gun pointed at the ground, and sobered abruptly.

"What th' hell? Who you, mister?"

"I'm the new sheriff. I'll thank you to turn the marshal loose now."

His eyes narrowed, belligerence flared in Grant's voice. "And what if we won't?"

Smoke spoke matter-of-factly. "Then one or both of you will be seriously hurt."

"We'll see about that, Sheriff." Grant swung his Colt up in line with the side of Grover Larsen's head and eared back the hammer. "You try anything an' we'll splatter the marshal's brains all over the street."

Smoke Jensen gave a slight shrug. "Go ahead, he doesn't mean anything to me anyway."

Confused by this unexpected attitude, Grant hesitated a moment. In that instant, Smoke pulled his Peacemaker with blinding speed and shot Grant in the right shoulder. The impact of the bullet knocked Grant's Colt off target and caused it to discharge harmlessly down the street. Grant dropped his revolver as though it had turned red hot. An astounding transformation passed over him.

Face red and puckered, he began to whimper and moan like a frightened infant. He let go of Grover Larsen and curled his body downward. A large, wet stain appeared in the crotch of his trousers. Drew gaped at his older brother and kept his weapon pointed carefully skyward. Forty-five still in hand, Smoke Jensen pointed at Grant.

"Marshal, take this whining baby to jail and get him patched up." Then to Drew, "You have two choices: give up or get a bullet like he did."

362 *William W. Johnstone*

For a brief moment, Drew tried to tough it out. "That's my brother. You shot him, you son of a bitch."

"And you're next if you don't do what I say. Lay down that gun and come along peacefully."

Sullenly, Drew did as he had been told. Smoke Jensen spun the boy and gave him a quick pat-down. Then he roughly shoved Drew in the direction of the jail.

An hour later, Harmon Eckers stormed into the small room that fronted the jail and served both sheriff and marshal as an office. His ordinarily ruddy features had been made even more scarlet by the anger that boiled under the surface. He cut accusing eyes from Marshal Larsen to Smoke Jensen in turn. His voice came out harsh and demanding.

"What's this about my sons being arrested?"

Marshal Larsen nodded and released a long sigh. "That's true, Harmon. They're both back there in a cell."

Eckers raised a hand in a threatening gesture and spoke through a thunderous outrage. "Then don't just sit there, Grover, get them out here."

Smoke leaned forward, heat radiating from his eyes. "Sorry. That won't be possible."

"Why not? And who the hell are you?"

Speaking softly, although bridling his rising temper, Smoke replied, "Because they broke the law. And I'm the new sheriff."

"You won't be long, by God, not unless you release my boys. I've broken tin-star punks like you a dozen times. If you don't have my boys out here within two minutes, I'll snatch you out of that chair and snap your miserable back over my knee."

That proved an instant mistake. Smoke Jensen came out of his chair like a lightning bolt, the barrel of his Colt Peacemaker a blur as it sped from the holster. He raised his arm in a swift blur and swung like a batter in Abner Doubleday's new game of bases. The barrel collided with the side of Harmon Eckers' head above his ear with a loud *clonk!*

He fell like a heart-shot deer. Not even a moan escaped his lips. Smoke looked from him to Marshal Larsen. He hooked a thumb over his shoulder. "Drag this piece of garbage out of here and put him in a cell.

They had to do something. Della Olsen realized that after the shock of her husband's murder began to wear off. For days she could not count, she had sat in a daze, seeing nothing, hearing nothing, not even caring. She dimly recalled that Tommy had cooked for his sisters, cared for her, saw that she kept her hands and face clean.

Through the miasma of her grief she recalled Tommy sweating as he dug the graves for Sven and the boy they had taken in, Elmer Godwin. Tommy's hands had been blistered and raw when he completed the sorrowful task. That had caused him to delay the burial until the next day, his throbbing hands smeared with salve and bandaged. Now, as she stirred herself to organize thoughts for their future, she heard in memory his sweet, child's voice singing Sven's favorite hymn.

"Rock of ages, cleft for me/Let me hide myself in thee." Now she sang aloud in the gentle morning sun as she turned her eyes to the dark mounds that rested under the spreading boughs of an ancient spruce. Tears sprang to her eyes, which she hastily brushed away.

"Come on, children, we have to collect everything we can find. They are—our memories."

Tommy had been a real man, someone to lean on in the time of her darkness. She looked now and saw the wagon he had repaired. How hard he had worked, sweating as he labored. With his shirt off, she could see his immature muscles strain and tremble with the effort to work the jack and raise the wagon bed. Sven had taught him well, she thought, as she dimly recalled him replacing two spokes and sweating the steel tire onto the damaged wheel.

It had taken all his strength to lift the heavy object into place. Then he had tightened the hub nut and freed the jack. The beaming pride that had shone on his face made her heart lurch even now. Della heard the sound of a horse's hooves and looked up in surprise. Her satisfaction in her son soared as she saw him leading their old plow horse up toward the barnyard.

"Look what I found, Maw," he called out cheerfully. "We can use the wagon now."

"That's fine. That's wonderful, Tommy. Put him in the corral and come help us collect what belongings we can find. Maybe we can leave yet today."

Tommy took his role of man of the house seriously. "In that case, I'll jist hitch up now."

With their scant possessions loaded, Della handed the girls up into the wagon box and took her place on the driver's seat an hour later. Tommy took the reins and slapped the rump of the swayback, old gelding, and they rolled down the lane. With only a brief, backward glance at the graves, the Olsen family left the ruins of their ranch.

Smoke Jensen had finished a cup of coffee and made ready to return to a stint of duty on the deadline when Boyne Kelso stormed into the office, Mayor Norton in tow. The officious Kelso wasted no time on amenities.

"Sheriff, you have to release Harmon Eckers and his sons. Right now if not sooner."

Smoke appraised him coolly. "Why is that?"

"You have no idea what you have here," Kelso blurted.

"What I have here, Mr. Kelso, are two wet-behind-the-ears squirts, drunk as skunks, and shooting up the town. And their father threatening to break my back like a twig."

"That's not important." Kelso ignored Smoke's mood. "Harmon Eckers is the most influential rancher in the area. He runs eight hundred head of cattle, and employs three dozen hands. And he has friends," Kelso concluded ominously.

"Then it's likely he'll not be seeing them soon," Smoke told him. "He threatened a peace officer, and his sons broke the no-guns law and shot up the property of other people. Now, you'll have to excuse me. I have a saloon to clean out of drifters and trash, then I'm due on the posting line."

8

Smoke Jensen entered the Trailside saloon and came face-to-face with an even dozen angry hands from the Eckers' ranch. A bull of a man Smoke figured to be the foreman took a step away from the bar and faced him.

"We're gonna mosey over to that jail of yours and take out our boss and his sons. An' there ain't a damn thing you can do about it."

Laughing, Smoke raised his gloved left hand in a stopping motion. "I beg to differ with that."

Two more who rode for the Eckers brand joined the first, which made him even more vocal. "There ain't no way we're gonna allow any two-bit, tin-horn lawman to stand in our way."

He completed the last of that boast well within reach of Smoke Jensen. Setting himself—a subtle change of position missed by the pugnacious ranch hands—Smoke took advantage of that. His right fist, encased in a thin, black leather glove, shot out and caught the Eckers foreman a fraction behind the point of his chin. Smoke put shoulders and hips into it, and the blow lifted the surprised cowman's boots off the floor.

His eyes showed whites before he hit the boards. Smoke followed up immediately while momentary surprise froze the two range hands. He chose the one on his right first and delivered a one-two punch to chest and jaw that put out the man's lights in a blink. By then the other cowboy was moving.

He made a grab for Smoke Jensen's left arm, only to close his fingers on air. Smoke turned so quickly the hapless youth did not even see the fist coming that knocked him back against the bar. Dazed, he shook his head in an effort to clear his vision, wiped blood from his split lip, then launched himself at Smoke again.

Smoke waited him out. He blocked the first wild blow, caught the other on a shoulder point, then snapped a short, hard right to the cowhand's face. Blood spurted from a mashed nose, and the icy blue eyes crossed for a moment. Smoke followed up with a tattoo of rights and lefts to chest and belly. His knees sagging, the young cowboy gave up any attempt to cover himself and fell forward into the arms of Smoke Jensen.

Smoke swung him to the left and dropped the groggy youth into a chair. At once the battered man slumped over and laid his head on the green baize table. Four more of Eckers' hands decided to enter the fray. They started toward Smoke, one of them drawing a knife from his boot top.

They stopped as quickly at the loud, double click of shotgun hammers. "That's far enough, boys," Marshal Grover Larsen said from the open rear doorway. He held a ten gauge Greener, the muzzles lined up with their bellies. Slowly they eased back against the bar. Smoke Jensen looked them over thoughtfully.

"Not a one of you went for a gun, which speaks well for you. I can understand hotheadedness. What I can't abide is a cowardly act." With that he walked over to the one who had pulled his knife.

Smoke reached out and plucked the blade from a numb hand. He raised it before the man's eyes and took the tip between thumb and two fingers. Slowly Smoke bent the steel until it snapped in front of the hilt. A fleeting smile played across his lips as he dropped the broken knife to the floor. He pointed a finger at the man's suddenly ashen face.

"This one goes to jail. The rest of you drag these two out of here and get out of town."

Abruptly, Smoke turned his back on them and walked to the door. Meekly, the knife artist followed him.

Night caught up to Della Olsen and her children before she wanted it. She estimated that they had barely made twenty miles from their burned-out ranch in the past two days. The tired old horse Tommy had rounded up had to stop and rest far too often. An hour ago they had made camp.

Sarah-Jane had gamely gathered wood and buffalo chips for the cookfire. The eleven-year-old had taken her father's death harder than the other children, though Della had to admit that her daughter's spirits had lifted since starting for Buffalo, the nearest town. Sarah-Jane looked on the journey as an adventure.

While Sarah-Jane brought fuel, Tommy unhitched the horse and slipped a feed bag over the nag's nose. Then he unloaded the wagon and made a ring of stones to contain their fire. Della busied herself slicing bacon on the lowered tailgate of the wagon, paring potatoes and cutting onions. It would be a spare meal; Tommy had not found any game to shoot.

"Maw, what are we going to do when we get to Buffalo?"

Della looked into her son's clear blue eyes. "I don't know, Tommy. I'll find us a place to stay, take work somewhere. You and the girls will attend school."

Tommy made instant protest. "Awh, Maw, do we have to?"

"Yes, son. Lord knows I've done the best I can teaching you at home. At least you all can read and write and do your sums. But that's not enough. There's a whole world of things to learn out there."

Tommy swelled his chest. "I should get work, too, Maw. I'm too old to go to school."

"Buffalo has a four-year upper school now. I'm sure they will welcome you."

Thunderstruck, Tommy gaped at his mother. "You mean people go to school even after they are too old for the eighth grade?"

"Of course. Some people, like doctors and lawyers, even go on to college."

Tommy's fair, freckled brow furrowed. "That don't sound like something I'd like to do."

"It isn't likely you will get the chance." Della cast a regretful glance in the direction of the ranch. "Although your father and I had our dreams."

After the meal, a sky full of stars brought back painful memories to the children of their father. Della busied herself with the cleanup, her concentration broken when she heard the sniffles and muffled sobs of little Gertrude. She turned to find Tommy seated between the girls, an arm around the shoulder of each.

"I know it hurts. I . . ." Tommy's voice broke. "I miss Paw, too. And Elmer. There's this great big empty place inside me. But we have to go on, you know. We have to look out for Maw."

Tears welled in Della's eyes, which she hastily wiped away. How strong her boy was. A thrill of pride ran through her.

"But, Tommy, we're . . . jist so little," Gertrude complained in a tiny voice.

Tommy's shoulders heaved as he drew a deep breath. "We're big enough. We have to be. Look, you two, dry your tears. We'll go roll up in our blankets. We can watch the stars cross the sky."

"What will it be like when we get to Buffalo, Tommy?" Sarah-Jane asked, rising.

Tommy paused a moment, sorting his thoughts. "There'll be wonderful things. Horehound drops and rock candy an' . . . an' real ice cream."

Right then, a coyote yowled mournfully. The girls squealed in sudden fright. Even Tommy shivered. Della knew, at that moment, that everything would work out all right. This man/boy of hers, only turned fourteen this summer, would see to that. While the girls scampered off to the wagon, Della walked over to her son and put her arms around his shoulders, hugging him tightly.

"Thank you, son. Thank you for helping with the girls. They need the comforting . . . and so do you."

"Me, Maw? Shucks, I'm okay. An' so are you, right?"

Della smiled to herself and tousled his hair with her chin. "Yes, son, I really am."

Once more the coyote howled as the family took to their bedrolls in the wagon box. Slowly the coals ebbed until only the frosty light of the stars shone down upon them.

Early morning brought more frontier trash to be expelled from town. Roused from only four hours' sleep, Smoke Jensen thought his head might be stuffed with wool as he hurriedly shrugged into trousers and boots. He pulled a shirt over his head and tucked it behind his belt. A wild yell and a gunshot reached his ears through the thin walls of his room at the Wilber House Hotel as he buckled his cartridge belt in place. The twin Peacemakers rode his frame like old companions. Smoke clamped his hat on his head and started for the door.

Out on the street, small knots of curious townspeople gathered to watch the unfolding of what was fast becoming a regular event. Down at the end of the block, Deputy Fred Chase faced six proddy saddle bums, a hand on the butt of his Colt. Smoke lengthened his stride.

He came up on the quarrelsome thugs from an angle that left them unaware of his presence. One, slightly in front of the other five, gestured angrily and bellowed in a rusty voice. It served well to hold the attention of Fred Chase. A mistake that Smoke noted at once. He would have to talk to Fred later. For now, his attention was riveted on another lout who sought to take advantage of the deputy's distraction.

Smoke stepped up soundlessly behind him as the young punk drew his six-gun. Smoke's arms darted out, and he grabbed the back of the man's shirt and vest. Unceremoniously, Smoke dragged him from the saddle. In a flash, Smoke had his .45 Colt in his hand and slammed the barrel across the head of the would-be sneak-shot.

Immediately, the others became aware of Smoke's presence. His eyes cut from one to the other, clearly defying them to make a move. None of them did. Quickly, Smoke waded in, yanked another from his seat and disarmed him. While he worked his way through them, Smoke wondered, not for the first time, if it was all worth it. From his right, Smoke heard a solid clunk and looked to see a grinning Fred standing over the supine figure of the self-appointed leader of the collection of garbage.

Smoke nodded his approval. "Send them on their way, Fred. I'm going to go see who is in for an early drink."

On his way to the Sorry Place saloon, Smoke came upon a quartet of surly, low-browed louts milling in the street outside the general mercantile. They turned sour looks in his direction. One of them, a lank shock of dirty blond hair hanging down over his nearly nonexistent forehead, poked a thick, stubby finger at Smoke.

"Who says we can't wear guns in town? The man in there"—he hooked a thumb at the general store—"said we had to give up our guns or get out of town."

"He's right. By my orders."

Another of the thugs pushed his way forward. "There's four of us and jist one of you. How're you gonna make us?"

With the skill of a conjurer, a .45 Colt Peacemaker appeared in Smoke Jensen's hand before the others could close fingers around the butt-grips of their weapons. "With this, if necessary."

The first mouthy one cocked his head to one side. "Who the hell might you be?"

"I'm the sheriff. T'name's Jensen. Folks call me Smoke."

Four faces drained of blood. "Awh, hell, we done got the wrong town," declared the second piece of trash.

"That you do," Smoke told him blandly.

A third one spoke up. "Damn, those people down in Colorado don't talk about nothin' but how good you are with a gun, Mr. Jensen—uh—Sheriff. We'll leave, an' we won't make no trouble, honest."

"I believe that. Now have a nice ride out of town."

Smoke watched them depart, then turned to observe that the shot-out window of Harbinson's Mercantile had been boarded up. While he idly inspected it, Eb Harbinson stepped out onto the boardwalk. He rubbed his hands industriously on his apron tail and produced a smile.

"Sheriff Jensen, I want to tell you that I was sure wrong about you and your posting law. Yessir, wrong as can be. You know, my business has actually picked up. Those advertising flyers you suggested have been a godsend. You're doing a good job. An excellent job, in fact. I want you to know that all the good people of town are behind you a hunnard percent."

Smoke gave him a quizzical expression. "If they are, how come none of them are rushing over to volunteer to be deputies, Mr. Harbinson? Tell me that."

Early in the afternoon, Smoke Jensen worked at his teeth with a whittled stick as he stepped out of the Sorry Place. The pig's feet had been tasty and tender, with just the right amount of vinegar pickle to them. He ambled along the boardwalk and noted with satisfaction the lack of hard cases and drifter trash. He had nearly reached the front of the Trailside when three shots blasted out of the interior.

Smoke reached the batwings in three long strides. Over the curved top of the louvered doors he saw a bulldog-faced hard case standing over the body of a local rancher, a smoking six-gun in one hand. Smoke stepped through the swinging doors, Peacemaker in hand.

"Put it down and raise your hands," he commanded.

Unwilling to comply, the gunman shouted his defiance as he tried to turn and fire at the same time. "Like hell I—" he got out before Smoke Jensen shot him through the heart.

Two other gunslicks, friends of the dead thug, took exception to Smoke's treatment of their companion and went for their guns. A bullet from Smoke's .45 crashed into the bar beside one of them; then the pair fired as one.

Smoke Jensen had already moved, spoiling their best chance. His third round found meat low in the belly of one shootist, which slammed the man back against the bar and turned him part way around. Dimly he saw the reflection of Smoke in the mirror behind the row of bottles on the back bar. He tried to hold himself up with his left arm while he struggled to raise his six-gun and get off a shot.

Meanwhile, Smoke had moved again. He traded shots with the third gunman and dived low behind a faro table. A slug from the rogue's Colt scattered chips on the layout. On his knees, Smoke shot back.

A thin, high scream came from the bewhiskered gunman, who dropped his weapon and staggered three steps toward the door. All at once he began to tremble. His body went rigid, and he crashed into the sawdust. Beyond him, the wounded brigand at last had his revolver in position. Cursing Smoke, he fired.

Though not before Smoke Jensen had ducked low and rolled across an open section of floor. The bullet went wild, shattered a coal oil lamp, and lodged in the wall. Smoke had far better aim with his second Colt.

Splinters flew from the rough pine planks of the bar when Smoke's bullet exited the chest of the stubborn gunhand. He looked down in surprise and blinked once, slowly, before his eyes rolled up and he teetered over the brink into eternity. Smoke came to his boots and looked around for further resistance.

He had none, he soon saw. Then he took in the gawkers, who peered into the saloon from the windows and over the double batwing doors, drawn by the sounds of the brief, deadly shoot-out. One of them he soon recognized as Mayor Norton, when that worthy entered, face beaming with relief and pleasure.

"You've done it, Sheriff Jensen. That's the last of them. There's not a piece of riffraff left in town. I never believed anyone could do it so fast."

"I had some help, Mayor."

"You're too modest. You're the one who put the back-bone back in Grover Larsen. Fred Chase was only doing his job. The credit is all yours."

Smoke Jensen cut his eyes to the three cooling corpses. "There's a lot of it I would rather not have had to do."

Corpses did not enhance a politician's popularity, so Mayor Norton hastened to close the discussion of the killings. "Of course, of course. I understand."

That, of all the things that had been said since he had come to town, rubbed Smoke the rawest. "No, Mayor Norton, I don't think you could possibly know how I feel." Smoke reached for his badge and pulled it from his vest front. "I'm through here. My job is finished. I have a herd to catch up to."

Twenty minutes later, Smoke Jensen had all of his possessions loaded into saddlebags and placed in the pouches of a packsaddle rig. After a few pointers to Fred Chase, he left the sheriff's job in his capable hands, mounted Cougar and rode out of town with a rented packhorse on lead. To his surprise, nearly the whole population turned out to see him off. But not all of the residents of Muddy Gap gathered to wish their recent sheriff a fond farewell.

Seated behind his desk, Boyne Kelso turned a hard

glower to the second-floor window, from which he could see the tall, lean figure of Smoke Jensen riding out of town. He wet full lips and tossed down a shot of bourbon. In the chair opposite him, his son, Brandon, sipped at a beer.

"You'll get yours, you bastard," Boyne Kelso growled as Smoke went out of sight.

"What do you mean, Paw? He ain't gonna be around here no more."

"Never mind, son. Where he's going, he is about to step into a hornet's nest."

Which brought Boyne's thoughts to the immediate. He had to get a message to Reno Jim Yurian to inform him that the owner of the herd of horses they intended to rustle was the notorious gunfighter, Smoke Jensen. His next thought brought Boyne a great deal of comfort. He had every confidence that Reno would know exactly what to do.

9

Smoke Jensen rode hard for two days. Unencumbered by a slow chuck wagon and the remounts, he covered considerable northward distance. When he topped a long swell in the high plains early the morning of the third day, he saw in the distance what appeared to be a wagon with a woman and three children on board. Smoke held back and looked around carefully for any sign of the woman's husband, or any other man accompanying them. When he saw none, he urged Cougar on at a faster gait.

Riding undetected to within twenty yards, Smoke reined in and hailed them, standing in his stirrups. He noted the cringe and frightened reaction. Something was decidedly wrong here. He called out again. "Hello, you folks in the wagon. I mean you no harm. May I ride up?"

A quick conference between the woman and a gangling boy, who might be sixteen, resulted in a hesitant invitation. Smoke rode in, careful to keep his hands clear of his guns. Two small girls looked at him with wide-eyed, solemn faces. The boy wore a frown, although more of puzzlement than anger. In his hands he competently held a .32-20 Marlin rifle.

"Howdy, folks. M'name's Jensen. I own that horse herd whose sign you've been markin' along the trail. I'm on my way to catch up to them."

"What got you behind in the first place?" demanded the auburn-haired, freckle-faced boy.

Under any other circumstances, Smoke would have found such impudence an affront. Considering that they were obviously alone, and frightened of something, he let it go.

"I got mousetrapped into cleaning out the scoundrels and saddle trash from the town of Muddy Gap."

"You are a lawman?" the woman asked suspiciously.

"I am. Deputy U.S. marshal. Though I'm not on government business at present," Smoke added.

"I see," Della responded, though she did not in the least. "Your horses are ahead of us, then?"

"Yes. Will you pardon me if I ask a blunt, personal question? Are you on your way to meet your husband?"

Della paled. "My husband—my husband is dead. He was murdered by outlaws who stole our cattle and burned our ranch."

Right on top of her words the boy spoke. "Why weren't you there to stop it, Marshal?"

Smoke curbed a flare of impatience. "As I said, I am not here on official business. I am sorry to hear that, Mrs.—?"

"Olsen. Della Olsen, Marshal Jensen. This is my son, Tommy, and my daughters, Sarah-Jane and Gertrude."

Smoke touched his hat in acknowledgment and made an instant decision. It was not safe for such vulnerable people to be out here alone. "Pleased to meet you. I'd appreciate it if you would tell me where you are headed."

Della considered a moment. "To Buffalo. It's not far actually. We should be there in two or three days."

"More like six, I'd say," Smoke countered. "I don't wish to be pushy, Mrs. Olsen, but do you mind if I accompany you? At least until we catch up to my horses?"

Relief blossomed on Della Olsen's face. "We would be grateful, Marshal Jensen. And, please, call me Della."

"Thank you, Della. Folks generally call me Smoke."

Tommy's eyes grew wide and bright. "Oh, my gosh! The gunfighter and lawman? I read about you in a dime novel."

Smoke seemed uncomfortable. "All greatly exaggerated, believe me. Truth is, I've been both, son. Right now I'm raising blooded horses and selling what I can of them." To Della, he went on to say, "This really is rough country for you to be traveling alone. I hope that revealing my identity does not change your opinion too much."

Della took a deep breath and settled her disquiet. "Not at all, Smoke Jensen. As a matter of fact, right now I can't think of anyone more welcome to accompany us."

Tommy fairly bubbled. "Good for you, Maw."

Rapid as his travel had been for the previous two days, Smoke now found his pace diminished to the painfully slow crawl of the aged plowhorse that drew the Olsen wagon. At the nooning, which Smoke would have ordinarily taken afoot, walking Cougar while he munched a strip of jerky and one of a dozen biscuits he had purchased at the Iron Kettle, Smoke made a suggestion.

"Della, what say we swap my packhorse for your critter for the time being. We could make a good twenty, twenty-five miles a day that way."

Still defensive around this living legend, Della chose to take offense. "If we're holding you up, Mr. Jensen, you can ride on alone."

"Now, that's just what I didn't want to happen. Don't take me wrong. I'm sure you are eager to get to Buffalo and settle in. I'm only trying to help."

Suddenly contrite, Della reached out impulsively and laid a hand on Smoke's forearm. "I'm sorry. All that has happened has . . . unnerved me. Yes, that is a good and practical idea. Generous, too. Thank you." She raised her voice. "Tommy, see to unhitching Barney and exchanging him for Smoke's packhorse."

With that accomplished, their pace picked up considerably during the afternoon. When Smoke indicated the place they would camp for the night, Tommy came to him. The lad had an eager expression that foretold his expectations.

"Mr. Jensen, my paw told me I'm a fair shot. What say I go out and find us some rabbits for supper?"

Smoke grinned broadly. "Fine with me. You have a shotgun along?"

"No, sir. Only my thirty-two-twenty rifle." Then Tommy added proudly, "I only make head shots."

"Then go ahead." Smoke reserved his praise for when the results came in.

Which, half an hour later, surprised and pleased him. He had heard only four shots, and Tommy came back with as many plump rabbits. Deftly, the boy skinned and dressed them, laid aside the livers for the frying pan, and laced the carcasses on green willow twigs, which he inclined over a bed of coals. After the meal, Smoke took Tommy aside.

"Out here, Tommy, it's important a man is able to fend for himself. I see you can provide for the table. Now, I want to give you something to help in protecting your family. I took these off a hard case who won't be needing them any longer," he explained as he opened one envelope of his pack rig and took out a .44 Colt Lightning, double-action revolver and a .44 Winchester.

"I can see no better use for them than that you have them," Smoke went on.

Tommy's eyes grew large and round. "I ain't got money to pay for them, Mr. Jensen."

"They're a gift, Tommy. Only one thing, always use them properly."

"Yes, sir. I promise. Is there cartridges for them?"

"What you see in the belt and another twenty rounds. It's not much, but a good shot like you can surely make them count."

Tommy's chest swelled, and he gulped as he accepted the weapons. "I'll . . . never do wrong with them, Mr. Jensen."

"I'll take your word for that, Tommy. By the way, how old are you?"

"F-fourteen."

For a moment, Smoke regretted his impulsive gesture, then considered the boy's size and sturdiness. He'd do. He remained satisfied with his decision until Della came to sit beside him later, after the children had gone to sleep.

"That was a generous thing you did for Tommy, Smoke. Though I must admit it worries me some. A boy his age with such powerful weapons."

Here it comes, Smoke thought to himself. But Della's next words surprised him. "Though if he is to be the man of the house, he must take upon himself manly things. It's decided, then. Tommy will keep the rifle and the revolver. And thank you. I feel safer just knowing that someone as considerate as you is around."

Smoke poured them both coffee. "Your loss is so recent, I don't suppose you feel like talking about it," he prompted.

"As a matter of fact, I don't. But I must face it. It was a gang, a big one. They came riding in like a band of wild Indians. Their leader was a fancy dresser, like a gambler, with a red silk lining in his black coat. My Sven was killed early on. It took a while to get poor Elmer."

"Your older son?"

"No. Elmer Godwin. He worked for us. Although we treated him like one of the family, goodness knows. An orphan boy."

"Do you know what caused the attack?"

"Not really. They were after the cattle, I suppose. They drove them off when they left. The children and I were in the root cellar. Tommy had his little rifle, but I don't think it would have done much against those monsters. They burned our house and the barn."

"Then you are wiped out?"

"Yes, Smoke. All we have are the clothes on our backs, a few sheets and blankets, that old wagon and a broken-down horse."

"And a mighty tough spirit, Della. When we reach Buffalo with the herd, I'll do whatever I can to help you get settled."

"You're a kind man, Smoke Jensen."

Smoke flushed slightly. "No. Only practical. There are a lot who would take advantage of a woman in your distress. They might find it more difficult cheating me."

Della studied him awhile in silence. "You are a most unusual man, Smoke."

They talked on until the moon rose. Then Smoke put out the fire with the coffee dregs and rolled up in his soogan, his head on his saddle.

Jerry Harkness had been uneasy since the previous afternoon. He did not doubt his ability to ramrod the drive. Yet, the responsibility of doing it had begun to weigh on him. At midmorning, with the sun warm on his right cheek, his discomfiture intensified to a full-blown premonition.

He did not like the looks of the treacherous ravine on the left, nor the steep hill to the right that forced the trail into a blind curve. Anything could be lying in wait ahead. Jerry pulled a long face and dropped back to alert the men. That left a young wrangler named Brad in the lead position. Jerry quietly informed the other hands. As usual, the eternal optimist, Utah Jack, made light of it.

"You goin' old maidish on us, Jerry? Hell, there ain't nobody out here but us."

"And a couple of thousand Cheyenne," Jerry reminded him. "Jist keep your eyes sharp. Don't overlook anything."

By then, the head of the herd had walked out of sight around the bend. Utah Jack, who rode drag, whistled to the stragglers to hurry them on. Jerry Harkness had just started forward when the first shots sounded.

Yancy Osburn bossed the left flank of the Yurian gang ambush. He spied the approach of the horses and felt a surge of elation. Here they came, by God. If only the fellers in the center held off long enough, the whole herd could be contained right there. The lone rider in the header position looked up right then and saw the barricade built the previous day. His startled expression faintly reached Yancy where he waited.

"What the devil is this?" Brad turned in the saddle to call back to the swing riders. "Hold up the herd. There's some kind of roadblock."

At once, the two swing riders nearest the head of the string of horses began to squeeze in, to stop forward motion. From his vantage point, Yancy Osburn saw two white puffs of powder smoke bloom behind the obstructing abatis.

A second later, the drover, whose name he did not know, threw his hands in the air and sagged crookedly in the saddle. His mount trotted nervously a few paces, then turned and looked about in confusion. Three more shots cracked from the palisade, and another wrangler went down. The remounts began to whinny and mill about.

That served as a signal for Yancy Osburn, on the left, and Smiling Dave Winters, who commanded the right flank. They jumped their horses into motion, followed by the ten men each commanded, Yancy in the lead, his flankers swarmed around the breastlike swell of the hill, intent on closing on the herd and preventing a stampede.

Smiling Dave did the same, leading his men up out of the ravine and directly against the middle swing rider. Two six-guns blazed, and another Sugarloaf hand went down. The loose remounts went straight-legged in shock, then bolted inward, against the pressure of mounted horsemen. The outlaws whistled softly and uttered soothing words in an attempt to prevent the explosive moment in which the animals bolted in all directions. Two hundred horses at forty dollars a head represented a good lot of money. On the far side, Smiling Dave watched as Yancy killed yet another of the drovers. So far, Dave considered, it had gone well.

Luke Britton came face-to-face with one of the rustlers. He fired instinctively and felt a jolt of satisfaction when he saw the front of the outlaw's vest jump and a black hole appear close to the heart. Moments earlier, Jerry Harkness had disappeared in a cloud of dust and powder smoke. Luke looked for his friend, avoiding death by a narrow margin when he jumped his mount forward unexpectedly. At once he swung on the bandit and fired his six-gun.

"Gotcha, you varmint," he shouted in satisfaction as the gunman fell from his saddle.

To Luke's right, another Sugarloaf rider cried out and fell across the neck of his touchy roan. This was quickly going from bad to worse, Luke decided as he ducked low and kneed his mount in the direction where he had last seen Jerry.

Seconds later, the two friends found one another in a wild melee. A red stain washed along Jerry's right side, from a bullet gouge along his ribs. Having exhausted their cartridges, three rustlers swung their six-guns by the barrels in an attempt to club Jerry from his horse.

At once, Luke shot one of the bandits, and the other pair pulled off to reconsider. Jerry took the time to shuck the expended cartridges from his Colt and reload three rounds before the murderous trash sprang forward again. He and Luke fired as one and drilled the nearer robber through one lung and his liver. He would not live to ride clear of the fight.

"There's too many of them," Jerry opined. "We've got to pull back."

Luke protested immediately. "But the horses. We'll lose the herd."

Frowning, Jerry revealed his hasty plan and the reason for his decision. "We're gonna lose them anyway. Alive, we can trail them. If we stand our ground, there won't be a one of us left. Go tell the others."

Caleb Noonan had his horse shot out from under him. He went down with a wide roll away from the heavy creature as it fell. Quickly he scrambled back and used the dead beast as cover. From that vantage, Caleb took aim and blew a rustler out of the saddle. He fired again; then a hot line burned painfully along his left side. The offending slug smacked into the belly of his mount a split second later. Caleb rolled and snapped off another round.

He heard a cry in the midst of the roiling billow that blanketed the majority of the riders and the horses. Noonan took time for a fleeting smile and looked for another target. Be damned if he'd let these yahoos take the herd.

Pop walker had come up with a sprained ankle and had been relegated to the chuck wagon and the duties of a cook. He grumbled about it, but secretly prided himself in the grub he turned out. To the chagrin of the regular trail cook, many of the men complimented Pop on his culinary endeavors. When the ambush erupted in their faces, he had been behind Brad Plummer when the young drover had been shot through the breast. Pop Walker hauled on the reins and tried to turn the wagon, while he shouted a belated warning.

Immediately, bullets began to crack into the side of the converted buckboard. Pop set the brake, dropped low under the driver's bench and unlimbered his six-gun. The old Remington conversion fired well enough, but the barrel locking pin had been weakened by the hotter, cased ammunition loads. That caused the barrel to wobble on discharge, which played hob with his accuracy.

He took careful aim and fired at the face of a shouting rustler. The bullet went low and smacked the outlaw's horse between the eyes. The animal reared and threw its rider, then dropped in place. The gunman swung free of his saddle and threw a hasty shot in the direction of Pop Walker. Splinters burst in a shower at the top of the highest board, and Pop felt their sting, like so many bees, on his face. He raised up to fire again, and pain exploded in his right shoulder. Heat and numbness quickly followed. Awh, hell, he thought in a dizzy moment, how would he cook now?

"We've got 'em on the run," a jubilant Prine Gephart shouted through the dust.

"What says?" came a defiant question.

"They ain't standin' their ground anymore. We've got the horses free an' clear."

Reno Jim Yurian answered him. "Not so free We've lost five good men so far. Tighten up those horses, don't let 'em run."

Suddenly, the fiercely fought ambush turned to equally desperate herd management. More dust rose to blind the Yurian gang and the Sugarloaf hands alike. An occasional shot blasted into the stillness of milling horses. An annoyed whinny usually answered it. Gradually the confusion diminished. A stiff breeze blew up from the southwest and carried away the brown cloud that had shrouded everything.

A moment after Pop Walker had shouted his warning, bullets flew all around Ahab Trask. Being saddled with the handle of the hated King of Judah gave him reason enough to use only his surname, he decided long ago. He ducked low and skinned his Smith American from its holster. From the volume of gunfire, Trask knew that this was no highway shakedown for tribute to use the trail.

These men had to be after the herd. The realization gave Trask renewed determination. He sought a target and at last sighted in on a pale face seen through a gap in the logs piled across the trail. He fired, and the face disappeared in a haze of red liquid. Once more he searched for an outlaw.

He did not have to look far. Brigands swarmed from around the side of the hill on his right, while more poured up over the lip of a draw on the left. Working drag, along with Utah Jack, Trask had the advantage of distance. He fired again, and one of the outlaws left his saddle. Then Trask looked at Utah Jack.

"We've gotta get these horses out of here."

Utah Jack spoke with authority. "No, Trask, we've got to hold them. If they stampede, we'll never find 'em all, an' the rustlers will have their pickin's."

Right then, a slug fired from the six-gun of Smiling Dave Winters cut a deep gouge along Trask's thigh and diverted upward to smash itself against the thick leather of his cartridge belt. It drove partway through the buckle and embedded there. Stunned and winded, Trask saw blackness swim up to engulf him.

Dapper as always, although his fancy clothes bore a patina of gray-brown dust, Reno Jim Yurian stood in his stirrups and surveyed the scene of carnage.

Not a sign of the wranglers with the herd. An old man lay slumped against the dashboard of a chuck wagon. He bled from his shoulder. Quickly Reno Jim counted the fallen opponents. Eight of them. There had been a dozen. Somehow, four had gotten away. No matter, he decided. He waved an arm at the milling horses.

"You boys get them lined out and headed for the canyon." Reno Jim eased back into the saddle.

"What about them that got away?" asked Yancy Osburn.

"Not our problem. No doubt they were wounded. Bound to die before they can get to any help. Same for that one in the wagon."

Yancy Osburn sent men to clear the obstruction across

the trail. They worked quickly and efficiently. Pop Walker lay still and watched them through slitted, pain-misted eyes. If what their leaders—a man Pop saw as dressed in fancy gambler's clothes—had said was true, he would be a goner soon. Damn, that rankled. He did not want to die out here all alone. Slowly, the herd came under control and moved on up the trail. Before the severity of his wound knocked him out, Pop heard one of the outlaws mention him.

"I still say we ought to finish that old-timer."

"No," the fancy-dressed leader responded. "Leave him for the coyotes."

10

Two days went by with the stolen herd getting farther away by the time Smoke Jensen and the Olsens arrived at the scene of the rustling. He hove into view a few minutes before eleven o'clock in the morning. Jerry Harkness saw him first. Although his ribs ached and burned from the infection that had invaded his wound, he raised his arm and waved eagerly to make certain Smoke knew someone had survived. Smoke turned to young Tommy when he saw signs of life.

"Bring the wagon along quick as you can. Those are my men down there."

Smoke cantered along the curve to within ten feet of the chuck wagon. There he reined in and dismounted, ground hitching Cougar. He made a quick count of heads while he strode toward Jerry. Five men. Only five left who were not seriously injured. At least they had managed to keep their horses. For a moment, Smoke tasted the bitter flavor of defeat.

"They ain't in any hurry, Smoke," Ahab Trask hastened up to inform Smoke. "An' they ain't hidin' their trail. We can catch them easy."

Silent, Smoke took in the injuries of his hands. He doubted that these men would be catching up to anyone soon. He spoke beyond the haggard group to Luke Britton. "Luke, I want you to take the most seriously wounded and strike out to the east for the nearest town. If you come upon a big ranch, that might serve. Get the injured taken care of and gather someone to help get that herd back. The trail leads along the south fork of the Powder River, through the Bighorn Mountains, and into Buffalo. Join us there."

Luke looked around in surprise. "Who is 'us,' Smoke?"

Smoke nodded toward Tommy Olsen as the wagon rolled up. "Me, Utah Jack and him. That's Tommy Olsen, he's a good shot and level-headed. He'll have to do."

"I'm going with you, Smoke," announced Jerry Harkness.

"No, you are not."

"Yes, I am." Jerry sat up abruptly and winced at the agony that shot through his chest. "I was only restin'. See? I can sit a saddle."

Smoke raised a gloved hand and pointed at Jerry. "You're not in that condition."

"It don't hurt that much, Smoke. It's getting better, really it is."

"Let me have a look."

Jerry knew better than to refuse, or even try to. He shrugged, pinched his features again and gave in with a sigh. Smoke climbed into the wagon and pulled Jerry's shirt away. The gouge cut by the bullet was scabbed, with oozing yellow pus escaping, bright red flesh all around. Long, scarlet lines, like the tentacles of an octopus, radiated out in two directions.

"I'm going to have to clean this, drain it and put a poultice on, Jerry. It's going to hurt like hell. But the only condition under which you are going along is that we get that infection whipped."

Eyes bright with a mixture of hope and sickness, Jerry looked intently at Smoke. "Go ahead. Whatever you do won't be any worse than what I've gone through so far."

"Don't be too sure of that. Luke, go to the nearest trees. Find some with moss. Then gather the yellow and gray parts. A whole lot of it. Also find some yarrow, if there is any, and bring the whole blossom. A double handful if you can get that much. Tommy, you go over to the creek and cut me an armload of red willow branches. Bring them back and we'll peel them."

Tommy looked at Smoke quizzically. "What's that for?"

"Red willow makes a good pain killer. We'll boil the scrapings from the bark and make a tea. I'll pour a lot down Jerry before I soak off that scab. He'll need it. Now, there's where you come in, Della. Find me some clean cloth, all you can spare, and tear it into strips. Those we'll boil to clean and bandage the wound."

In ten minutes, Smoke had a fire going. He examined all the wounded and treated the lightest injuries with liniment, bandaging them tightly when the boiled strips of a bed sheet had dried sufficiently. After half an hour, Tommy returned with a huge armload of willow branches. Smoke set him and his sisters to stripping the leaves, while he peeled and scraped the bark. He used a coffeepot from the chuck wagon, over mock protests from Pop Walker, who wasn't injured as badly as he thought, to begin to steep willow bark tea. When the boy finished cleaning the twigs, Smoke showed him how to peel and scrape the bark.

While they worked, Utah Jack Grubbs watched intently. At last he spoke. "That's Injun medicine you're cookin' up, ain't it?"

"Sure is, Utah. I learned it from Preacher when I was not much older than Tommy here."

"From a preacher, eh?"

"No, Utah. From the mountain man named Preacher. His given name was Arthur, but I don't think I ever heard his family name spoken."

Tommy looked up shyly from under long, auburn lashes. "He's the one you were tellin' me about the other night, sir—er—Smoke?"

"The same. He was quite a man. A real living legend."

"I've heard of him." Utah Jack pushed back into the conversation. "Wasn't he a bloody-handed murderer? They say he back shot more men than he faced down. Ambushed and kilt a whole passel of fellers."

"I don't know where you got such fool notions," Smoke replied lightly, attempting to disarm this scurrilous accusation. "I know better, because I was there most of the time. Preacher was no more a back shooter or a bushwhacker than I am. I learned my gun manners from him."

"Sorry, didn't mean to run down an old friend."

Smoke gave the equivocating horseman a frown. "There's not many men, living or dead, who could run down Preacher." Abruptly he came to his boots, poured a cup of yellow-red broth from the coffeepot and walked to where Jerry Harkness lay in the wagon.

"Here, Jerry, drink some of this."

"Do I gotta? That stuff tastes bitter."

Smoke shrugged. "Better bitter than not drink it and put up with what I'm going to do to you."

Jerry Harkness made a face and reached for the tin cup. He swallowed rapidly to get the liquid out of his mouth as quickly as possible. When he finished, he made to put it aside. Smoke reached out and took the container from him, filling it again.

"More?"

Smoke suppressed a grin. "More."

After the third cup, Jerry had about reached the gag limit. He licked his lips and made another sour face. By then, the medicinals Smoke required had been gathered and brought to the rough camp. Smoke rummaged in the chuck wagon again and came up with a wire basket popcorn popper. This he filled with the fungus and put it to dry over a low bed of coals.

With that in progress, he located a smooth, flat rock and piled the yarrow blossoms on it. He looked around and could not find what he wanted. He gestured to Tommy Olsen, who came to see what Smoke Jensen needed.

Pointing to the distant, tree-lined water course, Smoke made his request. "Tommy, go back to the creek and find me a fist-sized, water-smoothed rock. Wash it clean and bring it to me."

"Sure, Smoke," Tommy chirped. A mischievous, sly light came to the boy's eyes. "If I'm gonna get a good one, I bet I'll have to get in the water."

Having raised two sons and in the process of raising a third, Bobby, Smoke was wise in the ways of boys. "If you do, don't take more than ten minutes, and dry off good before putting your clothes back on."

Face alight with expectation, Tommy sped off after thanking Smoke for nothing more than acquiescing to the obvious. Smoke chuckled softly behind him. After all, he was not so old as to have forgotten his own boyhood.

Tommy returned with the rock twenty minutes later, his auburn hair a darker color, still dripping drops of water. His fair complexion, under the freckles, flushed a pink glow from the chill water of the creek. Proudly he handed Smoke a perfect stone.

Smoke thanked him and set immediately to crushing the yarrow flowers. He added more of the red willow scrapings and a bit of water to form a paste. This he covered with a strip of cloth from those drying on a thin line strung from the back of the Olsen wagon. During the process, he frequently checked the drying fungus.

When it reached the desired consistency, he added half to the poultice he had prepared and put the rest to soak in an especially strong liquor of willow bark. He looked up to see Luke Britton standing over him.

"I'll start off now with the wounded, if it's all right with you, Smoke."

"Do that. They're patched up as good as I can do. Take the best of your horses. We have two wagons. Pop Walker can drive one, Utah Jack the other. Tommy and I have horses. We'll get on the trail by mid-afternoon, and stick to the sign left by the herd. Join back up as soon as you can. And . . . good luck."

"It's you who's gonna need the luck, Smoke."

Smoke agreed readily. "Don't I know it."

Taking up his medicines, Smoke walked to where Jerry awaited his fate. With Della's help, he administered more of the potent tea and then took hot water and cloth strips and, using his sheath knife, began to scrape away the crust of dried blood that had scabbed over the wound channel. Jerry bit his lip and suppressed a cry of pain.

Smoke Jensen worked deftly and quickly, to peel open the long gouge along the ribs. While he progressed, at his direction, Della Olsen mopped up the yellowish matter that had collected under the surface. In a brief two minutes, which seemed like hours to Jerry, the whole raw wound had been exposed. With hands surprisingly gentle for their size and muscularity, Smoke bathed the savaged muscle tissue. Then he packed the groove with the poultice he had concocted.

Wonder registered on the face of Jerry Harkness. "It feels so cool. Like you'd rubbed ice on me, Smoke."

In the distance everyone heard two quick shots from the light .32-30 rifle carried by Tommy Olsen. "We'll change that in a couple of hours and then try to get some broth down you."

Pop Walker grumped his opinion. "What are you gonna make it outta? Most of our grub got flogged by those rustlers. We've been makin' do with corn bread and beans."

Smoke showed him an amused smile. "If I'm not mistaken, we'll have rabbit, or maybe some prairie chickens, might even be deer meat on the menu."

Pop looked surprised. "Y'mean that li'l tad of a boy's gonna fetch us our dinner?"

Smoke nodded. "Just so. I told you he is a crack shot. He never fires if he can't hit what he's shooting at. So, if I were you, Pop, I'd get to whipping up some of that corn bread. And see if you can't round up some onions, wild or otherwise. Anything to flavor a stew."

"Well, I'll be gol-derned." Pop Walker brightened. "I'll do that right away."

After they had eaten their fill, with Smoke Jensen urging everyone to stuff themselves and put aside what would keep, because it would be a cold camp that night, he changed the poultice and bandages on Jerry Harkness.

Smoke beamed down at his trustworthy ranch hand. "You may not feel like it, but you're looking a lot better. The poultice is drawing, and the infection is not headed for your armpit anymore. Another day or so and you can ride."

"That's good news. Say, the kid did a right smart job of gettin' that antelope. When do I get off this baby's broth and sink my teeth into some real meat?"

"By tonight, I'd say. I set the ribs to smoking over the coals. They should be ready by the time we break camp."

Jerry looked admiringly upon Smoke. "Do you ever not think of everything, Smoke?"

Smoke produced a wry smile. "Not since Preacher boxed my ears for leaving a perfectly good fireside trestle behind. He got right exercised by that."

Thirty minutes later, the refugees of the ambush started off after the herd. Most rode in silence. Tommy, atop the swayback plow horse, trotted up to ride beside Smoke Jensen. Smoke noted the boy had his Winchester along.

"What do we do when we catch up to your horses, Smoke?"

Smoke did not even have to think. "You fall back and protect your mother and sisters. That Model Seventy-three has range enough to make certain none of them get close. It'll be like shooting game. Make sure of your shot, never miss, and go for the head shots when you can."

Tommy went suddenly pale. "But, I . . . ain't never shot at a man before." His voice croaked from just beyond the threshold of puberty.

Smoke's reply, although candid enough, spared Tommy

the more gruesome aspects of the reality. "It's not nice, ever. And you never get over it. But a man has to do what he has to do. I'm not worried, Tommy. You'll be all right when the time comes."

Much relieved, Tommy heaved a sigh. "If you say so, sir. I'll try to do my best, Smoke."

Jerry Harkness had been sitting upright the last several miles, leaning over the left sideboard of the Olsen wagon, his eyes on the multitude of hoof prints. He called out to Smoke now, his eyes alight with confidence.

"It's them, all right. Unshod hooves an' all." An amusing thought suddenly occurred to him. "Say, those army farriers are gonna play merry hell with these critters when we finally get them there."

Merriment twinkled in Smoke's eyes, and he pulled a wry expression. "It's all part of the plan. At least that's my understanding from what Colonel Albright said in his letter. The shoeing of these horses is to be part of what the army calls On the Job Training. He's been burdened with green farriers. They need breaking in as fast as these mounts."

That brought a laugh from Jerry Harkness, which caused him to wince. Smoke trotted over to the wagon and climbed into the bed. He tied Cougar to the tailgate and went to his Cheyenne medicine supplies. Quickly he tended to the wound on Jerry's side and repacked it with fresh poultice. When the task had been completed, he cut his eyes to those of his ranch hand.

"You're doing better, faster than I thought. The red rays of infection have shrunk by half." He pointed to the formerly alabaster skin over Jerry's rib cage. "And you are taking on a more natural, pinkish coloring. For sure, by tomorrow you'll be driving that wagon, instead of riding in it."

"That's good news. Now, what's the bad news?"

Smoke sobered at once. "You won't be up to fighting form for at least three more days."

Jerry looked jolted. "Then you were right all along. I'm being a burden on all of you. I should have gone with Luke. A gimped-up man ain't no good in a fight."

Smoke sighed explosively. "If I had thought you were seriously wounded, outside of the infection, I would have made you go. Now stop feeling sorry for yourself and heal so you can carry your load in a fight." The last of that he said with a gruffness from the affection he held for this courageous young ranch hand.

That night, the small party settled into what would be the first of many cold camps. The generous portion of leftover antelope ribs, served out by Pop Walker, along with the remaining corn bread, biscuits and a pot of cold beans, left everyone with full bellies. While they ate, Tommy hunkered right up close beside him, and Smoke became aware of something that for the moment perplexed him.

Throughout the afternoon, Tommy had ridden resolutely at Smoke's side. In camp, the boy had stuck close to him; wherever he went, Tommy came along. No matter what chore he was given, Tommy went about it cheerfully and with an eagerness that belied the usual surly mood of teenaged children. While he conducted his labors, the lad constantly cut his eyes to Smoke to see if his efforts were being noticed. When his gaze locked with Smoke's, Tommy flushed furiously and looked away, suddenly burdened with ten thumbs. So frequently separated from his own brood, it took Smoke some time to figure it out.

No doubt about it, he allowed in late evening when the boy trudged along beside Smoke for a final check of the horses on the picket line. Tommy had transferred his need for a father figure to Smoke. *Damn!* Smoke thought. That was going to get the boy's feelings bad hurt before this was over. Somehow, that didn't seem right. For his part, rather than do the popularly accepted thing of spurning the youngster's devotion, Smoke responded by roughly teasing the boy. To Smoke's surprise, it seemed to strengthen the bond the lad sought to forge between them.

"Hey, Tommy, are you sure that water wasn't too cold this morning?"

A puzzled frown formed on Tommy's forehead. The water had felt wonderful. "Why's that, Smoke?"

"Your voice is a full octave higher than before."

Blushing, Tommy made feeble protest. "Awh, it is not. It's jist . . . sometimes it breaks, goes back to bein' a little kid again."

Smoke reached out and ruffled the youngster's tousled auburn hair. "Growing up is hell, ain't it?"

"Yessir, it purely is," Tommy agreed from the depths of his adolescent misery.

Early the next morning, Smoke's party lost the trail of the herd on a wide stretch of hard shale outcroppings. The wagons pressed on while Smoke and Utah Jack fanned out to search. Shortly before noon, Utah Jack cut their sign. He swung back to the wagons and fired three shots to alert Smoke. When the last mountain man arrived, Grubbs gave him the good news.

"I found them. They're headed for Powder River Pass up yonder in the Bighorns. The tracks look a whole lot fresher. They must be havin' trouble with the remounts."

Smoke considered that a moment. "That means they are straying away from our intended route. If that's the case, they have a place close by to hold the horses until a buyer can be found. That makes our job easy."

Utah Jack challenged this at once. "How do you figger that? There ain't but three of us fit to do any fightin'."

"Jerry can hold his own in that wagon. And as I said before, Tommy's a fine shot." Smoke looked up to find the boy at his side, eagerly soaking up every word.

"Yeah, but are you gonna take a little boy of fourteen into a fight with more'n twenty hard cases?"

He hadn't been any older when Preacher got him into a shoot-out with some angry Pawnee. Smoke almost spoke his thoughts aloud, though he refrained because he did not want to give Tommy any encouragement. Instead, he flavored his response with a frown. "I'm not going to get Tommy into any fight if I can avoid it."

"Awh, Smoke," Tommy protested. "You jist said I was a good shot. The sooner we get your horses back, the sooner you can get us on to Buffalo."

Momentarily stymied, Smoke pushed back the brim of his Stetson. "The kid's got a point, you have to admit."

Prine Gephart leaned over and tapped Garth Evans on one shoulder. With a grunt, Garth ended his mid-afternoon snooze and shoved his hat up off his face. "Huh? What is it?"

"Lookie over there. That's them comin'. You can bet on it, believe me."

Garth Evans rubbed sleep from his eyes and focused on the distant ridge. Two wagons labored down the facing slope. Three riders, one of them looking to be no more than a boy, formed a wedge in front of them. Dust boiled up from the wheels.

"Hummm. You might be right, Prine. If so, what do we do now?"

Gephart snapped testily. "What we was put here for. We're supposed to be lookouts, right? What we had best do is that you light a shuck outta here and catch up to the gang. I'll keep ahead of them and guide the boys in when they come. Now, best make tracks."

Garth Evans started to swing into his saddle. Prine Gephart roused himself to sit upright. "No, dummy. Walk your horse at least a mile before you mount up. You want them hearing you?"

"Uh! Never thought of that."

In minutes he had walked out of sight of the pile of carelessly strewn boulders. Prine Gephart went next, also walking his horse until well ahead of the slow-moving caravan. Then he took to the saddle and ambled along the wide path left by the horses. His confidence soared. He had counted heads. This little annoyance would be easy to get rid of.

Another cold camp. From a close examination of the hoof prints, Smoke determined that they had quickly closed the gap. The width of the trail indicated that the rustlers were indeed having trouble with the herd. Obviously not experienced wranglers, they let the horses spread out too far, making control difficult. Their nearness continued to gnaw on Smoke.

There would be no chance to retake the herd with so few able-bodied men. The best he could hope for would be to continue to keep watch and wait for reinforcements. After a supper of antelope ham and cold biscuits, Smoke felt it necessary to reassure Della. He took her aside.

"I don't want you worrying about Tommy, or yourself and the girls. I have no intention of going after those horses without a lot more gunhands than I have. We'll trail along, keep out of sight and wait."

"I'm so relieved." Della waved a hand in a half-circle gesture that encompassed the terrain and their condition as well. "All of this. It's . . . it's so bizarre. Outlaws stealing horses, raiding our ranch and burning it. Now chasing after these evil men. It was not like that back east. Not at all. We were—always so safe."

"Yes, but didn't you notice how much freedom you had to give up to be that safe?"

Della considered that as though a novel idea. "I never thought of that. A policeman on every corner. He knew everyone by face and name."

"He also knew everything everyone knew, said, or thought, right?"

Again a frown of concentration. "Yes. You're right. Any miscreant was soon hauled off the streets and questioned until he confessed."

Gently, Smoke probed farther. "Do you have any idea how those confessions were acquired?"

"N-no. Now that you mention it."

"Usually with boots, fists, and night sticks. Not that lawmen out here have found that method unworkable. It's effective; yet to me, it seems to take something fundamental out of the one beaten and the one doing the beating."

With an uneasy trill of laughter, Della dismissed the grim images. "That did not apply to our life. Sven had a good position at a large steel mill in Pennsylvania. He was an accountant, before becoming a pioneer."

"Your children were born there?"

"Tommy and Sarah-Jane. Gertrude came along after we moved west. First, it was Kansas. That's where Sven learned how little he knew about farming. Especially dry farming like they have to do there." She cheered slightly. "But he found he had a knack with livestock. Cattle in particular. We nearly lost the farm. Sven had a lucky streak when he found a buyer. We bought seed stock and started west. We ended up here in the territory."

Smoke listened sympathetically to her narration for the better part of an hour. When Della got to a recounting of her husband's death, she broke down and began to sob softly, hands clamped to her mouth. Solicitously, Smoke comforted her while she cried on his shoulder. The moon had set by the time she retired to the wagon, and Smoke rolled up in his blankets to sleep.

Shortly before dawn, five members of the Yurian gang ghosted into camp and fired shots in the direction of the sleeping forms on the ground. A second later, Smoke Jensen replied in kind, and all hell broke loose.

11

Sadly lacking in frontier skills, the Yurian gang had been heard crashing through the brush by Smoke Jensen several minutes before their attack. It had given Smoke time to prepare a nasty surprise. As the gang poured into camp, and fired at the dark forms rolled into blankets, they only served to pinpoint their locations. Answering shots came immediately, and from outside camp.

"Them ain't people," blurted Ainsley Burk.

Colin Fike added to their confusion. "They were layin' for us outside camp."

Thirty feet away from him, Jerry Harkness triggered a round from his six-gun. The man beside Colin Fike grunted and went down. Then a voice heavy with authority broke through the confusion.

Hub Volker barked his brief orders. "Forget them. Get that woman and the brats and let's get out of here."

At once the outlaws concentrated their attention on the wagon on the far side of the camp. Jerry Harkness dropped another thug, then gave covering fire to Smoke Jensen, who darted at an oblique angle toward the Olsen wagon. Three outlaws fired at his movement. Their slugs cut the air behind Smoke. Hub Volker and Smiling Dave Winters reached the wagon first. Hairy Joe tripped over a saddle, robbed of his night vision by muzzle bloom, and stumbled up next.

He reached the vehicle in time to take a round full in his face from the Winchester in the hands of Tommy Olsen. Reflex and impact flipped Hairy Joe backward, to land with his head in the softly glowing coals of the fire pit. The long, greasy strands of his black hair ignited instantly and formed a ghastly halo. Already dead, the now Hairless Joe did not feel a thing.

Smiling Dave lashed out and yanked the rifle from the grasp of the boy, who stared in disbelief at the destruction he had wrought. Sarah-Jane and Gertrude began to scream as the men climbed into the wagon box. Della fought with clawed fingers; her sturdy nails raked deep furrows along the cheeks of Garth Evans, who recoiled in astonishment. At once, Della snatched up the Colt Lightning Smoke had given her son and squeezed the trigger.

A .44 slug burned a hot, painful trail through the left shoulder of an incredulous Garth Evans, who howled and fell out of the wagon. Della looked around desperately to locate help. She saw Smoke's path blocked by two hard cases. Both had revolvers in their hands and raised them toward the last mountain man as she cried a warning.

Smoke's six-gun came up before either outlaw could fire a shot. The nearer one jolted backward and bent double as a .45 caliber bullet shattered the tip of his sternum. Without delay, Smoke triggered another cartridge. A thin, wavering cry came from the second thug as, gut-shot, he went to his knees. He dropped his weapon and began to try to stuff a bulge of intestine back inside his belly.

Behind him, Smoke Jensen heard a brief cry of pain as Jerry Harkness took another wound, this time a through-and-through hole where his neck met his shoulder. Smoke took a step forward only to see an obscure blur directly before his eyes. In the split second before the rifle butt crashed into his forehead, Smoke saw the grinning face of

Smiling Dave Winters looming over him. Lights exploded in his head, and darkness swept over Smoke Jensen.

Something cold touched the throbbing core of the pain in Smoke Jensen's head. Light flickered against his closed eyelids. His dazed senses registered wetness next. Cautiously he tried opening one eye.

Tall grass and a muzzy blue sky swam above Smoke. With a soft groan, he opened the other eye. The spinning slowed, then ceased. A startled grunt came, and Smoke vaguely realized that he had made it. Suddenly a blurry face appeared to fill the entire span of Smoke's vision.

"Man, am I glad you're back. I was afraid we'd lose you, Smoke." Jerry Harkness, his shoulder crudely bandaged, hovered over Smoke Jensen for a moment, then rose back to where he came into focus.

Smoke opened his mouth to a taste like an overused outhouse. His words came out in a croak. "Jerry . . . is— are the—the Olsens all right?"

Jerry's grim expression forewarned Smoke. "They're gone, Smoke. Those bastids took them, their wagon, everything. We're afoot, no chuck wagon nor a horse in sight."

Smarting at his failure to protect the vulnerable family, and shamed by his weakness, Smoke extended a shaky hand for Jerry's help in rising. "What about Pop Walker and Utah Jack?"

Sadness touched Jerry's features. "Pop's over there. They killed him, Smoke. I don't know about Utah. I can't find him anywhere. They may have taken him and killed him somewhere else."

Tentatively, Smoke touched his face. He found blood still crusted in his eyebrows and along his jaw line. "I've got to clean up. Then we'll bury Pop Walker and figure out what we do next. Is there any doubt that they were from the gang who rustled the horses?"

"None. But, Smoke, what can we do?"

"We can take stock and decide that later, Jerry."

With the help of his top hand, Smoke Jensen washed the blood away in a dented metal basin. Then he touched the bandage Jerry had put on his split forehead. A wave of nausea rose in Smoke's throat. He fought it back.

"We have to get something to eat."

"I'll dig a hole for Pop, Smoke. Are you up to a walk to the creek? Maybe you can catch us some fish."

Smoke nodded grimly. "Yeah. I follow that. We can't afford to waste ammunition on rabbits."

"You've got the right of it. I took stock while you were still out. You have your Colts and a Winchester. I've got my six-gun. Together we have about a hundred fifty rounds. You've got forty for the rifle, sixty-three for your revolvers. I have the rest."

"Sounds better than I expected." Smoke headed to where his saddlebags lay, their contents scattered on the ground. A small square of folded buckskin produced a coil of braided-twine fishing line and four hooks. Reclosing the container, he pocketed it and sought out a thin branch from a cottonwood nearby. He used it as a staff to aid his progress toward the stream. Behind him, he heard the steady chunk-chunk as Jerry Harkness drove a shovel into the turf. It could be worse, Smoke thought to himself. Though somehow he could not picture exactly how.

By the time Smoke had devoured three pan-sized bullhead catfish, his head had stopped swimming. It only throbbed slightly. He availed himself of some red willow bark and scraped a small pile of powder, which he washed down with water from the creek. Then he turned to the matter that had absorbed him since recovering.

"Jerry, I have to keep after the herd."

"Don't you mean we, Smoke?"

"No. You've been wounded twice so far. What I want you

to do is set out down the trail and find help. Bring as many men as you can."

Harkness had plenty of protest left. "You already sent someone east for help. I say we can do better if we stick together."

"I don't think so. The riders I sent are going to be waiting for us north of Sheridan. The herd won't be moving too fast. And with the Olsens, it will slow the rustlers even more."

"What I can't figure, Smoke, is why they took them in the first place."

"As insurance. Whoever is running that gang figures we will not try to take back the herd with a woman and children along. That's just their latest mistake."

"What was their first one?"

Smoke's hickory eyes narrowed. "Taking my horses in the first place."

While Smoke prepared to set out on foot, they talked of how he would leave sign if the herd changed directions. He would take his saddle and saddlebags along. Jerry would gather up anything useful when he returned with a posse. When everything had been decided, Harkness still had an objection.

"What if that head wound is worse than we think? I should stay with you in case you pass out again."

"That makes sense, but there are only the two of us. I have to keep after the rustlers. Now get goin'. And good luck."

Reno Jim Yurian found himself plagued by second thoughts. Burdened by the slow-moving horses, and the wagon with the hostages, the gang's progress had been slowed to a walk. Perhaps he should not have told Hub to grab the woman and her kids. Though they might make a good bargaining point. Another reflection gave him a sudden chill along his spine.

This Smoke Jensen had proven more stubborn than he had expected. Reno knew the name, of course. Jensen had himself quite the reputation. A gunfighter of the first order, who was supposed to have been raised by some mythical mountain man named Preacher, Jensen was reported to have killed his first man when barely fifteen. Or was it sixteen?

That detail didn't matter to Jim Yurian. Smoke Jensen was supposed to be so fast with a gun that only five men had ever cleared leather ahead of his draw. *That* worried Reno Jim more than he was willing to admit. If Smiling Dave had failed to bash in the man's skull, then as sure as the sun would rise tomorrow, Jensen would be coming after them. Reno didn't believe for a moment he would come alone.

Seeking distraction from such gloomy thoughts, Reno Jim turned his horse aside and waited while the lead gather of remounts walked past. The Olsen wagon came next, between the divided herd. As it rolled even, he touched the brim of his black hat with a gloved hand. A thin, teasing smile flickered.

"I trust you are comfortable, Miz Olsen?"

Della warred with herself over outrage at their capture and their apparent continued safety. She loathed this jaunty outlaw in his impeccable black suit and rakish tilt of hat. The pencil-line mustache on his upper lip seemed to mock her. Grudgingly she had to admit he was a superb horseman. He sat his mount well and flowed with its movements whether at a walk or a canter. The nickle-plated, pearl-handled revolvers he wore reminded her that although a dandy, he was a dangerous one. She did not want to answer him, but found that she must.

"So far we have not been treated too badly. Though I would like to give your underling, who slapped around my son, a lasting headache."

To her surprise the outlaw leader laughed. "I can understand your feelings, madam. Although you must admit that your boy did kill one of my men, as did you, I do believe."

He remained amused when Della started a hot retort. "I only wish—" Aghast at her temerity, she stopped.

"That it could have been more?" Reno Jim concluded for her, rightly gauging her intent. "Fortunately for you it was not. My men are fiercely loyal to one another. Had you been successful, they might have done . . . some violence to you all."

Shrewdly, Della checked him. "You would not have allowed that, now would you?"

Reno Jim made a show of being resigned. "You have me, madam. Truly you are my hole card. But, be assured, I will play you however it appears to my best advantage."

Della displayed her knowledge of card language. "You will forgive me if I say that I sincerely hope you lose the hand? Because, believe me, you are bucking four aces if you go against Smoke Jensen."

There was that cursed name again! Coming from this woman of considerable fortitude almost had him believing it. Perhaps if her faith became shaken, it would deflect from his own cold premonition. Maybe he should relax his prohibition somewhat and let the boys enjoy a trailside reward.

After plates of sow-belly and beans, flavored with hot peppers and vinegar, and skillet bread, several of the outlaws broke out bottles of whiskey.

When the liquor had made several rounds, one of the trail scum, fired by the raw rotgut, piped up to his companions. "What say we cut high card for who gets to do them gals tonight? First ace for the littlest, first king for the older one, and the first queen for the woman."

"What? Jist one each tonight?" complained Prine Gephart. "I'll bet the ol' woman an' the older girl can each take on at least four of us ev'ry night."

A snigger answered him. "Mighty likely they could, if we was all built like you, Prine."

Gephart took immediate exception. "Hey, you bassard,

that ain't funny." The chorus of laughter that rose said otherwise. That set Prine off on a single-minded course. "That does it, you smart-asses. For that, I'm gonna go over there and plow all three of them fields, all by myself."

His challenge met immediate response. Yancy Osburn came to his boots, hand closed around the butt-grip of his Smith American. "Like hell you are. It's gonna be fair share. Everyone gets a chance."

Gephart put on a pouting expression. Only his eyes showed his combativeness. "You gonna pull that thing, Yance? Reno said we could ride those fillies an' the mare to our heart's content. I aim to do exactly that."

"Draw for high card, dammit," growled Colin Fike.

Not nearly far enough away, Della Oisen clearly heard their angry voices and knew only so well what it was they intended. Quickly she reached out and covered her younger daughter's ears. She noted to her satisfaction that Tommy did the same for Sarah-Jane. Then the boy spoke with heated sincerity.

"If any of them so much as touches one of you, I swear, Maw, I'll make the sons of bitches pay."

Fear for her son's life blotted out her shock at his language and spurred her to dissuade him. "No, son. They—they'd kill you this time."

Tommy Olsen slitted his eyes. "Not before I got a lot of them."

Still determined to press for his equal right to pester the woman and her girls, Colin Fike pushed his insistence. "Cut the cards, Prine, we got a right."

Enraged by this defiance of his authority, Prine Gephart snarled at his subordinate. "As long as you're a member of my crew, the only rights you have are those I give you. You'd best learn that well." His anger crackled as he loosened the

Merwin and Hulbert in its holster. To his eventual regret, Colin Fike pushed once more, and too hard, for his rights. "I'm not your slave, by damn. Haul out that iron."

Brain fogged by whiskey, Gephart eagerly obliged him. Even drunk, Prine Gephart was faster than the befuddled Colin Fike. His Merwin and Hulbert .44 cleared leather in a blue-black streak, leveled, and the firing pin descended toward the waiting primer before a startled Colin even closed fingers around the butt-grip of his Smith American.

In the same instant, Yancy Osburn bellowed forcefully, "Noooool"

A gunshot blasted the night's silence. Prine Gephart's bullet struck true, burst the heart of Colin Fike and erupted through his back with a fist-sized hole. Instantly, the established herd leader let out a squeal of alarm, and whinnies of fright answered. Another bugle from the lead stallion, and the herd dissolved into a mindless, panicked mass of walleyed, terrorized animals. They jolted to the right, then back to the left, then in a second dashed away, tails high, in all directions.

"You idiots!" Hubble Volker bellowed over the noise of the stampede. "You goddamned idiots. Get to your horses, get after those critters. Move or I'll kill you myself."

And so it ended before it even started. Della stared in disbelief and relief as the outlaws raced for the picket line to throw saddles on their mounts and flog them after the splintered herd, all thought of rape driven from their minds.

12

Crouched down on the parched ground, Smoke Jensen searched for a small, smooth pebble. With a fiercely hot summer sun burning down over the previous afternoon and through most of his second day in pursuit of the stolen herd, Smoke had exhausted the contents of his single canteen. In the past he had gone without food many a time, and he knew that hunger was endurable. Now, plagued by thirst, Smoke stretched his perseverance to the limit by entertaining images of what he would like to do to the rustlers who had shot up every visible water container at his former campsite. He had to find an alternative or give up his quest. On his third try, he came up with a suitable, light brown stone.

Smoke used the last few drops of water from the canteen to wash the little rock, which he then popped in his mouth and worked under his tongue. At once, saliva began to flow. With his temporary measure in place, he began once more to trudge along the swath of disturbed turf that marked the passage of the stolen horses. So long as he found water by nightfall, he would be all right. Failing that, Smoke realized he could not survive.

* * *

Back in Muddy Gap, Ginny Parkins found herself restless and ill at ease as she tried to get a gaggle of ten-year-olds to understand the mysteries of long division. When a fit of giggling broke out among the fifth grade girls, she dismissed school early for the day. Her charges stormed the exit with squeals of jubilation. That still left Ginny with an empty feeling.

And, darn it, she knew the reason why. She had treated Sheriff Smoke Jensen most shabbily. No other word for it. He had only been doing his job. For a moment she wondered if he still enforced the law in Muddy Gap. The town had been so peaceful the past five days. Fortunately the riffraff had not returned after the final, brutal expulsion of the most unrepentant. No, Ginny chided herself, not brutal, rather necessary. Goaded by her conscience, Ginny Parkins left the former security of the schoolhouse on what she considered a delicate mission.

Her bustle swishing behind her, Ginny Parkins reached the downtown sector of Muddy Gap slightly out of breath. With a start, she realized she had been walking at twice her normal pace. Face set in a prim expression, she looked both ways before entering the office at the jail. To her surprise, she found Grover Larsen sitting behind his desk, and Deputy Chase in the sheriff's chair. She looked around a moment in consternation.

"Is Sheriff Jensen making his rounds?" she inquired.

Grover Larsen answered her. "He's not sheriff anymore, ma'am. He's moved on with his horse herd."

Ginny did not believe what she had heard. "What?"

Fred Chase offered assurance. "It's true, Miss Ginny. I've been appointed interim sheriff until the next election. Smoke left four days ago."

"I—I don't understand. I c-can't believe . . ." *That he would leave without telling you? After the way you treated him?* her mind mocked her.

Grover Larsen undertook to enlighten her. "Smoke

Jensen is a rancher. He raises blooded stock for the rich folks, and a large herd suitable as remounts for the army."

"But I thought he was some sort of gunfighter. A living legend."

Larsen smiled softly. "He's both, Miss Ginny. Let me tell you a little about Smoke Jensen. No one out here, but him, knows where he was born. His family was movin' west, out to Oregon Territory, when he got separated from the wagon train. He was a little tad, no more'n eleven or so. He managed to survive a few days on his wits.

"Some say he traded what few possessions he had with Injuns for food. They wanted to keep him, adopt him into the tribe, but Smoke had it in his head he could catch up and find his folks. That didn't happen. The old mountain man, Preacher, found young Smoke first. He took him in and raised him up. There's some argue it was a bad upbringin', that Smoke learned to fight and to kill. Supposed to have killed his first man at the age of twelve.

"Well now," Larsen continued, warming to his subject, "that ain't true. Preacher was through here a number of years back, when Muddy Gap was nothing more than a wide place in the road. I was a youngster then, myself, not more'n seventeen. I heard Preacher talkin' about Smoke Jensen. Said he got his name and the start of his reputation at the same time, when he was sixteen. That came from the man who should know. And in these mountains, Preacher's known to have never told a lie." Larsen flushed and waved a hand in dismissal. "There I go, ramblin' like an old fool."

Ginny protested at once. "No, please go on. I'm fascinated. I . . . never got to know Sheri—Smoke well."

"Well, Smoke grew up, like folks are likely to do. He learned Injun things, and their talk, too. Likewise, Preacher taught him to read and write and do his sums. Taught him to trap, skin and cure beaver hides, though the trade was fast dwindlin'. Smoke learned about horses from Preacher, also a lot about other animals, an' how to respect them and give 'em all space to live and move about. They say he's whipped the daylights outta more than one man who has mistreated animals. Seems quirky in a man who became a gunfighter an' eventual' a lawman. Don't you think?"

"I see nothing odd about a person who is fond of animals. After all, they need our care and protection," Ginny went on, taken up in her zeal. "They can't speak or write, so they can't stand up for their rights like humans can."

Young Fred Chase put in his outlook. "I can't agree with you more, Miss Ginny. The way I see it, animals don't have any rights because they can't nego—negotiate what they will do in order to get them. So a man who mistreats a horse or dog is the lowest form of inhuman trash." He looked defiantly at Grover Larsen. "An' that's a fact."

Larsen offered coffee, poured and they talked on for another half an hour about Smoke Jensen. Before Ginny departed, Marshal Larsen raised a staying hand. "Oh, before you go, Miss Ginny, there's something I have to give you. Smoke Jensen left this for you against the time when you might need it."

He reached into his top drawer and came out with a small .38 Smith and Wesson revolver. Ginny gaped, gulped, stammered and gingerly accepted the gift. "Thank you for giving me Smoke's present, although I'm certain I shall never have use of it."

Ginny left feeling somewhat better at having secured a promise that Marshal Larsen would send a telegram to the town nearest Smoke Jensen's ranch with her apology. Yet part of her felt worse, over becoming owner of a firearm. She would write Smoke, too, she pledged as she crossed the street to the general store. She would have to thank him for the gun, but also assure him that she would never use it. Idly she wondered if she would ever see Smoke Jensen again.

Sweat stained the armpits of the shirt worn by Smoke Jensen. The afternoon sun beat down relentlessly. It sapped him of the precious little moisture his body retained. For the past hour he had been watching the hazy, insubstantial outline of trees in the distance. Certain he had not circled and come back to the Powder River, Smoke fixed on the long file of greenery that indicated a watercourse.

Even the pebble failed to do its magic. The length of his stride had shortened, and his head throbbed. Slowly, the pale green leaves of cottonwoods began to swim into sharp focus. A creek all right. Smoke forced himself forward. Another fifty paces. His footsteps faltered.

Thirty paces now. Alarmingly, the sweat dried on his skin to a clammy coldness. His body had stopped producing moisture. Twenty paces now. The individual trunks of the trees could be seen. He could smell the water.

Stumbling like a drunken man, Smoke closed the last distance to the grassy bank that hung over a narrow streambed; below, the water peacefully glided past. Its surface reflected a cool, inviting green. With the last of his strength, Smoke eased over the bank and lowered himself to a sandy shelf. There he removed his boots and cartridge belt, then jumped into the water.

Its coolness embraced him. When his clothes had become thoroughly wet, he removed them and washed out the salt and dust. His thoughts snapped back to young Tommy Olsen doing exactly the same thing not so long ago. Wringing out his garments, he flung them up on the grassy bank. The cool water exhilarated him, and he noticed his skin had turned a rosy pink. Satisfied, he climbed out and let his effluvium drift away before filling the canteen.

Then he gained the embankment and spread his clothes on a hawthorn bush to sun dry. He would continue to use the pebble in order to preserve his water, he reminded himself. While he dried off, he drank deeply, but slowly, from the canteen. When his limbs stopped trembling, he returned to the creek to refill the canteen. He turned his clothes once and was soon dressed and ready.

Fastening his cartridge belt around his waist and easing his weapons into place, Smoke started off. He had a goodly ways to go before dark. Idly, he wondered what he might find to eat along the way.

Well over eight feet long, the sleek, fat diamondback lay torpid on a large, flat rock. Drowsed by the lowering sun, the serpent only vaguely felt pangs of hunger. It had killed and eaten a jackrabbit three days ago. Now the time had come to hunt and feed again. So enervated had the viper become from the late afternoon sun that it only sporadically employed its early warning system. After a long two minutes, the forked tongue flicked out, sensing the vibrations and flavors of its surroundings. Then it flicked out again, the creature suddenly alert.

So silently did Smoke Jensen move that the rattlesnake did not sense his approach until the man nearly came into sight. Lethargically, the viper roused itself and began to coil for a strike at what seemed a huge food source. Ancient instincts stirred, and it completed its spiral with renewed alacrity. The upper third of its body arched into the air; the snake swayed backward, prepared to strike.

That was when Smoke Jensen saw it. Despite the debilitating effects of no food and little water, a man of Smoke's prowess and speed had ample time to unlimber his right-hand Colt and blow the triangular head off the viper as it arched toward him. Deprived of command, the huge body writhed and twisted across the ground.

Instinct caused it to try to recoil, but the necessary command center no longer existed, and it all but tied itself in knots. Smoke stood well clear while the reptile's violent motions slowed, his .45 Peacemaker ready. He well knew that prairie rattlers like this one frequently traveled in mated pairs. A bull this size was sure to have a harem.

When the creature's spasms reduced to an occasional twitch, he grabbed the body below the rattles and held it at shoulder height while he walked quickly to a stunted oak that rode the top of a low knob. Using a fringe thong from his shirt, Smoke tied the snake upside down from a low limb. Expertly applying his Greenriver sheath knife, he slit the skin from neck to rattles, peeled it back, then opened the pinky white body from severed end to its bung. He used his boot heel to dig a small hole to dispose of the guts, then washed the meat with a little of his dwindling water supply. With that accomplished, he looked all around, scanning the horizon for any human presence besides himself.

Satisfied that he was alone, he made a fire ring, gathered deadfall from the oak, and kindled it to life from a tinder-box he habitually carried. When the blaze took, he fed it twigs until a decent bed of coals appeared. Nearly smoke-less, the fire under the spreading limbs of the oak gave off no telltale column of smoke. After threading the snake on a green branch he had cut, Smoke Jensen placed it over the fire. He wished for salt, then banished the desire. While his meat cooked, he located a chokecherry bush and stripped it of a handful of berries.

He would crush these and rub them into the meat while it roasted. The bittersweet tang of the fruit would make a fair substitute for salt. When all had been accomplished, he feasted ravenously on the whole body, buried his fire, and made ready to leave. He had a lot of distance to cover before dark.

Smoke Jensen's lean, muscular figure cast a long shadow to his right when he saw the dust cloud ahead. He had caught up to the herd. He grew more cautious. Deserting the trail, Smoke bent low and drifted through the tall buf-falo grass, skirted sage and hawthorn, and advanced obliquely on the rustlers. When the drag riders came into view, Smoke sank down and disappeared in the waving sea of grass. A quarter hour had gone by when he heard a faint "halloo" from far ahead. Those in the lead were halting the herd for the night. Smoke would wait until dusk to move again.

When the last thin, orange crescent sank in the west and only the afterglow fought against the encroachment of night, Smoke Jensen left his hiding place and made a circuit of the herd. It took him five minutes shy of an hour to complete the journey. He made careful note of the location of herd guards and, most importantly, their degree of alertness. While he ghosted from rock to tree to underbrush, Smoke concentrated on what choices he had. Looming large in his considerations was his need to know exactly how many men occupied the night camp. He would have to pay them a visit soon, but in order for that to happen, these outer guards would have to be drowsy and distracted.

Once he knew what he stood against, Smoke had several alternatives. He could run the herd off and make a break for it, leaving the Olsens to their fate. Or he could run the herd off, along with all the outlaws' horses, and possibly get the Olsens out with him.

Better still, Smoke reckoned, the ideal would be to locate the Olsens, get them mounted, and drive off all the other horses, leaving the rustlers afoot. He would have the remounts to Buffalo and beyond before the bandits could reorganize. From there, he would force the herd to greater speed, say twenty or twenty-five miles a day. At that rate, he would deliver them to the fort after a hard, three-day drive. Not bad. Smoke confidently believed that the stranded rustlers could not possibly close with them before then. Patiently, Smoke bided his time until shortly after midnight. Then he set out for the camp.

He slid past the inattentive herd guards with ease. Not until he drew close to the restive outlaws around their fires did he have to exert his greatest skill. They had picked their site wisely, Smoke noted. Two trees stood at enough distance apart to run a picket line to accommodate all of the horses not in use by the perimeter sentries. Good. That made his job much easier. Near the inner edge of the herd, Smoke caught a flash of a gray-and-black-spotted rump and recognized Cougar. At least they would all be properly mounted when the time came to take the herd.

Tommy Olsen had worked out in his mind what he could do to protect his mother and sisters. That being the case, he went in search of firewood rather than send Sarah-Jane. In the small stand of alders to one side of the camp, he searched the ground in the dim light. He had about given up for this night when his eyes picked out a gleam of starlight from the smooth surface of a rock.

At once, Tommy set down his armload of deadfall branches and used nimble fingers to pry the stone from the grasp of the earth. It came away at last and turned out to be slightly larger than fist-sized.

"Perfect," Tommy whispered to himself.

Quickly he rubbed it free of dirt and tucked it away inside his shirt. Tommy figured rightly that if any of the outlaws tried something funny, the rock could get him a gun, and that could sure fix any of them with designs on his mother and sisters.

"Yes!" he said aloud. "Yessss!" Visions of the rock crashing against the skull of a lustful hard case excited the boy. Then he would take the thug's gun and there would be hell to pay. Tommy never considered the very real possibility that he would be shot full of holes. When one was fourteen and just sensing the ebb and flow of manly sap within, one thought oneself immortal.

Two hours before dawn, Smoke Jensen considered that the optimum time had come for his move to recover his horses and free the Olsens. All during the night, while he waited and mentally rehearsed his actions, the sky to the northwest had grown incredibly black, and huge columns rose to blot out the stars. Ominous rumbles rolled over the craggy country in the foothills of the Bighorn Mountains. Smoke cast his gaze that direction more often as the hours wore on. Conscious of the impending storm, Smoke made a quick revise in his plans. When the thunder grew even closer, he used it to muffle his movements as he closed in on the slumbering gang.

13

A searing flash of forked-tail white split the sky asunder as Smoke Jensen stepped into the clearing where the gang lay. An instant later, a ripe crackling rippled the air, followed by a ground-shaking boom. With the swiftness of a mountain lion's pounce, a torrential thunderstorm broke loose overhead.

Fat rain drops fell wetly upon everyone and everything in sight. The torrent descended at a rate of three inches per hour, too fast to allow much water to sink into the parched ground. Rather it ran off to form miniature streams that gushed and gurgled. Smoke turned his back on most of the outlaws and froze in place. Grumbling, the rustlers wisely moved away from any trees, natural targets for lightning strikes.

In so doing, they exposed themselves to even more danger. With a loud clatter, like the unshod hooves of the demons in hell, barter-sized hail slashed down to bruise and punish flesh, even that covered by thick woolen blankets. The outlaw trash complained loudly, though few raised their heads to see the cause. Quickly the ice balls covered the ground with a two-inch-thick carpet of white.

Grumbling at this unexpected misfortune, Smoke Jensen eased his way out of a camp that was quickly becom-

ing aroused. Men had to be called out to help contain the
herd, or the storm would scatter them. His plan would have
to wait for a better time.

By dawn, the tempest was only a memory. After containing the livestock and waiting out the half hour of
determined rain, the soaking wet rustlers could not get settled down in soggy blankets. Instead, they took dry wood
from under the chuck wagon and the Olsen wagon and
kindled a large, roaring fire, then stood close to dry themselves. From his hidden vantage point, Smoke Jensen
observed the morning routine. When the first, faint streaks
of gray bloomed in the east, outlaw voices could be clearly
heard.

"Yer right. Not a sign of him."

"You're sure? No chance he's hidin'?"

"None at all."

"Turn out some of the men and widen the search."

From his observation place, Smoke Jensen studied the
flamboyant figure of Reno Jim Yurian. Again he felt a flash
of having seen the man somewhere in the past. Following
the exchange, the camp began to fume with activity. Several
men rushed about, peering behind bushes and into small
ravines. Still others grabbed up their horses and set out in
widening circles around the campsite. Curious as to the
reason, Smoke left his concealed spot to move in on a pair
of searchers, who sat their mounts and looked back along
the trail they had covered the previous day.

One of them removed his hat and mopped his brow.
High humidity, left by the rain, combined with a burning
sun to make it feel much hotter than the regular temperature. The hatless one spoke with fire in his voice.

"Damn that little brat. I'll bet he hauled his butt along
our back trail."

"Yeah, Darin, you might be right. He smacked Phipps

over the head with somethin', took his gun and stole a horse. Damn, how I hate a horse thief."

That brought a round of chuckles from both thugs. And it set Smoke to thinking along the correct trail. They had to be talking about Tommy Olsen. The gutsy little guy must have clobbered one of them and made an escape. Smoke pondered that a moment. Why hadn't he taken his mother and the girls? He would have to find the boy to learn the answer, Smoke reasoned.

No time like now to start that, he acknowledged. It would make it easier if he no longer had to go afoot. To solve that immediate problem, he must seek out a lone searcher. Smoke found himself one twenty minutes later and three miles from the outlaw camp.

Oblivious to Smoke's presence, Ainsley Burk ambled his mount past where the last mountain man lay in the buffalo grass that grew belly-high to a horse. When Burk presented his back to Smoke, the lean, hard man came to his boots and uncoiled his powerful leg muscles.

He vaulted onto the rump of Ainsley Burk's dapple gray, his Colt Peacemaker in hand and ready. It collided with the side of Burk's head and sent him off to sleepy times. Smoke shoved the unconscious Burk forward onto the neck of his horse, tied the outlaw's hands behind his back, and unceremoniously dumped Burk from the saddle.

With a horse under him again, Smoke felt much better. Even if it was a knot-headed gelding, it would make do. At once, Smoke Jensen set off in search of Tommy Olsen.

Tommy Olsen regretted his rash action when three of the outlaws struck his trail and came hard after him. He'd been riding all night, and his stolen horse was on its last legs. Still, Tommy ran him from gully to gully and over yet another ridge, in his effort to evade recapture. Inexorably the hard cases closed in on him.

In a last, desperate effort, Tommy began to take shots at

them, although he felt sure they remained out of range. He had eared back the hammer once again when a fourth outlaw appeared behind the others, riding hard to close the gap.

His fourth bullet kicked up dust at the forehooves of the lead bandit's horse. The animal reared and whinnied in fright. Tommy cocked the Colt again. When he started to take sight, he saw a puff of smoke appear at the end of the trailing rider's arm. The thug nearest to the stranger arched his back and then flung forward off his mount to land face-first on the ground.

And then the stranger ceased to be an unknown for Tommy Olsen. It had to be Smoke Jensen! That left the remaining three who rode hard toward Tommy. He took more careful aim and clipped the hat from the head of one man, then prepared to fire his final round. The firing pin fell on an empty chamber. A moment later they closed on the boy and surrounded him.

Though not for long. Smoke Jensen shot one through the shoulder and swung a wide loop from the lariat that had been attached to his saddle skirt. It settled over the shoulders of another hard case at the same time Tommy used the Winchester he had brought along, carried over his legs on the bareback mount. Without time to aim or fire, he wielded the rifle like a club to knock the third rustler to the ground with the butt.

An instant later, Smoke yanked tight the rope and hauled his target out of the saddle. The thug landed with a bone-jarring thud. Tommy kneed his mount over close to Smoke. "Smoke! Am I glad to see you."

"I imagine so," Smoke replied drily. "They are bound to have heard those shots back in camp. Let's gather up the horses and hightail it out of here."

Tommy gave him a blank, incredulous stare. "You mean, we're gonna run?"

"Just so. I counted a tad over thirty men in that camp last night."

"More like forty-two, by my count," Tommy added. "Still, we gotta get Maw and my sisters out of there."

"We will. But not if forty-some hard cases fall on us like these did. We need to be well out of sight by the time they get here. And, these extra horses will help confuse them as to who we are and where we went. We'll tie bodies on each of them so they have the weight of a man."

"Why do we need to do that?"

"To confuse them, Tommy. Even outlaws have smarts enough to be able to tell if a horse is carrying a rider or not. We'll take them out a mile or two and then send them off in different directions. That'll make the rustlers think there is a whole lot of us and we split up."

Tommy looked on Smoke with new awe. "You're right smart, Smoke. Think it will work?"

"If it don't, we'll be up to our a—ears in outlaws before nightfall. Now, get goin'."

Twenty minutes later, they rode away, the outlaws, the living and the dead, slung over their individual saddles. A quick look downward gave Smoke Jensen the satisfaction of noting the authentic appearance of the tracks left behind. Frequent checks of their back trail showed no sign of close pursuit.

Sundown found Smoke Jensen and Tommy Olsen in a cold camp amid a heaped mound of boulders. They had with them three outlaw horses, which had not strayed far from their course during the day. They had left the wounded hard cases tied up on the ground before they abruptly changed directions and headed northward, back toward the camp. While they munched on biscuits and fatback taken from two pair of outlaw saddlebags, Smoke listened to Tommy's account of his escape.

"I had gotten this rock, see? It was to use if any of them decided to pester my maw or the girls. Oh, they'd talked about that before an' I knew what they meant. I figgered to clobber one and get his gun. So when that storm broke out, I wondered why not get a gun and a horse, and come find you? It worked, sort of."

Smoke snorted in reply; then Tommy went on. "Oh, one other thing. That feller with you, Utah Jack? Well, he's a turncoat. Seems he was workin' with the rustlers all along. I'd like to fix him good.

Smoke gave him a short nod. "His time will come, right enough. Now, let me tell you how I figure we're going about getting your mother and sisters out of there."

For the next twenty-five minutes, Smoke went over in detail what he had in mind. He emphasized what he expected of Tommy by two repetitions and concluded with a third. "You will take the three extra horses to the spot I determine to be best and hold them there for your family. You are to do nothing, absolutely nothing, else. Now, repeat that for me."

Tommy did and Smoke pressed him further. "Is that clear? No room open for second guessing what I expect of you, Tommy?"

"It's clear, sir. I'll do what you say."

"Good. We'll be ready to head out at one in the morning. Now roll up and get some sleep."

Far from the foothills of the Bighorn Mountains, Sally Jensen watched from her darkened living room while three scruffy men, who even in her most charitable of moods Sally would have to call saddle bums, walked their mounts to the tie rail outside the bunkhouse. They dismounted and threw their reins over the crossbar and looped them loosely. They started for the door in the yellow light of a kerosene lantern hung from a peg in the front wall. As they progressed, they eased their six-guns in their soft pouch holsters.

Their earlier furtive actions had already decided Sally Jensen, even if she had not seen this latest threatening move, and she had crossed the room to an oak, glass-fronted, upright chest. She opened the hinged face piece and reached inside. She selected a light-weight, 20 gauge Purdy shotgun and plucked six rounds of No. 4 buckshot from a box, then dropped them into a pocket of her skirt.

She opened the front door as one of the prowlers reached for the knob to enter the bunkhouse. "Odd hour to be looking for work, strangers," Sally announced from behind them. Startled by the unexpected voice, and a female one at that, they stiffened, then turned toward her as one.

They found themselves confronted by the twin black circles of the shotgun muzzle. Immediately, they spread apart, one holding the center while the other pair took small side steps to put distance between them. The piece of trash in the middle raised a gloved hand and pointed at Sally, his face screwed into an expression of mean humor.

"Now, missy, that little-bitty scattergun ain't gonna do us a whole lot of harm, don't ya know?"

"I figure I can take out two of you even before my hands get a shot at the last of you trash."

Rat-faced and unshaven, the talkative one hooked a thumb over his shoulder. "You mean the *hands* in there, missy?" he sneered. "Why, they ain't there, now are they? They all rode out early this afternoon. We watched them go. That's why we decided to pay the place a visit."

Determined to keep control of the situation, Sally spoke confidently. "Then tell me why you were headed for the bunkhouse."

Nasty laughter answered her. "We jist wanted to make sure every one of them left. Since nothin's happened to us through all this palaver, I think we can be sure there ain't a soul at home."

"Yeah," the one on his right said through a giggle. "So we might as well get right down to the fun part. Be a good girl an' gather up all the hard money around the place. Bring it to us, along with any jewels you've got. After that, you can fix us up some grub. We're real hongry."

A sick giggle came from the other side. "He-he, tha's right, missy. We need to build our strength with some good vittles. 'Cause after that, we're gonna give you a whole lot of what you've been missin' for a while. He-he-he."

Sally had said her last word in argument. Instead, the Purdy spoke for her. A full load of No. 4 buck splashed into the chest and belly of the pig-faced satyr who had hinted at rape. He went down with a soft moan. A split second later, Sally unloosed the other barrel on the dirty, rat-faced trash in the middle. As he bent double in shock, he saw a flicker of movement at one of the windows of the bunkhouse.

A boy's face, under a mop of white-blond hair, appeared in the open space, along with a rifle. It barked twice rapidly, and the leader saw his last man go down, shot through the belly and his left thigh. His vision dimmed while Sally pushed the locking lever and opened the breech of the shotgun. Calmly she extracted the spent brass casings and inserted two more. Then she walked across the yard to stand over him, a shy smile on her lips.

Gasping, he looked up with blurred, close-set eyes. "You're a . . . a hard woman, Missy. Who—who is it that killed me?"

"My name is Sally Jensen. This is the Sugarloaf, the ranch of my husband . . . Smoke Jensen."

Already pale from blood loss, the drifter turned alabaster white, his jaw sagging. "Oh, Lord. Oh, Lord, have mercy on me."

"He'll have to be the one. I have neither the time nor the inclination. And you won't live long enough for me to develop them."

"But . . . I don't . . . want to—die!"

Ignoring the thug's mortal protest, Bobby called out exuberantly, "We got 'em, Maw. We got 'em good."

"Yes we did, Bobby."

From beyond her boot tips came the appeal. "Who's that? We didn't see anyone else around."

"That's Bobby, our adopted son. He killed your sidekick over there."

"My God, a whole fambly of gunfighters. What did we walk into?"

"Your doom." Sally bent down and retrieved his weapons. He shivered violently and groaned. Then his death rattle rose eerily in his throat.

That night, Smoke Jensen escorted Tommy Olsen to a strategic spot near the outlaw camp. He spoke briefly of the importance of controlling the three spare horses they had brought along.

"Keep a tight rein on them, Tommy. When I scatter the remount herd, many of them will head this way."

Tommy nodded vigorously. "I'll do it, Smoke."

"Good. You won't have much doubt when things get started."

With that, Smoke faded into the blackness and headed for the new camp. Due to the search for Tommy and their missing men, the gang had moved the horses less than fifteen miles that day. His first task was the same as the previous night.

Smoke located two outriders easily. They sat their horses, faced inward to the remounts, oblivious to any threat from outside. One rolled a cigarette while they talked about inconsequentials. Smoke dismounted and approached stealthily through the tall grass. A softly soughing breeze masked his movements.

After lighting his quirley, one of the outlaws queried his companion. "Rafe, where we takin' these critters?"

"To Bent Rock Canyon, Norm."

Norm drew in a deep draft of smoke. "Kinda a round-about way, ain't it?"

Rafe nodded agreement. "Way I hear it, the boss wants

to make the herd disappear somewhere over by Buffalo. Then we head south to the canyon."

"How do we make all these horses disappear?"

Norm did not get an answer. Smoke Jensen chose that moment to leap atop the rump of the horse Norm rode. Arms extended, he grabbed each outlaw by the side of his head and slammed them together with enough violence to ensure they would stay unconscious for a long while. When Smoke released the hapless pair, they fell to the ground.

Smoke dropped into the saddle and calmed the horses. Then he dismounted and tied the insensible men hand and foot. He led the horses off a distance and tied them to a sage bush. That accomplished, he set off to find more of the herd guards.

Smiling Dave Winters had little use for night herd duty. He looked upon himself as a leader, not a flunky. At least three of the men in his section of the gang had caught this turn with him. He had not encountered any difficulty in ordering around the other five. Which allowed him to make a circuit of the entire herd in a casual, relaxed mood.

That was until he discovered two men missing. Neither of them patrolled the sector he had been assigned to. At first it did not cause him any concern. With the horses quieted, no doubt they had wandered off to jaw with another of the sentries. Then he recalled who this herd was supposed to belong to. If true, there could be something very wrong with these missing men.

He became convinced of that when he found a third of the herd tenders swinging from a tree limb, at the end of a rope tied around his ankles. Quickly Smiling Dave dismounted and hurried to the side of this apparition. Hank Benson had been gagged, and his hands bound behind him, although he remained conscious. The fury that burned in his eyes told a clear story to Smiling Dave.

A quick look around failed to reveal to Smiling Dave a

darker, more substantial shadow among the many that surrounded him. With one hand on the butt of his six-gun, Smiling Dave reached for his sheath knife. With a hiss, the loop of a lariat settled over his shoulders. Before he could react, it yanked tight, pinning his arms at his sides. The bite end of the rope went over the same tree limb that suspended Hank Benson, and Smiling Dave Winters rose into the air. Top-heavy, he turned head down the moment his feet left the ground.

His hat went flying as his forehead struck the turf. He sensed light tugs that indicated the free end had been secured around the tree trunk. Then a human form, which appeared to be upside down to Smiling Dave, walked into view. The stranger deftly removed the weapons from the captive and studied his face closely.

Then Smoke Jensen spoke in a whisper. "You're the one who put a bullet in Jerry Harkness and killed one of my hands. Then you smacked me in the head with a rifle butt."

Although he didn't really need to ask, Smiling Dave blurted out, "Who—who are you?"

"I'm Smoke Jensen. And you are a dead man."

Smoke used Smiling Dave's knife to slit the outlaw's throat. Then he headed off to find the rest of the herd tenders.

14

Smoke Jensen had but a little distance to go in order to locate another sentry. He glided up behind him while the man stood on the ground, easing cramped leg muscles. With a single, swift blow, Smoke cracked him over the head with the butt of his Peacemaker. He tied the unconscious man and relieved him of his weapons. Then he glided off afoot to locate more.

By one-thirty in the morning, Smoke had located all but the final sentry. The outlaw sat his mount, one leg cocked up around the pommel of his saddle, rolling a quirley. Smoke eased in close and spoke in a low, though friendly, tone.

"Could you use a cup of coffee?"

"You bet. I'm obliged." He leaned forward as Smoke reached out with his left hand.

When the thug's head reached the proper level, Smoke swung his right arm and laid the barrel of his .45 Colt alongside the outlaw's cranium, a fraction above his left ear. The victim uttered a low grunt and continued earthward from his perch. Swiftly, Smoke Jensen secured him and started for the distant camp, his goal the picket line.

On the way, he worked through the remounts until he found his 'Palouse stallion, Cougar. The spotted-rump horse followed Smoke without need of a halter or reins. At the picket line, Smoke went from one animal to another, undoing the ropes that held them to the tether. He left Cougar there with a borrowed bridle and skirted the camp beyond the orange glow cast by the bed of coals. He emerged from the darkness when he reached the Olsen wagon.

Smoke awakened Della first, with a hand over her mouth to prevent a cry of alarm. He whispered in her ear, and she tried to turn her head. Smoke eased his grip, and she glanced left to verify that it was indeed he.

In a soft breath, Smoke explained his presence. "I came to get you away from here. Wake the girls and meet me out there in the dark, just beyond your wagon."

Della started to protest that their meager possessions would be lost, only to have Smoke shake his head sternly. "Would you rather it be your lives?" he asked harshly.

Smoke remained behind to cover their escape. When the youngest Olsen girl disappeared into the darkness, Smoke withdrew from the edge of the camp. He found them huddled together at the base of a gnarled cottonwood and led them to the picket line, where he lifted the girls atop two of the outlaws' horses. They settled astraddle with accustomed ease. Then Smoke turned to assist Della.

"I've not ridden bareback since I was little," she told him with a toss of her silver-frosted, light brown locks.

"You'll remember how easy enough," Smoke assured her as he made a step-up with cupped hands.

Della hoisted the hem of her night dress, placed a foot lightly in his grasp and grabbed a handhold in the mane of the horse. She swung aboard and settled in. Smoke vaulted to the back of Cougar and turned to take in the Olsens.

"Now what?" Della prompted.

Smoke waved a hand in the direction of the herd. "Now we stampede the herd."

He could not clearly see Della's reaction, but Smoke heard her gasp. Then she spoke in a reasonable tone. "Then we're going to need a way to guide these beasts."

So saying, she bent forward and formed a reasonably good hackamore out of the tie rope. With a steady hand, she eased over to her daughters and did the same for them, then spoke softly.

"You girls stay close by me, hear?" They nodded, and Della turned to Smoke. "We're ready."

Smoke drew his right-hand .45 Colt and eared back the hammer. A chilling wolf howl quavered from his lips, and he fired three rapid shots. The horses bolted at once. With wild whinnies, they raced off in the direction Smoke intended that they would take.

Several of the rustlers yelled in alarm, and two screamed in agony as the remounts thundered through the camp. One of the screamers grew silent after a fifth set of hooves pounded into his chest and belly, pulped vital organs and shattered ribs. Taking care to keep the Olsens in sight, Smoke pushed the herd from behind. The terrain proved an ally, as the startled animals swerved to avoid rock outcrops and disastrous ravines.

Thus channeled, the horses streamed toward where Tommy waited with the saddled mounts. Behind them, Smoke could hear the curses and uproar created when the outlaws found their own mounts missing. So far, he thought, not a bad night's work.

Smoke Jensen wasted not a second longer than required to retrieve his saddle and remount the Olsens on saddled horses. Then he gave them hurried instructions on how to bring the stampeding horses under some form of control. Over the days they had been together, Smoke had come to accept the fact that Tommy Olsen was mature beyond his years. He entrusted the left flank to Tommy and his mother. He took the two girls with him on the right flank. With only swing riders it would be difficult, yet Smoke trusted that the terrain of the foothills, which now narrowed the trail, would be to their advantage.

Which set Smoke to thinking about another matter. If they continued to Powder River Pass, it stood to reason that the rustlers would jump them again. They could head due north, to Granite Pass, which would bypass Buffalo on the far side, where the Olsens wanted to go. Or they could turn west, which would take them far from the Crow Agency and Fort Custer. All three courses had advantages, but the disadvantages outweighed choosing the lower altitude Powder River Pass.

Silently, he pondered his choices through the night. When the faintest gray ribbon spanned the eastern horizon, Smoke called a halt on the bank of the north fork of the Powder River. By then the horses had lost their fright and settled down in loose bunches under the herd leader and his subordinates. Comfortingly, to Smoke's way of seeing it, the largest gather, some seventy animals, led the pack. The stop would do everyone good, even the critters.

At least, they did not need any supervision to walk mincingly into the shallows and drink from the river. In the cool, mountain breeze, their coats steamed and their breath fogged the air. Smoke shared out some cold, hard biscuits and strips of jerky. He and the Olsens munched them industriously while the herd drank. At last, Smoke spoke what was on his mind.

"We've covered what I'd reckon to be fifteen miles from where we left the rustlers. I think we should get some rest here, then move on. Sleep awhile if you can."

Della Olsen looked at the rugged Smoke Jensen with a radiant face. "Oh, I'm much too exhilarated to sleep. Goodness, getting rescued is certainly exciting."

Sarah-Jane and Gertrude nodded eager agreement. "And we get to ride astraddle, like Tommy," Sarah-Jane declared in delight.

Della's eyes narrowed for a short moment. "Not too much of that, young lady. It is not proper for a woman to ride that way."

"But Momma, you're doing it," Sarah-Jane protested.

"Yes, but I've had three chil—" Della broke off abruptly and blushed furiously. "Oh! What am I saying? You must think me terribly brazen, Mr. Jensen."

Smoke hastened to reassure her. "Not at all, and it's Smoke, remember, Della? My wife rode side-saddle until after our second child was born." He gave Della a mischievous grin. "Although I could never figure out why."

Her embarrassment vanished, Della produced a relieved smile. "Oh, we women have our reasons, Smoke. Now, have you figured out what we are going to do for food?"

Smoke scratched idly at his chin. "After everyone gets the hang of handling the herd on the move, Tommy can take off and hunt for game. There's wild bulbs and plants we can gather, also. No one has ever starved out here unless the weather was against them or they were just plain stupid."

"Did you ever eat pine nuts, Smoke?"

"Oh, yes, many a time."

"My hus—Sven was exceedingly fond of them."

"They're a good source of energy."

With that revelation, they continued to eat in silence until the first thin slice of orange slid above the eastern horizon. With that growing, Smoke roused a lightly slumbering Tommy Olsen and called the family together.

"We're going to do this a little differently today. Della, you and your youngest will take the right swing, Tommy the left with Sarah-Jane. I'll ride drag."

Furious over the loss of the herd and their own horses, Reno Jim Yurian stood in the orange light of the new sun and cursed Smoke Jensen with fervor. When he at last ran down, he pointed a finger at Yancy Osburn.

"Yancy, take five men and spread out until you find some horses. Head north. I think I heard a couple whinny right at sunrise. If you find them, keep going until you have more."

"Sure, boss. Do we take saddles with us?"

"No, just bridles. We need those horses fast." Reno Jim

turned to the remaining gang members. "The rest of you, see what you can find to salvage in a camp that's been run through by two hundred forty-five horses."

With that, he kicked a crushed coffeepot and swore with renewed vehemence.

With only a boy, a woman and two small girls to control the herd, Smoke found little to celebrate, beyond the rescue of the Olsens. In daylight, with the horses refreshed and tested, difficulties began to crop up almost at once. First to impinge on Smoke's quiet reverie were the rebellious outlaw horses. A shout from Tommy alerted him to the problem.

"Hiii! Hiiii-yaah! Get back there. Get back," the boy yelled as he streaked along the left flank of the herd in pursuit of four fractious mounts with minds of their own.

Smoke veered to cut off the runaways. He and Tommy managed to contain three of them. The fourth put its tail in the air and streaked between them, back in the direction from which they had come. In disgust and defeat, Tommy spat a word that Smoke did not think the boy had in his vocabulary. He decided that a little fatherly advice was called for. He walked Cougar over and clapped a hand on the boy's thin shoulder.

"Better not let your mother hear you say that." At Tommy's grimace, Smoke went on. "We're going to lose more than one of those horses. They belong to the rustlers and will try to break away every chance they get."

Tommy made a face. "But they're worth some money."

Smoke shook his head. "They don't wear my brand, and I can't sell them to the army. The idea is to keep them out of the hands of the gang long enough for us to get clean away. And with this herd, that will be hard to do."

Pondering that a moment, Tommy spoke his inner expectation. "I thought maybe I could sell them and get a stake for Maw."

"A generous idea, though it would make you a horse thief."

Tommy cocked an eyebrow. "D'you think *those* guys paid for their nags?"

Smoke shrugged. "Probably. Out here they still hang a man for stealing horses."

A tinkle of laughter erased the frown on Tommy's forehead. "Imagine that, rustlers buying their mounts."

Smoke took a deep breath. "Now that is settled, I think we should cut out all of their animals and send them off at an odd direction."

"Why, Smoke?"

"Once the critters take it in mind to run off, the others will jump at the chance, too. We don't have the manpower to round up the entire herd if that happened."

That sounded reasonable to Tommy. "Sure, but how do we find the right ones?"

"My remounts haven't been shod. Look for the horses with shoes."

With that as a guide, Tommy soon cut out twenty-three broom tails and scattered them to the winds. Seven more refused to budge from the herd. Smoke appeared satisfied with that and rode on, wondering what would happen next.

Tommy Olsen discovered their next setback when they had advanced into the high, steep pass. Ahead of him, the leaders turned about and began to mill among the horses that came after them. He trotted forward, only to return at twice the speed, his eyes wide.

"Smoke, there's a big ol' tree up there, fallen across the trail."

"Does it look like someone cut it down?"

"No. It's dead. I think it just fell over."

Smoke looked at Tommy as they cantered forward. "We'll have a devil of a time getting it moved."

"Yeah. No saws or an axe."

After a moment's thought, Smoke offered a suggestion. "We do have ropes, and plenty of horses. If we fasten onto some larger limbs, we can maybe pull it away."

"Who'll watch the herd?"

"Your mother and the girls."

Tommy made a face. That brought a laugh from Smoke. But he wasn't laughing when he got a look at the downed tree—a large, old pine, which if it had not been dead a long time would have weighed tons. Even in its present condition, Smoke harbored a small doubt as to whether they could move it. He had little choice, so he set about it with a will.

Smoke put Della and the girls behind the herd, to calm and hold them in place. Then he and Tommy cut out three of the remounts and took ropes from each saddle. At Smoke's direction, Tommy fastened the ends of the lariats to stout branches high up the trunk. Smoke fitted the loop ends over the necks of the three horses, then took a fourth and did a dally around his saddle horn.

"Get your horse, Tommy, and dally off that last rope. Then we do a little pulling."

From beyond the herd, Della's voice reached Smoke's ears. "Smoke, they're trying to push past us."

"Walk your horse into a few of them, shove them back," Smoke suggested.

"I wish I had a buggy whip."

That gave Smoke an idea. "Break a leafy branch off a tree. Don't hit any of the horses with it, just swish it in front of their noses. Should work."

After a longer delay, while Smoke and Tommy readied the animals for their pull, Della called again. "It's working, Smoke. They're turning back."

Smoke gave Tommy a nod, and they slapped the rumps of the three unsaddled horses with their reins. All five creatures lunged into the effort. The lariats went taut, one vibrating with enough force to give off a low hum. The braided hemp stretched at first; then ever so slowly the constant strain caused the top of the massive barrier to move.

Snapped-off branches on the bottom side began to screech and groan as they gouged the ground.

Smoke dug his heels into the flanks of Cougar and spoke to Tommy. "Harder. Keep the pressure on the remounts."

Gradually the gap widened. Then the hooves of the horses began to lose purchase as the tree hung up on some unseen obstruction. Smoke got them stopped and dismounted.

"Tend to the horses, Tommy. I'll see what's gone wrong." When the ropes slacked off, Smoke went forward and bent to peer under the trunk.

At first, he could not see any obvious cause. Then he noticed a thin ridge of rock jutting above the ground. In moving the tree that far it had butted three broken branches against the stone. Smoke drew his Greenriver knife and attacked the first of these, whittling at it to form a notch. When he had cut better than halfway through, he sat on the ground and worked his booted foot into position. With all the effort he could exert in that position, he kicked the protruding partial branch.

Nothing happened. He tried again. Once more, no result. On his third kick, Smoke heard a satisfying crackling and the limb flew free. At once he started on the second. It would play hell with the edge on his blade, Smoke reckoned, and no way to hone it in the near future. This piece proved to be afflicted with dry rot and quickly yielded to the cutting edge of Smoke's knife.

When it fell away, Smoke went after the third. It proved to be stubborn, nearly as stringy as oak. Smoke remembered a lesson taught by Preacher about the growth of trees. "When a branch gets whipped and twisted a lot by wind, it gets springy. The fibers are long instead of close and compact. It gets so they are jist like hardwood."

Which might have been the case with this difficult stump. Heat radiated up smoke's arm as he cut at the defiant wood. He made little progress over several minutes; then the blade sank into the heartwood, and the rest became easy. In another two minutes he had cleared the final obstruction.

Back in the saddle, he nodded to Tommy, and they again set the horses in motion. The ropes stretched and sang, and the animals strained into their burden. Then, with a grinding crunch, the tip of the fallen pine lurched forward and opened a grudging space. Quickly the man and boy halted the remounts and their own horses. Fists on hips, Smoke inspected the opening.

It was disappointing at best. Barely three horses at a time could squeeze by the sheer wall of the pass and the obstruction of the tree. That would have to do, Smoke noted, because the thick trunk had jammed tightly against a boulder at the side of the trail. He looked back at Tommy.

"Let's get 'em headed up and moving through. We've lost more time than we can afford."

15

Glancing at the horizon, Reno Jim Yurian produced the first smile he had worn since the herd had been run off. Five men astride unsaddled horses trotted toward him. He estimated that the drove had a two-day lead on them, provided they could find the animals again. He had to admit, he had greatly underestimated this Smoke Jensen.

Reno Jim reviewed what he knew of the man. Few on the frontier, or back east for that matter, had not heard of him. Thanks to the proliferation of dime novels, Smoke Jensen had been a legendary figure long before he went on that lecture tour in New England and New York City. Not that his trip had lasted for long. Trouble had come looking for Smoke Jensen, and he had quickly obliged.

That much Yurian had read in the San Antonio newspaper. An account that lasted over several days. In an amused tone, its first installment recounted a chase through Central Park, with picnickers scattered and food crushed beneath the hooves of several horses. In his usual manner, the reporter had recounted, Smoke Jensen ended the altercation with a blazing six-gun.

Someone like that could be real trouble. Yet Reno Jim had discounted it as sensationalism. Well now, by dang, it seemed Smoke Jensen was indeed larger than life. And mean as a wet bobcat. Reno Jim abandoned his dark reflections to hail the approaching riders.

"You've done good, as far as it goes," he informed them when they halted before him. "Any sign of more of our horses?"

"Yep," answered Yancy Osburn. "Seen a few, but they shied. Thing is, boss, they ain't comin' from Powder River Pass. They showed up north of this trail."

"Well, then, saddle up and get out there and round up as many as you can. We're going after that herd. Smoke Jensen might be mean as hell, but he's only one man."

By nightfall, Smoke Jensen and the herd had nearly reached the 8,950-foot summit of Granite Pass. Tommy had bagged four plump squirrels. He grumbled ferociously over the difficulty of removing their skins. At one point, he looked up at Smoke Jensen, blood on both hands, one cheek and his little square chin.

"Why do these squirrels have to have their hides attached by so many of these darned thongs?"

Smoke took pity on the boy. "They are not 'thongs,' Tommy. They are erectile tissue. Squirrels need them to bunch up their skin in cold weather."

Eyes large with wonder, Tommy looked down at the creature he was working on. "Gosh, how did you learn all that stuff?"

"From Preacher. He knew all about animals. And at one time, there was a larger market for squirrel hides than beaver. Here, let me show you an easier way."

Smoke started at the back end of the animal and made a long cut from bung to neck, then worked the skinning knife in under one side. He cut through the elastic retractors down one side, reversed the blade and severed the opposite ones. He peeled back the hide and did the back.

"There. Think you can do it like that?"

Tommy thrust out his chest. "Sure. Let me at it."

"You've got to gut this one first; then I'll put it on the fire to roast."

Smoke took the carcass and doused it in the crystal stream that burbled over smooth stones alongside the trail. Then he began to thread it on a green stick. For a second, he flashed back four days to when he did the same with an eight-foot rattler. He had given the huge rattle—there were eleven buttons—to Tommy. The boy wrapped it in a strip of cloth and shoved it deep in one pocket of his overalls. A good thing, too, Smoke thought. Out in the open, it would have the horses spooked all the time. Della came over while Smoke propped the squirrel over the coals.

"Smoke, I wonder if there is anything we can do to get washed off. The girls and I, that is. We've been taking on a goodly lot of dust of late and . . . well, I feel grimy."

Smoke looked left and right, then nodded toward a bend in the trail below them. "You can go down there, around the bend, and wash to your heart's content."

"But who'll guard us from wild animals or—or men coming along?"

"Take Tommy's little rifle. You can stand watch while the girls bathe, then Sarah-Jane can be lookout for you."

Della still seemed unconvinced. "There doesn't seem to be much privacy that way."

Smoke stifled the chuckle he felt building. "It's the best we've got. After you finish, Tommy and I can take our turns."

Pulling a face, Della confided to Smoke, "If you knew that boy like I do, you'd be in there with him. It's near impossible to get him out of the water."

Smoke answered her drily. "Cold as this is, I doubt it will be a problem."

Squeals came from beyond the bend only a few minutes after Della and her daughters disappeared. Their cleanup lasted only a scant five minutes. The three came back with a rosy glow from the icy water. Smoke went next, and wisely stripped only to the waist to wash away the accumulated dust. The snowmelt stung his skin and sent shivers along his spine.

Tommy had finished the last squirrel when Smoke returned. Eagerly the boy headed for the bend. Della had been right about her son, Smoke noted when he clocked Tommy at a full fifteen minutes before he reappeared.

"I thought you'd frozen solid," Smoke remarked.

"Naw. It was jist right. Though it would have been better with the sun shining." A hiss and plume of steam rose from the fire as one of the squirrels dripped fat. Tommy sniffed the air and rubbed his belly. "I'm hungry."

Della turned the meat while she looked up at Smoke. "How much longer?"

"Three, maybe four more days. We'll be on the Crow reservation by then. Before midmorning we'll reach the summit. I want to take a half-day rest. It's all downhill from there."

"I thought we were going to Buffalo first."

"Can't risk it, Della. Reno Jim Yurian and his gang would be laying for us on that trail. Even if they don't recover any of their mounts, they know Buffalo is the closest place to get more. Then they will be after us."

Early the next morning the riders sent out by Reno Jim Yurian returned with a dozen more of their missing horses. At once, Reno Jim named off as many of his best men, including Utah Jack Grubbs. They quickly saddled the animals and stood waiting for instructions.

"I'm coming with you. That gives us seventeen men. We are going to track down Smoke Jensen and finish him off. If any man sees Jensen first, save him for me. I want to make him die slowly," Yurian told them ominously.

Hazy sunlight bathed the schoolhouse in Muddy Gap. Inside, classes went on as usual. Outside, Brandon Kelso

presented a far different agenda to his companions, Willie
Finch and Danny Collins. Only the day before he had been
released from jail by Marshal Larsen. His father had
promptly boxed his ears for allowing himself to be caught
in such a stupid way. Now he planned to get revenge

"Here's what we're gonna do. We're gonna go in there
and run all the kids out. Then we take care of that small t-ass
schoolmarm."

Not the brightest of youths, Danny Collins had to ask,
"How we gonna do that?"

Brandon grabbed his crotch and grinned wickedly. "You
jist follow my lead."

With that he marched to the front steps and climbed to
the stoop. Brandon's massive hand closed over the door-
knob, and he slammed the portal inward with explosive
force. Ginny Parkins looked up sharply to find her nemesis
framed in the opening. She bit her lip in trepidation, then
recalled the message that had accompanied her gift from
Smoke Jensen.

"You can march yourself out of here this minute, Brandon Kelso."

"Naw. Ain't gonna do that." Brandon waved to the up-
turned faces and staring eyes of the students. "All you kids
get out of here. This is a school holiday."

Willie Finch put in his bit. "Yeah, everybody out. Ex-
ceptin' you, Prissy Pants."

Brandon's face turned dark red with self-induced rage.
"That's right! Scatter . . . all of you." His beady eyes narrowed and fixed on Ginny as he advanced on her. "Not you,
though. We're gonna give you something you have obviously never had. But you'll surely appreciate it once we're
through with you."

Backed against the blackboard, Virginia Parkins fought
panic as she sought some means to defend herself. She
grasped a piece of chalk and hurled it at the face of her tor-
mentor. The white stick hit edge-on and cut a gouge below
his right eye. Enraged, Brandon charged her.

Nimbly, Ginny slipped under his grasping arms and dashed for her desk. Fighting to control her movements, she yanked open the top drawer and whipped out the small .38 Smith and Wesson given her by Smoke Jensen. She turned to face Brandon, and being inexpert in the use of the weapon, she fired it low.

Her first bullet ripped into the floor. The second smashed into Brandon's right kneecap and shattered it. A bellow of agony burst from the lout's lips as he went down on his good knee. Ginny turned her wrath on the other two.

"Take this little monster and get out of my school," she demanded in a cold, even tone. "Do it now or I'll shoot you, too."

"That won't be necessary, Miss Ginny," Marshal Larsen said from the open door, his shotgun held purposefully in both hands. "I saw them headed this way, and I thought I should come along and see what they had in mind."

"I'm glad you did, Marshal. They had every intention of—of having their way with me."

Marshal Larsen's face portrayed his disgust and outrage. "They'll not be any problem to you ever again, Miss Ginny. I'll take them from here."

"Arrest her, Marshal," Brandon blubbered. "She shot me for no reason at all."

"Shut up, you little bastard, or I'll use this shotgun to remove some of your teeth." To Danny and Willie, he commanded sharply, "Carry this filth out of here. You're all goin' to jail."

Behind them, little Jimmy Finch piped shrilly, "Three cheers for Marshal Larsen. Hip—hip—hooray!"

Shortly after halting at the summit of Granite Pass, and running a single-strand rope fence around the remount herd, Smoke Jensen heard a distant rifle shot. Ten minutes later, a grinning Tommy Olsen walked out of the stand of aspen that graced one side slope of the passage through the Bighorn Mountains.

"I need a horse," the boy announced.

"What for?" Smoke challenged good-naturedly.

"I bagged us a deer."

Tipping back the brim of his hat, Smoke gave off a low whistle. "I should have seen to it we got here sooner. A rack of venison ribs sounds mighty good right now."

Eyes sparkling from this fulsome praise, Tommy asked, "Which horse should I take?"

"How big is the deer?"

Tommy described the creature with wide swings of his arms. Smoke nodded and pointed to one of the purloined outlaw horses. "Take that one. He's the calmest of the lot. I'll get your mother started on making preparations, then go hunt down some wild onions and turnips. We can make stew out of the tougher parts of the legs."

"Umm. Sounds good. I'm hungry now."

Smoke reached out and ruffled the boy's tousled auburn hair. "You are always hungry."

"Uh—Smoke? When we get to the reservation will we see some real wild Indians?"

Smiling, Smoke shook his head. "The Crow are not all that wild. Never have been. They took a friendly outlook to us whites. They've provided scouts for the army for years." He laughed softly. "They can just about kill you with hospitality if you happen upon them during one of their social dances. They'll stuff you with food, heap tobacco on you, drag you into the dance circle, give you the place of honor to sleep in the lodge."

"Lots of whiskey, I bet," Tommy opined.

Smoke frowned. "Given their choice, most Injuns shun liquor. They don't have much tolerance for it."

"What's tolerance?"

"In this case it means bein' able to hold their whiskey. And many Injuns can't. To most it's like any of the other white man's diseases. In a way it's a good thing. Someone has to stay sober out here."

Tommy studied Smoke in silence while the boy slipped a bridle on the horse. "You don't seem to miss strong drink much, Smoke."

"Never developed a fondness for it. I drink a little whiskey, though not enough to make a saloon keeper a profit, and two or three beers is my limit."

A serious expression altered Tommy's face. "I don't think I'll ever drink."

"None of us knows for sure what we'll do later in life. But good for you if you stick to it. You know, the Germans call beer 'liquid bread.' They don't think of it as liquor."

Tommy furrowed his smooth brow. "Then maybe I'll have some liquid bread when I grow up."

They laughed together, and Tommy swung up bareback on the horse. Smoke handed him his rifle. After the boy trotted away, Smoke realized exactly how good some roasted venison would taste.

Well fed on venison and with the humans and animals alike rested, Smoke Jensen sent his amateur drovers down the trail that descended the northeast slopes of the Bighorn Mountains. Spirits remained high. Confident in their improving ability to manage the horses, Smoke put Tommy on drag and rode on ahead to scout the terrain they had to cover.

He had gone some five miles from the herd when he came upon two rather large men who took their ease outside a stretched canvas lean-to. Both had rifles ready at hand and revolvers stuck into the waistband of their trousers. Smoke counted three on one of them. Smoke reined in and greeted them in a friendly manner.

"Howdy to you, too, mister," the smaller, as compared to his barn-sized companion, replied. "Sorta off the beaten track, ain'tcha?"

"Could say the same for you two, I suppose."

A scowl replaced the earlier smile of greeting. "This here's our land, mister. We got papers filed an all, over to Sheridan way."

Trying to keep it light, Smoke observed, "An ambitious undertaking. You waiting for the trees to grow to build a cabin?"

Rather than take it in good humor, the larger man glowered and roused himself, to reveal a Cheyenne backrest that had been hidden by his slab shoulders. "That ain't none of your business," he growled. "But it is ours, as to what you're doin' on our place."

"Didn't know anyone had homesteaded out this way. But as it happens, I'm driving a herd of remounts north to Fort Custer."

"And you think to bring them through here?" the smaller one remarked.

Smoke found his patience a tad strained. "That's what I had in mind."

A head taller and a shade wider than Smoke Jensen, the smaller opportunist announced their avaricious intentions. "Well, then, there'll be the matter of a little toll."

"Yeah," the huge one joined in. "Say . . . two bits a head."

Smoke Jensen cut them a flat, deadly gaze. "I think not. This trail is a public throughway."

"You sound like a lawyer."

"I don't need a lawyer for this. The trail has been used freely since the Indians first got horses. We go through and there's nothing you can do about it."

With a low growl, the man-mountain started for Smoke. "Then we shut down the trail and shoot yer horses."

He lunged at Smoke, who did not even wait to dismount. Instead, he pulled one boot free of the stirrup and kicked the huge lout flush in the face. Blood spurted from a mashed nose and split lip. His eyes crossed, but he did not go down. Instead, he looked to his partner.

"B'god, Jake, he hurt me."

Jake, who apparently did not have the same confidence in his size, made an even more costly mistake. He went for one of the revolvers at his waist. In half an eye-blink, he found himself staring at the black hole in the muzzle of the .45 Colt in Smoke Jensen's hand.

"I don't want to kill you, but I will. Ease that iron to the ground."

"And if I don't?"

Smoke shrugged. "Your friend here can bury you."

A glint of cunning entered Jake's eyes, and he tried a new tack. "A real gunfighter never pulls his piece unless he's gonna use it. I think you are all bluff."

"He means it, Jake," cautioned the bigger man.

Smoke remained motionless, one corner of his mouth lifted in a mirthless smile. Almost casually he twitched his right index finger. The shot sounded thunderous, and Jake's Merwin and Hulbert went flying when the bullet struck his shoulder. Groaning, Jake dropped to his knees.

"Your friend was right. I did mean it. Now, shall we settle the question of a toll? If you fence off the trail, or take even one shot at any of my horses, I'll kill you both. In fact, if I even see either of your faces while we're passing through, I'll kill you. Do we understand one another?"

Their shame-faced, silent nods answered Smoke. Cowed for the time being, they turned away while Smoke Jensen rode back in the direction from which he had come. Defeated for now, Smoke knew full well he would have to be watchful of them when the herd came through first thing in the morning.

16

Even the canvas lean-to had disappeared when Smoke
Jensen and the Olsens brought the herd down out of the
pass and through the land claimed by Jake and his huge
friend. On a still slightly downhill grade, the wisdom of a
half-day rest proved itself. By one o'clock that afternoon,
Smoke estimated they had covered twenty-five miles. At that
rate, they would reach the main trail north from Sheridan
by evening. It couldn't be too soon, Smoke acknowledged.

He saw only one drawback to this increase in speed. The
dust kicked up by the horses formed a gigantic cloud that
rose skyward on a breeze from the southwest. That blocked
his forward view, but it kept a lot of it off the drag rider, a
position Smoke chose for himself when the gait picked up
to a quick trot. Like old hands, the Olsens kept the herd
in a long, narrow gather that only occasionally spilled over
the edges of the traceway.

Shortly before four that afternoon, his expectation of a
forty-mile day assured, Smoke looked beyond the herd to
see three men riding toward them. He stood in his stirrups
and called out to Tommy Olsen.

"Come back and take the drag. I'm going to go find out
who those men are."

Tommy looked forward, then back at Smoke, face puzzled. *He* hadn't seen any riders. But, if Smoke said they were there, they must be. When he reached Smoke's side, he received a nod.

"Keep 'em moving." Then Smoke rode off.

Smoke reached the front of the herd with only thirty yards separating him from the mounted men. He had no problem with recognizing a smiling Ahab Trask in the lead. Trask snatched his hat from his head and gave an enthusiastic, friendly wave.

"What are you doin' comin' at us from this direction?" Trask asked when they came within hearing.

Grinning, Smoke jerked a thumb behind him. "A slight detour. I managed to steal back the herd."

Trask appeared quizzically amused to see a woman and two small girls riding swing. "So I see. Who are your new hands?"

"A family named Olsen. Their ranch was raided by the same gang that rustled the horses. Della, that's the woman's name, told me that she and her son, Tommy, recognized the leader the first time they saw him."

"Dang, if that don't beat all." Trask flashed a white smile in his sun-mahoganied face.

"Where are the rest, Trask?"

"Over on the Sheridan Trace. We saw your dust and came over from there. It's only a couple of miles ahead. I— uh . . ." Trask paused, uncomfortable with what he had to say. "We could only get seven men, Smoke. They're borrowed from a rancher south of Sheridan who thinks highly of you. He'd also heard about the troubles in Muddy Gap."

Smoke looked at it philosophically. "That gives me ten more than I've had for the last three days. Send Bolt back for them, and we'll get headed for Fort Custer before beddin' down for the night."

Trask looked along the herd's back trail. "Any chance of those rustlers comin' after you?"

Smoke shook his head. "Only if they found enough of their horses."

* * *

Once settled down in camp, with introductions made around, Smoke found he liked the cut of these hands. They had worked the herd expertly, relieving Della and the girls of the necessity of keeping fractious animals in line. Smoke particularly liked the line foreman, Harper Liddy. Harp usually supervised the fence-mending crews for his boss, Solomon Blaire, who owned the sprawling Leaning Tree ranch.

Smoke had heard of it. Blaire was experimenting with the new English breed of Herefords. Squat and compact, the wooly-headed red-and-white cattle produced more usable meat than bone and hide, and seemed to flourish on the high plains. Smoke had looked into raising them before changing to horses. All considered, he had no regret. If the Herefords, especially the males, were not docked—their horns removed—they tended to do considerable damage to one another, even if altered into steers. When the new men settled around the fire for coffee, Harp Liddy talked about the breed.

"Some say their blood strain runs back to Iberian cattle, brought to England by the Romans. That's what makes them so aggressive."

Smoke found that doubtful. "After nearly two thousand years, they would have surely had that characteristic bred out of them. And, I've seen Iberian stock in Mexico. Most were black, with only a few a light, orangish brown in color. Not at all like Herefords."

Smoke looked up to see Trask pour coffee and come over to join him. Accustomed to working long hours and days without seeing another human being, Trask, like most ranch hands, did not say a lot. Only now did he bring up the subject of the missing hands.

"There was five of you when I left to find help, Smoke. What happened?"

"We came upon the Olsens first. Then the rustlers found

our camp. They killed all but Jerry Harkness and myself. Jerry was wounded and I sent him off to get help. They should be joining us soon. Oh, and Utah Jack, who turned out to be with the gang."

"That low-down snake. Did he . . . kill any of the boys?"

Smoke thought back to it. "I can't say for sure. I nearly got my brains knocked out."

"Smoke coulda got 'em all, but he was tryin' to protect my maw," Tommy Olsen came to the fire to say.

"Truth is there were too many for me." Smoke yawned and stretched. "We'll head out at first light. I'm gonna turn in."

After Smoke left the fire, the new hands drifted to their bed rolls or to herd watch duty. In less than a quarter hour, silence held throughout the camp.

Listening carefully to the words of the young warrior, Iron Claw's eyes glowed. The number of horses headed their way seemed impossible. And so few men driving them. The Cheyenne war chief clapped a hand on the bare shoulder of his scout and spoke thoughtfully.

"You have done well, Sees-the-Sky. This means there will be more soldiers on the high plains. There are too many already, pushing out onto our hunting grounds."

"We should not let them keep these horses," Sees-the-Sky suggested. "We could run them off, steal all we can."

"I have already thought of that. We could possibly get away with half of them. Think how that would swell our pony herd. And they would not be ridden against us that way."

He looked beyond the young warrior to where his large raiding party waited in patient silence. Iron Claw raised his voice so all could hear. "We will follow along out of their sight and see what good medicine the Great Spirit gives us."

Iron Claw swung atop his paint horse and raised a hand to signal his dog soldiers. Formed into a line three abreast, they silently rode parallel to the herd beyond a concealing ridge. Sees-the-Sky returned to keep the white men and their horses under watch.

Hubble Volker knew it would be the smart thing to do. When three more horses ambled back in their general direction, he had them gathered in and sent two men on through Powder River Pass to Buffalo. They were to use a bank draft Hub had forged with Reno Jim's signature to obtain horses for the rest of the gang and bring them back. He ordered the remaining men to walk through each day, bringing along their saddles and tack.

On the third day after the herd had been stolen, he saw his gamble pay off. Over a long swell in the prairie, the three he had sent on came fogging back with fifteen horses for the men afoot. Some good-natured cursing rose among the outlaws. They had visions of recovering their lost fortunes. Some of them complained, though, when Hub announced his decision not to pursue the herd.

"What do you mean we're not goin' after them?"

Hubble Volker kept a calm demeanor. "We are. Only we won't catch them by following the way they went. We know where they are going. The shortest route to get there is through the pass to Buffalo and north from there. You said yourself, Fred, that there is no sign those horses went through ahead of you. So they used the other pass. We'll catch them, don't worry."

They hastened to saddle the new horses and gratefully mounted. Hub took his place at the lead, then started them off. He reckoned that Reno Jim would appreciate his efforts.

Trudy Olsen lay in the bed of the buckboard brought along for supplies by the Leaning Tree hands. She had already thrown up three times this morning, and had been unable to control her bowels. She also complained of terrible thirst. Della suspected she had somehow contracted dysentery. The trek had been hard on all of them.

More so on Gertrude. Della worried most about Trudy, the youngest of her children. A thin girl, small for her age, Trudy had inherited her father's blond hair and large, square hands. Her precarious health had come from somewhere else. Colicky as a baby, she frequently took fevers and seemed to constantly have the sniffles, although that had markedly dried up since leaving the ranch. Della had no idea why. She rode with her daughter now, a damp compress to the child's brow.

"Momma, I feel sick again," Gertrude said weakly.

Della helped her to sit up and held her while she hung over the side and vomited. Could it be the water? Della wondered. Tommy rode forward from his position on swing.

"What's wrong with Trudy, Maw?"

Shaking her head in exasperation, Della answered her son. "I don't know, Tommy."

"Maybe I should get Smoke."

"He's a lot of things, son, but he's not a doctor."

Tommy looked shocked. "Is it that bad? Does she need a doctor?"

Della answered honestly. "I don't know. I think maybe so, Tommy." She thought for a moment, then spoke, a note of stress in her voice. "Yes. Bring Smoke back here. I need to talk to him."

When Smoke arrived, Della described the condition of her younger daughter. She concluded with an urgent appeal. "Please, can you route the herd past somewhere with a doctor?"

"I regret it, but I cannot."

"But why?"

Smoke seemed reluctant to answer. "There is nowhere along this trail until we get to the Crow Agency. No settlement that I know of."

"Then can't we turn back to Sheridan? It can't be more than a day's ride."

Smoke sighed. "For someone on horseback, yes. But with the herd and this wagon . . ."

"Oh, please. Isn't there something you can do?"

Smoke did not answer. For most of the day he had been seeing signs of Indians close by. He had no desire to further alarm Della, so he did not mention that. For her part, Della would not let it go so easily.

"Can't I send Tommy back to Sheridan for the doctor."

Shaking his head Smoke replied, "I'm sorry, I can't even allow that."

Della put quick, hot words to the thought that formed in her head. "You are absolutely heartless."

Still, Smoke would not speak of the potential danger. Tight-lipped, he responded curtly, "Not the way I see it."

Less than a day behind the herd now, Reno Jim Yurian and his sixteen men came down out of Granite Pass at a fast canter. Some five miles out on the prairie, they came upon the lean-to that sheltered Jake and his partner. The pair greeted Reno Jim familiarly.

Reno Jim responded in style. "Jake, Lutie, I haven't seen you boys in a while."

Jake made a face. "We got outta the outlawin' business. Gettin' to be too many lawdogs out this way."

Reno Jim cocked an eyebrow. "You goin' soft?"

Jake denied it. "Naw. Nothin' like that. Jist figgered it was time to settle down. Why, we even filed a homestead on this place. Got us a whole quarter section."

Lutie added his opinion of that. "At least what of it the Injuns don't camp on from time to time."

Giving their surroundings a quick examination, Reno Jim made a proposition. "Would you fellers object to makin' some real cash money?"

Lutie cut his eyes to Jake. They both read the same hunger. "Who we have to kill for it?"

"There may not be any killing," replied Reno Jim. "D'you have horses?"

"Yup. Speakin' of horses, a whole damn herd went through here a couple of days back," Jake offered.

"Those are the source of the money I'm offering you. We're gonna steal them back."

"You mean they's your horses?" Lutie asked.

Reno Jim produced a wicked grin and shook his head. "Not really. We rustled them from the fellers who have them now; then they stole them back. Far as we know, there's only one grown man, a woman and three kids with the horses."

"That's all we saw with them," Lutie admitted.

"Well, do you think that nineteen of us can take the horses from them?"

Jake swelled his chest. "Don't see why not."

Lutie cut his eyes from Reno Jim to Jake and back. "Uh—tell Reno what the big feller did."

Reno Jim leaned forward. "What was that?"

"Nothin'. Nothin' at all," Jake hastened to add.

Lutie looked hard at his partner, then turned back to Reno Jim. "He got the drop on us and runned us off."

Reno Jim nodded. "No surprise. That feller is none other than Smoke Jensen."

Both of the former outlaws turned pale. Jake spoke up hurriedly. "Well, then, Reno, you done lost you two extra guns. Ain't no way I'm goin' up again' Smoke Jensen."

"You astonish me, Jake. There's eighteen others of us. That's too many for even Smoke Jensen."

Jake canted his head to one side. "Oh, yeah? How is it, then, that he an' a woman an' some kids tooken that herd from you, Reno?"

That hit Reno Jim Yurian where it hurt. He glowered at the pair for a moment, then spat, "Then stay here and eat grass if you're so yellow. Come on, boys, we're wastin' daylight." With that, he turned his back on Lutie and Jake and trotted off.

"Wheew, I'm sure glad they're gone," Lutie stated in utter relief.

Jake had a different outlook. "I'm jist glad we didn't try to push it with Smoke Jensen."

Strain radiated from Della Olsen's face when she came to where Smoke Jensen squatted beside the cookfire. "Trudy is worse. And now Sarah-Jane is looking a little peaked. Have you no pity? We could have been in Buffalo by now and none of this would have happened."

Smoke looked at Della, completely at a loss for how to console the woman. In most situations, Smoke easily communicated with the ladies. But someone recently bereft by the death of her husband, with two ailing children, presented an entirely different predicament. Smoke nearly relented his refusal to allow Tommy to go after a doctor, in spite of his suspicion that they had been shadowed by Indians. He was about to speak his thoughts when high, shrill yelps and hoots came from around the herd.

"Injuns!" Harper Liddy shouted from that direction.

From his vantage point in a stand of cottonwood, Iron Claw watched the last of his dog soldiers glide into position around the horse herd. He switched his gaze beyond them to the two figures at the fire. The woman's posture spoke of some worry. Perhaps over the girl Sees-the-Sky told him about. The one who got sick over the side of the rolling lodge. He sensed the moment of indecision in the man. The time could not be better.

Iron Claw raised his face to the sky and uttered a piercing signal. "Kiii-yip-yip-yip!"

Cheyenne dog soldiers designated to move the herd whooped and howled in reply and began to flap blankets at the horses. Startled, the animals bolted. Yet, the white men who watched them did not lack courage. Several acted at once to channel the creatures as they thundered across the ground. Others sought the cause.

When they found it, gunshots crackled in the night. The sudden discharge served to prompt half of the remaining warriors to charge the camp. That, Iron Claw reasoned, would turn the herdsmen back to defend their brothers.

The darkness filled with shrieking war cries, arrows began to moan and hum through the air into the camp. Iron Claw watched as the big man smoothly shoved the woman to the ground and drew a long-barreled revolver. The white man went to one knee and fired in the direction of an arrow's flight. A brave cried out and began to thrash in the sagebrush, his hip shattered by the bullet. Iron Claw revealed himself at the edge of the copse and raised his rifle to signal the rest to join the attack. They responded with enthusiasm.

In seconds, Cheyenne warriors swarmed into the camp.

17

Smoke Jensen cocked his .45 Colt after shooting the warrior in the bushes and looked for another target. "Stay down, Della," he commanded.

From the wagon, a shot blasted into the night. Smoke looked that way. "Make sure what you are shooting at, Tommy. There are some of ours out there, too."

"Sure, Smoke. I'll watch careful. Yike!" The last came when an arrow thudded into the thick side of the wagon only three inches from Tommy Olsen.

Smoke snapped a shot at the warrior who had launched the arrow at Tommy and saw the Cheyenne flop over backward to twitch in agony from the shoulder wound. A quick check showed Smoke that the Leaning Tree hands had managed to channel what looked to be a little more than half the remounts into a ravine, where they held them in a milling, confused mass. Then came another outburst of war whoops, and more Indians charged into the clearing.

Trask and Bolt stood back-to-back and laid down a withering fire that caused the Cheyennes opposite them to recoil and seek a softer spot. They found none as other off-duty hands doubled up to defend themselves. Men whirled around as frantically as the horses.

Not many of the hastily fired rounds found a home in

flesh. Smoke watched as the Cheyennes rallied to charge again. It could only be a matter of time, he thought. There were far too many of them. They were about to be swallowed up in screaming Indians. From the slope to one side came a strident yell.

Suddenly, the attack broke off. Swiftly, the Cheyennes deserted the field. Smoke could only stand and wonder.

From his vantage point outside the cottonwoods, Iron Claw judged the progress of his warriors. More importantly, he gazed over the disappearing rumps of the horses that had been successfully driven off. He made a quick decision. Turning, he spoke to Spotted Feather, the dog soldier society leader.

"We have enough horses. To try for more will risk the lives of too many brave men. And it might be bad medicine to kill a white woman and those children."

Spotted Feather smiled grimly. "You are right as always."

"What is an older brother for, Spotted Feather?"

Iron Claw's younger sibling put humor into his smile. He spoke in the ritual manner of his warrior society. "You may stop them whenever you wish."

Iron Claw raised his voice in a sharp, barking hoot like a hungry coyote. At once the warriors ceased their fighting. Many withdrew beyond the limited light in the camp. Quietly they sat their ponies. Iron Claw stepped forward to where he could be plainly seen.

He raised his arm in the sign for a parlay. The big man at the fire pit repeated it and strode for a big 'Paloose horse. Iron Claw eased his excited, cavorting mount into a mincing circle as he watched the white man approach at an easy trot. When less than fifteen feet separated them, Iron Claw could not prevent the display of chagrin and embarrassment that washed over his face.

"I see you, Smoke Jensen."

"And I see you, Iron Claw. Why are you stealing my horses?"

Iron Claw shrugged and lifted the corners of his mouth in a smile. "Because they are here. And . . . I did not know they were your horses. They will be returned, old friend."

"Thank you, Iron Claw."

"Have your winters been light?"

Smoke produced a grin and a frown at the same time. "Now you want to get sociable? Yes, my winters have not been a hardship."

"I think of you often and ask the Great Spirit to watch over you and that black-haired wife. Your children are all grown?"

Smoke nodded. "Yes. Except for a boy we adopted recently."

Iron Claw raised eyebrows in surprise. "You are getting to be more 'Injun' every time I see you. He is a good boy?"

"I think he is."

"Then take your horses to where you were going and return to him, Smoke Jensen. The Cheyenne will not harm you more."

They exchanged the sign for peace, and Iron Claw turned his mount. He raised his feather- and brass-tack-decorated rifle to signal the dog soldiers. Without a backward look, they all rode quietly away.

Riding a lathered horse, his face beet-hued, Boyne Kelso ran recklessly down the main street of Muddy Gap. Flustered women put gloved hands to their mouths to stifle yelps of surprise. Men and dogs fled from his hazardous path. Kelso reined so viciously to the left that it drew blood from the tender mouth of his mount. Then he yanked up short in front of the sheriff's office.

Muttering angrily under his breath, he stormed to the door and slammed through. "Where's that idiot Larsen?" he demanded of a surprised Fred Chase.

"He's at dinner. Over to the Iron Kettle. What's got you so riled?"

"You damned well ought to know. I want my boy out of jail this instant."

"That ain't gonna happen, Mr. Kelso. Not with the charges against him."

Kelso shoved his mottled face toward the deputy. "And what might those be?"

Fred Chase made it clear he enjoyed this. "We'll take the minor things first. Brandon is charged with trespass, forced entry of a building, first-degree assault, and worst of all, attempted rape."

"What utter nonsense. My boy is not a criminal, nor is he depraved. Now get him out here so I can hear the truth of this."

"He stays where he is. No exceptions."

Kelso started to protest, then turned for the door. "Tell Larsen I'll be back."

Boyne Kelso had been at the holding pens in Bent Rock Canyon, happily counting their growing profits, when one of the Yurian gang brought word about his son being shot by Virginia Parkins and taken to jail by Marshal Larsen. It had taken him three days to get back. He'd be damned if it would take one minute more to free the boy.

To do so, he would have to have help, he reasoned. With a darkening scowl, he recalled the impudent smirk on the face of Fred Chase. How dare that stupid clod defy him? He started at once to round up supporters. His first stop would be the mercantile.

"What can I do for you, Deacon Kelso?" asked Eb Harbinson.

"You can come along with me. That mad dog lawman, Larsen, has locked up my son for absolutely nothing. And he's left orders that the boy's not to be let out for any reason. It came to me that a little moral persuasion is needed here."

"But, I . . . have the store to run."

"You've got clerks. I need you to back me."

Boyne made his next stop at the house of Mrs. Agatha

Witherspoon, president of the local chapter of the Ladies' Temperance League. She also held Bible studies for the church. Kelso had calmed somewhat when he presented his case to her. Although well aware of the actual situation, Kelso invented "facts" to support his position. Grover Larsen must have been successful in keeping the real events quiet, because Agatha Witherspoon reacted with genuine shock and indignation.

"That's simply horrible. Why in the world would he do such a terrible thing? Your boy is a little—ah—brash at times, but that's no excuse for someone to shoot him and put him in jail. Who is it that shot him?"

Kelso's face darkened again. "The brazen, damned, unmarried woman who flaunts herself in front of our children in that schoolhouse."

Agatha's hand flew to her mouth to cover a gasp. "Young Miss Parkins? I—I can't believe that. She is so gentle, so meek. She's at every Bible study bee. And I hear that the children adore her."

"I'll show you adore," roared Boyne Kelso. "She shot the kneecap off my son for no reason at all!"

"That—that's terrible. Oh, he must be in such pain. Has he seen a doctor?"

"He's in jail, Agatha. I don't know if the doctor has been to him or not. I'm not even allowed to visit him."

Agatha Witherspoon made up her mind with that revelation. "That will never do. Come along. We'll find Parson Frick. The marshal cannot deny him. He'll get a doctor for your boy."

Sweeping regally down the street, the Witherspoon woman led the way to the parsonage. From there they went to the home of Rachel Appleby, the choir director. Her husband, Tom, made an effort at objecting to precipitate action. He had heard a couple of rumors of late. And he had little use for that arrogant, pushy, spoiled brat, Brandon Kelso.

It did him little good. With Boyne Kelso's tale embroidered by Agatha Witherspoon, it galvanized Rachel Appleby into immediate partisanship. Parasol shading her from the broiling sun, she hoisted the hem of her ample skirts and joined the ranks.

With his entourage in tow, Boyne Kelso returned to the jail. He stomped through the door with the church elders and minister and confronted a surprised Grover Larsen.

"I demand that you release my son at once, Larsen."

Parson Frick added his two bits' worth. "Yes, this is quite distressing. Hardly the Christian thing to do, withholding medical treatment."

Brushing up against Smoke Jensen must have given Grover Larsen new backbone. Ignoring the minister, he balled his fist and extended a thick index finger, which he jabbed at Boyne Kelso. "That no-account, shiftless offspring of yours is in serious trouble."

"Nonsense!" Kelso thundered. "He may behave foolishly at times, but he's innocent of any real dishonesty."

"That's where you are wrong, Kelso. He's not innocent, and neither are the other two who are locked up with him. Now get out of here."

Kelso took on a shocked expression. "You have three boys locked up in there? This is an outrage."

"Not for what they're charged with."

"And what is that?"

"He, Willie Finch, and Danny Collins made improper advances to Miss Ginny. Your son attacked her in an attempt to carry them out when she refused."

Kelso snapped hotly, "I don't believe that."

"Why else do you think she shot him? He went after her in front of all the kids."

Beyond control, Boyne Kelso screamed with enough force that spittle flew from his mouth in a frothy, white spray. "That's a goddamned lie! I'll have your badge for that within twenty-four hours. And I'm going to have the territorial attorney charge that schoolmarm slut with assault."

* * *

For the first few minutes, Reno Jim Yurian could not believe his turn of luck. Hailed from behind them on the trail, Reno Jim turned to see Hub Volker and the rest of the gang headed their way. How had they caught up so fast? It came to him in a rush. Yeah, the horses came back, or they went into Buffalo and got more.

That would have put them on the way to this point for almost as long as he and his sixteen men. Now he had no doubt as to the outcome of their efforts to take back the horses. It would be simple with thirty-three men. They would wash over Smoke Jensen and the family with him like an ocean wave.

Believing themselves safe now, Smoke Jensen and his small band of drovers pushed the herd on northward the next morning. Shortly before noon, the missing horses returned under the guidance of Cheyenne warriors. The animals rejoined the gather without complaint. Smoke spoke words of thanks in the Cheyenne tongue and wished them well.

Tommy turned a big-eyed look on Smoke. "You can talk that stuff?"

"Sure, learned it young. It's an easy language."

"Could ya . . . teach it to me?"

"We won't be together long enough for you to get it all." At the boy's visible disappointment, Smoke relented. "I can teach you a few words, some expressions. Would you like that?"

Tommy beamed. "Would I!" He swiveled in the saddle and shouted to his sister. "Hey, Sarah-Jane, I'm gonna talk Cheyenne."

Smoke's confidence increased when they made thirty-four miles for the day. He located some herbs and blended them with sage leaves. This he had given to Gertrude Olsen, over the objections of her mother. By the nooning,

Trudy showed obvious signs of improvement. Smoke dosed her again.

By evening, she was sitting up and took some broth. She drank water thirstily to replace that lost to the diarrhea. Della restrained her in that endeavor and smiled for the first time since the child had taken sick. She even went so far as to apologize to Smoke.

"I think you have saved her life. I want to say that I am sorry for the way I snapped at you. It was grossly unfair. Why didn't you try the herbs earlier?"

Smoke gave her a knowing smile. "There weren't any of the right ones around. And you weren't desperate enough to allow me to use them."

Della looked shocked. "Why, that's a terrible thing to say. I would do anything for my children."

"Even if the remedy came from an Indian medicine man?"

Della gaped at him. "I never thought of that."

"I did."

"Smoke, I feel foolish."

"Not at all. You're just a very protective mother. That's a good sign. Your children know it and appreciate what you do for them. Now, I think Trudy needs more rest."

"Thank you again, and I am sorry."

Smoke turned his smile to a friendly one. "It's all in where you grew up."

That night, everyone slept soundly for the first time since the herd had been rustled. Smoke Jensen would soon find how beneficial that had been.

"We'll do it the way we did before," Reno Jim Yurian informed his gang. "It worked then, no reason it won't now. What we're after is the horses. Never mind the men, unless they offer resistance."

Yancy Osburn scoffed. "What kinda resistance can one man and some brats give us?"

"You have a point, Yancy, but from the tracks we've seen, it looks like Jensen picked up some replacements somewhere. Be prepared for trouble."

Hub Volker addressed the men who would be with him. "We'll split off now, swing around on the flanks. When the boss is in place in front of the herd, he and five of the boys will charge the herd. We swing down from the side and start pushin' them back along the trail. Those on the other side will hit at the same time. Get a movin'."

They departed in silence, with nothing to say until the fighting ended. Each of the outlaws had wrapped himself in his private thoughts. Ainsley Burk wondered about that pretty saloon gal who had waved to him back in Muddy Gap while they were robbing the stores. Maybe he'd drop in on her and spend some of his take.

Prine Gephart astounded himself by recalling the face of the wife he had left behind in Missouri and his three freckle-faced boys, stair-stepped between five and nine. He hadn't wanted to abandon his sons, but his wife had turned into a shrew, always complaining about not enough money. And when he had some, getting on his case about where he got it and how. Danged woman, she had driven him to robbing to supplement the meager income from their hardscrabble farm. Well, he'd shown her.

Virgil Plumm visualized the old, weathered ranch house in Texas where he had been born and raised. With the stake he would have, he could fix it up, paint it even. Then find him a good woman and raise a batch of young 'uns. Ranching was in his blood. His paw had put him atop a horse before he could walk proper. He had tried to rope calves the first time when he was five.

Awh, what the hell was he thinking? Outlawing was the only thing he had known since the age of sixteen. He'd never change now. The gray, warped siding of the house faded. He would just go get drunk, gamble away his profit and visit the bawdy houses until the last dime had been spent. Oh, and get his six-gun fixed. It had been hanging up of late. The recoil plate must be worn.

Bittercreek Sawyer saw a world entirely different from any of his fellow thieves. The soft yellow glow of gaslights played through his mind. Attractive young Creole women all in white lace and lawn hoopskirt dresses graced the wrought-iron galleries of the French Quarter and cast admiring glances at him as he rode in a spanking bright, black lacquered carriage along Saint Peter Street. A cotton-haired darkey drove the rig. Bittercreek wore a frilly white shirt, paisley vest, cutaway coat and top hat. A silver-headed cane rested in one gloved hand. The rich aroma of Cajun cooking wafted on a light, moist breeze up from Jackson Square. The bass hoot of a riverboat steam whistle startled pigeons off their eve roosts. All was well with the world.

With the impending fight drawing nearer, Lucky Draper concentrated on the scene of a smoky saloon, where he stood surrounded by his friends, who slapped him on the back and whooped for joy. He had just broke the bank. The faro dealer looked at him with a gaping mouth. Lucky's pockets bulged with double-eagles. He ran more through his fingers like grains of corn. A tall, willowy blonde ambled over, hips swaying in a skimpy dancer's costume.

She twined her arms around his neck and planted a big, wet kiss on his lips. Another lovely handed him a brimming glass of good rye. The cheering went on. Lucky tucked a twenty-dollar gold piece into the cleavage of each girl.

"Hold up!" came a low, but emphatic command.

It brought them all out of their dreams. Hubble Volker pointed at a low rise ahead. "Them horses are right beyond that ridge. We wait until we hear the first shots, then ride like hell."

Smoke Jensen's confidence continued into late afternoon. Then, before he knew what to expect, five men appeared on the trail ahead of them. They reined in momentarily, then came on at a gallop, weapons out and ready. The moment they came within range, they opened fire.

Tommy Olsen understood it all in a flash. "They're back!"

In a storm, the outlaws rushed beyond those in the lead of the herd. Smoke Jensen shot one out of the saddle, and then the horses stampeded. Gunfire broke out on the right flank of the panicked animals, driving them back on those behind. Eleven men streamed over the ridge in pursuit of the unsettled remounts. Most of them fired in the air, though a few directed bullets toward the hard-working drovers.

One of the Leaning Tree hands threw up his arms and wavered in the saddle. His horse scented the freely flowing blood and went berserk. It crow-hopped and sunfished until it dislodged the seriously wounded rider. Smoke Jensen swung in his saddle and fired directly at the shooter.

Smoke's bullet took him square in the chest. He flew from the saddle and disappeared under the hooves of the shrilling, stamping remounts. A bullet cracked past Jensen's ear, and he looked to see that the five riders who had attacked from the front now seriously worked at killing every one of his hands, himself as well.

18

Reno Jim Yurian and the four men with him halted at the edge of the boiling mass of horses and took careful aim at the men who attempted to control them. Another Leaning Tree hand slumped on the neck of his horse. A bullet cut through the jacket worn by Smoke Jensen and burned a hot line across his shoulder. Damn, Smoke thought in a flash, that shoulder had only recently healed. Then he gave himself over to the battle that brewed around him.

There would be no containing the horses, Smoke realized at once. Already the outlaws pushed them down the trail in the direction from which they had come. Clouds of dust and powder smoke roiled upward to cut off clear vision of the violent confrontation. Heat became oppressive. Sweat ran down Smoke Jensen's forehead and stung his eyes. He wiped with a forearm to clear them. Suddenly an outlaw loomed directly in front of him.

Smoke saw the muzzle rise to center on his chest; then he triggered his Colt. The bullet smashed into the open, screaming mouth of the gang member. The back of Prine Gephart's head flew off with his hat, and his dreams died with him. Then his Smith American discharged, and a shower of stars exploded inside Smoke's head. Immense pain shot down his neck, and he felt himself slipping from the saddle. Swiftly, blackness overwhelmed him.

Caleb Noonan found himself facing three determined rustlers. He knew the horses had to be controlled, yet the threat to his life forced him to draw and fire at one of the men. His shot went wild, and he recocked his Colt. Another outlaw took a shot at Caleb.

An aching line of fire ran along the outer side of Caleb's right thigh. Then his mount surged into a frenzied leap as the slug burned into its belly. Caleb shot again and put a bullet into the meaty part of one outlaw's abdomen. Then a giant pain exploded in his chest. All strength left him, and his horse threw him.

He landed hard enough to cross his eyes. When he straightened them, he looked up into the muzzle of a .44 Winchester pointed at his head. He saw only the first flicker of muzzle bloom . . . then blackness.

Granger Bolt saw Caleb Noonan go down. He twisted in the saddle and brought quick retribution to the outlaw who had killed his friend. That brought immediate attention down on him. To his regret, the surviving member of the trio who had gunned down Caleb turned his way. He and Bolt fired as one. To his surprise, in the face of the certain knowledge of his impending death, the bullet cracked past Bolt's head. All around, the air moaned and crackled with flying slugs. With new wonder he saw the outlaw jerk, then slump in his saddle.

He might get through this after all, Granger thought to himself. Then nine more rustlers joined the fray. They rode in with cold determination. One sighted on Bolt and put a bullet through his head from a range of twenty yards.

Granger Bolt died without a sound. The fighting went on without him. By now, nearly half the herd had been started back toward Sheridan, Buffalo, and Bent Rock Canyon beyond.

Pulling out of the swirl of the combat, Ahab Trask decided that these rustlers were seriously trying to kill them all. It hadn't been that way the first time. He tried to rally his muddled thoughts and make sense of what he saw. There seemed to be gunmen everywhere.

Worse, they fired with deadly accuracy. Another of the Leaning Tree hands went to the ground, his chest bloodied from a shot in the back. Ahab Trask took the time he spent in observation to reload his six-gun. At such short ranges, it would serve well. Two rustlers charged straight at him, driving ten head of remounts before them. Trask raised his Colt and fired.

Unfortunately for him, the close proximity of the frenzied horses set off a fear reaction in his own mount. It jinked to one side and threw off his aim. Then the remounts surged all around him. To his horror, his horse reared and spun on its hind hooves. Trask felt himself slipping, and then a rifle butt drove out of seemingly nowhere and slammed into his chest. He fell with a scream under the unshod hooves of the surging horses.

Ahab Trask's shrill cry quickly went silent. The remounts passed on. They left behind a lifeless ball of torn, bloodied clothes, bits of bone protruding from rents in the cloth.

A wicked smile playing on his lips, Reno Jim Yurian thought the whole plan had gone well. At the outset, not all of the men knew of his plan to kill everyone and leave no witnesses, or the chance of pursuit. Only those who rode with him, and those he placed on the left flank, had been aware of that.

He allowed himself a moment to gloat as those flankers crashed into the milling defenders. Two more drovers went down. One fell under the hooves of the remounts. Yes, well before sundown they would have the herd back together and under their control. Yancy Osburn rode out of the melee to join Reno Jim.

"They fight like wildcats, Reno. Ever'thing's so mixed up we're shootin' more air than men."

"So are they, remember. I don't see anything of Smoke Jensen."

"I think I saw him go down early on, Reno."

"Damn. I wanted him for myself."

"Anyway, he won't be a bother to us anymore. You have any spare cartridges?"

"In my left saddlebag. Take a box."

Yancy grinned. "If twenty rounds don't finish it, I'll eat my six-gun." Whistling lightly, he reached for the ammunition and returned to the fight.

"Give 'em hell, Yancy!" Reno Jim yelled after him.

Harper Liddy had a hard time keeping his mount between his legs. Gunshots cracked all around him. Ol' Reb, his trusty mount, constantly twitched his loose hide and made mincing side steps to express his discomfort. Everything was in such confusion. He could not prove it, but a moment ago it seemed as though the horses that had been driven off from the herd had started to return. How could that be? He had little time to speculate further.

A yowling rustler burst out of the miasma of dust and smoke and charged right at him. The hard case had a revolver blazing in each hand, his reins looped over the pommel. To Liddy's good fortune, the outlaw turned out to be a lousy shot. Hot lead flew past Liddy's shoulders, and one cracked overhead. A galloping horse provided a poor platform from which to fire a gun.

Harper Liddy took careful aim and ended Virgil Plumm's hopes of the good life in the French Quarter. Another, wiser gunhand shot Harper Liddy from a standing horse. The bullet cut through Liddy's chest from front to rear. Bad hurt and knowing it, Harper fired point-blank at the charging outlaw, turned in his saddle and killed the man who had mortally wounded him before he himself fell dead at the feet of his mount.

Intent on protecting the Olsens, Jerry Harkness fought his way from behind the rustlers toward the wagon. He and the five men he had brought along arrived only seconds before the attack. Two of the men died in the effort to penetrate the gang. Jerry had taken another grazing wound. Now he dismounted and crouched beside the frightened family. From above him, a Winchester cracked, followed by a shot from a lighter weapon, a Marlin, Jerry thought. He added his own firepower to it and saw immediate results.

A surging roan went down right in front of him, yanked from its front hooves by its dying rider. Jerry cycled the lever action of his .44 Winchester and fired at another outlaw. *These bastards don't care about the horses, they're more interested in killing us,* he realized at once. He centered on another bandit and squeezed the trigger.

Jerry's slug took the man in his hip. He howled and turned away from the fight. Another of the volunteers Jerry had rounded up died as a trio of the rustlers discharged their revolvers into him from three directions, not more than four feet away. Jerry bit off a curse.

Two hard cases swept past him, and the weapons above went off in a roar. One gunman fell. The other turned back and pointed his six-gun at the occupants of the wagon. Too late to take aim, Jerry thrust himself upward, arms out to deflect the revolver. He got his hand on the barrel and succeeded in his purpose, only to have hot pain explode in his palm when the Colt discharged. A second later, a shot came from his left and bored through his chest, bursting his heart.

* * *

Head throbbing, Smoke Jensen regained consciousness to find an eerie silence blanketing the battlefield. Had the horses been taken and the gang gone from there? Slowly he roused himself, conscious of a steady seep of blood down the side of his head. At least, he thought, it was the side and not his forehead. Slowly, Smoke gained control over the focus of his eyes. He saw a number of the outlaws sitting their horses and staring in horror off across the plains. What were they looking at? Smoke raised himself farther.

When his gaze moved to the ridge surrounding them, his features mirrored the same shock as that on the faces of the outlaws. He blinked, then slowly, painfully, came to his boots. He could hardly believe what he saw.

Ringing the entire swale, a double circle of Cheyenne warriors sat their ponies. They looked down in silence while the dust and powder smoke drifted from the scene of conflict. The horses driven off earlier milled in front of those on the south side. While Smoke Jensen looked on in astonishment, Iron Claw raised his rifle, and the Indians began a silent, baleful advance down into the shallow basin.

Iron Claw looked down on the slaughter below. Of all the white men who drove the herd, only Smoke Jensen remained alive. He and the boy and a woman held weapons in their hands. Iron Claw's keen eyes caught movement in the bed of the rolling lodge, and he made out two small girl children. All of the others had died. Had he not made the decision to come here when sounds of the fighting reached his ears and those of his dog soldiers, even his friend Smoke Jensen would have perished. He turned to his brother, Spotted Feather.

"We have come in time for our friend, Smoke Jensen."

"Not for the others," observed Spotted Feather.

Iron Claw shrugged. "They were white men. Now we will deal with the men who try to steal the horses of my friend. Then we will think on what is to be done next."

Iron Claw raised his feather-decorated rifle as a signal, and the Cheyenne began to advance.

Only Smoke Jensen knew the Cheyenne to be friendly. That resulted in utter chaos among the outlaws. Only escape filled their minds. The herd meant nothing now. Half a dozen took off to the north, to meet a wall of bullets and arrows. Recovered from his initial shock, Reno Jim Yurian shouted to the remaining outlaws.

"Band together, boys, we'll shoot our way out." He pointed the nose of his horse to the west and waited while the gang assembled behind him. When they had, with Utah Jack at his side, Reno Jim opened fire on the Cheyenne and spurred his horse.

Twenty-three hard cases began that fateful charge. Three got knocked from their saddles before they had covered fifty feet. The gang reached full gallop halfway across the slowly contracting ring of Indians. Abruptly, Reno Jim and Utah Jack reined in and let the others rush past them. As a result, the surviving outlaws took the brunt of the Cheyenne response.

Firing blindly at the Indians, the desperate hard cases crashed into the approaching ranks on a broad front. Rifles and revolvers fired an irregular volley that opened a narrow path through the Cheyenne ponies. Fighting at point-blank range now, the Yurian gang surged into the opening. More of the Indians moved to close the gap.

Before they could, Reno Jim spoke sharply to Utah Jack. "Now!"

They bolted forward and bulled their way through the rest of the gang, who struggled hand-to-hand now with the Cheyenne. Slowed to a walk, Reno Jim and Utah Jack shot two ponies out from under the last Indians blocking their escape. When the riders fell, the two white men spurred their mounts and broke into the open. They wasted no time. Turned to the south, Reno Jim Yurian leaned low over the neck of his horse and kept up a steady pricking with his big Mexican star rowels.

Back inside the contracting ring of warriors, Iron Claw started to call out for pursuit. Smoke Jensen stopped him with a raised hand. "No. Those two are mine."

Iron Claw nodded his understanding. "Go with good medicine, Smoke Jensen."

"I reckon I'll be needing some of that."

So saying, Smoke swung into Cougar's saddle and started south, after the outlaw leader and the traitor. The exertion of keeping in the saddle at a full gallop made his head spin again, and black spots rose before his eyes. Smoke had hastily tied a bandanna around his scalp graze, which had stopped the bleeding. For that he was thankful. Now all he had to do was catch up to his quarry.

Smoke ran Cougar about a mile, then slowed to a fast trot. It would be too easy to wind his mount and end up afoot. Considering the behavior of the fugitives, they might not take that factor into account, Smoke speculated. Ahead he could see the rising dust of their passage. With any luck, their horses would wear down soon and he could catch up. Only gradually did the realization of the effect of the attack register on him.

Too many good men had died back there. Jerry Harkness, Harper Liddy, Ahab Trask, Granger Bolt, Caleb Noonan and all those who had offered their help. The two he chased had a hell of a lot to account for. And Smoke reckoned to be the one to make them pay.

For a moment he felt an ache deep inside. It would grow, he knew, into an overwhelming sense of defeat . . . if he let it. No way he would do that, Smoke promised himself. He would track this pair to China and back if necessary. He looked forward to watching them hang.

19

Inexorably, Smoke Jensen traced the fleeing men across the high plains. Slowly he closed the gap. When he finally caught a first sight of them, Grubbs and Yurian walked their horses out of necessity. Even at that far distance, Smoke could see the flanks of the animals heave. White lather lay in rolls along their necks and around saddle blankets.

Fools, Smoke thought. They had gotten their horses completely blown. All the better for him. He gave Cougar a light tap of his round knob, cavalry-style spurs and picked up the pace. In no time, he closed the space between them to less than a quarter mile.

Then, abruptly and unexpectedly, the numbing pain returned to throb and gouge through Smoke's head. He swayed drunkenly in the saddle, his vision blurred and the world spun around him. A sudden spasm of nausea twisted his gut.

Groaning, Smoke bent over and vomited up a thin, green bile. His hand trembled as he reached for his canteen to rinse his mouth. Another shaft of blinding agony pierced his head. Smoke felt his balance gradually slip away. Darkness washed over him as he pitched out of the saddle.

* * *

Up ahead, Reno Jim Yurian and Utah Jack Grubbs watched in silence while Smoke Jensen fell to the ground. Grubbs pointed to the prone figure.

"I'll go back and finish him off, boss."

"Yes. I suppose that's the best way. I wouldn't get any satisfaction out of killing a helpless man."

"Nor will I. How the hell did those Injuns get mixed up in this?"

Reno Jim considered that a moment. "Probably had their eyes on the herd."

Utah Jack frowned. "From what I saw at the end, they didn't harm a hair on Smoke Jensen. In fact, their chief rode right up to him, and they talked real friendly like."

A grunt burst from Reno Jim. "I saw that. The damned savages must be friends of his."

A grim smile formed on the face of Utah Jack. "That'll make doin' for him easier."

"I'll meet you in Sheridan."

Utah Jack nodded in reply and set off on foot, at a walk, back toward Smoke Jensen. Reno Jim continued on south, leading his winded mount by the reins. They had lost the horses, he thought bitterly. Worse, his men had been slaughtered by the damned Cheyenne. Only six men were left back in Bent Rock Canyon with the cattle. He spoke aloud his frustration.

"How can I recover what I've lost? What kind of leader lets his men get trapped like I did?"

Only the low moan of a soft southwest breeze answered him.

A crunch of gravel under a boot heel brought awareness back to Smoke Jensen. He lay still, slowly opened his eyes and fought to focus. Above him, Cougar snorted a challenge. Another horse skittered its hooves and answered shrilly.

"Woah there! Easy, easy," a familiar voice soothed.

Smoke took the opportunity to raise his head and verify his suspicion. Though his head throbbed monstrously, he focused on the boots and rawhide chap-covered legs of Utah Jack Grubbs. Smoke looked higher. Grubbs was turned away from him, some twenty feet away, arms up to calm his nervous mount.

"Down boy. Down."

His attention completely off the man he came to kill, Utah Jack sawed at the reins. His sorrel gelding had been frightened by the 'Palouse stallion, and he had all he could do to regain control. As a result, he failed to see Smoke Jensen thrust himself to a sitting position.

Another wave of dizziness swamped him, and he had to sit a moment until it passed. Then Smoke reached out and gripped the right stirrup. Slowly, he dragged himself upright. Another black pool of dizziness engulfed him. He drew a deep breath through an open mouth to prevent it being heard. His vision cleared almost at once. He glanced down and silently swore.

Both of his Colts had fallen from the holsters and lay on the ground ten feet from him. He had run out of ammunition for his Winchester and left it behind. Then his left hand brushed the haft of the tomahawk he habitually carried on his saddle. Slowly he eased it out of the thong that retained it. In the next second Utah Jack settled his irritable horse. He turned again to face Smoke Jensen.

"So, you old bastard, you're on your feet." He cut his eyes to Smoke's revolvers. "Too bad you lost your irons. Without them, you're nothin'," Utah Jack scoffed, his mouth twisted in an ugly sneer.

He took a menacing step closer. "In fact, this is going to be so easy I think I'll do it with my bare hands."

Feeling not the least himself, Smoke answered in a low growl. "When pigs fly and cows sing."

"You've got a smart mouth, Jensen. If it wasn't for the prospect of gettin' that herd of yours, I woulda driven you into the ground like a fence post the first day on that stinkin' ranch of yours."

Time. Smoke needed every bit of it he could buy to get back even a little of his strength. To do so, he decided to bait Grubbs. "How are you going to do that, you mouthy little pile of horse crap? You gonna beat me to death with your tongue?"

"You'll find out in about a second. First, I'm gonna have my say. You're pathetic, Jensen. All that lovey-dovey stuff with that wife of yours. Askin' her opinion of ever' little thing. It made me sick. Any real man knows a woman ain't got no brains. You have to yell at 'em all the time and beat her at least once a month to keep her in line. And another thing. You never lay a hand on that towheaded brat. Ain't a kid that grows up right lest he gits whipped regular every day."

Smoke used all his willpower to hold his anger in check. He put a twisted smile on his face. "You're such a prime example of that."

"Damn right I am. My paw beat my butt raw at least once a week, took a belt to me ever' day. What really galls me is that you don't know anything about handling livestock. Horses has got to be whip-broke to properly tame them. Any fool knows that."

Taunting again, Smoke laughed at Grubbs. "Yeah, *any fool*. Are you through running that open sewer of yours?"

"Damn right," Grubbs barked. He started for Smoke again. To his surprise, Smoke beckoned invitingly.

"Come on, Grubbs, get right up close. I'm going to enjoy tearing you a new bung hole."

Utah Jack took two fast steps to close the distance, and he swung a slow, looping right. The moment he did, Smoke Jensen eased away from the support of Cougar and brought the tomahawk into sight. He swung it as Utah Jack's fist hurtled toward his jaw.

At the last second, Smoke jinked his head to the side as the keen edge of the blade sank into the arm of his opponent an inch above the elbow. It ground against the bone, dislodged a chip and then came free. Hot agony burned through Utah Jack, and he howled in anguish. Then numbness began to spread along his injured limb.

Grubbs backed off a few paces and fumbled the bandanna from around his neck. Clumsily he used it to bind his wound. Smoke Jensen came on. His arm useless, Utah Jack could not draw his six-gun. Smoke closed with him; blood dripped from the edge of his tomahawk.

"You're fast for an old fart."

"Not so old by half, you traitorous dog."

Smoke felt new strength surge through his body. It lifted him. He reached Grubbs and pounded him in the chest with a hard right. Utah Jack backpedaled. Smoke came on. The menace of the tomahawk remained, cocked and ready. Smoke's right lashed out again.

Blood sprayed across the outlaw's face as hard knuckles crushed his nose. His eyes crossed, and he momentarily lost sight in the left one. Mopping at it with his left hand, he tried to block the next blow. His effort failed, and his lower lip split in a searing flash of pain. Smoke pressed his attack.

Utah Jack tried to dodge to his right and felt the fiery bite of the 'hawk against his ribs. Then the darting right fist of Smoke Jensen drove sharply into the solar plexus of Utah Jack. Air gushed from his bloody lips, and for a while Jack Grubbs saw black.

Doubled over, Utah Jack's vision cleared, and he grasped feebly at the hilt of a knife in the top of his boot. Groaning, he came upright as far as he could and drove the blade with lightning speed toward the exposed loin of Smoke Jensen. Cold steel skidded across Smoke's cartridge belt and punched into his side.

Gasping, he fell away from his attacker. He landed on the ground and rolled toward his six-guns. Utah Jack advanced on him. Smoke's hand closed over the butt-grip of one .45 Colt, and he whipped it upward. Close to blacking out, he cocked the hammer and tickled the trigger.

"Noooooo!" Utah Jack wailed as he realized what Smoke had accomplished.

Smoke's bullet smashed into the chest of Utah Jack Grubbs. It drove rib bone ahead of it into his heart. The powerful organ spasmed, then began to rapidly pump in an erratic rhythm. Eyes bulged, Utah Jack looked down to witness his demise.

Grubbs fell dead as weakness washed over Smoke Jensen. He had to get the stab wound cared for. From the feel of it, the blade had missed his liver. How, he didn't know, but his gratitude to his Maker was genuine. Carefully, Smoke dropped his tomahawk and tugged his shirt from behind his belt.

New pain radiated through his torso as he pulled it higher. Another whirl of dizziness staggered him. He looked down, expecting to see the worst. He saw instead a small, two-inch incision. A thin ribbon of blood trickled over the bluish lips. Gently, he probed the pale flesh surrounding it. Little pain followed. Head still aching at each step, he returned to his horse.

From a saddlebag, he took some of the remaining moss that had been collected a week ago for the drawing poultice Smoke had used on Jerry Harkness. He wet it from his canteen, packed it in the wound and retrieved a length of buckskin strip from the bag. That he wound around his body and tied tightly. Then he washed the bullet gouge on his head again and rebandaged it.

Hobbling away from Cougar, he stripped the weapons from the corpse of Utah Jack. Smoke found the cartridge belt and revolver empty and five rounds in the Winchester. He gathered up his second Colt and replaced the expended cartridge in the right-hand one. He did not have the strength to throw the outlaw over his saddle, but he would not leave the horse out there to fend for itself. He led it back to where Cougar waited, mounted gingerly and put the 'Palouse in motion. With one rein around the pommel of Smoke's saddle, the sorrel trotted along peacefully beside Cougar.

Despite his recent head wound and the new cut in his side, Smoke began to feel stronger with each passing mile. He picked up the trail of Reno Jim Yurian readily and followed along at a fast trot. He had little doubt that Yurian intended to pass through Sheridan. Smoke wanted to catch him before then. Any hotel room or saloon front could become an excellent ambush spot. In a thoughtful mood, Smoke reached under the skirt of his saddle and extracted a softened piece of bison jerky.

He had obtained the dried meat from Iron Claw before setting out after the fleeing outlaws. "It will be good for your head," Iron Claw told him, pointing to the bandaged gouge with his chin.

"I doubt I'll need six strips."

Iron Claw insisted. "Eat them all. Then we get some hump meat. It will make you strong."

Smoke accepted this. He often recalled the story of the Kiowa war chief, Two Moons, who as a young man was reported to have taken thirty-six rifle and revolver wounds in one fierce battle with the cavalry from Fort Sill. At least two of them had struck him in the groin. The Kiowa subsisted almost entirely on bison. Not only did Two Moons heal up, but he sired seven children, and died at the age of eighty-three. That was enough to convince Smoke Jensen. There would be bison at the Crow Agency. He would get his hump meat.

Smoke bit at his lower lip to snap his focus back on what he had started out to do. His keen eyes fixed on the spot where Yurian had remounted. The depth of the hoof prints increased, and the space between them elongated. This time the rider kept to a trot. Despite the throbbing in his head, Smoke gigged Cougar into a canter. A mile farther, the tracks veered from the trail. Smoke looked back. He could not see the place where he had fought with Utah Jack. Reining Cougar to the left, he followed Reno Jim's sign.

Muted and made flat by distance, Reno Jim Yurian had heard the single shot. He knew it had to have been fired by Smoke Jensen. Utah Jack Grubbs would have pumped at least three slugs, as insurance, into so famous a gunfighter as Smoke Jensen. Accordingly, he left the trail to Sheridan and broke a new path cross-country. He knew that Jensen would be coming after him.

Deliberately he did not make any effort to cover his tracks. He had a definite plan. Reno Jim fixed his eyes on a distant line of trees that denoted a streambed. There he would find what he wanted.

When Reno Jim located it, he smiled a mean, thin-lipped smile. Perfect for what he had in mind. A deep, wide, twisting ravine ran perpendicular to the creek. Cut into the prairie by ages of runoff, it had grown to a depth he gauged to be fifteen or more feet. Quickly he backtracked to where he could negotiate the sloping side. Then he dismounted and led his horse down into the gully. He found the winding course to be ideal. It offered several places for a man to hide in wait.

Reno Jim picked his ambush site carefully. A limestone outcropping created a wide, gentle bend, and beyond it, a granite shelf forced a sharp turn in the dry waterway. The outlaw leader took his mount well beyond this and screwed a ground anchor into the sidewall. He tied the reins to this, pulled free his Winchester and returned to the angled curve. Then he settled in to wait.

Trees ahead, Smoke Jensen noted as he dogged the tracks left by Reno Jim Yurian. It would be the creek where they had camped two nights before. The place where the Cheyenne had tried to take the herd would likely be a couple of miles south. The irony was not missed by Smoke. Abruptly he made note of an overlay of tracks, one set returning across those that led to the distant creek.

A small alarm began to tingle in the back of his mind. If Reno Jim wanted to backtrack himself, he surely knew enough not to do it on his fresh trail. Not unless he wanted it noticed, Smoke's experience told him. Now, why would that be? He looked around, farther from the sign he followed. There, the return tracks cut away at a right angle from the trail he followed.

Then Smoke saw the broken ground at the lip of the ravine, where Reno Jim had descended. So that's it, Smoke thought grimly. He wants to lead me into an ambush. Might as well oblige the wily jackal. Smoke dismounted and tied Utah Jack's horse to a hawthorn bush. With that accomplished, he returned to Cougar and headed the animal down into the fissure.

Immediately, Smoke took in the nature of his new surroundings. Fine sand and small pebbles formed the bed of the cleft, its course a series of turns and bends. It had been carved out over what must have been centuries as water ran toward the creek. He judged himself to be close to eighteen feet below the level of the prairie. Reno Jim had left clear impressions of his boots as well as the hooves of his mount. Had the man wanted to hide his whereabouts, he would have come back and wiped out those telltale signs.

For all the harm done him today, Smoke could still smell an ambush in the making without effort. He chose to remain mounted, walking Cougar along slowly. He kept alert, his eyes moving constantly to detect any change in surroundings, or the glint of sunlight off a gun barrel. Man and horse rounded one twist in the defile and progressed along a relatively long straightaway. Another bend, wider than the previous one, waited beyond. For all his caution, it was not Smoke, but Cougar, who gave the first alarm.

A sudden shift in the wind brought the scent of Reno Jim's roan to the nostrils of the spotted-rump stallion. Undirected, he halted abruptly near the center of the curve, jerked up his head and snorted a challenge. A fraction of a second later, Smoke Jensen saw a puff of powder smoke beyond the second part of the double bend. Immediately he felt the sting of shards on his face from limestone blasted loose by a bullet impact, six inches from his head.

The slug had struck the rock at the exact point where Smoke's head would have been, had his horse not pulled up so short. At once, Smoke jumped the 'Palouse stallion to the left, behind the shelter of the rounded wall of the gorge. Quickly, Smoke dismounted and slid his rifle from its scabbard. He cycled the lever action and chambered a round. Then he eased the barrel out in the open.

He sighted at the spot from where the smoke had come and triggered two fast shots. They sang an evil duet as they ricocheted off the solid granite. Yurian fired again, this time hastily. A clump of dirt from above fell on the brim of Smoke's hat.

Then he answered the outlaw leader. One slug moaned off the slab and the other passed beyond. Reno Jim Yurian's shout sounded a bit strained. "I'm gonna get you, Jensen, you rotten bastard."

20

"Plenty have tried," Smoke answered flatly.

Yurian changed subjects. "What did you do to Utah Jack?"

"I shot him. Left the carcass for the coyotes."

Reno Jim swore viciously, then concluded with, "I suppose I shouldn't be surprised."

"You're wrong, Reno. Like you were wrong about taking my herd. If he hadn't stabbed me in the side, I could have put him on his horse and brought him along."

A long silence followed that revelation. Smoke Jensen strained to hear any sound of movement. After the early exchange, he knew he had only two rounds left for the .44 Winchester, and a cylinder load in each of his .45 Colts. He reckoned Reno Jim to be no better off. He looked sharply down the crevasse at the click of one stone against another.

Funny, it had come from farther down the watercourse. Smoke took another quick shot, then risked a dash to the sharper bend. He reached it without drawing fire. So far, so good. One round left in the Winchester. He grasped it by the receiver and let it hang from his left arm. Six-gun drawn, Smoke rounded the acute angle and found the ambusher's vantage point vacant. It would have to be the hard way. Making the best time he could, Smoke sprinted back to Cougar and put away his rifle. Then he led the animal back toward where Reno Jim had disappeared.

Standing beside his horse, Reno Jim Yurian stared with disbelief at the empty saddlebag. That left him with only the ammunition in his Smith Americans. A dozen rounds. He turned at the sound of a hoof striking a rock and drew with smooth speed. Before he could stop himself, the hammer fell, and he wasted one of those precious cartridges.

His bullet struck nothing. From beyond the turn he heard a soft, mocking laugh. Reno Jim moved away from his mount and fired again when he had a clear view. That slug struck the rock ledge above Smoke Jensen's head. Deformed by the impact, it moaned off harmlessly. A fraction of a second later, a .45 round cracked past Reno Jim's head, so close he could feel the heat. He dived for the ground. Slowly, the realization came to him that he had two choices. He could stay here and trade shots until they both ran dry. Or he could head for the creek and attempt to escape pursuit. The latter course sounded best.

Except that the only way to ensure success would be to make certain Smoke Jensen lay dead in this gully. He would have to out-wait Jensen. Time slowed down. It appeared to Reno Jim that hours dragged past before he sensed movement. At once, he fired in that direction. The derisive laughter came again. That broke his nerve.

"Goddamn you, Smoke Jensen. Show yourself and fight like a man."

Two shots crashed from beyond the curvature of the wall. One bullet kicked up shards of rock from the boulder Reno Jim crouched behind. The other burned a hot gouge across his right shoulder blade. A taunting voice followed.

"Show yourself, Reno, and fight like a man."

All reason abandoned, Reno Jim emptied his right-hand revolver in an attempt to banish his broken spirit. Quickly he changed over to the one on his left. A return to silence ridiculed his outburst.

For a long, sweaty hour, Smoke continued to toy with Reno Jim. He changed positions and used his ammunition sparingly. To keep the pressure on, he had to expend part of his dwindling supply. His strength increased steadily while he watched his enemy unravel. Suddenly Yurian appeared in the open, his face slack, eyes wild.

"I'm coming after you, Jensen. I'm going to leave your brains on this sand."

In a rush, Reno Jim charged, firing as he came. Smoke returned shots. Reno Jim jinked from side to side. One of Smoke's rounds clipped the heel from one of Reno Jim's boots. He sprawled in the sand and scrambled to get behind a boulder. With his body out of danger, he thought furiously for a means to gain an advantage. Slowly it came to him. He weighed it. Yes, it would work.

"Jensen? Can we talk?"

"I'm listening."

"Can we work this out? I can tell you where the cattle the gang rustled are located. I can tell you something else, too. Real important."

"What's that?"

"I have a partner. A very influential man, a regular pillar of the community."

Smoke Jensen kept his voice neutral. "What do you expect in return for this?"

Reno Jim Yurian's voice broke with the intensity of his emotion. "I—I want to live. I don't want to be shot down in this miserable wilderness. And I don't want to hang. I want to work a deal. Maybe a few years in prison in exchange for my information?"

Smoke thought it over a second. "I'll promise you this for now. You be straight with me and I'll not kill you."

"Remember this, I want to come out of this alive."

"Tell me what you have and we'll see."

"That's all I get?"

Smoke spoke drily. "For now. Give."

"All right—all right. The cattle are in Bent Rock Canyon, down near Muddy Creek. There are six men watching them."

"And this partner of yours?"

Reno Jim choked back his anxiety. "I'll really get to live?"

"I gave my word. I'll not kill you."

"All right—all right. You won't believe this, but it's true. He's —he's Boyne Kelso. The cattle broker in Muddy Gap. A deacon in his church, of all things."

Smoke blinked. He considered Kelso a windbag, over-willing to depreciate the criminal inclinations of his delinquent son, and prone to make too big a show of his rectitude. Yet a partner to Reno Jim Yurian?

"Tell me that again."

"My partner is Boyne Kelso. He has been for the past six years."

Smoke mulled it over in silence. "All right. Throw out all your weapons. Do it now."

Two nickle-plated Smith and Wesson Americans thud-ded out on the sand. A .41 rim-fire derringer followed. Then a knife. Slowly, Reno Jim Yurian rose from his shelter.

"Step out in the open."

When he did, Smoke Jensen came from his own cover and walked up to the gang leader. A fleeting smile flickered on his face as he held his Colt casually. All of a sudden, he balled his left fist and slammed a powerful knockout blow to the jaw. He looked down at the senseless man and spoke aloud.

"I didn't say anything about not hitting you."

Tommy Olsen and Iron Claw followed the tracks left by Smoke Jensen. The war chief studied the horizon after three hours at a moderate trot. He nodded and pointed with his chin.

"Up ahead. It is our friend, Smoke Jensen."

Tommy gaped at him. "Gosh, you can see that far?"

Iron Claw nodded. "I used to be able to see farther." He tapped his cheek, near his left eye. "The eyes get weaker with age." He laughed.

"We gotta hurry," Tommy urged.

Sage advice came from Iron Claw. "We will get there faster if we do not run the horses."

Tommy looked blank. "Oh. Yeah. Smoke said something like that, too."

"He learned well from White Wolf."

"Who?"

"The man your people call Preacher."

Less than a hundred yards separated them now, and yet Smoke came on at the same pace. "He is leading two horses," observed Iron Claw.

"I can see that. One has a tied-up man on it; the other has one across the saddle."

"That one is dead, I think," Iron Claw told Tommy.

Smoke hailed them and finally increased his gait. When he rode up, he explained the burdens tied and slung over the saddles. "I've got Reno Jim Yurian. Jack Grubbs is dead. And I have unfinished business in Muddy Gap."

"What kinda business?" Tommy queried.

Smoke canted his head. "I think we might get back your cattle, Tommy. Among other things. First, though, we have to get those horses to Fort Custer."

"Before that you have to have those wounds treated," Iron Claw injected as he looked at the bloody cloth at Smoke's side. "And we have a feast."

Tommy Olsen enjoyed the feast every bit as much as their Cheyenne hosts. Smoke Jensen appeared impatient throughout the affair. Upon the return of Smoke and the others, six of the warriors became hunters. They rode off from the herd, in search of bison, while Smoke supervised the burial of the dead. A surprise had awaited Smoke in the form of Luke and five volunteers, all deputized by the sheriff in Sheridan.

"I thought you would be strapped down in a hospital bed," Smoke told Luke.

Luke shook his head in rejection of the idea. "Ain't a doctor born who can put me down a minute longer than I want to be. 'Specially when my friends are in trouble." He pulled a long, sad face. "Smoke, I'm right sorry not to have gotten here sooner. We coulda swung the balance."

"I'm not so sure, Luke. There were near to forty outlaws, before the Cheyenne got here and took a hand. By then it was too late for most of us. The Olsens and I survived only because of Iron Claw."

"Well, then, I'll not belabor the point. But I still feel bad about it. What really hurts is losing Jerry. He was a friend."

Nodding agreement, Smoke added, "And a fine horse handler. We'll all miss him."

Smoke Jensen turned away from the last grave when the Cheyenne hunting party returned with a fair-sized bison calf. There came a moment of tension when they made it clear they expected Della Olsen, as the only woman in camp, to dress out the animal and prepare it for cooking. Smoke stepped into the breech.

He spoke in the musical language of the Cheyenne. "She is a white woman; she knows nothing of how to properly clean a carcass. It will take her forever. If you want to eat of it before it spoils, have two of your apprentice warriors skin and cut it up."

They thought that over awhile and decided it might be a good idea. Boys too young to join on the hunt often worked with their mothers at the preparation of the meat, which taught them the techniques needed. Spotted Feather selected two lads about thirteen years of age and assigned them to the task. They looked unhappy about it, but did a satisfactory job.

Meanwhile, other warriors built a fairly large fire for such open country and added wood to it periodically to produce a deep bed of coals. When only a few tiny blue flames flickered over the glowing orange mass, the hump and ribs went onto grilling racks, taken from the gang's improvised chuck wagon. In no time, fat from the hump began to drip and flare up on the embers. That released a delicious aroma that filled the camp. One warrior produced a small drum and began to compose a song of the battle.

"Dog soldiers came. See us! See us! Dog soldiers came. The dark ones came. See them! See them! The dark ones came. My friends of dog soldiers die in big fight. See it! See it!" The song continued as Della Olsen came to Smoke Jensen.

"Smoke, what did you tell them to get them to stop insisting I deal with that small beast?"

Smoke's eyes twinkled when he answered, neatly circumventing the exact truth. "I suggested that white people did not know the medicine of the bison and it might spoil the meat if you were to touch it in an uncooked condition."

"And they believed that?" Smoke nodded, and she went on. "That's outrageous, though close to the truth. I could have easily pierced the entrails and contaminated the meat. Sven always did the butchering for our family."

Smoke looked relieved. "Then nothing was harmed."

Della opened a new topic. "Tommy tells me you are going to Muddy Gap. When do you plan to leave?"

"After the herd is delivered."

Della looked anxious. "Would you . . . I know it is a lot to ask, but . . . would you allow us to accompany you?"

Smoke's expression did not hold encouragement. "I will be traveling fast. I'll be taking Luke and the men he brought with me. They have something else to tend to. I don't see any way you can keep up."

Disappointment clouded Della's eyes. "We know no one north of here, nor in Sheridan for that matter. Could you at least let us come with you as far as Buffalo? I have a shirt-tail relative there."

For a moment, Smoke considered this. "We'll see how fast the herd moves."

After she departed, Iron Claw came next. "You are going to need help moving all those ponies, old friend. Some of my younger warriors, and of course the boys, are excellent herdsmen. They will go with you."

Smoke visualized what that would be like: a herd of remounts, driven to an army post on a Crow reservation, by seven white men, and probably four times that number of Cheyennes. It beggared description. At last he clapped Iron Claw on the shoulder.

"Sally will never believe this, Iron Claw."

Only an isolated summer thunderstorm delayed the forty-mile journey to Fort Custer. And then by only half a day. The Olsens kept up and did not complain. Colonel Abernathy, newly appointed to command at the post, accepted the herd after only cursory inspection. His face registered cordiality, though his eyes betrayed his apprehension at the presence of so many technically hostile Cheyenne at the fort.

"You've made good time, although we did expect you some three days ago. Your explanation of the reason is quite satisfactory, and please accept my condolences over the loss of your men." He brightened, returning to the subject at hand. "The remounts are in excellent shape. Here is a draft on the government, Department of the Army, for the agreed amount, Mr. Jensen. You may present it for payment at any major bank that has accounts with the government."

"In Denver?" Smoke asked.

"Yes, certainly. The First Mining and Milling handles our payroll as a matter of fact."

"Fine then. I wish you good luck, Colonel. Those men who came out here with you look mighty green."

"They are. Never fear, my sergeant major will whip them in line in no time. Now, may I offer you the hospitality of the post for the night?"

"No, thank you. We have urgent matters south of here. Every hour is important."

Abernathy looked relieved. That meant the Cheyenne would be leaving soon. "I can appreciate that. The man you have as a prisoner. He looks dangerous."

Smoke answered levelly. "Believe me, he is. He and his gang nearly took your remounts from us."

That set Colonel Abernathy back a bit. "My word."

Smoke's cool, golden gaze fixed the colonel. "Yes. And now, if I have anything to say about it, he has a date with the hangman."

Along about ten miles outside of Buffalo, Smoke Jensen learned that the shirttail relative of Della Olsen was a stern, uncompromising brother-in-law. "He has never really accepted me. Bjorn believed that Sven married below his station. What did it matter that we loved one another? *He* was the older brother and expected Sven to do as bid."

Smoke looked her straight in the eyes. "Then the chances of a warm welcome are . . . ?"

"None. But I have nowhere else to go. And the children are his brother's."

"I've known my share of proud, stubborn men. My bet would be that it won't count for much with this Bjorn."

"So, then what?" Della had reached the limit of her hope.

Smoke hesitated only a moment. "How does Muddy Gap sound to you? There are people there beholden to me. I can put in a good word better there than in Buffalo."

Joyful optimism lighted Della's face. "Oh, Smoke. I—I don't know what to say. We—I've been such a burden. I would never be able to thank you enough."

"You already have. Your cooking has kept my hands' spirits high; Tommy has become a good friend. It will be my pleasure to extract some gratitude out of the good folks of Muddy Gap."

Della smiled radiantly. "Well. Now I can hardly wait to get there.

Smoke cut his eyes to the bound figure of Reno Jim Yurian. "Nor can I. I want to get this lizard behind bars and scoop up his partner in crime. Then we'll go recover your cattle. The sale of them will give you a nice little stake, I'm sure."

On the main street of Muddy Gap, which much to Smoke's surprise had been renamed *Jensen Avenue*, as proclaimed by newly painted and displayed signs, the small band of travelers split up. At Smoke's suggestion, the hands went to the Sorry Place saloon. The free lunch would provide them with food they had not tasted in a while. Della Olsen and her children went to the hotel to take rooms for the interim. Smoke, accompanied by the bound Reno Jim, headed to the jail.

There, he dismounted and dragged Reno Jim Yurian from the back of the outlaw's horse. Smoke frog-marched him up the steps and into the sheriff's office. Marshal Grover Larsen looked up with surprise and pleasure on his face.

Smoke spoke directly to the point. "Marshal, this is the man who murdered a rancher named Olsen and rustled his cattle, he also took a number of other beefs. And he's the one who stole my herd for a while. There are six men, all that are left of his gang, out at Bent Rock Canyon. My men and I are going after them when I've rounded up his partner."

Larsen blinked at the finery worn by the prisoner. "Why, that's Reno Jim Yurian. He's a former gambler who has turned to ranching. Quite prosperous, too. He does a lot of business with Deacon Kelso."

"I'll bet he does," Smoke said drily. Then he shoved Yurian into a chair. "Now, he has a story to tell you, Marshal."

When Reno Jim Yurian concluded his tale of robbery, rustling and murder—prompted by the efforts of Smoke Jensen—Marshal Larsen sat staring at the man as though witnessing for the first time the presence on earth of one of the imps of Satan. A sweating Jim Yurian cut his eyes from Grover Larsen to Smoke Jensen.

He lowered his gaze when he asked plaintively, "I've done what you've asked, and said what you wanted me to say. Now am I free to go?"

Marshal Grover Larsen screwed his full lips into an expression of pure disgust. "Nope. For starters, what you did to this town is enough to get you an appointment with the gallows. Then there's Sven Olsen. Oh, I knew him all right. A fine man. Horse thievin' and cattle rustling are hanging offenses, so's murder of express agents and shotgun guards. No, Reno, it looks like you'll swing, for certain sure."

Reno Jim Yurian turned to Smoke Jensen to plead his case. "But you promised."

Smoke looked at him, mischief alight in his eyes. "Yes, I did," he allowed. "That only applies to what you did to me and my men. I don't speak for Muddy Gap, or for the territorial attorney."

Reno Jim tried to come to his boots, hampered by his bonds. "You can't get away with this! It isn't fair! I'll beat this easy. I've got money, power, influence."

Smoke Jensen shook his head in refutation. "Right now it looks like all you have is a trap-door in your future. Now, Marshal, let's go get his partner."

"And who's that? He didn't say."

Smoke produced a grim smile. "It's Boyne Kelso."

"I'll be damned. I'm with you, Smoke," Marshal Larsen added, as he reached for his shotgun.

21

A highly agitated Slick Killmer, one of the six men Reno Jim Yurian had left to tend the cattle in Bent Rock Canyon, stood with hat in hand before the desk of Boyne Kelso. Oily beads of sweat had popped out on his forehead. He cut his eyes rapidly from corner to corner of the room and started violently when a noise came from out in the hall.

"That's right, Mr Kelso, I saw 'em with my own eyes. I was in for supplies, and a little Red Eye for the boys, when they come ridin' into town. Smoke Jensen, big as life, an' he had the boss as a prisoner. They went direct' to the marshal's office."

Boyne Kelso's eyes narrowed. "You could not have made a mistake?"

"No, sir. I told you jist what I saw. If I'd had more fellers to back me, I'd 'uv braced them right then."

"You keep saying 'them,' Killmer. Why is that?"

"Jensen had some rough-looking drovers along with him. Though they carried themselves like gunfighters."

A sudden chill filled Kelso. "How many?"

"Six, all together. An' there was a family along. A woman and three young 'uns. A boy half-growed an' two little girls."

Kelso sought to form a plan. With Jensen in town, and

Reno captured, he had a good idea what would come next. "Where did the family go?"

"I dunno. I reckon to the general mercantile. They had a wagon with them. Funny thing, it looked jist like the one the boys took with them when they went after them horses."

Boyne Kelso stifled a groan. That meant the gang had been wiped out, or at best scattered. Which could only mean Jensen's horses had not been rustled.

"Think, man. Where is that woman, and those kids?"

"Well—ah—they coulda—coulda gone to the hotel."

Kelso thought quickly. "Go to the Trailside. You know Butch and Docking and Unger? Tell them I want them to come here. There's work for them to do."

Slick Killmer gave him a fish eye. "What makes you think they'll drop everything an' come do your bidding?"

"You idiot, I *own* the Trailside. They work for me."

Not the brightest of all outlaws to have taken the owlhoot trail, Slick scratched at his noggin. "You do? Why, you're a deacon in the church. Ain't you Christian folk again' likker an' wimmin?"

Kelso brushed at the front of his coat. "There's some in our flock that take such things seriously, yes. I don't happen to be one of them. Now, do as I say. We have to find a way to get Reno out of that jail and finish Smoke Jensen."

Smoke Jensen and the marshal went directly to the office of Boyne Kelso. On the way up the outside stairs on the bank building, Smoke gave terse instructions.

"Cover me from the upper landing. I'll go in after Kelso alone."

Grover Larsen added a bit of caution. "He may have help in there."

A fleeting grin flashed on Jensen's face. "From what you tell me of that office, there can't be more men in there than I can handle."

Frowning, the lawman nodded. "It is small."

At the top, Marshal Larsen took a position that let him see in through the glass pane in the door and cover the alley as well. Smoke put his hand on the knob, turned it and went through into the hall. He unlimbered his .45 Colt as he stepped over the threshold. No resistance met him.

Five long strides brought him to the frosted glass panel in the door to Kelso's office. Here he stood to the side, reached over and freed the latch. When the portal swung inward, three rapid shots answered the movement. One struck the glass and shattered it; the other two smacked into the wall across the corridor.

Smoke Jensen bent low and entered in a rush, his Peacemaker leading the way. He saw the bulk of a man hunched behind the desk and the muzzle flash. A bullet cracked over his head. Then his Colt spoke.

His first round hit the man square in the chest. Driven backward by the powerful thrust, Art Unger crashed both elbows through the window panes before arresting his movement. He tried to cock his six-gun.

Another .45 slug drove into his belly, a fist's width above his navel. It doubled him over, and he pitched onto his face. The Colt Frontier in his hand slid across the floor. Smoke crossed to him. Large exit wounds made ugly blossoms on the man's back. Smoke rolled him over.

"Who are you and what are you doing in Kelso's office?"

"Art . . . Unger. The boss put me here to . . . stop you."

"Don't look like you did it."

Unger gasped, his death rattle already clear in his throat. "N-no. But it's too late for you anyway. Mr. Kelso an' a couple of the boys has got that woman friend of yours, and her brats. He—he's aimin' to make a trade."

"What's that?"

"Them for him an' Reno Jim goin' free."

Smoke bit off his words harshly. "That'll never happen."

Wincing at the pain, Unger screwed his face into an expression of defiance. "Th-then they're dead meat. An' so are you if you go after them."

Cold fury froze the face of Smoke Jensen. "Where are they? Where did Kelso take them?"

"That—that's for you to find out." With that, Unger went rigid, shuddered violently and died.

When Della Olsen answered the knock and found two men standing outside the door to her room, she did not know what to think. One of them touched the brim of his hat politely, then removed it.

"Mizus Olsen?"

"Yes, I am she."

"Smoke Jensen wants to see you and your young 'uns right away. We're to bring you to him."

"Why, whatever? Don't tell me he's found us a place to stay already?"

"I don't know, ma'am. Only that he said to come at once. We'll show you the way."

Della cast a glance over her shoulder. "Come on, children. We have to meet Smoke."

When they turned into a saloon, Della had immediate misgivings. By then it was too late. The two men fell back and blocked the doorway. Ahead of her at the bar stood a man she had not seen before. He wore the clothing of a prosperous businessman, and a satisfied smile that could almost be called a smirk. He nodded to her and waved a hand to encompass the room.

"Welcome to the Trailside, dear Mrs. Olsen."

"What? Where is Smoke Jensen?"

"No doubt searching my office for me about now."

"You're—you're Boyne Kelso?"

Kelso sighed. "Ah, it's a true pity that our Mr. Jensen has chosen to confide so much in you. I was afraid that might be the case. Whatever, you are to be my ace in the hole. You and the three jokers."

Anger suddenly drove away fear, and Della stamped her

foot. "I'll thank you to explain yourself in a manner that makes sense."

Kelso smiled and nodded jovially. "I have a friend, a business associate, who is currently languishing in the jail. Mr. Jenson put him there. I intend not to suffer the same fate. In fact, I expect to be trailing you and your offspring for his release and our continued freedom. Is that clear enough?"

Della's eyes narrowed. "Smoke Jensen will track you down no matter how far you go."

Kelso shrugged, indifferent to her threat. "Not if he is residing on that hill above town."

Eyes wide in horror, Della spoke the obvious. "You can't get away with that. The law would have you in an instant, rest assured."

A nasty sneer on his face again, Kelso advised Della. "The law in this town is an old man and a green deputy. With Smoke Jensen out of the way, they would do well to successfully swat a fly." He gestured to his henchmen. "Tie them up and put them over at that table."

"The Trailside." Smoke Jensen spoke the two words crisply as he came out onto the landing.

"Right. I heard the shots. Who is it?"

"*Was.* Someone named Art Unger."

Grover Larsen nodded. He had no doubt how that exchange had come out. Together they went down the steps to the walkway. Smoke used the descent to eject spent cartridges and slide in fresh ones.

Tersely Smoke told Larsen what he had learned from Unger. "Kelso has Della Olsen and her children. He intends to trade them for Reno and his freedom."

He and Larsen turned onto Jensen Avenue and started for the Trailside. Smoke motioned across the street.

"Over there, where you can cover the whole front."

Marshal Larsen was relearning things he had forgotten about being a lawman. He knew at once what Smoke had in mind. From across the way, he could cover the entire front of the saloon while Smoke went through the batwings. For a moment, Grover wondered why Smoke had not chosen for them to go in by two entrances at once, catch those inside in a cross fire. Then it came to him. First, the Olsens were inside, and second, Smoke had no idea exactly how many gunmen Kelso had in the barroom. He crossed the street.

Already, gawkers had begun to gather, careful to give the front of the saloon a wide berth. When the marshal reached the right position, Smoke cut to the center of the street. He strode to a position directly in front of the open door to the Trailside. He faced the liquor emporium and crossed arms over his chest. Then he called out to those within.

"Boyne Kelso! I know you're in there, and I know what you have in mind. Why don't you come out here and face me like a man?"

"You can go to hell, Smoke Jensen."

"What? Are you going to hide behind a woman's skirt, Kelso? Do you expect those children to protect you from what I'm going to do to you?"

Silence held for a while, during which more townspeople clustered in the dual crescents of curiosity seekers that extended out into the street. Then an aggravated Kelso offered a challenge to Smoke Jensen. "How'd you like it if I killed 'em one at a time and threw them out to you?"

Smoke gauged the likelihood of that. "Do you have any idea of what would happen to you after the last one got used up?" He paused a few seconds. "Have you ever seen what the Cheyenne do to someone who has deliberately harmed their women and children? Well, I'll tell you.

"They find themselves a bee tree and get some honey; then they find an ant hill, nice, big, red ants. Then they strip the ones who violated their families and stake them out over that ant hill. Next comes the honey. They smear it in every body opening. With a special lot around the eyes and the groin. Then they stand back and let the ants handle it for them. Sometimes they make jokes about the way the victims scream and writhe."

Smoke paused a long, dramatic five seconds, then threw back his head and bellowed, "THAT'S what I will do to you, you son of a bitch!"

No one spoke for a full, tense minute. Then Kelso called out, his voice colored by uncertainty. "You'd never do that, Jensen. You're too law-abiding."

"Don't try me, Kelso, because I swear by the Almighty that I'll make an exception in your case."

That did it for Boyne Kelso. His nerve broken, he pointed to Butch Jones and Ham Docking. "You two, take him. Do it now."

Ham Docking had second thoughts. "Mr. Kelso, I don't think . . ."

Driven by the power of his anxiety, Kelso snapped, "You aren't paid to think. Now get over there and kill that bastard."

Both of his henchmen started for the swinging doors. Della drew a deep breath and shouted. "Look out, Smoke, there's two of them coming at you."

"Shut up, woman," Boyne Kelso bellowed at the same instant that Smoke Jensen drew with his usual blinding speed and put a bullet precisely three inches to either side of the doorjamb.

Butch Jones shrieked in agony and went to his knees, his belly pierced by splinters and hot lead. Ham Docking howled a curse and spun away. Shards of wood protruded from his left arm. The slug had missed. Boyne Kelso blinked. It had all happened so fast. Enraged, he drew a nickle-plated .38 Smith and Wesson from a shoulder rig and took a step toward the huddled Olsens.

"I warned you, Jensen. I'm gonna start with the little girl."

"No, you won't." All at once, Smoke Jensen stood in the doorway, a .45 Colt in his rock-hard fist.

Boyne Kelso spun toward the opening as a moaning, terrified Ham Docking darted past Smoke Jensen to escape certain death and ran out the door. A shouted command came from outside. "Halt!" It was followed by the boom of a shotgun. The moaning ceased.

Smoke directed his attention to Kelso. "You have a gun. Use it."

Indecision caused Kelso's arm to sway between the Olsens and Smoke. "Nooo. I'm not going to try to take you, Jensen."

Smoke casually fired a round between his legs. "Use it, you gutless piece of dung."

Driven by mindless terror, Kelso swung back toward the Olsens and raised the Smith. "I'll kill them all, I swear it."

In a flash, Smoke Jensen shot Boyne Kelso through the side of the head. His brains sprayed on the rack of bottles on the back bar. For a moment, Kelso swayed on his boots, took half a tottering step, then fell face-first into the sawdust. Without a word, Smoke Jensen stepped over to the Olsens, freed them from their chairs, and escorted them to the door.

Outside, he took note of the crowd for the first time. Among them he spotted Ginny Parkins. Gasping, she rushed to his side and vied with Della Olsen for the privilege of first hug and kiss. In the end, Smoke got soundly bussed by each of them. Then Ginny spoke up, riveting Smoke with her words.

"I—I received your gift. And—I—I—ah—used it. I shot Brandon Kelso in the knee with it. He and his loutish companions tried to compromise me," she explained with a blush. "It has profoundly changed me. I have a different view of the use of force. Violence, I now believe, is sometimes necessary to the preservation of order and for self-protection. I've grown up some, Smoke. For that, I am grateful to you. You saved my life again, it seems."

Della Olsen took center stage then. "Smoke, we're going to stay in Muddy Gap. Somehow I think your coming to our rescue is all the recommendation we'll need."

"Well then," Smoke declared as he ruffled Tommy's hair and gave Ginny a friendly squeeze, "it looks as though I'm leaving the town in good hands."

Traveling alone, except for the burden of sorrow over the loss of so many good men, some who had been close friends, Smoke Jensen reached the Sugarloaf in only five days. His dark mood lifted when he saw Sally's raven hair bent over the kitchen sink. Before he could dismount, she sensed his presence and hurried out on the porch, wiping her hands on her apron.

"Oh, Smoke, it's so good you're back."

Smoke stepped from the saddle and produced a warm, genuine smile. "You've no idea how good it is for me. I've missed you, Sally-girl."

"It's good you're home." A bubble of laughter rose in Sally's throat. "I see you planned your arrival to be in time for noon dinner."

Smoke produced a fleeting smile. "I surely did. I've been dreaming of one of your pies since I left Muddy Cap."

Her initial joy passed as Sally noted the air of sadness about her man. Then she looked beyond him to where the returning hands should have been near the corral. "Did you ride on ahead? Where are the others?"

Smoke's delight at being home dissolved. "They— they're gone, Sally. Killed by rustlers. Let's go inside and I'll tell you about it."

Seated at the kitchen table, coffee mug in hand, Smoke related to his beloved Sally the ordeal he and his friends had undergone since they had left the Sugarloaf. When he concluded, Sally brushed a tear from the corner of one eye and cleared her throat.

"They're at peace now. Oh, Smoke, I'm so sorry." She went to him then and hugged him tightly, giving him the compassion and consolation he needed so badly, though he would never ask for it.

By then, the working hands had ridden into the ranch yard. All but one headed for the hot meal awaiting them. Bobby Jensen, who had seen Smoke Jensen's horse at the tie-rail, broke from the rest and raced to the main house. He burst through the kitchen door and threw himself at Smoke.

"You're home! I jist knew you'd be here today," the boy said.

"Did you now?" Smoke tousled Bobby's white-blond hair.

"Are you gonna take me along the next time?" Bobby asked through his pleasure at seeing Smoke again.

Suddenly Smoke's thoughts rebounded to Tommy Olsen. He reflected on how the boy, only a year older than Bobby, had become a man in the crucible of their shared hardship. He wanted so much that such suffering would never visit Bobby. But then, the lad was growing up. He held Bobby out at arm's length.

"Bobby, it is sometimes wise to be careful what one wishes for. You might just get it. As to going with me . . . not the next time. I think when you turn fourteen will be soon enough. We'll go find us an adventure then." *And a tame one at that,* Smoke promised himself.

Sally Jensen joined her husband and adopted son and embraced both her men. Smoke was home and wise as always, and all was well in her world.

THE MOUNTAIN MAN SERIES BY
WILLIAM W. JOHNSTONE

__The Last Mountain Man	0-8217-6856-5	$5.99US/$7.99CAN
__Return of the Mountain Man	0-7860-1296-X	$5.99US/$7.99CAN
__Trail of the Mountain Man	0-7860-1297-8	$5.99US/$7.99CAN
__Revenge of the Mountain Man	0-7860-1133-1	$5.99US/$7.99CAN
__Law of the Mountain Man	0-7860-1301-X	$5.99US/$7.99CAN
__Journey of the Mountain Man	0-7860-1302-8	$5.99US/$7.99CAN
__War of the Mountain Man	0-7860-1303-6	$5.99US/$7.99CAN
__Code of the Mountain Man	0-7860-1304-4	$5.99US/$7.99CAN
__Pursuit of the Mountain Man	0-7860-1305-2	$5.99US/$7.99CAN
__Courage of the Mountain Man	0-7860-1306-0	$5.99US/$7.99CAN
__Blood of the Mountain Man	0-7860-1307-9	$5.99US/$7.99CAN
__Fury of the Mountain Man	0-7860-1308-7	$5.99US/$7.99CAN
__Rage of the Mountain Man	0-7860-1555-1	$5.99US/$7.99CAN
__Cunning of the Mountain Man	0-7860-1512-8	$5.99US/$7.99CAN
__Power of the Mountain Man	0-7860-1530-6	$5.99US/$7.99CAN
__Spirit of the Mountain Man	0-7860-1450-4	$5.99US/$7.99CAN
__Ordeal of the Mountain Man	0-7860-1533-0	$5.99US/$7.99CAN
__Triumph of the Mountain Man	0-7860-1532-2	$5.99US/$7.99CAN
__Vengeance of the Mountain Man	0-7860-1529-2	$5.99US/$7.99CAN
__Honor of the Mountain Man	0-8217-5820-9	$5.99US/$7.99CAN
__Battle of the Mountain Man	0-8217-5925-6	$5.99US/$7.99CAN
__Pride of the Mountain Man	0-8217-6057-2	$4.99US/$6.50CAN
__Creed of the Mountain Man	0-7860-1531-4	$5.99US/$7.99CAN
__Guns of the Mountain Man	0-8217-6407-1	$5.99US/$7.99CAN
__Heart of the Mountain Man	0-8217-6618-X	$5.99US/$7.99CAN
__Justice of the Mountain Man	0-7860-1298-6	$5.99US/$7.99CAN
__Valor of the Mountain Man	0-7860-1299-4	$5.99US/$7.99CAN
__Warpath of the Mountain Man	0-7860-1330-3	$5.99US/$7.99CAN
__Trek of the Mountain Man	0-7860-1331-1	$5.99US/$7.99CAN

Available Wherever Books Are Sold!

Visit our website at www.kensingtonbooks.com